Back in the Game

Books by Holly Chamberlin

LIVING SINGLE

THE SUMMER OF US

BABYLAND

BACK IN THE GAME

Published by Kensington Publishing Corporation

HOLLY CHAMBERLIN

Back in the Game

Strapless

KENSINGTON BOOKS
www.kensingtonbooks.com

As always, for Stephen;
and this time, also for Erica.

Acknowledgments

I would like to thank Julia Einstein and Judy Sowa for their help with various parts of this project.

To those who have provided inspiration this past year, I offer all my gratitude.

Finally, I would like to thank my editor and friend, John Scognamiglio, for his ceaseless support.

Chapter 1

Jess

Recent statistics show that fifty percent of marriages in the U.S. will end in divorce.
—*Wake Up and Smell the Dirty Sheets: You Will Be Divorced*

He said I'd never loved him.

He was probably right.

"I don't know why you married me in the first place."

"Matt," I replied wearily, "we've been through this before."

Matt laughed and it sounded bitter. "No, Jess, we haven't."

He was right again. We hadn't talked through anything, but I'd been asking myself that very question—why did I marry Matt Fromer in the first place?—since the day I started the affair that ended my marriage.

I am Jess Marlowe and I am an adulteress. My crime is of Biblical proportions.

"I'm sorry, Matt." I was. I still am. But I was tired and wanted Matt to hang up so that I could go to bed.

"I don't give a shit," he spat. Matt was drunk. Matt rarely drank even a beer; his inebriated state was clear evidence of just how badly I'd hurt him.

If you didn't give a shit, I thought, you wouldn't have gotten drunk and called me. I said nothing. The divorce had been finalized that day. The papers to prove it lay next to the phone.

"What, you still have nothing to say?" he taunted. "I bet you had plenty to say to that kid, what's his name, Seth."

Matt was right, again. I had had plenty to say to Seth; he'd had a lot to say to me. Seth was only twenty-five but he had the toned, brilliant mind of a seasoned scholar. That's what attracted me to him in the first place, the words that came out of his mouth. The physical part just flowed from that.

It was inevitable.

It was wrong.

"You're really a bitch, you know?"

I had wronged Matt. But I didn't have to take this abuse. He was no longer my husband.

"I'm hanging up, Matt," I said. "I wish you the best."

Before he could reply with a scathing remark, I ended the call. I went directly to bed but couldn't sleep.

Guilt is a very noisy companion.

Chapter 2

Nell

Understand this: Approximately ninety percent of the sympathy you are shown is false. Your failure serves only to highlight another's smug sense of success.
—*They're Talking About Me: Surviving Your Friends, Family, and Colleagues Post-Divorce*

The day Richard and I got married it rained. Cats and dogs, my father said. The man loved a cliché.

The July sky opened up around three that afternoon and dumped rivers of rain on us until after midnight. When the reception was over, the rain finally stopped.

They say that rain on your wedding day is a good thing, a sign of luck, assurance of a blessed union.

For a little over twenty years our luck held, Richard's and mine. It held through good times and bad. It held through the birth of our two children, Clara, then two years later, Colin. It held through colds and chicken pox and scraped knees, through Richard's promotions and my ovarian cancer scare, and through the kids' graduations from high school. Our luck even held through the deaths of my parents in an awful car crash, and through Richard's mother's slow descent in Alzheimer's and then his father's fatal heart attack.

It held through the fabulous trip to Europe we took to celebrate our twentieth wedding anniversary.

But, as my father was fond of saying, all good things come to an end. Our union, blessed for so long, fell apart in a spectacular way the night I found evidence of Richard's affair—the night he admitted to being in love with someone else.

A man named Bob Landry.

My life as I knew it exploded that night. Almost a year later, I'm still finding bloody shards in unlikely places.

Like in the U.S. mail.

I'd spent most of the early spring afternoon walking, wandering really, with no goal in mind other than to eventually wind my way home. I was tired when I got back to the apartment but it was a good tired, the kind you feel in your bones. I hoped I would sleep well that night; since the divorce, sleep had been a hit or miss activity.

I shuffled through the mail I'd retrieved from the box in the lobby. A few bills. A letter from a colleague on the MFA's Annual Fund committee. A letter from my doctor, confirming what the technician at the hospital had already told me, that my mammogram was clean.

And then . . . I held the chunky envelope in fingers that were suddenly shaky.

Interestingly, some people still hadn't heard about Richard's emergence from a lifetime of secrecy and lies. Take, for example, the Smiths, a family who used to own an apartment in the building next door but who'd relocated to Connecticut five years earlier. Clearly they didn't know that Richard and I were no longer "man and wife" because there it was in my shaking hand, a wedding invitation addressed to Mr. and Mrs. Richard Allard.

Mrs. Richard Allard. The name mocked me; it mocked everything I had thought I had and was and would be until the end, until death parted Richard from me.

After the divorce I'd gone back to using my maiden name, Keats. Maiden name. An accurate term in my case as Richard was the first and only man I'd ever had sex with, and not really, not entirely, until after we were married. Until after the church sanctioned our union and we promised to love and cherish each other and to accept children willingly from God. Not until after we were made to listen to all that other crap Richard's Catholic church demanded we listen to.

Nell Keats. I am once again who I was a long, long time ago. Except that now, Nell Keats is a forty-two-year-old divorced woman, mother of twenty-year-old Clara and eighteen-year-old Colin, my children who still have their father's name, who in that way and more still belong to him. I could throw off the burden of Richard's name, the mark of his possession, but I couldn't ask my son and daughter to do the same.

Nell Keats. In what relation do I stand to those three Allards?

I tossed the wedding invitation from the Smiths on the hall table. It would have to be answered. I would have to explain yet again what I was so tired of explaining. And then would come the inevitable questions.

How are you feeling?

Like hell.

Are you okay?

No.

Did Richard at least take care of you financially?

Oh, yes.

A wild thought came to me then. Upon learning that Richard and I were no longer married, would the Smiths choose my ex-husband and his lover over me? Would Richard and Bob be invited to the Smiths' yearly Summer Splash pool party? Would I be left off the guest list?

Stranger things had happened to me since that eye-opening night when I found the scrap of paper in Richard's pants pocket as I sorted the laundry for clothes to be taken to the dry cleaners. I unfolded the scrap, thinking it might have been a receipt Richard might need to record, and instead found a note in a man's handwriting—I can always tell a man's from a woman's—and what it said exactly modesty forbids me to repeat.

I sat heavily on the edge of the bed. Richard wasn't home; he'd said he was working late. When Richard walked into the apartment at almost eleven, I was still sitting on the edge of our bed, numb. It never occurred to me, not for one moment, that the note was a piece of trash Richard had picked up from outside the building. Richard was always tidying up. Somehow, I just knew this note was evidence of something far more unpleasant than trash.

Richard came into the bedroom, smiled, opened his mouth to say, "Hi, Nellie." But nothing came out of his mouth. He saw the look on my face, saw the note I held in my hand, and knew the game was over. Thankfully, he didn't deny his culpability.

"I'm sorry," he whispered. He looked ill, scared.

I said nothing that night, I couldn't, but oh, by the next night the words were flying out of my mouth, questions, insults, protestations, cries for mercy.

Mercy. I felt like a victim, powerless, confused. Why me?

Eleven months later and I was still asking, why me?

I stared down at the Smiths' wedding invitation on the hall table. Let Richard handle it, I thought. Let Richard do the explaining.

I'm through.

Chapter 3

Laura

Everybody loves a victim. Be sure to embellish the tale of every domestic squabble to include his punching you in the nose.
—*After the Divorce: Lies to Tell Your Family, Friends, and Co-Workers*

Candace. Yes, Candace was a good name for a girl. But wait, I thought. People will be tempted to call her Candy, and no daughter of mine was going to have a name that was better suited to a porn star.

No daughter of mine.

I wanted, I needed to find just the right names for my children. And I wasn't even pregnant, not even divorced from Duncan Costello, my husband of eight years, the man who refused to give me my children, little Annabelle or Leon.

"Mrs. Costello?"

I looked up at the lawyer, startled back to the moment.

"I'd prefer if you called me Ms. Keats," I said. "I'll be going back to my maiden name."

That is, until I get remarried. Then I'll be Mrs. Lumia or Mrs. Makepeace. I really hope I meet a guy with a good last name!

The lawyer nodded. She had a nice face and a nice office. I'd found her in the Yellow Pages. One of my colleagues at the business and computer training school where I work as an administrative assistant teased me for using the phone book and not the Internet to find a divorce lawyer. But in some ways, I'm kind of old-fashioned. I might work for a school that trains people to build and repair computers, but that doesn't mean I want to build and repair them myself!

"Ms. Keats, then," she said. "Are you absolutely sure you want to go through with the divorce? Because your husband will be served the papers today."

I thought about my babies, the babies Duncan said he didn't want, and said, "Yes, I'm sure."

I left her office a few minutes later and took the elevator to the lobby. I walked out into the afternoon. It was early April. The winter had been really long and hard, with lots and lots of snow. But now that it was getting warmer, you could feel people's excitement. I felt my own excitement.

It was really happening. If Duncan came through on his promise not to be horrible, I could be officially divorced in a matter of months. On my own, single, back out there, back in the game and looking for love.

I stumbled. I suddenly felt really dizzy. What was I doing? Was getting a divorce worth it? Was it worth ending an eight-year marriage to a nice guy, someone I had fallen in love with completely, someone I'd been pretty happy with until . . .

I took a deep breath and felt a little better.

A marriage to someone I'd been pretty happy with until I hadn't been pretty happy with him. Until not long after the sudden death of my parents, until not long after my sister Nell's husband had announced that he was gay. That's when it dawned on me that what I wanted most in life was not Duncan but children. At least two children, hopefully a boy first and then a girl.

I took another deep breath and headed for the corner.

It isn't an unreasonable desire, you know. It's not like I'm crazy or something. I mean, every woman deserves a child, even if it means leaving her husband to get one.

As I waited for the light to change to green, I ran through

our past, Duncan's and mine, just to be sure I'd gotten things right, though I knew of course that I had.

Duncan and I met at a club. We liked each other right away and went on our first date the next night. Or was it the night after that? Anyway, we had a lot of fun and the next thing you know, we were an exclusive couple.

The subject of having a family didn't come up for the first six months of our relationship. I mean, we were having fun! And when the subject did come up, when one of Duncan's friends got his girlfriend pregnant and things got explosive, Duncan and I decided that neither of us really wanted children all that much. But neither of us rejected the idea completely. I mean, we just thought, what's the rush? We don't want kids now, so what's the point of talking about them?

I think Duncan and I had been together for almost a year and a half when we got married. It was a really fun wedding. I still remember how yummy the cake was and what really cool stuff the DJ played. My parents paid for most of it, which was really nice of them considering Duncan wasn't making tons of money and I certainly wasn't!

But that was my parents. Always doing nice things for their daughters.

I guess about a year after our wedding the topic of kids came up again, this time when one of my colleagues was struggling through a messy divorce and battling her soon-to-be-ex for full custody of their little girl. Once again, Duncan and I agreed that we were still up in the air about the whole "kid thing." That's what we called it. The "kid thing."

I started to cross the broad street, from one side of Boylston to the other. I don't like the word "kid" anymore. I like the word "child" better. It seems nicer and more mature, doesn't it?

Anyway, before you know it we were celebrating our fifth anniversary. And then the subject of children started to come up every month. I'd get my period and say, "Still just you and me, honey." Duncan would wipe his brow with the back of his hand, say, "Whew!" and we'd laugh. See, we weren't trying to get pregnant. We were trying to stay not pregnant.

And then it was year six. Duncan and I still hadn't come to any definite conclusion about the "kid thing." We'd end every conversation by saying things like, "Let's think about it some more" and "Let's wait until after Christmas to decide."

We were both pretty happy.

And then my parents, Mary and Lucas Keats, married over forty years, were killed instantly when a suddenly out-of-control tractor-trailer smashed into their small Honda. They were on their way to Florida for a week's vacation at Disney World. They loved Disney World. They went there every year. I have a whole collection of pictures with my parents and Mickey Mouse.

Not long after that terrible crash, I knew. I told Duncan that I wanted children. I told him that I needed to have children. He said, "Let's think about it some more." I said, "No more thinking." And then he said, "I'm sorry, Laura. I can't."

Well, it was a little more complicated than that, of course. There were a lot of big fights and I even begged him, but nothing would change his mind. He wouldn't say yes to starting a family even though it meant losing me.

I came to a dead stop in the middle of the street. My heart hurt. I felt all dizzy again. I wondered if I was having a panic attack.

"Lady! Move it or lose it!"

I don't know why people have to be rude.

The taxi driver's shout got my feet moving and I reached the sidewalk safely. I thought about going into Marshall's to browse the children's section. I remembered all the cute outfits I'd bought for Nell's children when they were little. I love being the adoring aunt.

Nell is smart; she always has been. She had Colin and Clara in her early twenties. And now that a bad thing has happened, now that Richard, the love of her life, has left her for a man, the love of his life, Nell still has Colin and Clara. She isn't alone, not really, the way I would be someday if I didn't hurry up and have a baby.

I turned left and hurried down the sidewalk to Marshall's.

Chapter 4

Grace

If love means always having to say you're sorry, divorce means finally getting to say, "It's all your fault, you idiot."
—*Looking on the Bright Side: One Hundred Great Things About Divorce*

My mother used to tell me that I was a pushover. "Grace," she'd scold, shaking her head, a look of keen disappointment on her face, "you're a pushover. You're just a ball of fluff being tossed around by the wind."

She was right. I was a spineless creature. I saw that about myself from the start.

My mother, however, didn't share my consciousness. As much as she hated my tendency to comply, she never saw the same tendency in herself. My mother, Eva Lynch Henley, was the classic pushover, the woman anyone, especially a man, could get around with nothing more than a smile, a caress, a puppy-dog look.

I should note that I never took advantage of her the way other people did, probably because even as a child I was already professionally pleasant.

But my mother, oh, she'd warn me that I would be hurt out there in the big bad world unless I toughened up. "Grace," she'd say, "where has your self-esteem gotten to?"

I never told her that my self-esteem hadn't bothered to show up in the first place.

And I never, even when I was in college and hating her, I never pointed out that my behavior was almost an exact copy of hers. I never pointed out that I had been her trainee.

I hated my mother but I was too nice to act on that hate. It seemed rude to remind her that my father, her husband, treated her like a dim-witted cleaning lady rather than like a partner in life. It seemed rude to point out that she allowed his bad behavior, that she seemed to enjoy bending over backward when he brought over friends for dinner at the last minute. It seemed rude to point out that she didn't yell and scream when he spent their vacation money on a touring bike. It seemed rude to point out that she hadn't fought back when without consultation he installed his ailing mother in my mother's sewing room, forcing my mother to make the custom shirts my father preferred in a cramped corner of the garage he had always promised to clean and never did.

All those years I said nothing.

I'm not blaming my mother for making me into anything I wasn't already by accident of birth. Well, maybe I am blaming her, just a bit, but I keep my anger in this regard to myself. It's too late, anyway. It would do no good to say, "Thanks a lot, Mom, you set a really fine example" to a grave.

My mother died when I was twenty-one, just barely out of college, and since then I've mostly been doing her proud, first by falling in love with and then marrying a moody artist named Simon Trenouth, by putting up with his numerous affairs, by paying all of his bills. Yes, I did divorce charming Simon after too many years of his casual abuse, but true to my mother and to myself, I continued to "be there" for him, letting him sleep on the couch when his girlfriends threw him out, paying his rent when he forgot to, holding his hand when artistic inspiration just wasn't there.

But the credit card bill was the final straw.

I looked down again at the blue sheet of paper. I felt the urge to scream but I didn't. It might annoy the neighbors.

There had been other surprises on other credit card bills—clothing from the Armani store (a suit he never wore), caviar from a mail-order company (food he never ate)—but nothing like this, nothing so enormous, nothing from Rothman Brothers, an exclusive jeweler. Simon was in big trouble.

I didn't even bother to question the purchase with the credit card company. Years of tending to a deeply immature man had given me a sixth sense, an ability to tell when he was at fault, and when I was going to have to pick up the pieces yet again.

I dialed Simon's cell phone, wondering if he'd run out of minutes, remembering how he could never seem to keep track of such details. Simon answered; his voice sounded hoarse and I noted it wasn't yet noon, his usual waking hour.

"What did you buy at Rothman Brothers?" I said.

"Gracie?"

"What did you buy?"

Simon sighed the tortured sigh of the long-suffering artist. "Gift," he said. "For Jane."

"Who the hell is Jane?"

"Girlfriend. Nice kid. You'd like her, Gracie."

"Return it," I said. "Because I'm not paying for your girl-friend's baubles. And if you ever use my credit card again, I will report you to the police."

Simon made a gurgling sound of protest and I hung up.

What did I expect, really? I'd trained Simon all the years of our marriage to be helpless and irresponsible. Sure, he'd come to me pretty much that way, but I'd helped mold an amateur slouch into a professional bum.

I could be mad at Simon, but I could be madder at myself.

I took a deep breath, straightened the stack of opened mail, and thought about treating myself to a croissant at the bakery on the corner. I decided against it. Too expensive. Until Simon returned that bauble and my credit card bill was adjusted, I'd have to be very, very careful.

There was two-day-old bread in the kitchen. I ate that.

Chapter 5

Jess

So he left you for a younger, more beautiful woman. It's a fact;
accept it. No one respects a whiner.
   —*What Now? How to Pick Up the Pieces and Save Your
   Pride*

"Hi," I said, tossing my bag on an empty chair. "It's been
ages. Why are we all so busy?"

Nell smirked. "Contemporary society tells us we have to be
busy. If we're busy, our lives must be important. Busyness, I am
told, helps fill the emotional and spiritual void most of us find
ourselves condemned to. Hello, Jess."

"Aren't you in a chipper mood," I commented.

Nell just shrugged.

She'd arrived at the restaurant before any of us; she's always
just a bit early. She says she was punctual even as a little girl,
punctual and in charge.

I met Nell a few years back at a charity event she was cohosting.
We hit it off when a particularly rude woman at our table was
told off by the waiter she'd been abusing. Nell and I spontaneously
applauded and met for lunch later that week. Though our lives
were playing out very differently—Nell was married and I wasn't;
Nell has kids and I don't; I teach sociology at Northeastern while
Nell has chosen a more traditional manner of career as a full-

time mother and volunteer—we had enough of the important things in common to make a friendship grow.

A love of reading, an interest in the arts, a sometimes wry approach to life, and a tendency to applaud when justice is served.

I never really got to know Richard, Nell's husband, the man she'd been with since college. I saw him rarely and my general impression was of a quiet, intelligent, well-mannered guy, a tiny bit hesitant or secretive, or maybe just private. It was clear to me from the start that Nell adored him; they were best friends, really, and for a brief time I was almost jealous of their union. I remember thinking: that is what marriage should be. Somehow, Nell and Richard got it right.

Grace arrived at the restaurant just after I did and took the seat against the wall; she always does. She likes to people watch; she can hold an intense conversation with someone while at the same time noting minute details of passersby. I imagine this ability to focus on one thing and yet observe another is essential when you're a teacher of nine- and ten-year-olds.

Grace and I met almost eleven years ago when I was seeing a guy named Carl, a jazz saxophone player. One night Carl introduced me to his friend Simon, and to Simon's wife, Grace. Simon was a painter, supposedly gifted—not that I would really know; I appreciate art but don't really know what I'm looking at—and sexy in that charming, bohemian kind of way. While Simon was charismatic, prone to dramatic gestures and a roaring laugh, his wife was more guarded in her behavior, self-contained. For a while I wondered if Grace was intimidated by her show-stopping husband, but when I learned she taught art at a prestigious, private middle school, I figured the discipline her job required informed every aspect of her life.

The long story short is that Grace and I became close and the guys didn't last. Carl and I broke up—he was far too carefree for me—and Grace, finally tired of Simon's infidelity and other costly antics, divorced him.

Around the time Grace filed for divorce, Nell invited me to a cocktail party at her beautifully appointed apartment on Marlborough Street. Temporarily single, I brought Grace along. That night we both met Nell's younger sister, Laura, and her husband, Duncan. Duncan seemed a nice enough guy and made a nice enough impression on me. Laura and Duncan seemed well suited, as did Nell and Richard.

Well. It wasn't the first time I was wrong and it won't be the last.

Laura finally arrived at Café Alice. Her tendency to be late or to slip in just under the gate is only one of the ways in which she's different from her older sister.

Nell is tall and slim, aristocratic in her bearing, though certainly not in her attitude. She has a delicate beauty, with fine features, sapphire blue eyes, and sleek blond hair. Laura also has blond hair but it's thicker and darker than Nell's. She's medium height and slightly plump in a way that might be a problem later but which suits her perfectly now. Laura's eyes are wide and blue green and somehow innocent.

Grace is small and slim. Her hair is dark, almost black, and she wears it in a bob reminiscent of Louise Brooks. Her eyes are brown and doelike; her style, urban sleek.

As for me, at five foot nine inches I tower over Grace. I've never been shy about my height; I like being tall, though it can be difficult finding pants that fit properly. The rest of me is unspectacular. Brown hair to my shoulders, brown eyes. End of story. Well, I have heard that I have a good smile.

"Well," Nell said when we had ordered a round of drinks, "I don't know about you gals, but I've had quite a week."

"What happened?" Grace asked.

Nell told us about the wedding invitation from the Smiths.

"That's awkward," I said. "So, did you ask Richard to respond?"

"I didn't ask him; I told him to respond. And to explain to Mr. and Mrs. Smith that he now prefers the company of men. Rather, that he has always preferred the company of men but was too scared to admit it. So, what's new with you, Jess?"

I related the sad tale of my conversation with Matt.

"So, it's official," I said. "We're divorced and I'm single and Matt is miserable."

Nell, not terribly demonstrative, patted my hand. "I still

think we should raise a glass to the whole nasty business being over."

It had been a nasty divorce, though it could have been worse. Much worse. My lawyer was very good and very expensive. The settlement was fair and equitable; my personal finances hadn't taken too bad a blow, but my insides, my heart and soul and sense of myself as a decent person, felt crushed.

We raised a glass. The toast was restrained.

"Well, I've got some news," Grace said then. "I've cut Simon off and before you say 'again?' let me assure you that this time it's for good. No more taking him back, no more lending him money, no more help of any kind."

Laura frowned. "I'll believe it when I see it," she said. "Seriously, Grace, sometimes I think you'll be dragging Simon around like a bad smell for the rest of your life."

If Grace was stung by this remark, she didn't show it. "You'll see," she said. "This time he went too far." And she told us about the outrageous charge on her credit card.

"How did he get the card in the first place?" Nell asked.

Grace blushed. "I let him use it. Once. Maybe twice. I suppose he assumed he was free to use it any time he liked. It's my fault, really—"

"No," I said fiercely, "it's not your fault! Simon is a bum!"

"How did he get away with it, anyway?" Nell asked. "What happened to security measures like a picture ID? Who would believe his name was Grace?"

"Simon is charming." Grace smiled ruefully. "He always gets what he wants."

"Until now."

Grace nodded at me. "Right. You know what the worst part is? The bauble he bought was for his new girlfriend. I swear in all the years we were married he never spent even a fraction of that amount on me!"

"Good riddance to bad rubbish," Laura pronounced.

"Well, I wouldn't call him rubbish—"

Laura cut Grace off with her own news update. "Duncan was served the divorce papers," she said.

The three of us just sat there; even Nell, quick-witted Nell, had nothing to say.

"Well, aren't you happy for me?" Laura demanded.

Grace and I mumbled something incomprehensible; I certainly didn't understand us.

"Well, I'm happy." Laura looked pointedly at her sister. "Not happy like I'm jumping up and down, but I'm glad the divorce is moving along. The sooner I'm free, the sooner I can start my new life."

I thought for a moment that Nell would have to be restrained. It was no secret she thought her sister's divorcing Duncan was a huge mistake. We all did.

Nell's continued silence was bothering Laura.

"Do I have to explain it all again?" she said plaintively. "It's just that I see myself as a mother. It's what I want more than anything. Why should I give up my dream? What do I get in return?"

Nell pretended to consider. "Well, let's see. How about the love of a good man?"

"If Duncan loved me, he'd make me pregnant. He'd give me my baby."

"Laura," I said, finally finding my voice, "if you loved Duncan, you wouldn't force him to do something he didn't want to do."

"I didn't force Duncan. I gave him an option. Either give me a baby or we're through."

"That's harsh." Grace shrugged. "I'm sorry. It strikes me as harsh."

"Becoming a father isn't like sitting through a chick flick," I said. "The flick is over in two hours. The paternity lasts until the day he dies. Maybe Duncan just needed more time to think things through. Most people don't respond well to ultimatums."

Laura frowned down at her Cosmo. She always orders sweet, colorful drinks.

"I don't know why you just didn't get a dog," Nell said." You could have dressed him in little outfits and carried him around with you. Besides, dogs are a lot cheaper than kids. No college tuition, for one."

Laura looked up. "I don't want to talk about Duncan and me anymore."

"Fine," I said, eager to restore some peace.

"So," Nell said with false brightness, "here we are, four single women. Back in the game. Back on the market."

Grace frowned. "We're commodities?"

"Yes. Whether we like it or not, we're commodities on the market and players in the game."

"What ever happened to romance?" Laura mused.

I figured Duncan and Matt were probably thinking the very same thing.

"It died a slow and agonizing death some time around the turn of the nineteenth century." Nell paused before adding, "Maybe earlier."

"Romance is still alive," I said, though I wasn't entirely sure I believed what I was saying. Was romance just a pretty word for lust? If so, yes, romance was alive and I'd encountered it recently.

Nell finished her glass of wine in one long draught. "If I'd known my marriage would end in the way it did," she said then, "I would never have gotten married in the first place."

Laura gripped her sister's hand. "What about Colin and Clara? If you'd never married Richard, you never would have had the children."

Nell removed her hand from Laura's death grip. "I know, I know. I'm just venting. You always take everything so literally."

"No one goes into marriage thinking, hey, what the hell, if it doesn't work, I can get a divorce, no big deal. Not even me." I laughed; no one laughed with me. "It's so much work even to get to the point of talking about marriage, let alone planning a wedding and a life together. You have to believe that marriage is forever. You just have to, in spite of all evidence to the contrary."

Nell smiled ruefully. "So, everyone who gets married is an idiot?"

"Blinded by visions of lacy veils and lush bouquets?" Grace suggested.

"Naive?" Nell said.

Laura drained her Cosmo.

I shrugged. "Maybe. Or maybe just hopeful. To be human means to be weak and hopeful. Though hope, I suppose, is a sort of courage."

"Weak, hopeful, and newly single. Or in my case," Grace went on, "not so newly single. Just newly committed to getting on with my life post-Simon."

"You know," Laura said suddenly, "divorced women with young children are really at an advantage."

Nell shook her head. "Excuse me?"

I hoped there weren't any single mothers within earshot. But of course there weren't. Single mothers were at home paying the bills, cleaning the toilets, and helping the children with their homework.

"No, I mean it," Laura said. "Because they can meet divorced men with children through school activities and soccer practice and Boy Scouts and Girl Scouts. Children are even better than dogs when it comes to attracting attention."

"Maybe," Grace said carefully. "But life isn't exactly rosy for single parents of little kids. Even if they do manage to get re-married, there's a good chance they'll have to deal with a blended family. And that has to be exhausting."

Laura rolled her eyes. "Duh, remember *The Brady Bunch?* Blended families can work just fine."

Really, at times I wondered if Laura's already tenuous grasp on reality wasn't beginning to weaken.

"Sure," Nell said, "on television anything can happen. Aliens can be fuzzy smart alecks and astronauts can keep genies in their living rooms."

"By the way," Grace added, "in real life the actor who played Mike Brady, all-American dad, was gay."

"You know, I always thought he was the only character on the show with half a brain." Nell turned to Laura. "So, as a single mother of college-aged kids, I'm out of luck?"

"Not necessarily," Laura said, missing, as she often did, her sister's sarcastic tone.

"Speaking of kids," I said to Nell, "how are they faring? I'm sure they have opinions about the divorce and their father's new life. And I'm sure they're not shy about voicing them. Kids that age don't seem to be shy about anything."

Nell shrugged. "Remarkably, both Colin and Clara have been pretty quiet about the whole thing. I know Richard's coming out and our divorce must have shaken them up, but so far, I haven't seen much fallout. We'll see. Maybe they're having a delayed reaction. Maybe when they're thirty or forty they'll go after Richard with an axe."

"Colin and Clara love the both of you," Laura protested. "They understand."

"Kids never understand their parents' divorce," Nell said. "Not really. They have to blame someone. With my luck they'll probably decide I'm the one they hate for breaking up the family."

"But, Nell," Grace protested, "Richard is gay. He's in love with a man. You had no choice. You had to get divorced. You're not to blame."

Nell's face took on a hard look. It was a look I'd seen too often since Richard's bombshell. I looked forward to the day when it would go away for good.

"I could have figured things out a long time ago," she said. "I could have been smarter; I could have been not so embarrassingly stupid. I can easily imagine my kids having no respect for me. I mean, what kind of example did I set for them? Why would either of them ever want to get married after the debacle that was their parents' marriage?"

"Richard was very deeply in the closet, Nell," I said carefully. "You couldn't have known."

"I should have known," Nell replied fiercely. "I was his wife, for God's sake! How could I not have known? I was so wrapped up in my own life I never really saw the person on the other side of the bed. And yet, I loved Richard; I thought I was being his true partner."

"You were his true partner," Grace said. "Don't blame yourself for his choice of secrecy."

Nell ignored her and ranted on. "I swear I still don't know when he was having all this anonymous sex because we spent almost every night together, from dinner through Jay Leno. Sure, sometimes he had to work late, but when he came home, he never smelled of anyone else's cologne! I'm furious with myself for being so blind. I'm furious with Richard for tricking me so thoroughly. And I'm furious for having wasted twenty years of my life as Mrs. Richard Allard. Who was she, anyway? Who was that sorry woman?"

I wished I had an answer to that question, something smart and also comforting, but I didn't. Neither, it seemed, did Grace or Laura.

"Um, I have a date next weekend," Laura said.

Grace rolled her eyes.

Nell poured more wine into her glass from the bottle on the table. "In spite of my sister's freakish success in the dating game," she said, "I believe that the four of us are at a disadvantage. We've been off the market for too long, and yes, I know I'm mixing metaphors. Single women our age who've never been married or who've never been in a long-term relationship know the rules. And you can bet they're not going to share insider information with us. They'll view the four of us as an additional threat. We're swelling the already swollen population."

"Why thanks, Nell," I joked lamely. "You've really lifted my spirits."

"Sorry. Anyway, I have no interest in dating just yet. Not much interest, anyway. God, it's not like my dating someone is going to make Richard jealous!"

Grace looked troubled. "I've been wondering. What kind of man is available to women our age? And to women the age we're going to be in a few short years? Men in their thirties and forties—if we can find them—are either married or looking for younger women."

"Some younger men are really into dating older women," Laura said. "You know, because it's hip."

"Dating is the operative word," Nell pointed out. "Most young guys aren't going to stick around for marriage and menopause."

"And older men?" I said. The oldest man I'd ever been with was twenty years my senior. I was just out of college. I thought I was being terribly adult, about to embark on an affair with an "older man." Visions of foreign cigarettes and dry martinis and expensive lingerie danced in my head. And then we had sex and I discovered that the reality was far less interesting than the fantasy. He wore faded boxers. Alcohol made him break out in hives. His smart suits hid a significant roll of fat around his middle. When he called me a few days later, I told him I'd gotten back with an old boyfriend. It was a lie.

"Well, that depends on the man, I guess," Nell conceded. "If he's tired of life's nastiness, if he's learned the value of true companionship, he might be interested in meeting a contemporary."

"It's all so unfair." Laura pouted; it made her look about fifteen. "Women have the advantage for such a short time. The minute we hit thirty we, like, stop being desirable to a huge part of the male population. Men grow into the advantage. A man in his fifties—even if he's not filthy rich—can still get a woman in her early thirties. If he is filthy rich he can get a woman in her twenties. It's ridiculous!"

I wondered how carefully Laura had considered this fact when she dumped Duncan.

"But, consider the mature man," Grace said. "I mean, someone not looking for a trophy wife, someone looking for love. If I met a man in his fifties who wanted to go out with me, I'd say yes. Assuming, of course, he seemed nice. And had a job. And wasn't an artist."

Nell laughed. "Yes, you've had more than your share of the creative types. Still, think about the baggage an older man is sure to be lugging around. Like bitter ex-wives and greedy kids. And, if he's been living alone for some time, nasty bachelor habits."

"Everyone has baggage," I said. "We'd be terribly boring if we didn't."

"True," Nell agreed. "But with age come health problems. Once a man reaches fifty the illnesses start coming on fast and thick. Heart problems are almost guaranteed. Weight gain. Prostate troubles. Erectile dysfunction. Then a man reaches his sixties—if he reaches his sixties—and it just gets worse. Before you know it, you're a forty-five-year-old with an invalid on your hands."

"That's not always true," I protested. "The general population is healthier than ever."

"Except for the obese," Laura added, nodding none too discreetly toward a table at which sat a hefty couple. "There's an epidemic, you know."

"People live longer lives. Medical care is available." Grace paused before adding: "For those who can afford it."

Nell shrugged. "I'm just trying to make a point. Sure, older men are appealing in a way, but in another way, they're simply not."

"Well," Laura said, "older men aren't an option for me, anyway. I need a man who's young and virile, someone who wants to start a family. I don't want my children to have a doddering old man for a father."

"Heaven forbid," Grace murmured.

"He needs to be able to help with midnight feedings and take the kids to soccer practice. He can't be falling asleep at the dinner table and in bed by eight."

"Here's a news flash, Laura." Nell leaned close to her sister, as if about to impart a vital piece of information. "All parents fall asleep at the dinner table and yearn desperately to be in bed by eight. You have no idea what you're in for."

Laura made a dismissive motion with her hand. I noticed her empty ring finger and wondered what she'd done with the set Duncan had worked so hard to afford.

"I remember when Colin and Clara were little," she said. "It didn't seem too bad."

Grace and I shared a look. It was hard to know if Laura was truly dim or just besotted with the notion of having a cute, cuddly baby of her own.

"Because you went home at night and left the demons to me!" Nell laughed a bit harshly. "You were the fun, young aunt.

I was on the front line; I was the mean, crabby mommy. I was the one who cleaned up vomit and went to boring teachers' conferences and made the rules the demons struggled mightily not to follow."

Laura looked deeply distressed. "How can you call Colin and Clara demons? They're your pride and joy! Aren't they?"

For a second, only a second, Nell's eyes glimmered with tears. "My children," she said, "are my life. Now that Richard isn't."

I called for the check.

Chapter 6

Jess

When your date tells you that his divorce was uncontested and without bitterness, don't believe a word of it. It's the guilt talking. He was a dirty, lying cheat and will always be a dirty, lying cheat

—*It Was Just One of Those Things: The Myth of the No-Fault Divorce*

I remember when it first came to me that my marriage would be over before long.

It was less than a year after the wedding. I'd driven to Ogunquit for a weekend at a colleague's beach house. The weather was good. Each of us spent an afternoon on our own; most academics enjoy solitude. I was sitting on the sand, gazing at the water, which was very flat, very blue. A big pink beach ball drifted along lazily, and the extreme calm of the scene was comforting and at that exact moment I knew I'd be divorced from Matt.

And the thought didn't kill me.

Later, as I was getting ready for bed in the tiny, sparse room I'd been assigned, I remembered the flat blue water and the big pink ball. Yes, I thought, I won't be wearing this diamond ring for long.

I knew I wasn't going to set out to destroy the marriage, but at the same time I knew I was waiting for it to end. I didn't know how it would end, but I knew it would soon be over, and not because of death or any other noble or tragic thing. I felt very calm about the whole prospect, too.

You see? I was doomed from the start. The first day back in Boston after that trip to Ogunquit I met a new assistant professor in the bioengineering department. His name was Seth Morgenstein and he was a mere twenty-five years old. Seth was—is— everything Matt is not. He's communicative and witty; he's an intellectual; he's passionate. Seth listened to me.

We started an affair within weeks of meeting each other. I enjoyed it enormously, for a while. Finally, the guilt got to be too much to bear, but only after I'd exhausted every ounce of passion between Seth and me. That process took four months.

And now? Now I'm left with the dark realization that I can't trust myself, and the darker realization that I can't be trusted.

It's said that some people aren't cut out for marriage. I think I know what that means. I like the idea of commitment, the comfort, the goodness of that. But I don't think I'm capable of putting that idea into action. And I don't think I'll change with "the right person." Nothing was wrong with Matt. He's an okay guy, a decent guy, most of the time, anyway. His only serious flaw is that he married the wrong woman—me.

He should have married someone—well, someone more like Laura, someone less demanding and "interesting"—someone more like him.

Matt is a corporate accountant. He makes a lot of money, though to hear him talk, you'd think he was starving. Matt's life revolves around "getting ahead" and football. The getting ahead part, the desire to climb the corporate ladder, was always a bit foreign to me. As an academic, I know the pressure to publish or perish; I guess that's my version of "getting ahead." But the money part, the part that interests Matt so much, isn't there for me in the first place and honestly, I don't care all that much about getting rich. I don't want to starve; I want to be comfortable and more, I want to be secure, but I lack the desire to upgrade my car, my home, my vacations on a yearly basis.

And the football. Okay, I've never been interested in sports, though I can enjoy a Super Bowl party as much as the next person who's not entirely clear on what teams are playing. So before we moved in together, I considered Matt's rabid interest in the game kind of cute. His face would light up when he scored tickets to a game; he'd stumble over words when trying to describe to me an "awesome play"; he'd jump out of his seat when a player did something spectacular.

And then, Matt moved into my apartment. Things were okay at first; Matt was respectful of my space and I of his and there was virtually no football to be found on television. We were married that August.

And then it began. Before two weeks had passed, I had become the proverbial football widow. If Matt wasn't watching a game, he was taping one. If he wasn't watching a commentary show, he was on the phone with a buddy, sharing his own commentary. If he wasn't parked in front of the living room television, he was parked at a local sports bar, watching a game on a wide screen.

Matt didn't seem to care that I didn't share his obsession. He didn't need me; he needed football. So he could never understand why I would want him to attend a lecture with me or to go out on a Thursday night to hear some blues or jazz. Before long I realized I was even more alone than I'd been when I was single. Because when I was single, there was no one person I was supposed to be able to rely on as a companion. But now there was that one person and he had virtually no interest in being my companion.

We never fought about this. I realized right off that arguing, cajoling, discussing would get me nowhere. Matt was happy; why should he change?

Certainly not for love of me.

Why, I began to wonder, did I get married in the first place?

And the sex, our "love life" as it used to be so euphemistically called, it wasn't so good. Frankly, the sex was average, even boring. Passion hadn't brought us together; passion hadn't compelled us to link ourselves legally until death did us part.

The truth is I'm still wondering why I got married in the first place, and why I married Matt. I try to remember how I felt when I said yes to Matt, how I felt just afterward, but I can't remember, not clearly.

I do remember that my parents were happy. I remember my mother saying it was "about time I settled down." But what I can't remember is what they said over the years—if anything—about my being single. Had they been exerting a subtle pressure on me to choose a husband all along; and if so, had I been at all aware of the pressure?

No. I can't blame my parents for my saying yes to Matt. I can't blame anyone but myself, certainly not societal norms or the pressure of my peers.

After all, I'm a professional person with a stack of degrees to prove it. If I can't be trusted to stand apart from the group and think for myself, who can? I observe society's ever-changing mores; I don't blindly accept them.

Or do I?

Chapter 7

Nell

He likes football, you like figure skating. He likes refried beans,
you like salad. He likes action movies, you like foreign films.
What the hell were you thinking?
  —*Incompatibility and You: You Married the Wrong Guy*

Mrs. Smith, she of the wedding invitation, sent me a gracious note on thick, expensive paper, written in a precise
and feminine hand. She mentioned she had spoken to Richard.
And she wondered if I was attending the wedding. Enclosed was
another reply card. I checked the line marked "regrets" and
popped it in the mail that afternoon.

The last thing I was in the mood for was a wedding.
Weddings are so—stupid.

Divorce? Now that was interesting. I took Richard to the
cleaners in our divorce. I'm sure his lawyer is still shaking his
head. The money doesn't make up for the insult, but it helps.
Still, I feel like I won't ever be able to trust any man ever again.
If I remarry, it will be all for money, that's all, and he can keep
a separate bedroom for all I care; in fact, I'd rather it.

But why would I even bother to remarry? I'm fine alone. At
least I can't betray myself.

Richard says he had known all along, since before he married me, that he was gay. Why didn't I sense something was
wrong? Why did I believe he thought me the love of his life?

The funny thing is I know for a fact that Richard liked being seen out in public with me. He liked being seen with me because I'm tall and thin and pretty and because I dress well.

I guess I was a good cover. I should have gotten fat and sloppy; that would have driven him crazy.

Sex?

Our sex life was occasional after the first years of our marriage, but I didn't care all that much about sex and Richard never pressured me. True, on occasion I got crushes on a movie star and once I got a crush on a man in the building next door, but I never acted on those romantic feelings. I was married; fidelity was part of the deal. Besides, Richard was the only man I'd ever slept with, and you know what they say about not missing what you've never known.

Anyway, while I was at home redecorating the kids' rooms and watching movies and reading novels, Richard was out on the town meeting guys and getting laid. Luckily, all sex between us had stopped before the seventh year of the marriage, so there was little if any chance Richard might have made me sick. Still. I was such a fool.

A fool and an excuse.

For a long time I suppose I was Richard's excuse for avoiding his real life. "I can't cheat on my wife; I'm married; I'm a father; I made a vow." I suppose I was quite convenient. But I guess his true self, the self that needed men, finally became too strong to ignore. So Richard starting having sex with men but still refused to leave the kids and me.

Until Bob. Bob the electrician. I know I'm being mean, but I can't help but picture my ex-husband's lover as the children's TV character, Bob the Builder, a blocky figure in a stupid yellow hat.

I miss my parents. It was horrible the way they died, but on some level I'm glad they didn't have to witness Richard's coming out and the subsequent dissolution of my marriage. I'm not sure they ever would have understood; I know they would have been heartbroken and terribly worried about me.

And they'd probably want me to remarry as soon as possible. The thought of marrying again mystifies me. The thought of creating a whole new life with someone not Richard seems impossible. I have no idea of where I'd even start.

Well, I could start with a date, of course.

I think I want to date. At least, I—I what? I would like to have someone to take along to weddings. It would be nice to have someone to go out with on a Saturday night.

But do I want someone sleeping in bed with me every night? No. Absolutely not. Maybe. But in the far distant future.

Because first, I have to address the troubling issue of sex. I think I might want to have sex. I'm attracted to men, not all men, of course, not the slovenly or the overweight, but particular men, mostly on-screen but occasionally someone I pass on the street or meet at a function. But I'm scared out of my mind at the prospect of taking my clothes off in front of a man. Actually, terrified is a more accurate word.

I, Nell Keats, am a born-again virgin. I've been revirginalized. This is what happens after thirteen years without sex. I hardly remember what it was like being with Richard. How am I supposed to imagine what it would be like with another man?

Will it hurt? Will I be expected to do things I certainly never did with Richard? Will a man know it's been so long and find me suddenly unattractive? Will I ever feel desire?

I wonder if convents are still accepting middle-aged women. I'm not Catholic even though I was married in the Catholic church, but what's conversion compared to the trauma I've experienced?

Chapter 8

Laura

Die young and leave a good-looking corpse. Divorce young and be able to afford lots of plastic surgery.
—*The Smart Woman's Guide to Divorce*

The apartment looks a whole lot bigger now that Duncan's stuff is gone. His stuff. After eight years of marriage, figuring out who owns what is really hard, believe me.

All our money was in joint accounts. Duncan made more money than I did, true, but that was never an issue when it came to buying things. If I wanted new placemats and candles, I just went out and bought them. If Duncan wanted a new stereo system, he just went out and bought it.

Duncan took the stereo. I kept the candles and placemats.

Other things, things we'd bought together, things we both decided we wanted, well, they were harder to divvy up. The king-sized bed, for example. We were both crazy about it. It barely fit into the bedroom; Duncan had to shimmy sideways against the wall to climb in at night. And king-sized bedding can be a lot more expensive than queen sized, let me tell you! But we'd had a lot of fun in that bed.

Duncan really wanted it when he moved out. He never said that, but I knew. The problem was the apartment he was renting was far too small for the bed; you couldn't even squeeze it into the living room. So the bed stayed put. Which is kind of a shame because I can't bring myself to sleep in it anymore. Not that I miss Duncan. Not all that much, anyway. Not that I regret anything.

Maybe by the time the baby comes, I'll be okay with the bed. Little Caroline and I can sleep in it together. And my new husband, of course.

My new husband. A shinier model man, one who wants to be a dad.

Nell thinks my leaving Duncan was a mistake. She's still trying to get me to take him back. It drives me nuts. I just can't convince her I know what I'm doing.

See, Nell thinks that our parents' dying the way they did, so suddenly, so violently, somehow screwed me up and made me obsess about having a baby.

It did not screw me up. Well, maybe in the sense that it made me incredibly sad. I cried for days on end. Poor Duncan. He was really wonderful during that time. But I got over the shock and yes, I miss my parents so much. I used to talk to them every day, but just because I feel really alone sometimes since they've been gone doesn't mean I'm trying to replace them with a baby! I mean, that doesn't even make sense.

But poor Nell has had a terrible shock with Richard. She lost her parents and her husband, and though I know she doesn't consciously want me to be unhappy, I think somehow she doesn't want me to have children because that's one thing she has that I don't. Except that now I don't have a husband, either, but I will have one soon.

I have plans.

Nell says I'm going about looking for a man like I'm a general at war, mounting a campaign. But what's wrong with that? Who has time to waste?

I've written down a list of questions to ask on the first date. Mostly medical questions but a few other questions about lifestyle, like does he enjoy sports and how much time does he spend on his grooming each day. If his answers aren't the ones I'm looking for, I won't see him again, no matter how cute or charming he is.

One thing I know. I refuse to be a stepparent. I want my own children and only my own children. I don't see why I should have to raise some other woman's child. Nell pointed out that most people have children and that my chances of finding an eligible guy without a son or daughter are slim. But I don't care. I've come this far; I've left Duncan; I'm not going to compromise now.

Nell, the spoilsport, also pointed out that at thirty-four I have far fewer eggs than I had at twenty-four. Duh. Of course I'm aware of this. It's why this quest is so urgent, why I have to act like I'm a general mounting a campaign.

Anyway, I know I can conceive, I just know I can. Okay, I've never gotten pregnant, even when I was careless (only a few times) and didn't use birth control. I guess I've just been lucky. I'm sure the fact that I'm almost the only woman I know who hasn't ever been pregnant has nothing to do with my womb being hostile or anything.

What a horrible thing a hostile womb must be! You have to walk around knowing there's something mean inside you, something that refuses to allow a life to take hold.

I'm a friendly person. I just know there's nothing hostile about me, inside or out.

I just know it.

Chapter 9

Grace

The so-called Seven-Year Itch actually starts sometime in the fourth year. Keep this in mind when researching your next spouse.

—*Getting In and Getting Out: The Cycle of Marriage and Divorce*

I saw his cell phone number on the screen and let the voice mail system take his call.

In spite of my recent vow, I still didn't trust myself to talk to Simon directly. Years of backsliding, years of being lured back into the role of indulgent caretaker had made me wary of my weakness. And now, days after finding the outrageous charge on my credit card bill, my anger had cooled. It was still there but no longer red-hot. Simon would hear the change in my voice and take advantage of my softer mood.

I watched the phone, volume turned down, until a red blinking light indicated that Simon had left his message. I raised the volume and listened.

"Gracie, if you're there, pick up. It's me. Pick up, Gracie. Come on. Okay. Whatever. I have to run. Meeting Jane. I just wanted to let you know I need your card to return that thing I bought. The guy at the store was a real asshole about it. So, maybe you should give me your card, just for the day, and I'll take care of things. Okay? I'll come by later to pick it up."

No thanks. No good-bye.

I had to get out of the apartment. I knew Simon all too well. I knew he would pound on the door and issue pitiful pleas until I broke down and let him in. The only way I could be safe was to leave my own home and take my credit cards with me. I'd changed the locks—again—but Simon had been known to pick a lock. I scanned the apartment for anything valuable he might steal—or "borrow," as he would claim—but there was nothing left to steal. I kept no secret stash of cash; I kept what little jewelry I had at Jess's apartment. Simon wasn't above pawning the gold bracelet my favorite aunt had given me for high school graduation. I loved that aunt and I loved that bracelet and Simon was not getting his hands on it. He'd already sold my wedding ring, though it was a shoddy thing to begin with and I can't imagine he got any real money for it.

I went to my favorite art supply store on Huntington Avenue. The day was sunny and dry with a refreshing breeze, perfect for walking. I'd grown up in a suburb of Boston. Everybody drove everywhere. Until you got your driver's license, you were virtually captive in your own home. It was only when I moved to the city that I discovered the joys of walking, that my legs were good for more than depressing the gas and brake pedals.

I wish I could walk to work, but that's impossible, given the school is located in Brookline. Instead, I take a commuter train. I could drive but having a car in the city is a hassle; parking is hard to find and traffic is always crazy. I tried for a while, but in the end I sold the car. I got very little for it. Simon had been in several accidents with it; I'm still surprised he hadn't managed to total the machine.

Life on a teacher's salary doesn't allow for a new car every other year.

I like teaching; I've been doing it since graduating from the Massachusetts School of Design with a master's in art education. I like teaching, though there's definitely a burnout factor to consider. A few older teachers at my school have taken sabbaticals. And I've learned that one of two things happen after a sabbatical. You come back refreshed, armed with new ideas and bursting with creative energy, or you don't come back at all.

I used to wonder if I'd know what to do with a sabbatical of

my own. Where would I go? What would I accomplish? I like to
work; I need to work. I need to be taking care of someone or a
roomful of little someones. What would I do if the only person
I had to take care of was me?

A few years back I stopped wondering about sabbaticals.

A high-pitched voice to my right made me flinch. Two young
girls, maybe about sixteen, brushed past me. They were dressed
as if it were already summer. Their fat bellies hung over their
low-slung, flouncy miniskirts; their hot pink and green flip-
flops smacked the spring sidewalk smartly. I suddenly remembered all the times when Simon and I would be walking along,
in the middle of a serious conversation or simply enjoying each
other's company, and an attractive woman would pass. Simon
would stop, stare, even compliment her as if I wasn't there, his
wife, the woman supporting his career.

More times than not the woman responded with appreciation.

Are women their own worst enemies? So much for sister-
hood.

Simon.

I caught up with the carefree teens at the next corner. One
wore sunglasses that covered three quarters of her face; they
were tinted purple. Was this, I wondered, the new style? If so,
I'd need to buy a new pair of sunglasses or settle for looking old
and frumpy this summer.

Summer.

The light turned green and I stepped into the street. What
would I do with myself this summer now that I no longer had
Simon to look after? How would I fill my time? There were options, of course. I could take a class, find a part-time job, sleep
late, see my friends, maybe take a few road trips to museums—
the Portland Museum of Art, the Ogunquit Museum of American
Art, the Farnsworth, DeCordova. I could eat some lobster if the
prices weren't too outrageous this year.

Lots of options and yet, none of them seemed particularly
enticing. It was only April but already the summer loomed as a
long and lonely stretch of time.

Jefferson's Paints. I pushed open the door and walked inside. As always, I gravitated first to the aisles of paints—oils, acrylics, watercolors. And suddenly, I felt a wee spark of excitement, maybe even inspiration—at least, I felt the desire for inspiration.

Yes, I thought, maybe this summer I would even work on my own art. I reached for a tube of cobalt violet. It's a beautiful color, but difficult to use and for my budget, very expensive. I wondered if I dared to buy it. I remembered reading about the color in a paint catalogue; the ad said that cobalt violet had been used since 1664 by various Dutch masters.

I frowned down at the tube of paint in my hand. I was no master, Dutch or otherwise. I thought of my bank account, underfed and in poor health. And I decided that there was no point in my buying the paint.

Desire, I reminded myself, is not the same as need.

Simon needs to paint. I like to paint, but it hadn't felt like a need for a long, long time. Maybe it never had; I realized I'd forgotten a lot about myself. Why had I put aside making paintings after I was no longer required to make them to earn my degree? It's true that my job involves lots of creation, but my own work, what was once my serious work, is not what I do with my students.

My serious work.

With a sigh I put the tube of paint back in its place on the shelf.

The truth is that Simon is far more talented than I am. And Simon needs tending; his spirit needs succor; his inspiration needs to be protected. With my work ethic and his gift, we'd make the perfect successful artist, if by successful one meant an artist who creates and shows regularly.

We certainly hadn't made the perfect husband and wife.

I turned to leave the aisle and stepped right into a person.

"Oh, I'm sorry!" I cried. It was a young man, maybe in his early twenties, wearing a T-shirt that said LIFE IS GOOD.

The young man smiled. "No, please, it was my fault."

"No, I wasn't paying attention."

"Well, neither was I. So, we are both at fault, okay?"

"Okay," I said.

I expected the young man to move on but he didn't; he stood there and smiled at me again. "What are you buying?" he asked.

"Oh. Well, nothing." I gestured to the shelves of oil paints. "I was just looking at a tube of cobalt violet."

"It's a beautiful color. It conveys passion."

"Yes," I agreed, "it does. But it's so expensive and I don't really have any immediate plans to paint so . . ."

The young man lightly, briefly touched my arm. "I think you should buy it anyway," he said, "even if you do not use it right now. If it is in your home, your studio, maybe it will inspire you to work. I am Alfonse, by the way."

Alfonse—I'd detected an accent—held out his hand and we shook.

"I'm Grace. Nice to meet you."

Alfonse smiled again and I found myself engaged in a lively conversation about painting in general and a current show at the Fogg Art Museum in particular.

Maybe it was the smile, maybe his generally warm manner and good conversational skills, maybe it was thoughts of a long and lonely summer. For whatever reason, I bought the tube of cobalt violet and a few new brushes.

Alfonse accompanied me to the cashier and then outside onto the sidewalk.

"Well," I said, "good-bye."

But Alfonse had another idea. "Would you come with me for a coffee?" he asked.

Of course I won't come with you for a coffee, I thought. I don't know you and . . . What will people think?

What people, Grace? A voice from inside me posed this question. I'd never heard the voice before. What people, indeed? So what if someone thought this boy was my—nephew? Simon dated women barely out of their teens and no one batted an eyelash.

Why couldn't I do the same? This boy—young man—was

adorable and sexy and he looked at me with such intensity, but not the creepy kind, the kind that makes you go weak in the knees. It had been a very long time since a man had made me go weak in the knees.

"Sure," I said. "Okay."

Alfonse smiled that lovely smile. He offered to carry my package and I let him. He walked on the outside of the side-walk, protecting me from any cars that might leap the curb. He had been trained well. I wondered how old his mother was. And then I pushed that thought away.

We found a little café, somewhat dingy, just down the block. There I learned that Alfonse had been born in Frankfurt, Germany, and that he'd been in Boston for a year, working as a graphic designer at a small firm owned by an American ex-change student he'd met back in college.

"So," I asked, "do you like it here in Boston?"

Alfonse nodded. "Yes. I have work and there is much to do here for fun. But I miss my home. I am close to my sister and her children."

We talked then a bit about our jobs and about another cur-rent exhibition at the Museum of Fine Arts. After a while, Alfonse checked his watch.

"I'm sorry," he said. "I have to go. I'm meeting a friend to see a film."

We paid for our own coffees. I doubted Alfonse had much money and I was tempted to pay for his coffee, but I didn't.

"Thank you," I said. "I enjoyed our talk."

"As did I. Will you see me again?"

There was something so sweet about the way he phrased the question. Not "Wanna have dinner sometime?"

I glanced again at his slim, expressive hand resting on his thigh and at the other one cradling the tiny espresso cup. And I did something entirely shocking.

"Yes," I said. "Let's get together tonight?"

"Face it, Grace. You're an idiot."

I stood naked in front of the freestanding full-length mirror in my bedroom. The mirror was an antique, far too large for the tiny room, but it had been such a deal I just couldn't pass it up.

Now, looking at my nearing-forty-year-old reflection in its glass, I wished I had.

I turned away and grabbed my robe from the bed. It was utterly insane to even consider going on a date with a guy almost half my age! I flashed back to those young girls I'd seen earlier, just before meeting Alfonse at Jefferson's Paints. Weren't they more the kind of girl he should be dating: nubile, carefree, and wearing flip-flops?

But then again, Alfonse had asked me out, not those belly-baring girls.

Me!

Was he on drugs? Had the paint fumes altered his perceptions?

I sat heavily on the bed and took a few deep breaths. It would be easy enough to call Alfonse and beg off, make some excuse and avoid any suggestions about a rescheduled meeting. It would be easy enough; he'd given me his cell phone number. Twentysomethings lived by their cell phones; there was no way Alfonse would miss my call and wind up waiting all alone for me at the restaurant where we'd agreed to meet.

I reached for the slip of paper on which I'd written his number. It sat on my nightstand, right by the phone. I looked at the neat handwriting and smiled. No doubt about it, Alfonse was sweet. And he was sexy, in that unconcerned, unaffected way some young men have. I was attracted to him. I enjoyed our conversation.

But could I go out on a date with him?

Maybe, I thought, I should call Jess and get her opinion. She went out with a much younger guy. I reached for the phone, then stopped. I wasn't sure reminding Jess about her affair with Seth, the event that had led to the breakup of her marriage, was such a good idea. Besides, I thought, you're an adult, Grace. You can make this decision on your own.

An adult. A grown woman with the beginnings of a middle-aged tummy and lines around her eyes and an occasional gray hair. What business did I have spending time with a guy who could—technically speaking—be my son?

Business. What business? What, I wondered, did having dinner with a man, even a very young man, what did that have to do with business, with right or wrong, with rules and regulations? Was I so—flattened—by years of tending to Simon that I'd completely forgotten how to do something purely for the pleasure of it?

Yes. Yes, I was so flattened.

And then the phone rang. I hurried into the living room where the machine was hooked up. I turned up the volume and waited. If it was Alfonse, would I pick up? Maybe he was calling to cancel, and if so I'd be glad, really.

"Gracie! Where were you today? I told you I'd be by."

Simon. Of course, Simon.

The sound of a car horn cut off his next words and then, yes, I heard it distinctly, the giggling of a woman, a young woman, the woman for whom he'd bought that expensive bauble.

"Jane, stop," Simon said, and I pictured him halfheartedly pushing away her grasping hand.

"So, I'll come by tonight, okay? Be there, Gracie."

And then Simon was gone and I was alone again in my living room, wrapped in my robe, facing another night all by myself or . . .

I marched back into my bedroom and flung open the closet. If the Diane Keaton character in *Something's Gotta Give* could do it, well, why couldn't I? If Demi Moore could do it in real life—well, the Hollywood version of real life—why couldn't I do it, too?

I was going out on a date with a much younger man.

I went into the bathroom and studied my face in the vanity mirror. An extra dab of moisturizer around my eyes and lips might just do the trick. And I prayed for low lighting at Rose Café.

* * *

"And so, now that I have told you about my obsession with eighties dance music, why don't you tell me about your obsession with whatever it is you love and are embarrassed to admit you love?"

I smiled at Alfonse. He was adorable, self-deprecating within reason, and oh, so sexy. In the low and—yes—flattering light of Rose Café his face took on a maturity it lacked in the light of day.

"Jellybeans," I said. "I am obsessed with jellybeans. I've tried every flavor imaginable, even some horrible ones. I don't know what it is about them that attracts me."

Alfonse lifted my hand and kissed it. "Your dread secret," he said with mock seriousness, "is safe with me."

The conversation all through dinner was like that, light and pleasant, such a contrast to dinners with Simon where he'd bemoan his lack of money, lament about the sorry state of the Boston art scene, rant about his latest nemesis—and never once ask anything about me. And never once want to talk about the state of our relationship.

And never, ever pull out his wallet when the bill came.

Alfonse, twenty-one-year-old Alfonse, paid for our meal. Out of habit I suppose I insisted on leaving the tip. He was gracious about my offer. I wondered if this were the last meal he'd ever pay for but pushed the thought away. Alfonse wasn't Simon. Even if he proved to share some characteristics with my ex-husband, he was not my ex-husband.

The very fact that he held the restaurant door for me proved that.

When we came out onto the sidewalk, I shivered. Alfonse put his arm around my shoulders and gently squeezed. "Are you cold?" he asked.

"A little," I admitted.

His arm felt good around me. We walked like that, close and side by side, for blocks. We didn't talk much. Bright green buds glowed under the streetlamps. The air was fresh as it is only in April.

When we reached the corner of my block, I stopped and turned to him.

"I live just a few doors down," I said. I don't know what I wanted to happen then. Suddenly, I felt terribly shy.

Alfonse leaned down and kissed my forehead. "Let me walk you to your door," he said. "It would make me happy to know you are home safely."

I nodded and we continued down the block. And my mind raced.

Come up for coffee, come up and see my etchings, want to come up and fool around?

What should I say, I wondered, and should I say anything at all?

Sex. Suddenly, it loomed large. I hadn't had sex in well over a year and then, once; it had been with Simon, a slip on my part. I'd regretted it for weeks.

Was I ready to have sex again, and with this very young man? Calm down, Grace, I told myself as we drew nearer to my building. Don't be crazy. If you invite Alfonse up to your apartment, it doesn't necessarily mean you have to have sex. All it means is that you could have sex if you choose to. If he wanted to and if you wanted to and . . .

"Grace?"

I started and realized we had stopped walking.

"Is this your building?" Alfonse asked.

I looked to my left, then back to Alfonse. "Yes," I said. And then I really looked into his eyes and liked what I saw there, someone honest and sweet and funny. And then, somehow, I found the courage to say: "Would you like to come up for a while?"

Alfonse didn't seem at all surprised. He smiled back at me and said, "It would be my pleasure."

I looked over my shoulder, half expecting to see Simon loping toward me, hand outstretched for my credit card. But the street was empty.

"Okay," I said.

I tripped on the first step outside my building. I fumbled with the keys to my door. I couldn't find the light switch on the wall in my apartment.

"I'm sorry," I mumbled into the dark.

Alfonse drew me to him. I felt his hard chest beneath his jacket.

"For what?" he whispered into my ear.

And then he kissed my ear and then my eyes and my cheeks and then my mouth and I forgot all about the lights being off and forgot all about Simon hurting me and forgot all about everything and was aware only of that moment and of Alfonse's lips on mine.

Ah, yes, I thought before all thought ceased, pleasure. If this was what pleasure felt like, I'd been depriving myself for far too long.

Chapter 10

Nell

Forget the Yellow Pages. Forget the Internet. The best way to find the right lawyer to handle your divorce is to ask around. Listen to the stories of your divorced friends and colleagues. Who's vacationing in Hawaii? Who's eating spaghetti from a can?

—*Finding the Perfect Divorce Attorney*

"**Y**ou don't look very good."

Jess sighed and dropped into the seat next to mine. The four of us were meeting for dinner at Le Chat Noir.

"I don't feel very good."

"What's wrong?" Grace asked.

My sister was eyeing her pinky nail as if she'd just discovered a colony of minuscule aliens on it. I wondered if she was aware Jess had joined us.

Jess sighed. "I'm sorry. I'm fine. I'll get my act together. Let's have a nice evening."

"Friends are allowed to destroy a good mood," I pointed out. "Not that we were swinging from the chandeliers before you came."

"Thanks, Nell. How about I order a drink first?"

She did and when it was served and sipped, she said, "Here's the thing. I'm plagued by guilt. It didn't even feel this bad when I was embroiled in the affair with Seth. It's getting worse as time goes by."

Laura finally looked up from her nail. "It hasn't been that long since you came clean to Matt," she said unhelpfully.

Jess ignored her. "Some days," she said, "the guilt feels like a physical thing, like a cancer, something chewing up my insides, something that really can and will kill me. I'm embarrassed to look at my own face in the mirror. I feel like a freak. I feel evil. I scare myself. If I could cheat on my husband, what other horrible thing am I capable of?"

Poor thing.

"Infidelity is not an atrocity," I said with conviction. "It's not an admirable thing, not something one should aspire to, but it doesn't make you a criminal. At least, in this country and in this day and age, infidelity is not a crime. No one is going to brand you with a scarlet letter. The men in the village aren't going to beat you to death."

Grace patted Jess's hand. "I hate that you're feeling such guilt, Jess. You've got to work past it."

"I'm trying," she said. "Sort of. Not really."

"Look," Grace went on, "the experts say that when a spouse has an affair, it's not really about the other person, the bimbo secretary or the milkman or whoever. It's about what's lacking in the marriage. And yes, of course I've considered that maybe one of the reasons Simon cheated on me all the time was that I really wasn't the right woman for him. The point is, Jess, that you're not entirely to blame. Matt wasn't the right man for you."

Jess nodded. "I know that. I know that now, anyway."

"Seth was a convenient way for you to leave Matt," Laura announced, as if she'd been rehearsing the thought and its delivery. "Have an affair, confess, get a divorce. Simple."

I glared at my sister but she refused to be cowed.

Jess laughed awkwardly. "Oh, great. Now I feel guilty about having used Seth. Which was not my intention, believe me."

"Didn't you tell me that by the time you ended the affair, Seth was already eyeing some other lady professor?" I asked her.

"Yes. But is that the point? Anyway, I've been wondering. Maybe I'm addicted to falling in love, not to being in love."

"That's ridiculous," I said brusquely. "You're not addicted to anything. Tell me, was Seth your first affair?"

"Yes. I was always one hundred percent monogamous in my relationships before Matt. But I was never married before Matt."

"Maybe marriage just isn't for you," Grace suggested.

"Or," Jess said, "maybe it is, maybe it can be with some other man, someday. I'd like to know for sure. I'd like a crystal ball to show me the answer."

"You'll know the answer when you next fall in love. You'll know then how you feel about marriage and if it's a good choice for you."

Jess didn't look too sure about Grace's optimistic vision.

"See a therapist," I told her. "Go to a support group. See a minister if you have to. Get some perspectives other than those of your friends. And above all, promise me you'll get rid of this ridiculous guilt."

Jess nodded but didn't voice any promises.

We needed to lighten the mood. "So, Laura," I said, "how's the daddy hunting going?" My sister's escapades were sure to amuse us.

Laura shrugged. "Well," she said, "I can't say I've made any real progress. Last night, I went to a singles mixer—can you believe it? It was really called a mixer, like something from the fifties!—in the basement of a church."

"A Catholic church?" Grace asked. She had been raised in the Catholic Church and, though she didn't practice the faith, she retained a keen interest in its comings and goings.

"No. It was some new denomination, I think. Something like the Second Church of Good God . . . No, that's not it. The Third Church the Sacred Candle . . . I forget. Anyway, I won't be going back!"

Jess barely restrained a grin, which must have been hard since it was probably the first time in days she'd felt like smiling.

"Oh?" I asked. "Why is that?"

"Well, we had to sing hymns. And they weren't good hymns, either."

"You would know what constitutes a good hymn?" I asked.

"I know 'Amazing Grace' and that's a great hymn. Everyone says so." Laura made a face. "But these were sort of—stupid. Like the writers were trying to be cool or hip or something but they just didn't get it."

"So," Jess asked, "what happened after the hymns?"

"Not much. They had some disgusting punch with, like, a pound of sugar in it. I mean, I like sweets but this was gross. And the guys were all seriously nerdy, like they still lived at home with their mothers or something. It was kind of creepy. Plus, I was the only woman in pants. Everyone else was wearing some loose flowery dress, like a sack." Laura shuddered. "It was like a scene from what's that old show, *Little House on the Prairie.*"

"Well, did you talk to anyone?" Grace asked.

Laura nodded. "This one guy looked fairly normal, so I went over to him and we started chatting, you know, about the weather and what we did for a living. And . . . well, I don't know how it came up, but I mentioned that I was getting divorced and it was like I'd just admitted to being a child molester or something."

"Oh," I said. "What did he do?"

"He marched right over to some people behind the punch table—I think maybe they were the priests or something—and they all started to glare at me like I was some evil criminal. One even pointed his finger at me! Ugh. It was horrible."

"Did they try to stone you?" I inquired sweetly.

"It wasn't funny." Laura pouted. "I was really scared. So I just grabbed my jacket from the back of a folding chair and ran. I mean, I actually ran."

My sister, I thought, *is an imbecile.*

"What were you doing at a Christian singles event, anyway? You haven't been to church since grammar school. And by the way, Mom and Dad were Episcopalian."

"Whatever. I don't have time to waste. I have to find a guy soon. I've got to stay open to new ideas."

Ideas old or new were never my sister's strong suit, but I felt no need to point that out.

"I've got," she said, "to have that baby."

"A baby," Jess replied, "isn't going to guarantee anything other than more expenses. A baby can't grant you eternity. A grown-up child is not necessarily going to take care of you when you're old. Remember your Shakespeare: 'How sharper than a serpent's tooth it is/To have a thankless child.'"

"My sister never read Shakespeare," I said.

"I did, too! I took a class in college!"

I bowed my head. "My mistake."

"A baby," Laura said, "is going to love me."

Poor Laura. "Sure," I said, "he's going to love you at first because he has no choice. He has to rely on you for everything: food, shelter, changing his diaper. But he might not love you when he grows up."

Laura waved her hand dismissively. "Maybe other people's children don't love their parents. That's their problem. Those parents probably did something wrong in the first place. My child will love me for his entire life. Or for her entire life."

"It sounds exhausting," I quipped. "Poor little kid."

Jess leaned in toward my sister. "Really, Laura, what do you want from a child? Be careful not to load an awful lot of responsibility onto a very small person. You can't ask a child to save you from loneliness or whatever it is you want to be saved from."

"I don't want to be saved from anything," Laura snapped. "I just want a baby. Does there have to be some deep dark reason?"

"I'm sorry, Laura," Grace said. "We're just trying to understand."

My sister threw her napkin on the table. "Why do you have to understand? It's my life, not yours. Why does everyone have to be so mean?"

"I'm sorry," Jess repeated. "It's just that we like Duncan. We love you. We thought you two were good together. This situation is just a little hard to absorb."

I don't know why I can't leave well enough alone with my sister. But I can't.

"And," I said, "it's a little hard to believe you really want another husband. You had a perfectly good one and you tossed him away. If you really just want a baby, you can have one without a husband. Without a boyfriend, even. It's done all the time."

Laura rolled her eyes. "Of course I want a husband. I want a traditional, two-parent family."

"And adoption is out of the question?" Jess asked.

"Absolutely. I don't want someone else's baby. I want my own."

Maybe, I thought, Laura's baby would get Duncan's brain. I hoped so.

"But first you have to get pregnant," Grace said, "and that's not always easy. Really, Laura, would it be so horrible if you don't—if you can't—have a child of your own? Do you really think your life would be empty and meaningless if you don't give birth?"

Laura stared at her discarded napkin. I wondered if she'd considered the actual giving birth part. Laura had always been squeamish. The sight of even a drop of blood sent her swooning.

"I know it's hard," Grace went on in a gentle tone, "but try to imagine not getting the one thing you want more than anything—and then try to imagine surviving. Lots of people don't get what they want. But they survive. And they find creative ways to make their lives feel rich and meaningful."

Laura looked away from the napkin. "What do you want more than anything?" she challenged us.

Jess and Grace were silent.

"I don't know what I want now," I admitted. "I know what I wanted when I was a girl. I wanted to meet my Prince Charming, fall madly in love, get married, and live happily ever after. And I got that. My wish was fulfilled. At least, most of it was. At least, I thought it was. Now? I just don't know."

"Well," Laura said, and it was impossible to miss the note of triumph in her voice, "unlike you all, I have a goal. I have a dream and I'm going after it."

"Good for you," Jess murmured.

Grace leaned forward. "I've read about women who have a baby because their relationship with their husband is lacking in emotional depth or on shaky ground. They believe a baby will cement their union somehow, you know, by providing a common topic of concern. They believe a baby will provide the emotional stuff they really need from their husbands."

"They're just being silly," Laura said self-righteously. "I would never do something so dumb."

Add self-delusional to the list of my sister's flaws.

"Let's get off the topic of babies," Jess said. "I'll be dreaming of diapers and formula all night."

"Excellent idea," I said. "Grace, what's been going on with you since Simon's banishment?"

A grin came to Grace's lips. "I'm seeing someone."

"Not Simon, I hope!"

"No, Laura, of course not! Not anymore. I am completely over him."

"So?" Jess said. "Tell us about him."

"Well, his name is Alfonse and he was born in Germany and he's a graphic designer."

"Is he divorced?" I asked. "Does he have children? How long has he been in the U.S.? Is he a citizen?"

"No, no, a while, yes." Grace grimaced and hunched her shoulders, as if bracing herself against a blow. "Here's the thing. He's only twenty-one years old."

Laura clapped. "Cradle robber! I didn't know you had it in you, Grace."

Neither did I.

"Well, this is a little weird," I said, "considering I have an eighteen-year-old son and the thought of him with a woman in her thirties is a tad disturbing. But I'll get over the weirdness. I always do."

"The sex is fantastic," Grace blurted. "Sorry, Nell."

"No, no, go right ahead. I'm already adjusting. Just because I haven't had sex in over a decade doesn't mean that you have to be celibate."

That dampened the mood for about a second.

Grace sighed. "It's just that I'm having so much fun. I feel kind of ashamed, kind of dirty, but—there it is!"

"How *Sex and the City* of you," Jess said. "How Samantha Jones."

"Am I a cliché?" Grace asked worriedly.

"Who cares if you are? I suppose I was a cliché by having an affair with Seth. He's only twenty-five."

"So," I said, "you're fully aware this relationship isn't going to last?"

"Of course I'm aware. But I don't get the sense that Alfonse is going anywhere soon. I think he's going to be my summer companion."

I wondered.

"I hope you have some other activities planned," I said. "Just in case the young man disappears before Labor Day. Besides, you can't stay in bed all day having sex."

Or could you? I wouldn't know.

Grace frowned. "Actually, I'm not sure what I'm going to do this summer. Now that I don't have Simon to babysit."

"Make sure you keep it that way," Laura admonished. "Don't let him come sneaking back."

"Simon doesn't sneak. He barges in. He's not subtle." Grace turned to me. "What about you, Nell? What do you have lined up for the summer?"

Ah, the first step of my new life.

"I'm hereby letting it be known that I am an available single woman. I've already notified my colleagues on the museum and symphony committees and they're on watch for an eligible man."

"Good for you," Jess said.

"Why don't you sign up with a dating service?" Laura asked.

How could my sister begin to understand the horror I felt at the prospect of letting strangers arrange my romantic life?

"I am absolutely not putting an ad in a paper or signing up for an online dating service or going through any other channel but my friends," I said. "I'm willing to be introduced to a man through a friend or colleague. It's the only way I can handle this—this whole new world."

"Okay," Jess said. "So, what are your requirements? You know, in case I meet anyone in my vast and exciting travels on the T."

"Just a few," I said. "He can't be too old." I looked pointedly at Grace. "And he can't be too young. Can you imagine what my children would think of me if I went out with a twenty-one-year-old?"

"This is not about your kids," Jess pointed out. "This is about you."

I sighed. "There is no real me apart from my kids. Not entirely. But I know what you mean. Anyway, he can have kids of his own, of course. He can be divorced. Who isn't divorced these days? I would be happy to go on a first date, gather some important details, and then decide if I want to see him again."

"What kind of details?" Laura asked.

"Well," I said, "for example, does he talk about his job incessantly? Does he consider his children more of a burden than a joy? Is his ex-wife horrid? And if she is, does he take the high road and keep his mouth shut, or does he talk badly about her to anyone who will listen? Things like that, important things. Widowers are fine, too, again, depending on the details."

"Like an obsession with his dead wife," Jess suggested.

"Yes, like that."

"Anything else?"

"Yes," I said. "Financial solvency. I am absolutely not supporting a man. Good health, within reason. Good grooming habits. I refuse to teach a man how to trim his nose hair. Intelligence is a must. A sophisticated sense of humor is also a must. No little-boy toilet humor for me. Good moral character, of course. Brown eyes would be nice."

Jess laughed, finally. "Is that all? Piece of cake. I meet a million perfect men every day of the week. You'll be married before the end of the month."

"Oh, I'm not saying I want to get married. Yet. Maybe ever. I just think I should go on a few dates. I just think I should see what it feels like to have dinner with a man other than Richard."

Laura beamed. "I think it's a great idea."

"Are you nervous about being back in the game?" Grace asked.

"Ladies," I announced, "I'm terrified."

Chapter 11

Jess

Is the judge a man? How old is he? Is he married or single? Does he have children? Find out the answers to these questions and dress accordingly.

— *What to Wear to the Divorce: How to Influence the Judge in Your Favor*

It was called Women of Divorce. I found it online. The group met on Wednesday mornings at ten o'clock, which was not really convenient for me as I was usually in my office by nine, but I went anyway.

At the foot of the stairs leading from the sidewalk to the church basement there was a door. On it was posted the name of the group and a wiggly WELCOME. One last chance to run. I opened the door and went inside.

A ring of folding chairs had been set in one corner of the large, recreation-type space. Three women were already seated. One rose and waved me over.

"Women of Divorce?" I asked.

"That's us!" The woman handed me a blank name tag and a pink marker. I should have known right then that this group was not for me. Pink has never been my color. But I'd promised my friends to give it a try. And I always try to keep my promises. Except when I don't.

"I'm Patty," she said, tapping her own name tag. "And this is Marianne and this is Heidi."

I smiled tentatively at the other two women and took a seat across from them, a wee bit closer to the door.

Over the next few minutes the rest of the group gathered. It was a motley crew: a few women seemed to be in their fifties; one woman looked no more than twenty-five. Everyone was nicely dressed; after all, the meeting was taking place in the Back Bay. No underprivileged here.

I looked down at my five-year-old suit; it had been an expensive purchase for an academic. I wondered what I had in common with these women, other than our sex and being divorced. I thought again of fleeing but before I could take action, Patty introduced me as the newest member of the group. The women nodded or released tight, inquiring smiles.

"Jess," Patty said, "would you like to tell us about yourself?"

No, I thought. I would not. And then, words, unrehearsed, just came pouring out of my mouth.

"One day," I said, "I looked in the mirror; I was brushing my teeth, no big deal; and suddenly, I realized I didn't know who I was any longer."

I looked at Patty. Her smile remained fixed and she gave a slight nod.

"Everyone's heard that cliché," I went on. "'I looked in the mirror and I realized I didn't know who I was.' I've seen ads for recovery programs that use that phrase or something like it. Well, that morning I learned the scary truth behind that cliché and I started to think about the strange process of alienation. It's slow and subtle and sneaky and you just aren't aware of it happening, until one day you look for yourself or for the person you're supposed to love and you can't see them without squinting. Instead of right next to you, they're miles away, little dots on the horizon, and receding ever farther. You shout, 'Hey, come back!' but most times they can't hear you and maybe, used to silence, they aren't even listening."

I felt a flush coming to my cheeks. I sat a bit straighter in the folding chair. I didn't see the women around me anymore; I saw my face in the bathroom mirror that important morning.

"And then," I said, "I began to wonder if there was a way to recognize this process of alienation early on. I began to wonder if there was a way to stop it. I began to wonder if we're all doomed to live and die alone, apart even from ourselves.

"Right then, right at that moment, standing at the sink, toothpaste dribbling down my chin, I vowed to start paying attention—to me, to other people, to everything. It might, I realized, be my only hope of—of happiness."

As abruptly as the words had come, they were gone. I looked around the circle of the Women of Divorce. No one was nodding sympathetically. No one was smiling encouragingly. The woman named Heidi looked angry.

I was puzzled. Weren't we here to talk things through, even if we didn't make complete sense?

Finally, Sally offered a practiced smile. "That's—nice. But let's get down to business."

"I'm sorry?" I said.

A woman named Ellen spoke. "What Sally means is, what did your nasty ex do to you? Mine left me for my sister. He destroyed my family and tainted my past. Just so you know."

"Mine developed a cocaine habit." Diane snorted. "So retro! We lost the house and I barely got out with the few pieces of antique furniture I'd brought to the marriage."

"You won't believe this," a woman named Aggie said. Her eyes glittered with anger. "My creep of an ex-husband had a second wife and kids in New Hampshire. Evil bastard."

Oh. I felt my shoulders slump just a bit. I folded my hands on my lap. What had my nasty ex-husband done to me?

Matt was obsessed with football. He didn't laugh much. He spent too much time at the office. But you couldn't blame the end of a marriage on sports or a poor sense of humor or even workaholism. Could you? I shot a look at Sally, who seemed to be the leader of this gang.

"So?" she urged. "Tell us."

Here it was. The moment of truth.

"Well," I began, looking at no one in particular, trying for a casual, yet not a flippant tone, "actually, the long story short is that I . . . I had an affair. When I told Matt, he demanded a divorce. So . . . we got divorced."

There was dead silence. Really, everything felt dead, heavy. And then the woman named Ellen leaned forward, her neck stretched like that of a starving baby bird, eyes blazing.

"What gave you the right?" she demanded. "Here we are, so many women being betrayed by their husbands and you have a perfectly fine husband and you cheat on him!"

It took a moment for her words to sink in. "Um," I said finally, "are you saying that because you were unhappy, I didn't have a right to be happy? That's like saying . . . That's like your mother telling you to eat all your vegetables because there are starving kids in Africa."

"It's about being grateful for what you have," Aggie snapped. "You should have been grateful to have a husband in the first place. You should have been grateful he wasn't a jerk."

I felt a surge of anger like a wave of boiling oil in my head. I probably should have left the room right then rather than subject myself to further abuse, but I was far beyond sensible thinking.

"First of all," I said, voice trembling, "you know nothing about me, not really, so how dare you lecture me on my personal happiness! And how do you know my husband wasn't a jerk? For your information he was a jerk, just like every other man can be a jerk. And, and, I should have been grateful? What is this, the days of Queen Victoria? A woman has a right to be happy, not just grateful."

Eyes rolled but no one argued my point.

"What did he ever do that was so bad?" the woman named Aggie suddenly challenged.

What, indeed?

"He changed the access code to one of our joint accounts to CHEATER," I said. "That was uncalled-for."

Sally glared at me. "You *are* a cheater. He was just telling the truth."

Clearly, she hadn't accepted Jesus as her personal savior. "Let him who is without sin cast the first stone."

My self-preservation instincts kicked into higher gear.

"You're preaching pick-and-choose morality," I said, fixing Sally with a glare of my own. "If I had been an abused wife, no one would blame me for cheating. Are you saying it's acceptable to cheat because you have a black eye but not acceptable because your soul is bruised?"

"So," Sally said, with a wicked gleam in her eye, "now that we know Matt's not a wife beater, can we have his number?"

A few of the women laughed uncomfortably. Sally, I realized, wasn't kidding. I felt stunned.

"I don't have it," I said. "It's unlisted. We're not in touch."

Sally turned to her neighbor with a smirk. "Who can blame him?"

By the time I got home that night—after a long departmental meeting, after a stalled train—I was wiped out, a dishrag, a wet noodle.

The women's message had been clear. Men who cheat are despicable but normal. Women who cheat are whores. Worse, they are potential threats to all other women, especially those who are married. After all, if you'll cheat on your own husband, what's to stop you from stealing another woman's husband?

I tried to eat something but had little appetite. At eight-thirty I got ready for bed. In the bathroom I saw Matt's shaving equipment on the sink. It wasn't really there but I saw it anyway, like an accusation.

I looked straight in the bathroom mirror and spoke these words aloud: I broke my marriage vow. I did something wrong. But I believe, deep down, that I am a good person, a good person who has done a bad thing. I am not an aberration of nature, no matter what the Women of Divorce think.

I am not an aberration.

Chapter 12

Nell

Tip #348: Redirect the money you reserved for charity to your Personal Plastic Surgery Fund. Remember: As a middle-aged single woman in America, you are in much more need of help than orphaned plague victims.

—*You Need All the Help You Can Get: Dating in Middle Age*

"So, little lady, what will it be?"

I smiled tightly. I really wanted to leap from my seat at the white-clothed table and run, but I sat tight and smiled tighter.

"I think," I said to the red-faced, overfed specimen across from me, "that I'll have the broiled fish."

I hoped my choice of entrée would put him off. I assumed he'd try to bully me into eating red meat, and that the more I refused the more he'd realize I was not the "little lady" for him.

I was wrong. I'd never been up against this particular breed of man before.

"Now that's what I like to hear!" he boomed. "A lady taking care of her looks, watching her weight so her man can look across the room when she makes an entrance and know that every other man in that room is crazy with jealousy."

What, I wondered, had Jane Roberts, someone I'd known for years, someone I thought sane, what had Jane been thinking fixing me up with this caricature?

Over the salad—which Mr. Longhorn barely touched—I was

informed that a pretty little thing like me shouldn't be all on her own in a big city like this. "I don't know what that ex-husband of yours was thinking when he took off on you," Mr. Longhorn said, shaking his head sadly. "That homosexuality, it's a disease is what it is, a disease and a crime against God and man. And against all the little ladies like you."

Have you ever been so shocked, so appalled by the words coming out of someone's mouth you can't even protest? You're frozen, you can't imagine where you would even begin to argue.

"Uuuh," I said.

Over dessert and coffee—I made sure to order the double portion of cheesecake in a last-ditch effort to repulse him—Mr. Longhorn promised me my very own horse. I protested that I didn't ride. He laughed loudly and assured me that if he had anything to do with it, I'd be sitting tall in the saddle before long.

The check arrived and Mr. Longhorn signed with a flourish. I began to rise but Mr. Longhorn reached for my hand and anchored me to my seat. He leaned in and his expression turned serious.

"Now, what you need," he said, "is a real man to take proper care of you, a real man to give you all the nice things you deserve like pretty clothes and sparkly jewelry. Little lady, I am that man. Now, I'm also a gentleman; nobody will tell you otherwise. So I'm prepared to offer you my guesthouse, which, by the way, has a Jacuzzi and three bedrooms and a pool and all the other amenities, until you feel ready to move into the big house with me."

Central casting. I was out with a character from central casting. Where was the director to yell "cut"?

I nodded weakly. "I'll think about it," I lied.

Mr. Longhorn released my hand and grinned. "Little lady, I'll expect your answer in the morning."

Later that night, safely at home, sitting by a window overlooking beautiful Marlborough Street, I wondered.

Suppose Richard wasn't gay.

Would we have stayed married forever? Or would we have gotten divorced at some point along the way?

There was no way to know.

I suppose it hadn't been realistic to think that Richard and I could, that we would stay together our entire lives, from the age of twenty, and be happy, fulfilled, challenged in our relationship.

I suppose it's never realistic or even reasonable to think that a person can be really happy with one other person forever after.

How many married couples who stay married until one of them dies can honestly say that they weren't terribly bored at times?

How many can honestly say that they never fell in love with someone else along the way, someone they didn't pursue because they'd made a vow to stay with their spouse? How many would say they regretted that choice?

How many people married until the end of a life can honestly say that they were perfectly content?

Well, I thought, whoever is perfectly content? And who ever said anyone had the right to be perfectly content?

Life is hard. Life is lonely.

If I'm honest with myself, and I'm trying to be in this process of emotional recovery, I can admit to times during my marriage to Richard when I felt very lonely. Only now am I realizing—or am I inventing this?—that I would have liked more passion in our relationship. All those nights watching romantic movies on DVD, watching men sweep women into their arms and kiss them hungrily . . .

I had none of that, not since the very beginning with Richard, and even then, though there was intense love, there was never intense passion.

Maybe I was unhappy for a lot of my marriage but didn't even realize it. Why? Because I had so many things, I still have so many things: beautiful furniture, stylish clothes, gorgeous jewelry. Lots of things. And I have a career of sorts, volunteer work but meaningful work. And I have Colin and Clara and a house to run and parties to give and friendships to maintain. She who is busy has no time to realize unhappiness.

Now I have to wonder: why was I so busy in the first place? To fill a void I suspected was there but was afraid to acknowledge? Maybe. I might not ever really figure out the past, my past before Richard and my past with Richard.

And what about the present? It feels tender and raw. The future? It feels dark; it feels frightening, not in the least bit promising. I hope that before too long that changes.

One thing I do know about the future. It is not going to include Mr. Longhorn.

Chapter 13

Laura

Ask yourself these tough questions and be sure to answer honestly: Isn't it about time your lazy-assed ex-husband took some responsibility for the kids he helped create? Isn't it about time you got every weekend and all holidays to yourself?
—*What to Do with the Kids: Custody Advice from Professional Divorcées*

"What is this?"

Jerry looked down at the stapled pages on the table in front of him.

A girl at work had set me up. Jerry Truman was her accountant, divorced with no children, thirty-six years old. He was balding, wore glasses, and was a teeny bit overweight. He looked like a nice man, the kind just made for bouncing a toddler on his knee.

Right then we were sitting at a table for two at a high-end restaurant Jerry had suggested. It was good to know he could afford to eat at expensive places. That meant he could afford to keep me and my baby in a nice house in a nice suburb.

"It's just a little questionnaire I came up with," I explained, "you know, to help me evaluate a man. The questions are mostly about your health, some stuff about family history, you know, all the basics. Do you need a pen? I have one if you do."

Jerry shook his head. I don't know why he seemed so shocked or baffled. Good health is important in a potential sperm donor. I mean, in a potential father.

"I'm not filling this out," he said finally. "I don't even know you. What right do you have to be asking me such personal questions? This is supposed to be a date, not a visit to the doctor."

"I'll give you another moment to think about it," I said. I excused myself to go to the ladies' room. And once there I began to wonder. Maybe Jerry had a point. Maybe the first date was too early to be asking such probing questions about a family history of mental illness. Jerry seemed like a nice guy; he came well recommended; maybe, I thought, I should let him wait until our second date to complete the questionnaire.

I leaned over the sink and looked at my reflection in the mirror.

My eyes were still bright; the whites were still white. My hair was still thick. My skin had retained its elasticity. But below the shoulders my biological clock was ticking wildly.

Why, I wondered, couldn't men understand this? Jerry, I realized, was just like Duncan, just like all the rest. Men have all the time in the world to make a baby, but we women aren't so lucky.

I washed my hands vigorously. Germs are everywhere.

Maybe, I thought, there's another reason Jerry refused to fill out my questionnaire. Maybe he's hiding something like a deadly infectious disease! Isn't it illegal not to tell a potential sexual partner that you're ill? If not actually illegal, it's definitely unethical.

I dried my hands carefully and reapplied a little hand lotion from the bottle I always carry in my purse. Men like a woman with soft hands.

I walked back to our table. It was empty. I assumed Jerry had gone to the men's room. I sat and waited and sipped my wine. I noticed that Jerry's glass was full; he hadn't taken even a sip. Maybe, I thought, he's not a drinker. That was another good quality in a potential father.

Minutes passed.

"Miss?"

I looked up at our waiter. He held out a white letter-sized envelope. "The gentleman asked me to give you this."

Inside the envelope was twenty-five dollars. It covered the two glasses of wine and a tip. The waiter melted away. I left the money and the envelope on the table and caught a cab home.

Later that night I picked up the most recent issue of *Mommy* magazine and tore out a subscription card. It helps to be prepared and, given the fact that I hadn't been around babies since Colin and Clara were small, I felt I really needed some reeducation.

Plus, with the subscription you got a free sippy cup.

I met Larry in the produce section of Star Market. He was well dressed, well groomed, and filling a plastic container at the salad bar. I noticed that he avoided the high-fat choices like the avocado slices in favor of low-fat items like the sliced tomatoes.

Tomatoes and tomato-based products are very good for the prostate. This guy looked no older than thirty-eight or thirty-nine, too young to be actively worried about his prostate, but obviously he was mature enough to take preventative measures.

A strong candidate for fatherhood if I'd ever seen one!

I followed him to the peaches and admired the way his manicured hand gently squeezed the fruit for freshness.

"I just love peaches," I said. I picked up a jumbo-sized peach and sniffed it.

The guy half smiled and turned to walk away.

"Could you help me pick a good one?"

The guy half turned.

"Were you talking to me?" he asked.

I smiled dazzlingly. "Yes. If you have a moment, that is. Would you help me pick a good peach?"

He hesitated. And then he said, "That one you have in your hand has a brown spot."

I looked at the fat fruit. So it did.

I laughed tinklingly. "I'm so bad at choosing fruit!"

Well, I had him from there. He took a half step forward, stopped, then came right on over to me.

A few minutes later I left the store with a bag of peaches—

which I don't really like all that much—and Larry left the store with his heart-healthy lunch and my phone number.

We met a few nights later at Bar Europa. The questionnaire was in my purse. This time, before springing it on my date, I decided to address the issue right up front. As soon as we'd ordered a drink, I told Larry that I was getting a divorce from a man who wouldn't give me a baby. I told him that I was looking for a husband and a father to that baby.

Most men like the direct approach.

Larry laughed. "I don't know if I'm flattered or offended," he said.

"You should be flattered," I told him. "I'm very choosy."

Larry drank down half of his scotch. Then he looked right at me like I was a piece of fruit he was assessing for potential sweetness. Then he shook his head.

"You're too old to be having kids," he said.

I wasn't sure I'd heard him correctly. "Excuse me?" I replied. I suddenly noticed that the light in the bar wasn't the most flattering. Was there a weird grayish cast to my skin or something?

Larry laughed again. "Look, when I'm ready to get married, I'm going to pick a woman in her midtwenties. That's when a woman should have kids, when she's young enough to get pregnant without all those expensive medical procedures. I don't want to have to pay a doctor to get my wife pregnant. Besides, young women get their figures back. Someone like you? Well, let's just say I'm not interested and leave it at that."

Do you know what? No one had ever said anything so horrible to me in my entire life. I really didn't know what to say or to do. So I stated the obvious.

"I guess this date is over."

Larry slipped off the barstool. "Yeah. But, you know, good luck with finding a guy who'll go along with this whacky scheme. Hey. You don't expect me to pay for the drinks, do you?"

"Of course not," I replied, with as much dignity as I could, considering I felt absolutely awful, fat and old and stupid.

Why, I wondered, as Larry hurried off, had he ever gone out with me in the first place?

* * *

When I got home that night, I made myself a cup of tea and went online. After some searching I found what I was looking for—a chat room for Mothers of Advanced Maternal Age. Though I was still only thirty-four, I'd be thirty-five before long and then I'd officially qualify for this group.

I stayed in the chat room until almost midnight. The women were nice and very comforting. It didn't matter what Larry had said. What did he know, anyway? I was not too old to have a child, maybe even two children. The members of this chat group knew the truth. They knew that a woman could have a baby well into her forties.

If she has enough money and isn't afraid of needles.

Chapter 14

Grace

When the tedium of everyday life with your spouse becomes unbearable, file for divorce. You'll be thrown into a whirlpool of acrimony, accusations, and anger, all of which will leave you anything but bored. And when the chaos has receded and the tedium of everyday domestic life lived all alone becomes unbearable, propose to the first man you meet!
—*Serial Marriage: The Perfect Solution to Boredom*

"**D**o you want me to answer?"

Alfonse nodded toward the phone. I'd seen the number flash on the screen. It was Simon's cell phone.

"No," I said. "Let the machine pick up."

But I'd forgotten to turn the volume down. And there was Simon's voice, filling my home, again.

"Gracie? Hey, are you there? Look, I know you didn't forget my birthday; you never do. It's next Wednesday and a bunch of us are getting together at Café Trash. I haven't seen you in ages. Be there? Around ten."

Alfonse touched my shoulder. "A friend?" he asked.

Was he jealous? I turned to look at my young lover. No, no dark emotions in his eyes.

"Not really," I said. "He used to be."

Alfonse smiled and grabbed his backpack from the floor by the door. "I can come by tonight?" he asked. "After work?"

I smiled back, distracted, thinking mostly of Simon. Simon never asked. Simon always took. "Sure," I said. "I need to be up early tomorrow though."

"Okay. We will go to bed early, then!" He winked and was gone, my boy toy.

The apartment seemed terribly quiet all of a sudden.

I turned on the radio. It was set to NPR. But after a few minutes of depressing news from a starving continent, I turned it off again.

I'm not proud of the fact that at that moment my personal problems felt more important than the problems of hungry children. But they did.

I looked at the door to the bathroom. You could hardly see where I'd patched the hole Simon had kicked in it. Living with Simon had made me quite skilled in home repair.

Simon.

I could bring Alfonse to Simon's little gathering, I thought. There was no reason I couldn't. But even in the depths of that lonely moment I knew that the only reason I'd show up at Simon's birthday party with Alfonse was to show him off, to make Simon jealous, which, I was pretty sure, would be a futile effort.

Simon is not the jealous type. He doesn't care enough about anyone other than himself to be possessive.

Who knows, maybe that's a good thing in the end, not caring.

I walked over to the phone. My finger hovered over the "erase all messages" button.

Besides, whether I went to the party alone or with Alfonse, I knew what would happen. One by one Simon's friends would slip off into the night, say they were going outside for a cigarette and not return, and I would be left with the bill. It had happened too many times for me to doubt it would happen again.

I depressed the button. No more Simon.

The program was called Art for All. The Web site informed me that the program was new, privately funded, and free to all kids twelve and under. There would be two summer sessions. The staff was mostly volunteer. The director position hadn't yet

been filled. The duties included helping to design the mini-
courses, handling administrative matters such as grant writing,
and working directly with the kids. The salary was nominal.

It didn't matter. If I'd wanted to make a lot of money, I
wouldn't have gone into teaching in the first place.

I applied for the job via the Web site.

Two days later I received a call from the Art for All founder,
a Cambridge-based philanthropist. She asked me to come to
her home in Porter Square for an interview.

I did. She offered me the job on the spot. I said yes.

It certainly wouldn't be a relaxing summer, but that was okay.
The way I figured it, the busier I kept myself, the less time I'd
have to wonder what Simon was up to.

Chapter 15

Laura

Tip #65: There's always a man older than you. So, you're forty-five? Go for a sixty-five-year-old. So, you're fifty-five? Find yourself a seventy-five-year-old. What do you care if his ass hangs down to his knees? You're in it for the money, honey.
—*So She Married a Millionaire: How to Beat Those Whores at Their Own Game*

"He has no butt," Nell whispered.

It was true. Alfonse was boyishly slim. But that didn't seem to bother Grace, who, let's face it, weighs like ninety pounds herself.

"Since when do you notice men's butts?" I asked.

"Since I've been back in the game, I've realized that I like a man with a nice butt."

"You don't want one too big," I said.

Nell gave me an odd smile. "Of course not, Laura."

We were at Grace's apartment for a little party. Grace wanted us to meet Alfonse. Personally, I thought the whole thing was a big waste of time. We all knew Alfonse would be gone before long. But, you know how it is. Sometimes you have to humor your friends.

Grace joined us, a smile on her face. On the other side of the living room, Alfonse and his three friends stood in a huddle, drinking some foul-looking stuff from odd-shaped bottles. I guess it was one of those hip drinks you see advertised on television. You know, in commercials where everyone looks like a super-gorgeous model. Anyway, since we'd arrived, the three friends hadn't said more than "hey" to us, and even that "hey" was said like they didn't mean it.

"Grace," Jess said, "the place looks really nice."

Grace smiled again. I had to admit she seemed pretty happy since Alfonse had come along. All that sex, I guess.

"Thanks," she said. "I finally got around to repairing some of the damage Simon caused." Grace pointed to our right. "I re-painted this entire wall. Remember the time he used bicycle grease to make a self-portrait?"

"Ah, yes," Jess said. "The great bicycle grease experiment."

Grace rolled her eyes. "The great medicinal marijuana ex-periment. An altered state of consciousness might help some people create, but not Simon. Even he thought the drawing was horrible. When he recovered two days later. But of course he was too lazy to paint over it."

I popped another pig-in-a-blanket in my mouth. I'd brought them and so far I was the only one eating them. People can be so weird about food. Like there's something wrong with a clas-sic like pigs-in-a-blanket? My mother served them all the time!

I looked at the newly painted wall. It was a shade of green I couldn't name. Not my taste at all. Anyway, I tried to imagine a picture of Simon in bicycle grease. I couldn't. I swear, I really don't know how Grace put up with all that nonsense from Simon. If Duncan had ever scribbled on a wall, I would have called the men in white coats.

Then, again, Duncan wasn't the type to act out. Really, he'd never once embarrassed me in public or left the toilet seat up when I asked him to put it down or farted at the dinner table. He even wiped the sink clean every time he shaved.

I shoved aside the somehow disturbing memories of Duncan's many positive traits. I would find another man with even more good qualities. Soon. Think positive!

Alfonse called out to Grace just then and she went scurrying off to join him.

"Doesn't Grace see that Alfonse is just another version of

Simon?" Nell said in a stage whisper. "When is she going to stop dating boys and find herself a man?"

I watched Grace and her boy toy interact. He touched her cheek fondly. She kissed his cheek in response.

Well, Alfonse was okay. I mean, he was polite and all and he definitely looked cleaner than his friends. He gazed at Grace a lot. I personally don't like that sort of thing; it kind of creeps me out, but Grace didn't seem to mind it.

But like I said, Alfonse's friends were another story. I frowned at them. They thought they were so cool but I thought one was skankier than the other.

"That one with the soul patch is very rude," I said. "Did you see the way he pushed past Grace in the kitchen before?"

"They're beyond rude," Nell said. "They're indifferent to us. They know we exist, but they just don't care. They're not the least bit interested in us as women."

Jess frowned. "They're not the least bit interested in us as people. Has one of them said a word to you besides that half-hearted greeting? Has one of them asked any of us a question? Even offered a social smile? It's disgusting. I hate being so ignored."

"On the other hand," Nell said, "do we really want to be recognized and acknowledged by these kids? Who are they? Why should we care about them?"

"We shouldn't care about their opinion of us, but it's hard not to."

"I have an idea," I said. "After this, let's go to Bar Loup. It's just full of single guys and it'll be fun. Really. Maybe we'll all meet someone!"

Jess shook her head. "No thanks. I've heard of Bar Loup. It's a meat market. Besides, after this I'm going home to bed. It's already ten o'clock and I've got a busy day tomorrow. There's end-of-semester work piled on my desk."

I looked to my sister. "Come on, Nell, how about it?"

"And run the risk of bumping into one of my kids' friends? No, thanks. But you go, Laura. Have fun. Maybe you'll meet your baby's father."

"I can't go to a club alone! I'll look—desperate."

Nell smirked. "Aren't you?"

I know she's my sister but sometimes I really hate her.

Anyway, Alfonse and his friends left soon after that; they were going to hear a friend of theirs who performed experimental music, whatever that is. We girls stayed and helped Grace clean up.

"Don't you want to go with Alfonse?" I asked. I picked up a soiled napkin with my fingertips and dropped it in the trash. Ick.

Grace laughed. "I might be comfortable being with him in the privacy of my own home, but I'm not entirely comfortable being out in public with him. I know, how provincial of me, but I'm doing what I can. Besides, he and his friends stay out way too late."

"Aren't you afraid he's out flirting with other women?" I asked.

"No," Grace said, "I'm not afraid. He probably *is* flirting with other women. But I can't really do anything about it, can I? I mean, we don't have a commitment. I don't want a commitment, not with a twenty-one-year-old. And frankly, if he's flirting with a nineteen-year-old, I don't want to know about it."

"What if he's sleeping with a nineteen-year-old?" Nell asked.

"Then I definitely don't want to know about it."

I looked at Grace, shocked. "You don't care if he's seeing other women?"

"Of course I care," she said, dumping half a glass of beer in the sink. "We have protected sex, but if he's sleeping around, there's still a risk I could catch something. Okay. Can we change the topic? I'm feeling all queasy now."

"You know," I said, "dating services are allowed to screen for STDs. Anyway, I think they can."

Jess laughed. "Everyone lies in personal ads and with dating services," she said.

Sometimes she's so cynical.

"Not everyone," I protested.

"Everyone. It's the extent of the lie that matters. I mean, if you tweak the truth, if you describe yourself as voluptuous instead of fat, that's just good marketing, that's smart self-promotion. But if you claim to be forty when you're really sixty, well, that's false advertisement."

"A lie is a lie," my sister said. "But I see your point."

Grace leaned against the counter and folded her arms across her chest. She's really flat, maybe like a 32A.

"I read somewhere recently," she said, "that non-Jewish men and women are looking for dates through Jewish dating services. Sometimes, they're open about being Christian or atheist or whatever they are. Sometimes they even promise to convert. But sometimes they say nothing about religious affiliation until they're actually on a date with someone. And then, 'Hi, I lied; I'm not the nice Jewish man you hoped I was.'"

"That's just wrong," Nell said. "What kind of woman would stay with a man who starts a relationship with such a big lie?"

Jess shrugged. " A desperate woman. A woman with no self-esteem."

I considered. A nice Jewish man. Why not?

"You know," I said, "the Jewish tradition is very family oriented. Maybe I should try one of their dating services. I would join their church. I don't really care about God."

My sister gave me one of those annoying looks, the kind that make you feel like you just said something really stupid, even though you know you haven't.

"What?" I challenged. Nell turned away and began to load glasses into the tiny dishwasher.

"You'd have to agree to raise your children in the Jewish faith," Jess pointed out. "And in that case you'd have to at least pretend to care about God."

"Well, duh, I wouldn't marry a really religious man, like someone who keeps kosher, or someone who's, I don't know, Orthodox."

Nell whipped around to face me. "News flash, Laura. A religious man wouldn't marry you, either."

Grace unfolded her arms. "But what if Laura happens to fall in love with a man who keeps kosher?"

"She won't," Nell snapped. "This quest of hers isn't about falling in love. It's about having a baby. The man really doesn't matter. Only his seed matters."

I felt like I'd been slapped. "That's a horrible thing to say! And it's not true. Of course I want to fall in love again."

"Do you?" Nell turned back to loading the dishwasher.

Jess patted my shoulder. "I'm calling it a night. Does anyone want to share a taxi?"

I thanked Grace and left with Jess. I didn't say good-bye to my sister.

Chapter 16

Jess

Forget fad diets. Forget programs that charge an arm and a leg for tasteless frozen meals. The best way to lose weight is simply not to eat.

—*The Post-Divorce Diet: How to Shed Those Unsightly Pounds You Put On Over the Years of Your Miserable Marriage*

It was bound to happen sooner or later.

I'm not usually in the Downtown Crossing area but I needed a new pair of navy pumps. Stylish navy pumps are almost impossible to find, but I figured that somewhere within those twisting, busy streets a pair might be lurking.

Besides, shopping for shoes, even basic, sensible shoes, is always an uplifting experience. Is this something to do with female hormones or simply social conditioning?

I took the T to the Downtown Crossing stop and emerged into the uncomfortably humid afternoon. I headed toward the DSW store. At the next corner I stopped with the crowd to wait for the green light.

And there he was. Matt. My ex-husband, hand in hand with a woman.

The woman was beautiful in that all-American way, tall and blond, far more attractive than me. Even I could see that she fit better with Matt than I ever had.

I stood to Matt's left, an old woman between us, waiting for that light to change. And suddenly, I felt scared. What if Matt saw me, what if he confronted me? I was just about to slide away when Matt turned his head.

He saw me. I know he did. I felt my mouth form a small, involuntary smile.

His sunglasses hid the expression in his eyes. His mouth indicated no particular emotion. He looked away. The light changed to green and he and his companion stepped into the street.

I didn't cross with the others. I watched him go and as I did I realized that seeing Matt with another woman hadn't caused any feelings of deep regret or overwhelming sadness. Mostly what I felt at that moment was relief that he hadn't shouted, "Adulteress!" or something worse, something obscene, not that Matt was prone to using foul language, but still.

And, of course, I felt a renewed wash of guilt.

Always guilt.

For the first time since I was a moody teenager mad at the world, shoe shopping failed to lift my spirits.

There was a bomb in the mail when I got home that night. Not a literal bomb, of course, a figurative one, but one that caused some bloody maiming nonetheless.

The letter from my mother was addressed to Mrs. Jessica Fromer. I had never taken Matt's name, but my mother had never accepted that. Now, I was divorced and she was still referring to me as someone I had never been.

I don't remember my mother ever sending me a letter before this one. Birthday cards, Christmas greetings, even the occasional newspaper clipping, but never a letter.

I opened the envelope with some trepidation. The trepidation was warranted. My mother had taken it upon herself to scold me for the divorce. In her mind, my inability to stick with the marriage was related to my inability to stick with anything.

In her words:

In short, I'm concerned about your inability to stay with anything you start. In third grade there was ballet. You refused to go after the third lesson.

Yes, I remembered. Because one of the girls was a horrible bully and I was scared. Mom didn't seem to remember that part of the story.

The summer you were sixteen you bought a book about chess and a chessboard and never touched either once school started in September. That was a real shame as you had so much talent at the game.

No, I didn't have talent. I was completely untalented. And the other reason I abandoned chess that fall was because my course load was enormous what with all the Advanced Placement credits I was determined to earn before starting college.

Did my mother remember that I saved my parents the price of twelve college credits by working myself senseless that senior year?

And I'll never understand why you left that nice young man you dated your sophomore year in college. He was so serious about you and you broke his heart. Your father and I were so disappointed . . .

I couldn't read any more. I wondered if my mother had ever known me, even just a little bit.

That nice young man I'd dated in sophomore year of college, Bart, hadn't been serious about me; he'd been obsessed, insanely jealous of any other male within yards of me, horribly suspicious of my every move. When he finally threw me against a wall for talking to a fellow classmate about an assignment, I'd had it. And my father had been there to support me through the process of reporting Bart to the campus police and getting a restraining order and then helping me get through the rest of the school year, avoiding Bart's menacing presence.

Where was my mother through all this? I wondered now if my father had kept it all from her, knowing she would become part of the problem and not part of the solution. Maybe she had known what was going on but had found it convenient to forget the ugly truth.

Whatever the case, I felt stunned and hurt. Why had my mother felt the need to reopen all those old wounds? The memories had scarred over nicely but now, all these years later, they felt raw and tender again.

I reached for the phone. It was another first; I don't think I'd ever placed an emergency call to a friend. What was happening to me? I wondered if I was breaking down completely.

"Nell," I said, "I need to talk. Are you free?"

She was. I told her about running into Matt. And she tried to make me believe that my lack of emotional response to seeing Matt with another woman was nothing more than an instinctual response.

"Your self-preservation instincts kicked in," she said. "That's normal. Just because you didn't fall weeping to the sidewalk doesn't mean you're incapable of love, or whatever it is you think you're incapable of."

"Maybe," I said. Then again, maybe not.

Then I told Nell about the letter from my mother. It lay where I'd tossed it, on the coffee table.

After a few sounds of outrage, Nell offered her advice. "As for the letter," she said, "throw it in the garbage. It's invasive and hurtful and completely out of line. And I say that as a mother myself, one who tries very hard not to cross the line between valid concern and unhelpful intrusion."

I smiled at the wall. "My mother never could keep her mouth shut. It drives my father crazy."

"And that's why you're in Boston and she's in Florida. You don't have to listen to her, Jess. Tear up the letter, hang up the phone, delete the e-mail. You have the power."

I laughed. "Have you been watching *Oprah?*"

"No, but I am reading her magazine and I love it."

"Maybe I should pick up a copy."

"Maybe you should. And I should go to bed. Long day."

I said good-bye to Nell and hung up. And then I stuffed my mother's words into the garbage, as advised.

Chapter 17

Nell

Men are lazy. They fall into habits and stay there like a wheel stuck in mud. If you think a separation will make your husband realize how much he misses you, you're just plain stupid. One week on his own and he's an entrenched bachelor.
—*Trial Separation: Is It for You?*

His name was Charles Taylor. He was retired as the CEO of a small manufacturing firm. He'd lost his wife to ovarian cancer five years earlier. He had two grown sons. And Dr. Lakes had assured me that he had a fine moral character.

What she had failed to mention was that he was old.

I'd always been fond of Dr. Lakes. I'd been going to her since just after Colin's birth. For almost twenty years I'd been a loyal patient. So, how did she figure I deserved this interesting surprise? Was Dr. Lakes a secret sadist? Was she fond of playing cruel jokes on unsuspecting single women?

"Nell?"

"Hmm? Oh," I said, embarrassed. "I'm sorry. I didn't mean to be rude. My mind just wandered for a moment."

Charles Taylor cocked his head and smiled. He had good teeth. I wondered if they were his own or an expensive set of dentures.

"It's my age, isn't it?" he said. "Dr. Lakes didn't tell you that I was seventy-nine?"

"Seventy-nine!" The words came out in a bit of a shriek. I was mortified. "I'm sorry," I said hurriedly. "I thought you were maybe seventy. You . . . You look great. Really. And no, Dr. Lakes didn't mention anything about your age."

And I was going to wring her neck for it.

"But you agreed to go out with me based on what she did say?"

"Yes," I admitted. "I liked what I heard. Though I must admit that for a minute or two I did wonder about the ethics of the situation."

Charles laughed. The skin on his neck jiggled only slightly. "Don't worry," he said, "Dr. Lakes hasn't revealed any of your medical secrets. I'm sorry about this."

I tried to laugh, too. I wondered if anything on me was jiggling.

"Don't be," I said. "It's not your fault."

"Oh, I know it's not my fault. I just mean that I'm sorry things worked out the way they did. I like you, Nell Keats."

"And I like you, Charles Taylor." It was easy to say. I did like him.

"And you'd like me better if I were, say, fifty-nine."

"Yes," I said. "I'm sorry."

Charles sat up straighter in his chair. He had good shoulders.

"No more apologies. Would you like to stay for dinner or should I take you home now?"

Why couldn't this nice man be forty-nine? Even fifty-nine?

"Let's stay for dinner," I said. "The food here is wonderful."

"And of course, the evening is my treat."

"Charles," I said with a sigh, "you're killing me."

I was home no more than ten minutes when the phone rang. It was Richard.

"I called earlier but you didn't pick up," he said.

"I was out."

"Oh."

Richard wouldn't ask where I'd been. I wondered if he was afraid to know.

"Why are you calling?" I asked.

"Nell, I have something to propose. Now, please just listen to what I have to say. Let me finish before you say no."

"Richard," I snapped, "just get to the point." Why, I wondered, does he pussyfoot around me? Oh. Right. Because since he told me he's gay, I tend to yell and scream at him.

I pictured Richard taking a deep breath. "Bob," he said, "has a very good friend, a guy he's known since college. They were roommates and they've stayed in touch ever since. His name is Jeff and he's a lawyer in a small firm downtown. Well, Bob was thinking . . ."

"Yes?" I said. Let Richard say it. I was not going to help him.

"Well, Bob thought that you and Jeff might hit it off. You know, at least enjoy a nice dinner together."

My husband was setting me up with another man. What would Oprah say about this, I wondered. I really wanted to know.

"How do I know this guy Jeff's not gay, too?" I demanded.

"Bob says Jeff has always been involved with women. He was even married once. He's one hundred percent straight."

I laughed meanly. "Yeah, well, that's what I thought about you and I was seriously wrong."

Richard was silent for a moment, no doubt recovering from my latest blow.

"Nell," he said finally, "you're missing out on a chance to meet a very nice guy."

Really, could I be blamed for exploding?

"Don't you dare tell me what I'm missing out on! You know nothing about what I'm going through, Richard, nothing."

"Nellie—"

Nellie. Only Richard called me Nellie. It was his name for me, right from the start. Tears welled and spilled.

"Just leave me alone, Richard," I said thickly. "Unless you need to talk to me about the kids, don't call me. Do you understand?"

After a moment, Richard spoke again. He sounded weary. Well, I was beyond weary.

"I'm sorry, Nell. About everything, this call, all those years . . ."

I put my hand to my head. It suddenly felt very heavy.

"Good night, Nell."

I hung up. And then I said, "Good-bye, Richard."

Chapter 18

Laura

He says, 'Jump,' you say, 'How high?' He says, 'I want sex now,' you say, 'The red or the black negligee?' He says, 'I'm going away for the weekend with my buddies,' you say, 'Have a good time, dear.'
—*Luck Has Nothing to Do with It: How to Keep the Man You Married*

"Look, Laura, I wasn't entirely honest with you last night." Whenever a man begins a sentence with the word "look," you know you've been screwed. Whenever a man says he hasn't been "entirely honest" with you, you know he's told a massive lie.

I had met Marcus only the night before. I know I shouldn't have slept with him right away, but he was so handsome, so incredibly gorgeous. Every other woman in the room was eyeing him hungrily, but he chose to talk to me. Me!

Right up front I told Marcus about Duncan and me. I told him I wanted to get married again and have a baby. It was an incredible coincidence. Marcus wanted children, too. Just like Duncan, his ex-wife hadn't wanted a family and, though Marcus had begged her to reconsider, she'd held firm.

It seemed Marcus and I were made for each other.

So I took him home with me. We made love in the king-sized bed Duncan had been so eager to install.

And then, morning came.

"Oh," I said.

Marcus made a goofy, sort of apologetic face. "I do have kids," he said. "Three of them. They live with their mother in Lincoln."

I looked at the crumpled sheets. I would throw them out. I would buy a new mattress pad. I would sell the bed.

"You lied to me," I said. It was a stupid thing to say.

Marcus sighed and hung his head. How many times had he been through this little speech? "I know, and I'm sorry, but man, you looked so good in that dress and we were having such a good time . . . I wanted to tell you before we came back here but . . ."

I backed against the dresser for support. Also, a heavy lamp stood just to my right. If things got really ugly, I thought, I could use it as a weapon.

"But you just wanted to get laid," I said. "You don't care at all about me. What else did you lie about, huh? You're HIV-positive? You're still married? What else!"

Marcus slipped on his boxer shorts. Always protect the goods when dealing with an angry woman.

"Whoa, calm down, it's not the end of the world."

Strange. To me it felt just like the end of the world.

"I am . . ." I could hardly form the words. I tried again. "I am so angry. You . . . I want you to leave, right now."

Marcus took a step forward. In an almost-whisper he said, "Come on, Laura, can't we talk about this?"

It was dangerous, his coming any closer.

"Get out! Get out, get out, get out!"

Marcus clapped his hands over his ears. "Jeez," he said, totally annoyed, "you don't have to be so shrill!"

"Yes I do!" I screamed. "Yes I do!"

He was dressed in less than a minute. He didn't even ask to use the bathroom.

I slammed the door after his sorry butt. And then I opened it and slammed it again. And then I threw on sweatpants and a jacket, grabbed my wallet and ran, literally ran to the CVS store five blocks away, where I bought three home pregnancy kits. I mean, we'd used a condom but you never know. The pregnancy kits cost me over forty dollars. If I'd known Marcus's address, I would have sent him the bill.

I took the first test as soon as I got home.

Not pregnant.

I took the next test the next morning and the third on the day after that. Not pregnant both times. I felt such huge relief. I mean, I wanted a baby but not with some idiot who clearly had no intention of marrying me!

After that I vowed, I swore, that I would never again have sex with another man until there was an engagement ring on my finger and a serious family plan in place.

I vowed.

And I started to research obstetricians.

Chapter 19

Grace

Never disclose the full reality of your situation on the first date. Let him fall in love with you before you tell him you stood trial for the suspicious death of your second husband.
—*Dating After Divorce: The Fine Art of Information Control*

A lfonse disappeared from my life bright and early on a Monday morning. He kissed my cheek and with a jaunty wave walked out of the apartment and, no doubt, into the apartment of some other lonely woman nearing forty.

No explanations. He simply didn't call or return my calls. After two days I understood. And in spite of my claim to knowing full well what I was doing by getting involved with Alfonse, my heart hurt. Not a lot, not like it had hurt so often with Simon, but it hurt.

As if sensing my vulnerability, Simon called that afternoon when I got home from work. I saw his number and I picked up anyway.

"You didn't come to my birthday party," he said. "And I didn't get a card. Gracie, what's wrong?"

"Hello to you, too. Nothing's wrong," I lied. "I just forgot. I'm very busy. The semester's almost over and there's a lot to wrap up. And I was just hired as the director of a summer program for city kids at—"

"Great," he said, cutting me off. "Cool. Listen, I need you."

I didn't want it to happen. But a tingle of excitement, of anticipation, passed through me.

"This amazing thing has happened to me, Gracie, and I need your support, you know. The Auster Gallery gave me a solo show and I'm, like, freaked. I need you to help me out, like you always do, you know, I need you to be there."

Like I always am.

In truth, the gallery was an important one; a solo show there could really launch Simon's latent career. My helping him prepare for such a show would be a good thing, a generous, productive thing.

All alone in the living room I was overcome with embarrassment at my inability to resist Simon completely.

"I'll think about it," I said carefully.

"Excellent! I'll call you back with details. My girlfriend just walked in."

Without a good-bye, Simon ended the call.

Typical.

And then I was furious that Simon had assumed I would say yes to his cry for help. I'd said I'd think about it. I'd made no promises. But Simon had heard only what he wanted to hear.

I took a deep breath. I thought of all I wanted to change about myself. And I realized I'd made very little progress.

And then I felt defeated.

Face it, Grace, I thought. We both know the "I'll think about it" means "yes."

Like it always does.

Chapter 20

Grace

Face facts: No man wants the responsibility of a financially devastated woman, especially when he's got an ex-wife and kids to support. If you're in debt, get out or risk being alone for the rest of your sorry life.

—*Financial Solvency and Love: Perfect Partners*

"Someone start talking," I said.

Because, I thought, I don't want to hear only my grim thoughts.

The four of us had met at Café Retro. Dinner with my friends was pretty much my only social life since Alfonse had gone off.

It made me wonder. Had tending Simon all those years eaten up so much time that I'd lost what personal interests I'd once had? When, I thought, was the last time I'd gone to a movie or to the theater? When was the last time I'd gone to hear a concert?

"I'll start," Laura said, and she told us about the guy who lied about having children. We all agreed that Marcus was the lowest of the low, a bum, a jerk.

"You sure know how to pick them," Nell said with a phony smile.

"It could have happened to anyone."

"Not to me. I don't make a habit of going home with a guy I've just met."

"You don't make a habit of going home with any guy," Laura

snapped. "Maybe if you had been more interested in sex, then Richard—"

"Don't say it." The look on Nell's face stopped Laura cold.

"So . . ." Jess said. "Anyone seen any good movies lately?"

I laughed. "Not me."

"Me, either," Laura said. "I'm too busy looking for Mr. Right. So anyway, I met another guy, just last night. I went out with a girl from work to Café America, and we talked for a while, and do you know what he told me? He told me his ex-wife and two children live in New York somewhere. And before I could ask how often he got to see his children, he told me that their living in New York was as good as his not having children at all because he didn't have to see them that often."

"Yikes."

"Well," Jess said, "there's a guy with a healthy ego. 'Hi, I'm a jerk, want to go home with me?'"

"Can you imagine?" Laura went on. "What's wrong with men these days? Either they don't want a family in the first place, like Duncan, or they go ahead and have a family they don't really want!"

I felt sorry for Laura, I did, but my sympathy was tinged with an uncomfortable feeling of annoyance. Hadn't we advised her against leaving Duncan; hadn't we suggested she reconsider such a rash act?

But who was I to judge?

"That's too bad," I said lamely.

"What kind of woman would be attracted to a man who doesn't want to see his own children?" Laura asked.

Jess shrugged. "A woman who doesn't want to be saddled with another woman's children. A woman who wants to be the center of a man's attention at all times. A woman who doesn't want any children of her own."

Ah, yes, I thought. There's someone for everyone.

"A man like that is toxic," Nell said. "He's all about his own gratification. If he can ignore his kids, he can ignore his wife or his girlfriend. If someone's inconvenient, ignore her and move on."

Laura suddenly looked defeated. "I don't know. I'm not giving up or anything, but sometimes . . ."

"Look," Nell said, "this is the last time I'm going to suggest this, I promise. Please consider talking to Duncan before the divorce is final. Maybe there's some way for you to work things out."

Laura stiffened. "You think I'm destroying my life."

"I didn't say that."

"But it's what you're thinking," Laura insisted. "Fine. Think what you want. But I'm not compromising on this issue. I'll find another man, a good one, I'm sure of it, and I'll have my baby."

There was another awkward silence; our conversations seemed to be full of awkward silences since divorce had come tearing into our lives.

"On another, less volatile topic," I said, "you might be interested to know that Alfonse is history. At least, I think he's history. I don't really know what he is because I haven't heard from him in almost a week."

"Have you called him?" Laura asked.

"Yes. No return calls. It's pretty clear to me he's moved on to some other pitiful single woman."

"Don't say that, Grace." Jess squeezed my hand. "You're not pitiful."

Maybe. Maybe I wasn't pitiful regarding Alfonse. But regarding Simon?

I decided to keep Simon's most recent call to myself. I knew what everyone would say. And I wasn't quite in the mood to hear it.

But Grace, you swore things would be different this time.

Where's your self-respect, Grace?

"So, Nell," I asked, "what's been going on in your life?"

Nell told us about Richard's call and his attempt to fix her up with one of Bob's friends.

"Do ex-husbands ever really go away?" I wondered aloud.

"I think it's kind of sweet of Richard to try to set you up," Laura said.

"I think it's kind of sick." Nell shuddered. "Who is he to hand me off to another man? It . . . It feels like prostitution somehow. I know he's no longer my husband. Still . . . I didn't want to be dating in the first place. If Richard hadn't—If I hadn't found that stupid note, everything would be fine—Oh, God, what am I saying?"

"Enough about Richard," Jess said. "I want to hear about your date, the one your gynecologist set up."

Nell told us. Jess and I laughed awkwardly. Laura seemed appalled.

"I can't believe Dr. Lakes set you up with a guy almost forty years older and didn't even tell you about it!" she cried. "Why would she think you were interested in diapering and spoon-feeding some old coot?"

"I don't know what she was thinking," Nell admitted. "The sad thing is that he was really nice. Very smart and fit—at least, he looked fit in his suit, but who can tell what clothes are hiding."

"Getting old is not for wimps," Jess said. "The body begins to deteriorate at an alarming rate. Things sprout. Things spread. Things sag. It's horrifying."

Nell laughed unhappily. "I've said it before and I'll say it again. Once a woman turns forty, she begins to fade to invisibility. It doesn't matter what she's accomplishing in her career or her personal life or how physically beautiful she is, men simply stop seeing her. Unless they're seventy-nine, and then I suppose a forty-two-year-old like me looks perfectly appetizing."

"What I find more disturbing," I said, "is how young women, women in their twenties, look at us with, I don't know, with pity, like somehow we've failed by growing older. Like somehow they've won the game. But that doesn't make any sense!"

"Of course it doesn't," Laura said gloomily. "But young women are arrogant. What young women forget is that someday their breasts will be as saggy as ours."

"Speak for yourself!" I laughed. "There's some benefit to being small."

Nell sighed. "I suppose I really don't mind getting older. The alternative isn't too cheery. But I refuse to wear a purple dress with a red hat. If that's the way to get attention, forget it. I'll take invisibility. It's far more sophisticated."

"Oh, I agree. But I don't want to go gently, anonymously into death, either. I don't want to look at the world someday and feel nothing sexual." Jess shook her head. "I don't want to be content with only a cup of sugared tea and a plain cracker. I want to drink martinis and eat Mexican food until the day I die. I might get old, but I dread having to feel old."

"Would you rather die now, before you're even forty?" Laura asked with real concern.

"Well, I would leave a prettier corpse. I don't want old-woman skin. It's horrifying."

"Jess!"

"Relax, Laura," Jess said with a laugh. "I'm not planning on departing this world any time soon."

"What you need," Laura told her, "is a man. It'll take your mind off gross things like age spots and liver spots, whatever they are. Go ahead, look around. There are lots of men right here in this restaurant. Well, there are some. Maybe you'll see a man you like and he'll like you and then you won't feel like you're getting old."

Nell shook her head. "Ah, if only life were as simple as Laura seems to think it is."

"I am getting old whether I feel it or not," Jess pointed out. "Besides, a restaurant isn't a good place to meet a man. I just want to enjoy my meal, not worry about how wobbly my chin looks when I chew."

"That's one of the good things about marriage," I said. "You can stop worrying obsessively over your appearance. Your husband knows you have a double chin, and you know he has a spare tire, so big deal. No more surprises, nasty or pleasant. There's some appeal in the usual."

Though with Simon, I thought, even the usual, the everyday, was never dull. Exhausting, but never dull.

Nell sighed. "I don't think I have the energy to get married again. I don't know if I have what it takes anymore to get to know a person so thoroughly. It's an awful lot of work and for what?"

For living with the man you adore.

"Wait until you fall in love again," I said, hating the words as I spoke them. "Love makes everything seem doable. Love gives you energy."

"Love gets you into trouble," Nell replied speedily.

Yes, I thought. It most certainly does.

"Don't you mean lust gets you into trouble?" Jess said.

Nell smirked. "Aren't love and lust really the same thing?"

Yes, I thought. In many ways they are.

Chapter 21

Jess

Perception #12: The grass is always greener. Remind your married man that, unlike his bitch of a wife, you like it when he farts at the dinner table.

—*Dating the Married Man: How to Get the Man You Love to Divorce His Wife*

I picked up the phone out of habit. In retrospect it was a stupid thing to do. I've since ordered caller ID. One's home is one's castle, at least it should be, and I'm all for the installation of the modern equivalent of a moat and draw-bridge.

It was Matt's older brother, Mike. I'd never liked Mike much. Then again, neither had Matt.

"Is everything okay?" I asked. Of course he had to have called because something was wrong with Matt. Or maybe one of Matt's parents was ill. Or maybe Mike was calling to curse me for having broken his baby brother's heart.

"Yeah, everything's cool, you know."

"Okay," I said.

"So, how you been?"

"Okay," I said.

"Cool. I was, you know, just wondering. You wanna go out sometime?"

This, I thought, has got to be a joke, a cruel joke.

I laughed, nervously. "Okay, Mike, very funny. I've got to go now."

But Mike was serious. "No, wait, Jess. I mean it. I always liked you; you're kind of hot, you know. So, whaddya think?"

What did I think? Good question.

"I think," I said carefully, "that going out with you is a very bad idea."

Mike chortled. "How come? We're both single."

It seemed I really was going to have to explain to Mike why his suggestion was in seriously poor taste.

I explained and was careful not to make him angry. Mike had a temper and even over a phone line it could be nasty.

"But Matt and I aren't even close or anything," he replied.

"Still."

"And you cheated on him. It's not like you're a saint or something."

Mike's voice was steady, his tone, almost conversational. He wasn't attacking me; he was just pointing out a sorry fact.

"Look," I said, feeling all buzzy and sick, "I really have to go. Sorry." And I hung up.

Mike had hurt me but I'd done worse. I'd committed an enormously hurtful act. A good person who'd done a bad thing? Right then I wasn't so sure.

I called Nell. Poor Nell. She had enough to handle without my crying on her shoulder.

Of course, she was furious on my behalf.

"Mike's a jackass, Jess. Didn't he get arrested once for drunk and disorderly conduct?"

"Yes." I'd forgotten about that. It was just after I'd met Matt; he'd put together the bail and not spoken to his brother for a month afterward.

"Jess," Nell went on, "I remember that on more than one occasion you told me you felt lonely in your own home. You didn't recklessly destroy something that was perfect to begin with. You dismantled a faulty structure. Maybe that wasn't your conscious intention when you met Seth, but that's what resulted."

My unconscious, it seemed, had a lot to answer for. "Yes," I said, "that's what resulted. A marriage in ruins."

"Anyway," Nell went on, ignoring my self-pitying comment, "who are these people to think they can just call you up or send you a letter and tell you what they think you're doing wrong with your life! It's incredible, really."

It was incredible. It was hard to believe. But it was real.

"I don't think Mike meant to insult me," I said. "He was just stating a fact. I did cheat on his brother."

"But what gives him the right to bring up the past to you?" Nell argued. "You were never his friend. He was entirely wrong in calling you at all."

"Yes," I said. "He was wrong to call, but he was right about my cheating on his brother."

Nell groaned. "Maybe if his brother had laughed a bit more or hadn't spent endless hours in front of the boob tube, you wouldn't have had the time or the inclination to stray. Stop taking all the blame for what happened."

Who else was there to blame? Was Matt guilty because he wasn't "there" enough? Was he guilty of what the Catholics call a "sin of omission"?

I don't think so.

"It's very generous of you to help me deal with this," I said, "particularly given what you went through with Richard."

"What, because I was the person cheated on? Every relationship is different, Jess. If I equated you with Richard just because you both had an affair, I'd be pretty simpleminded. Besides, Matt and I couldn't be more different. I'm far prettier than he is."

"And a far better friend," I said. Tears threatened. I don't like to cry. "Thanks, Nell. I'll let you get back to whatever it was you were doing when I interrupted."

"Ah, yes, my exciting life. I was ironing if you must know. I love linen, but it's hell to maintain."

Call it what you will: poking the wound, wallowing in self-pity, slogging through shame . . . Later that night I took out a box of photos of Matt and me. For some reason—lack of interest, probably—I'd never gotten around to putting the pictures in albums. In fact, aside from our official wedding album, every photo I had of Matt was in that box. I'd never even framed one for my desk.

Well, if that isn't telling, what is?

The photos were bound to cause pain and discomfort. I dug right in and came up with a few shots taken on our honeymoon.

Getting Matt to agree to Paris as our destination was a real coup. He'd wanted to go to a tropical island and do the whole sweet fuzzy drinks and cabana thing. But I'd made my case for the most romantic city in the world and convinced him.

In one photo Matt stood in front of the Arc de Triumph. He wore a baseball cap backward. I remembered being embarrassed by the hat, but I hadn't asked him to take it off. A good wife, I'd thought, supports her husband in all ways, even his poor sartorial choices.

I looked hard at Matt's boyish face and thought about how I'd dragged him from museum to museum and how he'd followed along gamely, good-naturedly. Maybe he knew the trip was the only one he'd have to make to Paris; probably he was thinking about all the football that awaited him stateside.

I wondered: Had I ever really loved Matt? Maybe I had, in the very beginning. Why, why else would I have married him?

But then something must have gone wrong because if I'd continued to love him, I would never have cheated on him with Seth.

Right?

I grabbed another handful of photos and spread them out like a deck of cards. Matt at a New Year's Eve party given by one of his colleagues. Matt on a ski weekend in Vermont. Matt and his buddies at a football game, the Patriots' symbol painted on their faces.

In all of the photos Matt was smiling.

I gathered the photos and crammed them back into the box. At ten o'clock I went out to Bar Loup. I ordered a martini and then another. I chatted with a guy in a navy blazer and khakis. Chatting led to flirting and another martini.

I took him home. We had sex but I don't remember much of what actually went on. He left me his number, which I immediately tore up.

One more night to regret.

Chapter 22

Nell

People make mistakes. Get over it. You thought he was Mr. Right but you were wrong. He thought you were his angel but he was wrong. Dwelling on the past will get you nowhere.

—*Oops! My Mistake! What To Do When You Marry the Wrong Person*

"Mrs. Allard?" The voice on the other end of the line was downright chirpy.

"It's Ms. Keats now," I corrected.

"Oh, yes, Ms. Keats. You are Colin and Clara Allard's mother, right?"

"Are my children all right?" I demanded. "Who is this?"

The chirpy voice giggled. "Oh, I'm so sorry. This is Ms. York from Colin and Clara's former middle school. Melinda York. Of course you're wondering why I'm calling."

I glanced at the clock above the hall table. I had an appointment for a facial in twenty minutes.

"I assume it has something to do with the school's scholarship fund. The board wants my help?"

"Oh, no," Ms. York said, "nothing like that. You know Mrs. Sheridan?"

Nineteen minutes. "Barbara Sheridan?"

"Yes. Well, she still has a son here, little Justin. I was chatting with her the other day when she happened to mention that you and your husband . . . Well, that you're divorced."

Barbara Sheridan had nothing better to talk about than my divorce. Not surprising. Her own life was sadly distorted; everyone knew her husband had a mistress; he even vacationed with her, back in her native Argentina.

"Yes," I said, with some annoyance. "I'm divorced." What did the school want me to do? Give a talk on the evils of homosexuality? No, thanks. The sanctity of marriage? Absolutely no, thanks. How to find a good divorce attorney? That I could do.

"Great!" Ms. York yipped. "Oh, I mean, well, what I mean is that I know an absolutely wonderful man for you. He's an old friend of my husband and gosh, I've known him now for almost eight years. He's just wonderful."

Fifteen minutes and counting. There was no way I was going to jeopardize my appointment at the spa.

I picked up my purse. "Thank you, Ms. York, but I really don't think I—"

The chirpy voice interrupted. "Oh, just give it a chance. I really do think you and Roger are perfect for each other."

"Really, I appreciate the thought but—"

"Now, Mrs. Allard—"

"Ms. Keats," I corrected. Damn good breeding. I should have slammed down the phone right then.

"Yes, of course, Ms. Keats. Certainly. Now, Ms. Keats, I really won't take no for an answer. May I give Roger your number?"

"Yes, yes, fine," I snapped. "I'm sorry but I have to go."

Ridiculous, what I had to do to get this annoying woman off the phone. This Roger person had to be easier to put off than the twittering Ms. York.

I made my appointment with only a minute to spare.

Roger called that evening and in spite of my firm intentions to disappoint him, I found myself succumbing to a voice that was deep and rich and slow. How awful could the man that belonged to such a sensual voice be? Even when he suggested we meet at a popular restaurant in Waltham, a good hour from downtown Boston, I agreed.

Oh, the stupid things good breeding and hormones make us do.

I handed the valet parking attendant my keys and stepped inside the noisy, cavernous restaurant. Roger had said he'd meet me at the bar; he told me he'd be wearing a dark suit with a white shirt and no tie.

He wasn't hard to miss. He was very handsome in a sort of slick, Cary Grant way, tall and well built with thick hair expertly cut. And the suit was beautiful.

Richard would love to know his tailor, I thought.

Richard! No more thoughts of Richard, especially not on a date with a handsome man.

Roger smiled and stood as I approached.

"Nell?"

"Yes."

He extended his hand. "You're even more lovely than Melinda said you were."

Well, I thought, he certainly knows how to greet a gal.

We were led to our table and an officious waiter took our drink order. A glass of Prosecco for me, a neat bourbon for Roger.

A manly drink, I noted.

"So, Nell," Roger said, "tell me a bit about yourself."

I did. And then he told me a bit about himself. And immediately it was clear that we had virtually nothing in common beyond being residents of the Commonwealth of Massachusetts.

I enjoy watching tennis; Roger thought it was a boring sport. I read a novel a week; Roger reads only nonfiction. I am a Democrat; Roger is a Republican.

Why had the chirpy Ms. York thought Roger and I would click? What was this obsession with matchmaking some women couldn't shake?

Roger put his empty glass on the table with some force. "So," he said, "what do you think?"

I had no idea what Roger had been saying. "I'm sorry," I

said. "My mind must have wandered. What do I think about what?"

"About coming home with me tonight. My house is only about fifteen minutes from here."

How convenient for you, I thought. I smiled falsely but politely. "Oh, I'm—"

"You look like the kind of woman who likes it doggie style." Roger winked, grinned.

"What?" I blurted.

And then he barked. Loud enough for the man at the next table to snicker. Loud enough for me to feel utterly humiliated. And angry.

I stood. "Go to hell," I said, with a large and lovely smile on my face. And I left Roger there, no doubt already eyeing the bar for another woman who looked like the type who liked to do it while suspended from a bridge.

I was starving. I had been looking forward to the swordfish special posted on a chalkboard over the bar.

I took off my dress and heels, made a peanut butter and jelly sandwich, and decided to become a recluse.

Why not? It was becoming increasingly clear that I was not cut out for dating and all its many ugly aspects.

Like sex with someone you hardly know.

Suddenly, I remembered something Laura had said not long before. I'd cut her off but her meaning had been clear enough. Maybe, she'd suggested, if I had been more interested in sex, Richard wouldn't have—left me.

Ridiculous.

I know the facts.

I know you can't make someone gay. I know people are born gay or not gay.

Still, right after finding that note in Richard's pocket, I had wondered if Richard's interest in men was somehow my fault. Not that his interest in men is in any way wrong. But I had wondered about my own role in his emerging life.

What woman in my position wouldn't have wondered?

I finished the sandwich and opened a pint of mint Oreo ice cream. It's my biggest vice, that ice cream.

I dug right in. And I wondered what doggie style would be like.

Chapter 23

Laura

Don't kid yourself. The process of extricating your life from his will take years and might never be totally completed. Like a bad smell, the ex-husband lingers. Practice holding your nose.
—*Unraveling the Ties That Bind*

I swore I wouldn't do it.

Five hundred dollars is an awful lot of money.

But I was getting nowhere fast dating men I met in produce and men my colleagues thought were so perfect. Really, what were they thinking?

So I wrote the check and signed up with a dating service called Happy Couples. Their office was really bare and plain. Nothing about the place said romance. There were no flowers in glass vases or photos of couples strolling the beach at sunset.

Maybe, I thought, this is a good thing. Happy Couples is all about business, all about getting men and women out of the singles scene and into a nice ranch house in the suburbs.

Although personally, I'd like a two-story colonial.

A pale, skinny woman in an outfit clearly from Dress Barn sat behind a big metal desk in what at first I thought must be the reception area; eventually I figured out it was the entire office. She introduced herself as Ms. Berber and told me she would be my facilitator. Without meeting my eye she thrust a stack of pa-

pers at me and told me to fill out the Happy Couples manda-
tory questionnaire. I sat on one of the metal folding chairs lin-
ing one wall of the room and began to read.

The lengthy questionnaire was totally humiliating, not like
the one I'd come up with at all. No, Happy Couples wanted to
know if I had a body odor problem; if I used a depilatory cream
on my face; and if I had any skin tags. Skin tags! Happy Couples
wanted to know my height, weight, and fitness routine. (Well, I
lied a bit about my fitness routine because I didn't have one.)
Happy Couples also wanted to know if I had any visible scars
that would prevent me from wearing a bikini. Sheesh.

When I had answered the two hundred questions, I handed
the questionnaire to Ms. Berber. I noticed the diamond ring on
her left hand was really big but kind of dull.

"We'll review your chart," she said, already eyeing my check
marks, "and get back to you as soon as an eligible match can be
found."

I nodded and said thank you.

I was at the door, my hand on the knob, when Ms. Berber
spoke again.

"And Ms. Keats? One final note. Lose ten pounds. The cab-
bage diet works quickly."

Four nights later I was out with Match #1. His name was
Barry and his profile clearly indicated that he was looking for
Ms. Right. Or so that skinny Ms. Berber told me.

Barry suggested we meet at Bar Louis. I hesitated before
agreeing. Bar Louis is a hangout for twentysomethings, a notorious pickup joint. But it was supposed to have good mixed
drinks and I hadn't had a Fuzzy Navel in ages, so I said okay.

I dressed carefully to make just the right first impression. I
wanted Barry to take one look at me and see a serious woman,
a woman ready to start a family. I wore a crisp white shirt and a
fitted linen skirt that came to the knee. I wore my hair in a neat,
sleek ponytail, which took about a pound of product to accomplish. I wore a strand of tiny pearls.

And from the moment I walked through the door of Bar

Louis I felt like the biggest frump. Partly it was because every other woman in the place was half-naked; at least half of them wore exposed thongs and flaunted firm brown bellies. Partly it was because not one man looked at me, not even once. But mostly I felt like the biggest frump because Barry could not keep his eyes off the other women, all of whom were younger than me by, like, years.

Ten minutes into our lame conversation I realized I'd gone from frumpy to invisible.

"How was your day?" I asked.

Barry, his eyes following a girl in skintight, low-rise jeans, replied, "Huh?"

"What do you do for a living?" I asked.

Barry, salivating over the cocktail waitress's huge breasts, replied, "What?"

"Are you originally from Boston?" I asked.

Barry, tossing his napkin on the table, replied, "I'll be right back."

And I watched him make his way through the chattering crowd to a tall, slim black girl. I watched him give her a business card.

I sat absolutely still and watched Barry make his way back to our little table.

He sat back down and grinned. "Miss me?"

"You just gave that girl your number."

His grin remained firmly in place. "What?"

And then the anger just surged through me. "Don't deny it," I cried, "I saw you! We're on a date. You're supposed to be paying attention to me. How can you even know if you like me if you spend the whole time staring at other women?"

Barry's grin ran away. "Hey, ease down. We're not married, okay?"

"Don't tell me to ease down! I'm reporting you to the agency. You lied. You don't want to have a baby. You want to date a baby!"

I threw my napkin on the table and stormed off. I'm not sure he even noticed I was gone.

* * *

The next afternoon during my lunch hour I took the T to the Back Bay. I'd read about a new high-end children's clothing shop called Fleur but hadn't gone because, well, it was high-end.

The shop was cool and scented with fresh lilac. The clothing was handmade in France. The prices were astronomical. I mean, they had this thing called a layette that cost almost as much as my monthly rent!

I fell in love with everything and had a really hard time choosing, but finally I decided on a sweet little set. It was absolutely adorable, a blush pink knit sweater and leggings, just perfect for a bright New England fall day.

It did occur to me that if I had my baby in, say, December, by the next fall she would be too big for the sweater and leggings. And if my baby turned out to be a boy, well, he wouldn't be able to wear the outfit at all.

But it was so sweet.

I know I shouldn't have spent the money.

I know.

Chapter 24

Grace

Just remember: Forever is relative. What one person sees as three years can feel like a lifetime to another.
—*Did I Say Forever? Reinterpreting the Marriage Vows*

"Good morning. Welcome to the Auster Gallery."
I knew I wouldn't run into Simon; he always sleeps until at least noon. But I hadn't anticipated running into the owner of the gallery.

Everyone connected to the Boston art world knows Evan Auster, even a person who teaches ten-year-olds how to hold a paintbrush. I recognized him right away; I'd seen his picture often enough in magazines, newspapers, on television. He appeared to be a handsome man, about fifty, with very blue eyes and very dark hair, a clean-shaven face, fit, and well dressed.

The photos, I realized with a bit of a shock, didn't do him justice.

"Good morning," I said.

Mr. Auster smiled winningly. "If I can be of any help, please let me know. Are you interested in a particular artist?"

I glanced quickly around the space. Yes, I thought. But not in the way you mean.

I looked back to Mr. Auster. I noted that I came up only to

his shoulder. "I know the artist you're featuring in your next solo show," I said. "Simon Trenouth."

Mr. Auster nodded. "I see. You're a friend?"

Was Simon my friend? Was I his?

"Well, actually," I said, "we were married for twelve years. But we're divorced. Amicably . . ." When I'm not furious with him for abusing my credit cards and calling at all hours of the night. But Mr. Auster didn't need to know the whole story.

"So," he said, "you're here because you want to get a sense of Simon's work in the space?"

I nodded. "Yes, exactly. I haven't been to the gallery in a while. I've been pretty busy with work." And with a young German. But that's over.

"Really? What is your work?"

Mr. Auster was a polite man. He didn't need to ask a question that, for all he knew, might have resulted in a lengthy or boring answer.

"Oh," I said quickly, "I teach art at a private middle school in Brookline."

"That sounds interesting. And exhausting."

"It is," I admitted. "Both things."

"So you must be glad summer is almost here." Mr. Auster smiled. "What do you usually do with your time off?"

Take care of Simon. But not this year.

"This year," I said, "I'm going to be the director of a new program called Art for All. It's for kids twelve and under. It's privately funded and free to the participants. We've already got close to a hundred kids signed up for the two sessions."

Mr. Auster seemed genuine when he said, "That's great. Congratulations. I'd like to learn more about the program. It sounds like a worthy cause."

There wasn't a trace of phoniness in his tone or on his face. Mr. Auster wasn't just making polite conversation. He really was interested in the program.

"Oh," I said. "Well, I could give you the Web site address . . ." I reached into my bag for a pen and piece of paper.

"That would be great." Suddenly, Mr. Auster laughed. "I'm sorry. I haven't introduced myself. I'm Evan Auster."

I looked up from my search. "Yes," I said. "I mean, I recognized you. From photos."

"And you are . . ."

An idiot.

"Oh. Sorry. I'm Grace. Grace Henley."

Evan put out his hand; it was a very nice hand. We shook and he didn't squeeze too hard.

Finally, I found a pen and wrote the Web site address neatly across the back of one of Evan's business cards.

"It's been a pleasure to meet you, Grace. Would you like to have dinner some time this week?"

I was completely surprised by Evan's offer. I think my mouth might have dropped open because Evan added hastily, "To discuss the show, of course. And your program."

Of course.

"Sure," I said. "Yes. That would be fine."

After taking my number and giving me another of his cards to keep, Evan excused himself to speak with an older couple who'd come in moments before. They had the look of serious art buyers about them; her tasteful jewelry alone would have paid my mortgage for years.

I walked back to my apartment in a sort of stupor.

Evan Auster, a big name in the gallery world, had asked questions about my work. My work. Not my job. Work sounded so much more meaningful than a mere job. Simon never asked about my work, not even in the beginning, not even as a means of getting me into bed.

Simon hadn't had to do a thing to get me into bed. Simon was Simon and that had been enough.

Had been enough, once upon a time. Wasn't enough anymore. I had to remember that.

By the time I reached home my thoughts had begun to spin off in an odd direction.

What if Evan and I started dating and then had a bad falling out? Evan might cancel Simon's show in retaliation. Worse things had happened in the sometimes vicious world of art. What if I were the one responsible for destroying Simon's big chance?

I sat on the couch and sank into its cushions.

Crazy thoughts! Here I was putting Simon's welfare above my own happiness, again.

Here I was imagining a future with Evan, a man I'd met only an hour earlier.

Grace, I told myself, sinking even deeper, get a grip.

Chapter 25

Jess

An old term for a husband or wife is yokemate. Do you really want to be compared to a pair of oxen? There is no freedom in restraint.

—*The Old Ball and Chain: Why Marriage Feels Like Prison*

"Where do people meet if not at work? I mean, adult people, people with jobs and health concerns and aging parents. People with mortgages."

I was feeling glum. The psychology department's assistant had announced her resignation that afternoon. It seems she'd met and fallen in love with an assistant from another department and was moving with him to Seattle. I was happy for her, in a sort of removed way, but not happy to be losing her valuable skills.

"Even meeting at work is tricky," Nell said. "Sexual harassment laws are getting stricter. In some places it's not even acceptable to date someone at exactly your level. It seems crazy to try to legislate love or sex, but there it is."

"People meet at the gym," Grace said.

"That's so nineties!"

I looked at Laura. She comes out with the oddest things.

"People have to join a gym first," I pointed out. "Besides, I don't want to be worried about how I look when I'm on

the StairMaster. I just want to work out. Well, I don't actually want to work out, but if I did, I wouldn't want some guy
sizing me up as I'm furiously pedaling on the stationary
bike."

Laura shrugged. "You don't have to exercise. You could just
sort of hang around, maybe meet a guy at the juice bar. Most
gyms have juice bars."

"Oh, please." Nell laughed. "Can you really imagine Jess hanging out at the juice bar, eyeing the muscle heads in shiny span-
dex?"

"I guess not."

"People meet at bars," Grace said.

"People get drunk at bars." People get drunk and invite
strangers into their home for sex they can't even remember the
next morning.

Grace nodded. "True. But not everyone hangs out at a bar to
get drunk. It's a social place, a meeting place. Bars can be very
friendly."

And they can also be very dangerous.

"I just don't see myself as a barfly," I said. "Besides, a single
woman hanging out at a bar alone looks pathetic and easy. It
shouldn't be that way but it is."

"Speaking of alcoholic beverages . . ."

The waiter arrived with our drinks, something neon green
for Laura, a glass of red wine for me, a glass of white for Grace,
and champagne for Nell.

"And if you go to a bar with a girlfriend," Laura said when he
was gone, "and one of you meets a guy and he wants to talk to
you and you want to talk to him, then what's your friend going
to do? Just sit there all alone?"

Nell put her hand to her head as if it hurt. "You'd abandon
your girlfriend to talk to some stranger who probably only
wants to get into your pants?"

"I wouldn't," Laura protested. "But some women would."

"A woman can't go to a bar alone to meet a guy because
she'll look cheap," I said. "And she can't go to a bar with a girlfriend because if she does meet a nice guy, she won't be able to

talk to him, not without hurting her friend. It's a no-win situation; it's ridiculous."

"I think," said Nell, "that we should eliminate bars altogether as possible places to meet the love of your life."

"Galleries," Grace said. "Museums. You could meet a man at an opening."

I think I made a face. "I'm not comfortable with the notion of art as social lubricant. I want to look at the art, not at the other viewers."

"You're impossible!" Laura said.

"Maybe," I agreed. "Anyway, there's just no point in my dating. What I mean is, there's no point in my looking for love. It doesn't happen that way for me. Love—or lust, or whatever you want to call it—finds me. Suddenly, there's a man and we're undeniably drawn to each other and—that's it. No questions, no dancing around the issue. But it's a rare occurrence. I might be alone for months, for years before the next—force of nature—finds me."

"Maybe you can change that dynamic," Grace said gently.

"Maybe. But why would I want to?"

Laura rolled her eyes. "Uh, because time's running out?"

Now Nell rubbed her temples. Maybe she did have a headache, and we'd brought it on.

"I don't mean to sound like a sappy greeting card," I said, "but I really believe that love knows no age limit. I believe an eighty-year-old can fall in love as easily as a twenty-year-old."

"But," Laura argued, "what man is going to fall in love with an eighty-year-old woman, besides, maybe, a man in his nineties. And there aren't a lot of those around!"

"I'm not sure I agree with you, Jess, about the old falling in love." Nell looked to each of us in turn. "It seems to me that new love requires a degree of innocence, a willingness to be vulnerable, that age and experience can kill. I suspect that by the time most people reach fifty, maybe sixty, they're just too weary to fall in love."

"Then so be it," I said. "I just can't get married again to assure there's someone in bed with me every night. It's simply more essential to me that the person in bed with me be the right person. I'm perfectly capable of sleeping alone. Sometimes I'm lonely, but who ever said that life was going to be a slice of peach pie?"

Grace smiled. "I don't think I've ever had peach pie."

"It's wonderful, but very sweet, very intense. A little bit goes a very long way."

"I think I'll treat myself to dessert tonight," Laura announced.

I looked to Nell, expecting to see her rolling her eyes—which she was—and suddenly noticed the small gold locket around her neck. "That's pretty," I said.

"It was my mother's," Nell explained. "When she died, Laura and I each chose a piece of her jewelry to keep. She didn't have much, really, and most of what she did have wasn't my style. But I thought the locket was sweet. It's the first time I'm wearing it."

"Who's inside?"

"Colin and Clara, of course."

"I never asked," Laura said. "What did you do with your wedding set, Nell?"

Nell looked at her naked ring finger. "I put my wedding ring in my safe-deposit box. My 'engagement' ring, my diamond, which Richard couldn't afford until our fifth anniversary, is in there, too. Someday maybe Colin or Clara will want it. I don't know."

"What about you, Jess?" Laura asked.

I felt a twinge of discomfort. I'd never talked about this.

"I gave my engagement ring back to Matt," I said. "The stone had been in his mother's family for generations. I couldn't very well keep it."

"Of course not," Nell agreed.

"But I did keep the wedding band. It's silly. I can't imagine I'll ever use it. If I get remarried, which is unlikely, I don't think I'd be comfortable wearing a ring that was supposed to symbolize my lasting union with another man. And I can't see wearing it as a meaningless piece of jewelry. It's full of meaning. I don't know. Maybe I should just sell it and use the money for something practical, like paying a bill."

"Or," Grace suggested, "you could use the money to buy another ring, something that symbolizes your commitment to yourself and to your own life."

"It's a nice idea," I said, "but I'm not that into jewelry. Besides, I'm not sure I do have a commitment to myself. I'm feeling rather unmoored these days."

Nell turned to her sister. "So, Laura, what did you do with your wedding set?"

"Oh, I kept it. Duncan wanted me to have it."

"Because he's a generous man?" Nell inquired with a false smile. "Or because the set is a bitter reminder of what he had and lost?"

"There's no need to be nasty. What Duncan actually said was that he had no use for the rings. Of course he doesn't. It's not like he can wear them or give them to some other woman. Anyway, I'm thinking of having the diamonds reset in a totally different way."

"You're not going to save the rings for your daughter?" Nell asked.

Laura looked at her sister as if she were insane. "No, no, of course not. My daughter will use a set from her father's family. Duncan has no connection to my children. He's my past. My children are my future. I think I'll have the chocolate tart!"

Nell put her head in her hands. Grace rolled her eyes. And I wondered.

What would it be like to dismiss the past as easily as Laura seemed able to do?

Chapter 26

Jess

Ninety percent of men want to bail at the first sign of trouble, such as your breast cancer or your mother's moving in with you. When it comes to women, men prefer to flee rather than to fight.

—*For Better, For Worse—Exploding the Myth of Marriage*

"I've been into S & M for about ten years now. It's really changed my life. I'm so much more open to my emotions now, really in touch with my feelings."

"I see," I said, but I didn't see at all.

Dr. Neal Smith is smart, fit, and forty. He's a respected research scientist with a small private practice. When he stopped by my office earlier that week and asked if I'd like to have dinner with him, I was pleasantly surprised. I had no idea Neal was interested in me.

In spite of having told my friends there was no point in my dating, I agreed to have dinner with Neal. Maybe, I thought, something nice will happen for us. Not marriage, not love, not even sex, just something pleasant. At the very least, it would get me out of the house for a few hours. All I seemed to do at home was mope.

We met at Bistro Noir. We shared a bottle of Merlot. The duck was wonderful. Our conversation was easy and wide ranging.

Things were going well until he suggested we go back to his place. And until he told me about his fondness for bondage.

"I visit a dominatrix once a week," he was saying now. "It's far better than therapy. I feel utterly refreshed when I come out of the Mistress's lair."

"Oh." Was Neal putting me on? Was this all some sort of sick joke? I took a long drink of water. It didn't help.

"I've got all the equipment we'll need: nipple clamps, restraints, whips, so you—"

I put up my hand. Joke or no joke, things had gone too far. "First of all," I said, "I hardly know you. I don't go home with men after a bowl of pasta and an espresso." If that wasn't strictly true, it was certainly true for that night.

Neal had the good grace to say, "Fair enough. Maybe after a few more dates we can—"

"And second . . ." I leaned a bit closer to him and spoke in a softer voice. "I'm sorry, but I'm not into anything kinky or alternative, especially not with someone I don't know. Or trust."

Neal sat back and grimaced. "Yikes," he said. "Okay. It's just that, well, I know you've been around some and I thought you might be open to sexual exploration."

I shook my head. "What do you mean, I've been around some?"

"Well, you're divorced and I heard you had an affair and—"

Really, was everyone out to give me a heart attack?

"And you know nothing about my life at all," I hissed. "How dare you make assumptions about me!"

Neal sat back as if afraid my hissing would turn to slapping. "Whoa, Jess, look, I'm really sorry. My bad. Can we just forget this whole night ever happened?"

"Gladly." I tossed my napkin on the table and reached for my purse.

"And, well, I'd appreciate it if you don't tell anyone at the university about my preferences. You never know who's going to freak out on you."

Like me, Jess Marlowe, gal about town.

"Your secret," I said acidly, "is safe with me."

* * *

Later that night I lay in bed, not sleeping, staring into the dark, thinking.

Why, I wondered, did people feel they had the right to humiliate me? Or was I the one doing the humiliating, giving people the power to make me feel like dirt?

And it had all started, this strange phase of my life, when I destroyed my marriage.

What had I done by cheating on Matt, by setting us up for a fall? I'd never considered all the possible consequences, all the ramifications. How could I have? Who has that vivid and wide ranging an imagination?

Here I was judging Laura for what I considered a rash decision to throw away her marriage, but hadn't I done much the same?

At least Laura had left Duncan for a real, solid reason. Laura wanted something concrete that Duncan wouldn't or couldn't give her; now, she was in search of that something herself.

What had I wanted, specifically, that Matt wouldn't or couldn't give me? What was I in search of, what was my goal, what the hell was I doing with my life?

I turned out the light. I thought about the papers I needed to finish grading before noon and about the meeting I had to attend and about a colleague's book I had promised to review.

Work.

The only constant in my life, I realized, was work, and it would continue to be. No more romantic entanglements, I prayed to whoever would listen, at least for the rest of the decade.

Especially not with men who carried their own nipple clamps.

Chapter 27

Nell

Your faith in love has been shattered. Your worldview has been rocked. Everything your church told you about fidelity was a lie. Cheer up! It's always darkest before the dawn.
—*This Too Shall Pass: Surviving the First Few Months of Divorce*

"We'll have a bottle of champagne, the Veuve Clicquot." The waiter moved off noiselessly and Trina flashed me a dazzling smile. "After all, darling Nell, we are celebrating."

Trina Donohue—she'd kept her maiden name—was somewhere in her midforties and already on husband number four. Rumor had it she was having an affair with a tax attorney in New York and getting ready to divorce the "old coot," as her current husband, Miles Collins, was popularly known. Miles wasn't a particularly nice man; still, I wasn't sure he deserved a punishing divorce.

And if Trina's history was any indication, the divorce would indeed be punishing.

Trina had called me earlier that week and suggested we meet for lunch. I was surprised and not entirely happy that she'd called. Trina and I had nothing in common besides a uterus. Assuming Trina still had one.

The waiter returned with the champagne and poured us each a glass. Trina raised hers in a toast.

"Darling," she said, "welcome to the club."

I raised my glass as well. "What club?" I knew the answer, of course, but I wanted to hear Trina say it.

Trina touched her glass to mine. "The divorcée club, darling! In spite of what people think, we're not at all dreary and bitter. We're a devil-may-care group, darling. We're seizing the day!"

I didn't feel like seizing a piece of bread from the plate in front of me, let alone an entire day.

"I don't want to be part of this club," I said.

Trina smiled brightly. "But you are, darling Nell, you are. You might as well make the best of it. You might as well learn to enjoy your new position. And by the way, darling Nell, frowning does great damage to the firmness of your skin."

"You're married," I said, ignoring her beauty advice. "You're not part of this—club—anymore."

"Once a member, always a member," Trina said, rolling a ring around her finger with her thumb. There were enough diamonds on the ring to satisfy a hundred greedy brides. "Besides, darling Nell, I won't be married much longer."

"Does Miles know what's coming?" I asked.

"Darling, he doesn't have a clue. He's senile, you know. Has been for the last year."

"Is it Alzheimer's?"

Trina laughed. There were virtually no lines around her eyes. Her face had been plumped. Her hair shone; her teeth gleamed. "Oh, no, nothing official. He's just become even more of an idiot than he was when I married him."

"Why would you marry an idiot?" I blurted.

"Darling Nell, sometimes idiots are very, very rich."

Well, of course. What other answer could there be?

"Family money?" I asked.

"Oh, yes. The estate has very good management. I made sure to investigate thoroughly before I signed on for the job."

"The job?" I asked.

Trina looked at me slyly. "Darling Nell, you were married for over twenty years. You can't tell me that marriage isn't a job."

I thought for a moment. Finally, I said, "Marriage is hard work sometimes, most times. But it's more of a vocation than a job. It's something you want to do. A job is something you have to do."

"And my job," Trina said, "is to marry wealthy men and relieve them of the money they don't really need."

I might have thought Trina was joking if I hadn't known her marital history. It was ample proof she was speaking her version of the plain truth.

"I've never met a woman with such a cavalier attitude toward men and marriage," I said.

Trina nodded, as if I'd given her a great compliment. "I've perfected my art."

Now her job had become an art form?

"So," I asked, "you don't believe in love at all?"

"Of course not, darling." Trina looked almost shocked that I'd bothered to ask such a ridiculous question. "Love is fine for some people, people who have no ambition, for example, but not for me."

"I married for love," I said.

"And look where it got you."

Single and forty-two. Doubting my sexual appeal. Feeling victimized. Maybe romantic love didn't necessarily make for a good marriage. But then, what did?

"My parents had a happy marriage," I said. At least, I thought they had. But what did I really know about what went on behind their closed doors?

Trina cocked an eyebrow and took a sip of champagne. I noted again her couture, her Hermes bag, her diamonds. I thought of the clothes and bags I'd bought with money Richard had earned. I pictured my own small but expensive collection of jewelry. Was it possible Trina and I had more in common than I'd first thought?

"I don't know if I like you very much," I blurted.

Trina smiled. "I'll admit I'm an acquired taste."

"I'm sorry. I shouldn't have said that."

"Really, Nell, it's quite all right."

"On the other hand," I said, "I find myself compelled to sit here and listen to what you have to say."

"I often inspire conflicting feelings of attraction and repulsion."

Like a boa constrictor, magnificent and deadly.

"You say you don't believe in love. But have you ever experienced it?" I asked. "Have you ever loved a man? Has a man ever really loved you? I wonder if you'd recognize love if it was offered."

Trina put down her glass. "Darling Nell," she said. "When I was sixteen I fell in love with a charming, fascinating man. He was married, of course. I believed every word that came from his smiling lips. And every single word turned out to be false, of course. It was then I decided that if love caused such unpleasant feelings, I wanted no part of it."

Trina picked up her glass and drained the last of the champagne.

"One adolescent heartbreak and you gave up on love?" I asked. "I find that hard to believe."

"Nevertheless," Trina said, "it's the truth. Now, let's be decadent. Let's order dessert."

Maybe it was the champagne at noon, maybe it was the fabulously rich tart, but by the end of lunch with Trina Donohue, I felt as if a new woman was about to emerge from the old Nell Keats. And I wondered who that woman would be.

I thought about Trina all the way home.

She drove me crazy. She fascinated me. I couldn't wait to see her again.

Chapter 28

Laura

The question of whether or not to maintain a post-divorce relationship with your ex-spouse is entirely yours to make. If the very mention of his name induces projectile vomiting, your course is clear. Stay away from the bum.

—*Negotiating the Rest of Your Life: It's a Long Road 'Til Death*

"Would you like more water?"

I looked up at the waiter. He was about twenty and annoyed.

Well, I wasn't going to order a drink before my date got there! He was supposed to pay for drinks and dinner; I wasn't taking any chances on getting stuck with a bill.

As it turns out, I made a smart decision.

"No, thank you," I said stiffly. "My date has been unavoidably delayed. I believe I will wait for him outside."

The waiter smirked and slipped off.

One hour.

I squinted at my watch to be sure. Yes, no mistaking a sixty-minute revolution of a watch hand. Match #2 wasn't late. He had stood me up.

As soon as I got back to my apartment, I placed a call to Happy Couples. My hand shook with anger.

A recorded voice blared in my ear. The number was no longer in service. There was no forwarding number. I contacted the Better Business Bureau. A bored-sounding woman informed me that they had already received fifty-two complaints about Happy Couples and that they were investigating the whereabouts of its owners.

"Isn't there something you can do? Like, now?" I cried.

"Like what? Refund your money. Sorry, but that's not our responsibility."

I hung up the phone.

Five hundred dollars down the drain and for what? For a big fat dose of humiliation.

It was the straw that broke the camel's back. I don't really understand that expression. I mean, why is there straw on the camel's back? But I know when to use it, and that night I realized that I'd had enough of single life. I'd had enough of the misery that is dating.

Nell would smirk and be all smug about it when she found out. She would say, I told you so, but I didn't care; I could handle my sister's nastiness.

I called Duncan.

Okay, so I abandoned my pride. What choice did I have?

It was clear, painfully clear that I'd made a huge mistake in filing for a divorce before giving Duncan and myself some time to think things through.

But it wasn't too late to fix everything. The divorce wasn't final.

It just couldn't be too late.

I suggested we meet at a Dunkin' Donuts by Downtown Crossing. It was Duncan's favorite fast-food place. He was crazy about their bagels. I thought that if our meeting went well, I'd buy him a dozen bagels to take home. Maybe he'd invite me over to share them.

I got to the store a few minutes before ten, bought a cup of coffee, poured in lots of milk, and sat at a corner table, facing the door. I was a bundle of nerves, just a mess, but I refused to let Duncan see that I was desperate. I guess I hadn't abandoned my pride entirely.

At ten on the nose the glass door opened and in walked Duncan. He looked relaxed, like he always looked. He looked unconcerned.

I stood and gave a little wave, though he'd already seen me. I wondered if he would kiss me hello. I wondered if he would give me a hug. I'd never expected a handshake. It was really awkward, me leaning in for an embrace and Duncan thrusting his hand toward me as if to ward off my more intimate touch.

I took his hand but I couldn't look him in the eye.

"I'll be right back," he said.

I sat down while Duncan strode to the counter. A few minutes later he came back with a coffee and a muffin.

"I thought you liked the bagels," I blurted.

Duncan shrugged. "I'm kind of over them. Now I'm into the muffins."

"Oh," I said. It didn't feel like a good sign, Duncan's changing his mind about something he used to like so much.

"So," Duncan asked, "why did you want to see me? My lawyer says everything's going fine, the divorce is in process, no bumps in the road."

"You called your lawyer about meeting me?" I asked in surprise.

"Sure. You and me, we're on opposites sides of the fence here, Laura. We're not just two people, we're a legal issue now. I needed my lawyer to know I was seeing you."

"But you just said everything was going smoothly," I said. "Isn't it? Have you changed your mind about something?"

Yes, Laura, I have changed my mind. I don't want the divorce, I want you back and I want a family.

Yes, Laura, I have changed my mind. I want to play hardball. I want your doll collection in return for the crap you made of my life.

Duncan shook his head. "If I'd changed my mind about anything, my lawyer would have contacted your lawyer already."

"Oh," I said. "Of course." I unfolded the paper napkin. I refolded it. "So, how are you? You look great."

Duncan grinned. "I am great. I mean, considering I'm in the

middle of a divorce that took me totally by surprise. I met someone, Laura. She's fabulous."

You know that old expression, "you could have knocked me over with a feather"? That's what I felt like, totally shocked, like if someone blew on me, I would crumble into dust.

Not once had it occurred to me that Duncan might be dating. I don't know why.

"Oh," I said. "That's—wonderful."

"Yeah, it is, isn't it? I mean, only a few months ago I felt like my life was over. I was really screwed up, you know? And then I met Anne. It was like—magic. Love at first sight and all that. It was the first time that ever happened to me, you know, just— bam!"

The first time? I wondered what Duncan had felt when he'd first met me. Maybe he'd told me once. If so, I'd forgotten. Not love at first sight, though. That was for Anne.

"So," I said, trying but failing to sound okay, "you think it's a good thing I asked for a divorce?"

Duncan took a sip of his coffee before answering. "Maybe. In the end. Who knows? Sometimes life has to really suck before it gets radically better than it ever was."

All I knew at that moment was that my life felt radically worse than it ever had.

Duncan took a big bite of his muffin and chewed enthusiastically. I used to find Duncan's enjoyment of food sweet. What, I wondered, did Anne think of his eating habits?

Duncan wiped the crumbs from his lips. "So," he said, "don't you want to know anything about her?"

No. Of course not. I don't feel even a shred of morbid curiosity.

"Okay," I said.

"Well, she's a bit younger, twenty-six to be exact. And she's divorced; who isn't these days, right? And she's got a three-year-old girl named Edie. God, Edie is adorable. I swear she's the cutest little girl I've ever seen. She totally takes after her mom."

"That's nice."

Why, I wondered, is he doing this to me?

"Anne's ex is an idiot," Duncan went on. "He sends a check every month but wants nothing to do with either of them. Anne's got full custody and the father even waived visitation rights, which is fine by me. I don't want Edie spending time with that jerk."

Since when had Duncan become so paternal?

"So," I asked, unnecessarily, "things are serious between you two?"

"Oh, yeah," Duncan said with enthusiasm. "Like I said, I've never felt this way before. Things are just different with Anne. I can't explain how or why. They just are."

Different. Different means better; everyone knows that.

"Oh," I said.

"Yeah." Duncan leaned forward and fixed me with his eyes. I'm not sure I'd ever seen him look so serious. "Laura," he said, "when you left me because I didn't want kids, well, it really got me thinking about the whole thing. Now, with Anne, I feel really ready, really excited about being a dad. We hope to have a baby of our own before long. Right after we get married. I don't know, maybe I just needed some time to process my own feelings, you know?"

My entire body began to buzz. I thought I might faint. "So," I finally said, "if I had waited a few more months before serving you divorce papers, maybe you would have changed your mind? Is that what you're saying?"

Duncan seemed to ponder. Since when had he become a great thinker?

"No," he finally said, "not really. Something tells me I probably wouldn't ever have wanted kids with you."

I pushed my coffee cup toward the middle of the table. The thought of food or drink was nauseating.

"I'm sorry," Duncan said, "I don't mean to be harsh. Look, maybe it's just hindsight talking; maybe it's just my way of getting over the pain you put me through. Jesus, Laura, you turned my life upside down, both of our lives. You had no faith in us as a couple. You threw away someone who loved you for someone who didn't even exist."

Someone who loved me. Past tense.

Different means better.

Duncan laughed. "Anyway, look at me, I've been doing all the talking. So, what did you want to see me about?"

I wanted to ask you to take me back.

"Oh, it's . . ." I smiled shakily and waved my hand. "Nothing, just . . . nothing."

Duncan had known me too long to believe I was telling the truth.

"Hey, Laura, are you okay? I hope I didn't sound cruel or anything—"

"No, no, it's fine. I'm fine. Really."

Duncan looked at me again, closely, but asked no more questions. "Okay, then," he said, and his voice was somehow softer. "I should go. Anne and Edie are meeting me just outside. I promised I'd take them to the aquarium."

I nodded. No more words. Duncan stood and hesitated for a moment. I kept my eyes on the Formica table. And then he left.

I didn't want to look. I shouldn't have looked. But I did, and what I saw made me so sad I thought I would die right there in Dunkin' Donuts.

Duncan stepped out into the late morning sun. He put his arm around a small, plumpish woman and squeezed. She beamed up at him. The toddler she held in her arms reached for Duncan and he took the little girl. He kissed the little girl on the nose.

And then I watched my life walk away.

"You look like hell."

I don't remember how I got to Nell's apartment. I don't even remember her opening the door. But she did, and when I didn't say anything in response, she took my arm and led me inside.

"Sit," she said, and I did sit on the big comfortable couch.

Nell went away for a minute and came back with a glass of water. I shook my head. Nell put the water aside, crouched on the floor, and placed her hands on my knees.

"What happened?" she asked. "Laura, talk to me."

I wanted to say something, I did, but I couldn't because suddenly I was sobbing these big, painful sobs. Nell sat next to me then and held me against her while I cried and cried all over her nice blouse. I'm sure I ruined it but she didn't say anything about it afterward.

"It will be all right," Nell said in that soothing voice I remembered her using when the children were little. "Everything will be all right."

I shook my head and managed to croak, "No, it won't!" before another bout of sobbing overtook me.

Finally, finally, the crying stopped, suddenly, like all the tears were just drained from my body. Nell went away again and brought me a box of tissues, most of which I used blowing my nose and mopping my face. She handed me two ibuprofen tablets and the abandoned glass of water and I choked the tablets down.

"You're going to have a whopper of a headache," she said. "When you were a little girl, you always got headaches when you cried this way."

I attempted a smile, but I bet it was a pretty lame one.

"Are you going to tell me what happened?" Nell asked again.

I looked at my sister and took a shaky breath. Somehow the words got out. "I saw Duncan," I said.

Nell's expression remained neutral. "And it didn't go well."

"It was horrible. I wanted to . . . I wanted to ask him if he, you know, if he wanted to get back together."

I had to stop there and sob some more. Nell waited patiently; at least she didn't rush me. When the sobs went away again, I told her the rest, how I had never gotten to ask Duncan about getting back together because first he told me all about how happy he was with that woman and how he was going to get married and have babies with her.

When I was done, Nell looked almost sick. "Oh, Laura," she said, "I'm so sorry. And here I was, urging you to talk to him . . ."

"Don't feel bad," I said. "If I'd taken your advice weeks ago, I might have had a chance with Duncan. I guess . . . I guess I just waited too long."

Nell and I sat quietly for a while, side by side on the couch. Finally, Nell sighed. "Laura," she said, "I have a meeting at three but I'll cancel and stay here with you if you want."

I shook my head. "That's okay. Go. But can I just stay here for a while? Can I lie down here and not move? I don't think I can move just yet."

"Of course." Nell got up slowly and helped me to lie down. She brought a blanket from the linen closet and tucked it around me, nice and tight.

"Try to sleep," she whispered. "I'll be back as soon as I can."

I did sleep.

And I dreamed that the truck that killed my parents was crashing into me.

Chapter 29

Grace

You harbored dreams of growing old together, of breakfast on the porch, of reading poetry aloud to one another, of holding hands by the sea. But those dreams were shattered like a fragile glass thrown to the floor by an angry drunk. Now, sweep up the shards and get on with your life.

—*It's Not Pretty: Facing the Reality of Divorce*

"Grace? Is something wrong with your entrée?"

I stuck my fork into a piece of something and lifted it to my mouth. "Oh, no, it's fine."

I chewed but tasted nothing.

"Good," Evan said. "I thought you might like this place. It's unpretentious all around, don't you think?"

"Yes," I said.

My language skills seemed to have failed me. Try as I might, I couldn't seem to make normal conversation. Evan had to notice my odd behavior, but he didn't seem bothered by it. He continued to introduce interesting topics and to ask questions about my life as if I were actually capable of responding with more than one- or two-word answers.

See, I was terribly attracted to the man across the table.

It happened the moment I walked into the restaurant and spotted him waiting for me at the bar. I don't mean to sound dramatic but it was a dramatic moment, one of those pivotal moments in life, a moment after which nothing is ever the same, for better or worse. I suppose you could argue that every moment changes you forever, but I'm talking about those moments you remember vividly, the ones you replay in your head with wonder.

The moments, I reminded myself, that you most often regret.

I poked at the pile of herbed rice on my plate and wondered if I could get a forkful to my mouth without it all spilling. Sexual attraction tends to make my hands unsteady.

And they were trembling now. I hadn't felt so drawn to a man since I'd met Simon. I hadn't known I could feel this way again. Alive. Sexual. Intensely interested in everything Evan had to say, in the way his hair swept off his forehead, the way the cuff of his shirt accentuated the breadth of his hand. His very skin was compelling. The reading glasses he slipped on to consider the menu made me wild. He looked so serious and strong.

I felt myself staring. I wanted to gaze into his eyes; I wanted to know him.

I lowered my eyes to my plate. What was I eating? Herbed rice. And, oh, yes. The duck. I wondered then if desire after the age of thirty-five is always accompanied by mental illness.

Evan was saying something about the last show the gallery had produced.

The gallery.

I hadn't felt so compelled by Evan when we'd met at the gallery. Maybe I'd been intimidated by the space, by the notion of Evan's reputation, by his professional expertise. But away from the gallery, in a casual setting, Evan was just a man and I was just a woman and I felt dangerously close to throwing myself on him and begging him to make love to me.

"So," Evan was saying, "would you like dessert?"

"Yes," I said. "Okay."

We shared a piece of cake. I think it was hazelnut. Or maybe it was almond. I don't know.

The check came. I reached for my bag.

"This is my treat," Evan said. He slipped a credit card from his breast pocket and inserted it into the leather folder.

Simon had never paid for my dinner. He'd never paid for anything. Not once, not ever.

"Our waitress was good, don't you think?" Evan was saying. "A bit unsure of herself; she must be fairly new, but she seems to have the instincts to do the job."

"Yes," I said. Our waitress had forgotten to bring the water we'd asked for. She'd dropped a knife. She'd misrepresented the preparation of Evan's entrée.

But all Evan saw was the fact that she was trying.

Simon, on the other hand, would have been a boor about the whole thing, making a scene and demanding a free meal.

"Are you ready to go?" Evan asked.

"Yes," I said.

Evan rose. I rose. We walked to the door of the restaurant. He opened it, held it as I walked through.

On the sidewalk Evan asked if he could get me a cab home. I said, "Yes, thanks," and he stepped out into the street. A moment later he was opening the cab's back door for me.

"Thank you, Grace," he said. "I had a lovely time."

He smiled down at me. I tried to smile up at him.

"Yes," I said. "Thank you."

And I ducked into the backseat.

The cab took off with a lurch. I snuck a look over my shoulder. Evan was watching us go.

I turned around and tried to take a deep breath. It was hard to do with my heart pounding violently. I put my hand to my chest and willed my heart to slow, but it wouldn't, not until I was lying in bed an hour later.

I wondered. Had I just fallen in love with a man? I mean, a man, not a little boy, not an unruly, self-centered adolescent, but a man? Someone responsible for his own life, someone who had his own needs enough under control that he had room in his heart for the needs of another person?

You can't do this, Grace, a voice inside told me. You don't know how. You're too old to learn.

It's never too late to learn, another voice said. You simply have to apply yourself.

I turned on my side and curled up, covers clutched in my hands. I felt both very old and very young, a person who had no language to express herself beyond the ability to whimper, a person suddenly aware she was in need of great care.

Evan called two days after our dinner date. I was surprised; I was sure my less-than-engaging behavior had put him off.

I was also pleased. I also felt like I was going to throw up.

"Is this a good time to call?" he asked.

Simon never cared if he interrupted my life.

"It's fine," I said. "How are you?"

"I'm doing well, thanks. And you?"

I'm confused. And scared.

"Okay," I said. "You know, busy."

"A teacher's life is a tough one."

"Yes."

Simon never showed any interest in my job, my career, my work.

"I had a good time the other evening," he said.

My hand around the receiver was tense. I found myself staring at a spot on the floor, seeing nothing.

"Me, too."

"I'm glad you liked the restaurant."

"Yes."

There was a beat of silence and then Evan said: "I was wondering if you might like to get together again, maybe this Saturday? If you like, we could have dinner at that new seafood place in the North End."

Simon always insisted we eat at his favorite restaurants. I always paid the bill. It's what I did.

"Grace?"

"I'm sorry," I said, a bit too loudly. I looked up from the floor. "I can't. I mean, thank you. I have plans."

"Oh. Okay then." Evan's voice was pleasant and even. "Maybe some other time?"

My heart thumped in my chest; it felt like it wanted to get out and run.

"I'm sorry," I said. "I don't think I can. Good-bye."

Chapter 30

Nell

When it comes time to determine custody of your pets, ask this most important question: Who cleans the litter and scoops up the poop? This person is the true custodian of the cat and dog.

—*Dividing the Spoils: Getting What's Rightfully Yours*

"Jess, darling, what's your story?"

Trina cocked her head, held her martini aloft, and eyed Jess as if she were a specimen in a lab. It was the first time Jess, Laura, and Grace were meeting Trina. My apartment, in actuality quite spacious, suddenly felt terribly cramped.

And Jess looked terribly uncomfortable.

"You don't have to talk about it," I said hurriedly.

"I cheated on my husband," Jess blurted. "We got divorced. I'm consumed by guilt. I just don't know how you can not feel awful about having an affair, about—about living the way that you do."

Trina was unfazed. She took a sip of her martini. "I have my moments, darling," she said. "And I have my priorities. They're not everyone's priorities, to be sure."

It was a Saturday evening in May. And for the past hour Trina had been regaling us with stories from her outrageous life. Four marriages, each to a wealthy and powerful man. Numerous affairs with an astonishing variety of men, including a well-known aging rock star and a Washington politician with the president's ear.

Grace seemed to find Trina amusing. "I can't be like you," she said at one point. "I can't take love or romance or marriage so lightly, but I have to admit I find your attitude refreshing."

Trina laughed. "I'm glad I entertain you, darling."

"Oh, I didn't mean to be insulting! I just—"

"You haven't insulted me, darling. Now, you were saying that you can't take romance lightly."

Grace nodded. "I can't, but sometimes I wish I could. It's just that I've gotten lost in love. I've let it blind me. I've let it lead me around like a dog being led by a leash. The thing is that I believe in love, I want love, I think I might even know where to find it, but I'm scared it will overpower me again and make me do stupid things."

"What do you mean you might know where to find love?" I asked. "What haven't you been telling us?"

Grace colored. "Never mind. It's nothing. Nothing's going to happen."

Jess reached for a shrimp from the iced platter on the coffee table. "The lady protests too much."

"Believe me," Grace said, and I thought she sounded sad, "I've already destroyed any chance I might have had with this man."

Trina poured more champagne into Grace's glass. "A real man isn't so easily put off, darling Grace. They know how to practice patience. Is he a real man?"

Grace blushed. "Yes. I think so."

"Then don't underestimate him."

So far, so good, I thought. Five very different personalities gathered around one coffee table and so far no one had thrown an ashtray.

Of course, I don't have an ashtray in the house; almost no one does these days. Still, if there had been an ashtray, especially a heavy glass one, my sister just might have thrown it. Her disapproval of Trina was stamped all over her face. I wondered if Laura was truly horrified by Trina's casual approach to marriage or just jealous of her ability to gather husbands.

It was a mean thought, but there it was. My sister too often inspires mean thoughts.

After a third glass of champagne, Trina tripped off to the bathroom.

"I don't know how you can be friends with someone like that," Laura hissed the moment she was out of sight.

I feigned ignorance. "Someone like what? Someone who knows how to find a husband?"

"No! You know what I mean. She's so . . . so shallow!"

"I don't think she is shallow," Grace said. "I think she's thought a lot about how she lives her life. She's in control of everything she can be in control of. She's living her life consciously, deliberately, which means she's thought things through."

"I wish I had some of her hardness," Jess said. "Or her carelessness, or her independent spirit, or whatever it is that allows her to function so blithely."

Laura folded her arms across her chest. I noticed a roll of fat around her middle. My sister, I thought, had better start watching her weight if she expects to succeed in the brutal world of middle-aged dating.

"Nell," she said, "I don't like you spending time with her."

My little sister, acting like my mother? Laura, it seemed, was practicing her maternal skills. This was new. But after the debacle with Duncan—which Laura had made me swear not to mention to Jess or Grace—her mood had been erratic.

"I'm sorry you feel that way," I said. "Because I intend to spend a lot more time with Trina Donohue. She's helping me to wake up. She's helping me to start over."

"We don't help you?" Laura demanded.

I took a sip of my martini before answering. "Not in the same way. Don't be offended. I'm not abandoning my sister and my closest friends for the popular new girl in school. I'm just adding her to the mix. For now."

Laura didn't look too sure.

Trina came tripping back into the living room. "Talking about me, darlings?"

"Yes," I said. "You make for an interesting conversation."

"I do, don't I?" Trina sat next to Laura on the couch and looked her right in the eye. "Now Laura. Nell tells me you're looking for a man to father your child."

Laura glared at me. "And to marry me, of course."

Trina patted Laura's thigh with her perfectly manicured hand. I made a mental note to ask her about the sapphire chunk on her third finger. A gift from a previous husband or a treat she'd bought for herself?

"Of course, darling," she said. "Would you like me to give you any pointers? I am awfully good at landing a man."

"No," Laura said, jumping up from her seat as if she'd been bitten by a bug. "Nell, I have to go."

Without saying good-bye to the others, my sister stomped out into the night.

Jess and Grace left soon after, Jess looking slightly glum, Grace expressing hopes of seeing Trina again.

When everyone had gone, Trina sighed dramatically. "I'm afraid your sister doesn't approve of me."

I poured a final drink for us both. "Don't tell me that bothers you."

"Of course not. But I am bothered by the fact that she seems so unhappy." Trina fixed me with unusually serious eyes. "Believe it or not, darling Nell, I care a great deal about my fellow females. Especially those who pose no threat to my business."

"The business of snaring incredibly wealthy men."

"Yes. And though your sister is pretty, she's a tad too fat to be competition."

"Even though she's probably ten years your junior," I pointed out.

"Oh, yes. The rules of my world are quite strict. Better an anorexic fifty-year-old than a fat thirty-year old. Fat just doesn't work with couture."

No, I thought, I guess it doesn't.

Chapter 31

Jess

You were wife number four. Why are you surprised that wife number five is giving dinner parties in what used to be your dining room?
—*Learn to Read the Warning Signs: How to Avoid the Serial Monogamist*

A compulsion. An urge. A craving.
A thought pops into your head and it won't go away until you acknowledge it, deal with it, or succumb to it.

This is fine if the thought that pops into your head is "I want a chocolate chip cookie." Eat a chocolate chip cookie and your mind is on to something else.

This is not fine if the thought that pops into your head is "I want to send my ex-husband an e-mail."

I was at my desk. It was about eleven. And try as I might, I couldn't concentrate on the paper I was trying to outline, at least not once it occurred to me that I could contact Matt in a relatively unobtrusive way.

The people who invented e-mail should be punished. They can't have had any idea what havoc their creation would wreak.

I got up and closed the door to my office, as if what I was about to do constituted a crime. Back at my desk I created a file. I wrote a message, deleted it, wrote another one, tweaked it, deleted again. After twenty minutes of editorial madness I had it.

Hi, Matt. I hope this finds you well. I wish the best for you. Jess.

I copied it, then pasted it into the body of an e-mail. And I sent it to Matt's office account.

The moment it was gone I regretted my action. Of course I did; I knew I would. And I wondered: Would I ever be through punishing myself?

Two days and there'd been no word from Matt, no return e-mail or phone call or letter. Part of me was relieved. Part of me was anxious.

I wondered if Matt was furious with me for disrupting the new life he was trying to build. I wondered if maybe my e-mail had gotten lost in cyberspace so that Matt had never received it. Then again, maybe he had received my e-mail, but his own reply had gone missing.

Maybe, I thought, Matt is out of town and not checking his e-mail. No. A ridiculous notion. Matt was as attached to his laptop as any other red-blooded American male in a suit and tie.

Finally, it occurred to me that maybe Matt simply had nothing more to say to me. Ever. Somehow, that possibility hurt more than a stream of scathing accusations.

My mind continued to race. I continued to obsess about Matt's possible state of mind. I had to talk to someone or jump off the Tobin Bridge.

I called Grace.

"I did something stupid," I said.

I could hear her taking a deep breath. "Okay. What?"

"I sent an e-mail to Matt."

Grace laughed. "Is that all? For a minute I thought you were going to say that you slept with him. And I know what a disaster sleeping with your ex can be."

I sat heavily on the edge of the couch.

"I know you know," I said. "I'm sorry, but it's why I can admit this to you. You and Simon had your own unique relationship, nothing like what Matt and I had, but still, I know you understand the need to connect somehow, even when the marriage is officially over."

"I do," Grace said. "It's a real need and a real pain in the ass."

"I'm making no sense these days, Grace. I don't know why I'm doing anything I'm doing. I'm not sleeping well."

"Jess, what were you hoping to hear from Matt?" Grace asked the question gently.

"I don't know," I admitted. "I guess I'd like to know that he forgives me. Not that I feel I deserve to be forgiven, not entirely."

"Oh, Jess. What are we going to do with you?"

"Bear with me? I promise I'm trying to get past the negative feelings."

"Of course we'll bear with you. There's no question of abandonment, Jess."

I believed that. It was good to trust something, someone.

"I have an idea," Grace said suddenly. "It won't solve anything, but it might give you a few hours of peace. Let's go for massages tomorrow."

"The way I feel, I'll probably fall asleep on the table."

"So? Your body will still benefit from the massage. And the sleep."

I got up from the couch and stretched. "Okay. What time?"

"Around four? And Jess?"

"Yes?"

Grace paused a moment before saying, "If Matt does e-mail you back, promise me you'll delete the message before reading it. Don't risk more pain."

I paused a moment before saying, "Okay."

I didn't say, "I promise."

Chapter 32

Nell

Your stepdaughter adored you when you gave her a closetful of designer clothes. Your stepson thought you were awesome when you gave him his own car. So why, now that you're divorced from their dad, haven't they returned your calls?

—*Blood Is Thicker Than Water: The Thankless Role of Stepparent*

"A size six should do nicely."

"Okay," I said to the saleswoman eyeing me from the waist down.

She walked off to a rack on which hung a variety of leather pants.

I'd never worn leather pants. I wasn't entirely sure I would wear them even if I bought a pair. But Trina had encouraged me to sex up my wardrobe—of course, that's her term. I agreed to do so, but in a classy way. That was my condition. She then suggested I start with a pair of tailored black leather pants.

"Can I call them slacks?" I'd asked.

Trina had laughed. "Whatever makes you comfortable, darling Nell."

So there I was, in Louis of Boston, shopping for a pair of tailored black leather pants. I mean slacks.

The saleswoman returned with two pairs. I took them into a dressing-room stall and locked the door behind me. And then I stood looking at myself in the mirror, holding the two pairs of

BACK IN THE GAME   151

pants, and wondered again what sort of woman Nell Keats really was.

Thoroughly embarrassed, I tried on the first pair. I closed my eyes, afraid to look at my transformed reflection.

"Do you need any assistance?" the saleswoman called from just outside the dressing-room stall.

"No," I almost shouted, startled by her voice. "Thank you." And then I opened my eyes.

Have you ever caught your passing reflection in a store window and for a split second not recognized yourself? And you wonder if the face in the glass is the face other people see, not the face you see in your own bathroom mirror. It's a strange sensation; it disrupts your assumption of self in some way.

The Nell Keats standing before the full-length mirror in that stall was not the Nell Keats I'd seen in the bathroom mirror that morning. This Nell Keats—can I say it?—looked hot. This Nell Keats looked fabulous.

It was hard to look away, hard to finally take the pants off and try on the second pair. If possible, they fit even better than the first pair. I felt slightly drunk. I felt slightly euphoric.

Can you be slightly euphoric? Or is that like saying you're slightly pregnant?

Reluctantly, I redressed in my Ann Taylor A-line skirt. And then I bought both pairs of black leather pants, and a few fitted blouses, the kind not meant to be tucked in neatly, and an armload of new lingerie, not underwear but lingerie, complete with lace and satin and silk.

And then I went home.

Two nights after the shopping expedition that changed my life—I'm being consciously dramatic here—I went out with a man named Oscar Perkins.

Trina had introduced us at a cocktail party she'd given a week earlier. Oscar and I had chatted for a good deal of the evening. We'd talked about Boston politics and the most recent natural disaster in Asia. He'd told me he'd started his own law firm fifteen years earlier, not long after making partner at the firm that had given him his start. From the gorgeous suit he was wearing, I'd assumed his business was a success. I'd told him about my work for the MFA and various local charities. He'd told me he had three children from an early marriage. I'd told him about my own early marriage and children.

Just before I'd left Trina's apartment at a little before eleven, Oscar had asked for my number. I'd given it to him with no hesitation.

Oscar had called the very next day and we'd made plans to meet for dinner at the Flowering Tree. I wore a pair of leather pants.

Again, the conversation was easy and wide ranging. Oscar had a quick wit and regaled me with a few outlandish stories of his rise through the criminal court system. We discovered a shared interest in medieval art and artisanal cheeses. Oscar paid for our meal.

After dinner I invited him back to my apartment for a nightcap. I knew something romantic might happen. I wanted it to and I dreaded it would.

Once inside I poured us each a glass of scotch. Oscar took his neat and he rose in my estimation. We sat next to each other on the couch, turned to face each other. Oscar clinked his glass with mine. We each took a sip.

And then he leaned in and kissed me.

I let him. And then, I began to kiss him back.

"You call the shots," Oscar said against my lips. "We'll take it slow."

"Okay," I said.

Our lips touched again, tentative, soft, and then more sure.

Oh, I'd forgotten what a slippery slope physical desire is! I remember my mother telling me when I was small that "kissing leads to babies." I had no idea what she meant until years later, of course. But that night with Oscar, I remembered.

Later, when Oscar had gone home, I lay in the bed Richard and I had shared for so many years. I could still smell Oscar on my skin. I could still feel his touch. I squirmed with remembered pleasure and wondered if I was becoming debauched.

Yes. Hopefully. Why not? It was far too soon to risk more heartache.

I stretched and grinned and for the first time in ages I felt content and excited and—alive. Maybe someday I'd be ready for love, but now it was time to sow the wild oats I seemed to have been storing for the past twenty years.

Yes, I thought. Sex is good.

Chapter 33

Laura

You love his mother. You adore his father. His sister is like the sister you never had. Is divorcing the convicted criminal worth losing his fabulous family?
   —*Look Before You Leap: Is Divorce Really Worth It?*

"Oooh, he's so cute! What's his name?"
   The woman stopped and beamed. On the end of the leash she held was absolutely the most adorable golden retriever puppy I have ever seen in my entire life. I mean, ever.
   "Frasier," the woman told me. "After the TV show."
   I bent down and let the puppy sniff my hand. His tail began to wag furiously, rocking his furry little body.
   "How old is he?" I asked as Frasier stood up on his hind legs and barked excitedly.
   "Just eight weeks," his mommy trilled. "Isn't he precious!"
   "Yes he is! He's the most precious little boy in the whole wide world!"
   After a while the woman took Fraiser off for his walk in the Commons. I watched them go.
   A puppy, I thought, might be just the thing! I could get a small breed because my apartment wasn't huge and maybe a breed that didn't shed really badly. If he was really tiny, I could carry him around with me like all those stars carry their little

doggies and maybe even train him to go on newspaper so I wouldn't have to get up so early in the morning or take him out in bad weather.

Yes, I thought, a puppy would be just the thing.

And then I thought of the money.

I walked on down Newbury Street. Coming toward me was the woman I wanted to be. She wore a sundress with a Pucci-like print and she was pushing a stroller I recognized from an online catalogue. It was outfitted with every imaginable safety feature and sported imported fabric and extra-thick padding for comfort and style. And it cost seven hundred dollars.

Seven hundred dollars! Well, if I had seven hundred dollars to spend on a stroller, I would spend it, but I didn't and I still don't and I'm pretty sure I never will.

The truth is I hadn't really thought through my post-divorce financial status. I know it sounds stupid and maybe it is. Suzy Orman would have a heart attack if she found out about me. Anyway, since Duncan had moved out, I'd been spending an awful lot of money I shouldn't have been spending. I'm not sure why. I do know that after a shocking Visa bill and a depressing bank statement, I promised myself I would make and stick to a strict budget.

I glanced over my shoulder at wealthy mommy and child and walked on. Still, I thought, a puppy would be great. People would stop me on the street to talk. I could carry him almost like I would carry a baby.

And then he'd grow up and be my best friend.

Everyone needs a best friend.

I knew I could get a dog or a cat from the Animal Rescue League of Boston for very little money, and I supposed I could buy generic brand food in bulk, but how would I afford the yearly visits to the vet? And what would happen if the dog or cat got sick between visits and needed medicine or surgery, what then? Would Nell lend me money for my pet's medicine or surgery? Would Jess?

An elderly man passed, walking slowly, his old mixed breed hobbling along by his side. I wondered how long they'd been together. They almost looked alike in that way people and their dogs do after lots of years together.

Some couples look alike after lots of years together, too.

Suddenly, I felt so alone. Alone and poor. But I'd be a little less poor once I'd returned the adorable pink sweater and leggings to Fleur.

I climbed the stairs to the second-floor shop and pushed open the door. I was greeted by their signature lilac fragrance. It's a very calming scent, lilac.

The sales clerk was the same young woman who had sold me the sweater and leggings. The expensive layette was gone from the shelf above the counter.

"I'd like to return this, please," I said. I put the little bag on the counter and removed the sweater and leggings.

She gave me a funny look. "I'm sorry," she said, "but we don't accept returns."

"What?" I pushed the sweater a bit closer to her. "But I don't want these anymore."

The sales clerk pushed it back. "What's wrong with them?" she asked, her expression bland. "Are they damaged in some way?"

"No, no, it's just that . . ."

Just that I could use the two hundred dollars they cost me because the husband hunting isn't going too well.

The sales clerk's expression remained bland. "Yes?"

"It's just that the person I bought them for doesn't need them anymore. She's . . . She's not having a baby."

The sales clerk's expression changed instantly to one of practiced sympathy. "I'm sorry to hear that," she said, "but I'm afraid there's nothing I can do. The store's policy is clearly stated on your receipt. No returns. We'd be happy to exchange the merchandise for—"

"But the tags are still on."

"I'm sorry. Would you care to look around for a similarly priced item?"

"No," I said. "No, thank you." I stuffed the little pink sweater and matching leggings into the fancy little shopping bag and hurried out of the shop.

* * *

It was Matt.

Matt Fromer, Jess's ex-husband, standing just a few yards away by the white leather sofa and the chrome and glass coffee table.

Boy, was I glad I'd come to the party!

After such a depressing afternoon I really wanted to stay home that night and watch my DVD of *Working Girl* and order a pepperoni pizza and eat every last bite of it. But a bit of the real Laura, the one with a fighting spirit, the one determined to have her baby and a husband too, spoke up and made me get off the couch, dress nicely, and show up at a party given my colleague Betsy and her husband Ryan.

At first glance the other guests seemed all paired up. I looked harder and finally saw a few single men; at least, they were alone at the party. I'd have to be careful. There was a good chance one of them was married and stepping out on his wife!

I went over to the bar—which was really a table covered with a white tablecloth—for a glass of wine. I would have preferred a chocolate martini, but you usually can't get that sort of drink in someone's home. No sooner had I turned away from the bar with my glass than I spotted Matt.

I noted he was drinking a bottle of sparkling water and remembered that Matt rarely ever drank. A sober man was just the kind of man to make a good father.

I choked a little on my wine. Matt as my baby's father. It was a strange thought. I felt weird, kind of guilty for thinking it, but then I said to myself: Why should I feel guilty? As far as I know, Matt is single. I'm single. Doesn't that make us a potential match?

Yes, it did.

I slipped through the throng of partygoers and appeared at his side. I tapped his shoulder.

"Hi, Matt."

Matt was startled; he visibly tensed. I remembered him as a little stiff, so unlike Jess.

"Oh," he said. "Hi. Laura. Wow. This is, um—"

I laughed. "I know. This is a bit awkward."

Matt relaxed a bit. I'd forgotten how cute he was. Kind of boyish, like a younger Tom Cruise.

"Yeah."

"But it shouldn't be," I said hurriedly. "Right?"

"Right. I guess." And then a tall, lanky woman with professionally streaked blond hair slipped her arm through Matt's.

I felt very conscious of my at-home streaking treatment. I'd kind of messed it up the last time and I knew my roots needed a touch-up.

"Laura," Matt said, "this is Patrice. Laura is—an old friend."

Patrice smiled lamely. I couldn't fail to notice that Matt hadn't called her his girlfriend.

"Well," I said, "I'm going to, um, go talk to someone I know over by the bar."

Patrice made no response. Matt said, "Nice running into you, Laura," and the two turned away.

For the next hour I sipped a second glass of wine and kept my eye on Matt and his date. The moment I saw her walk off toward the powder room, I slipped through the crowd and appeared again at his side.

"Hi, again," I said brightly.

"Hey, Laura." Matt's smile was genuine, easier than it had been earlier.

"So, who do you know here?"

Matt shrugged. "The host. Ryan and I work at the same firm. You?"

"His wife, Betsy. I work with her."

There was a moment of silence and then Matt blurted: "I'm not really much of a party guy. But Patrice really likes to dress up and go out so . . ."

"Oh, me, too," I said. "I mean, I don't like parties much either. I'm kind of a homebody, you know. An old-fashioned girl."

Matt smiled again. "Yeah, I guess I remember that about you."

"Look," I said, "I have to run but, well, I was wondering, if, you know, you might want to get together some time for coffee

or whatever. Maybe talk. You know, I'm going through a divorce myself and—"

Matt's face instantly took on an expression of sympathy.
"Laura, I didn't know. Hey, I'm so sorry."

I smiled a sad little smile, shrugged, and sighed. "Yes, well,
sometimes people aren't who you think they are."

"Don't I know it!" he said.

I looked up into Matt's eyes and he looked down into mine
and at that moment something happened. I knew I had him.

"I should go before your date comes back," I said softly. Do
you see? The words implied that something illicit was about to
happen between Matt and me.

Matt's eyes still held mine. "Who?" he said. "Oh, right, Patrice."

I handed him a slip of paper on which I'd printed my home
number. (I'm always prepared!) "Anyway, here's my number if
you want to get together. You know, and talk."

Our fingers touched briefly. Matt slipped the piece of paper
into his jacket pocket. His smile was really very nice. I imagined
that smile on a little boy of my own.

"Thanks, Laura," he said. "I'll call you. Take care, okay?"

I lightly touched his forearm. "Thanks," I said, with a bit of
breathiness. "You, too." And then I left.

Once in the backseat of the cab I took a deep breath. My
stomach was fluttering with excitement.

What, I wondered, am I doing? I'd just made a pass at my
friend's ex-husband.

My friend's single, eligible ex-husband who just might want
to settle down with a sweet, blond, family-oriented woman
named Laura Keats.

After all, I thought, all is fair in love and war.

Chapter 34

Grace

You've got a mink. You've got a Tiffany diamond. You've got a house in Tuscany. Why can't you overlook a little philandering on the part of the generous man who makes your life so comfortable?

—*Think Twice: How Not to Make a Rash Decision When It Comes to Divorce*

"Oh, my God," Brittany screamed as she burst into the room, "guess what? I just read that Simon Trenouth is having a show at some gallery in, like, three weeks!"

I looked up from the worktable where I was laying out origami paper for the afternoon's project.

"Get out!" Brianna screamed back as she grabbed Brittany's fleshy upper arms. "We so have to go!"

Brittany and Brianna, my summer interns, were fine art majors at Boston University and they were totally unlike any art majors I had known in my own college days. Two more mainstream, pop-culture addicts you'd be hard-pressed to find. Two less tortured souls did not exist in Boston.

That they read art journals came as a huge surprise, until I learned it wasn't the articles and critiques and quality reproductions that interested them but the notices of openings and other events at which they could drink for free and, more important, meet cute guys.

Guys like Simon Trenouth. I'd never mentioned my connection to Simon. There seemed no reason to tell these girls my life story.

Brittany bounced on her toes, which was impressive considering she was wearing chunky wedge sandals.

"I mean, Simon Trenouth is just so amazing," she cried. "He's so awesome. He's like, he's like my idol or something!"

He's something, all right.

Brianna put her hand over her heart. "I heard he's really great in bed. I know someone on my floor who knows someone who slept with him once and she said it was, like, awesome."

I turned away to hide a grin. Huh? That someone who knew someone on Brianna's floor—I assumed she meant in her dorm—must have confused Simon with another man. The sexual Simon I knew was a lot of flash and little substance.

But I knew the appeal of flash. It blinded you to the reality. That is, until your eyes adjusted.

"Oh, I so am going to try to meet him!" Brittany vowed. "I mean, the opening is probably private, but maybe I can find out where the after party is and be there. God, I would die if he, like, liked me!"

There was some squealing.

I was sorely tempted to burst Brittany and Brianna's happy little bubble and tell them the dirty truth about Simon. That I'd been his wife for years and that he was a lying, cheating bum, yes, a talented bum, but an emotionally abusive partner who had drained our bank account and destroyed our apartment and damaged my self-esteem until finally, finally I kicked him out. And divorced him. And continued for way too long to cater to his every need.

I was tempted. But I said nothing. Let Simon retain his gloss in these girls' eyes. Let them learn the hard way that once the gloss wears thin, and it always does, what's left is pockmarked and pimply.

"The Auster Gallery show," I said, interrupting the squealing, "certainly will help Simon's career."

Brittany cocked her head. Brianna squinted and scrunched up her bobbed nose. "What?" she said.

"The Auster Gallery. Simon Trenouth is showing there."

Brittany nodded vigorously. "Oh, right."

See, I thought smugly. This is the difference between these girls and me. I had—still have—great respect for Simon's talent. It wasn't all about the sexy persona. It never had been.

I'd made the sacrifices I made in the name of Simon's work. If he could come home to a clean house, if he had access to money to buy paint and canvas, if he had the freedom to stay away for days without explanation, then he could concentrate on the work.

Or so I'd told myself.

"Do you have the article?" I asked the girls. "I'd like to see what it says about Evan Auster."

"Who?" Brianna asked.

It must be all the fast food young people eat these days that causes a constipation of the brain.

"Evan Auster," I said carefully. "The owner of the Auster Gallery."

Brittany shrugged. "Oh. Right. I only read the parts about Simon. Anyway, I put the magazine back in your office."

"Thanks," I said. "Can you girls help me move this table against the wall?"

That night I read the article that had sent Brittany and Brianna into fits. It included a fairly lengthy interview with Evan Auster. I was impressed by his simple evaluations of Simon's paintings and his lack of bogus art world mumbo jumbo. Articulate, intelligent, attractive, and successful.

This was the man I'd turned down.

In contrast, Simon's quotes were almost incomprehensible. Here's a sample:

What I do in my painting, what I try to, like, say, is that we all, you know, and it's not even about getting a message across, I hate that. It's more like, I just want to let the paint, like, say what it needs to say, be free or whatever. You know.

To be fair, I thought, people really shouldn't expect an artist to explain his work. That's a job usually better left to the critics. Still, the contrast between Evan's considered words and Simon's rambling spoke volumes to me.

I put the magazine on the bedside table and turned off the lights. And I wondered if I was ready for a relationship of simplicity, clarity, and sense.

Chapter 35

Laura

So you slept with your soon-to-be ex-husband. So he suggested you do it again. This doesn't mean your relationship is salvageable. It only means your soon-to-be ex is getting free sex.

—*Getting Out for Good: How to Break the Nasty Habit of Backsliding*

"So," Nell said, "my darling offspring are coming for a visit."

"When?" Jess asked.

The four of us were having dinner at a brick-oven pizza restaurant I'd suggested. The prices were reasonable and the salad bar was free. I'd skipped lunch because I'd forgotten to bring a sandwich with me from home and there was no way I was going to pay eleven dollars for a sandwich from a shop! Not anymore.

"Soon."

"For how long?" Grace asked.

"Two weeks. Unless they get bored with sleeping until noon and shopping all afternoon, and then I suppose they'll head off to campus early."

"Gosh, I've missed them," I said. "I'll have to come up with an idea for a fun excursion."

"Laura," Nell said, "they're not ten. Don't be disappointed if they can't find the time to spend with their aunt. Eighteen- and twenty-year-olds have very busy schedules that rarely include family."

A cool, fun aunt isn't the same as a boring old mother, I replied silently. "They'll stay with you, right?"

"I suppose."

"You don't sound very happy about this visit," Jess said.

Nell shrugged. "It's nothing. It's silly."

"Oh, come on, Nell."

"All right. I'm a bit hurt by their lack of sympathy for me. Don't misunderstand," Nell said. "I don't want my children to pity their mother. And I don't want them to hate their father, either. The divorce should not be their concern; I know that. I guess it's just that I still feel so fragile. I'd like a little bit of sympathy from at least one of them."

"I'm not sure they're capable of sympathy," Jess said. "I think they're too young to understand the depths of emotion you feel. Has either of them ever been in love?"

Nell considered for a moment. "Not that I know of. Colin usually hangs out with a crowd of boys and girls and God knows what they do for fun. Clara dated someone last year for about two months. It was a record for her."

It was true. Colin and Clara had never been in love. They would have told me, the cool, fun aunt, about a serious relationship, even if they kept it from their mother.

"See?" Jess said. "Besides, maybe they feel a lot more than they're letting on. Maybe they just don't know how to take care of a mother who's always taken care of them. You've been a very strong person for Colin and Clara. It might be confusing or even depressing for them to see you in pain."

Nell sighed. "I know. I do know, and I understand. I'm still trying to be strong for them. The last thing I ever want to be is a burden on my children."

"Nell," Grace said earnestly, "it's not in your nature to be a burden on anyone. We're the burdens on you!"

Well, Grace could speak for herself and maybe for Jess, but not for me! I'd never been a burden on my sister.

"There's another thing," Nell said with a grimace. "God, I hope it doesn't make me a bad mother to say this—to feel this—but I'm glad the kids are only coming for two weeks. I'm enjoying being on my own. I'm enjoying the freedom of making my own schedule, answering to no one, tending to no one."

Well, I thought. Miss Perfect Mother isn't so perfect after all! I just know I'll always be thrilled to spend time with my children, even when they're being all icky and teenagey.

"Oh, Nell," Jess said, "you're not a bad mother or a bad person. You're normal. And for the first time in your adult life, you have the time and the space to think about your own needs."

Nell laughed. "Well, I guess I have something to thank Richard for! You know, I wouldn't be surprised if Clara decides to stay with Richard. She's always been a daddy's girl. Now that I've been eliminated as a rival, Clara really is the only woman in Richard's life."

"So," Jess asked, "does that make Colin a mama's boy?"

Nell shuddered. "God, no. I tried very hard not to ruin him for other women. I want his future wife to thank me, not curse me."

I made a mental note to find a book about raising emotionally healthy boys. Girls, I thought, were a snap. I'm a girl. I know what we're like.

"Nell," Grace said, "I just have to say that you look fantastic. I've never seen you wear something so clingy. And leather pants!"

I frowned. I thought Nell looked—well, I didn't really like her outfit. "I thought leather pants were only for winter," I said. There was one piece of pizza left on the platter. I slid it onto my plate.

"Oh, no," Nell said. "They come in all weights and finishes and colors. Leather and suede are appropriate all year round. You just have to know the right styles and where to buy them."

"You've become quite the expert on animal skins, haven't you?" Jess said.

Nell laughed. "I'm working on it. But seriously, there's something else I'm working on becoming an expert at, something far more important to my well-being as a woman."

"What?" I asked. "Are you taking up knitting?"

Nell looked at me with one of her annoying I'm-so-much-smarter-than-you looks.

"What?" I asked. "Is there something wrong with knitting?"

And then Jess slapped the table, something I'd never seen her do.

"You didn't," she said. "You did!"

Nell grinned. "I did."

"What?" I asked, annoyed by this secret code or whatever was going on. My sister can be very rude. "What are you talking about?"

Jess leaned across the table and stage-whispered, "Nell had sex."

I took a sip of water. The pizza sat like lead in my stomach. Why, I wondered, had I eaten that last piece, and so quickly?

"Oh," I said. Well. Sex certainly wasn't knitting.

"What was it like after so many years?" Grace asked. Like Jess, she seemed all excited and happy for my sister.

Before Nell could reply, Jess said, "Who is he? Are you seeing him again? Where did you meet him?"

"What's he like?" Grace asked. "What's his name? Did you go to his apartment?"

I took another sip of water and wondered if I had any antacids in my purse.

"No, no," Nell said, "I took him to mine. I read somewhere about the home-turf advantage and believe me, I was nervous enough. There was no way I was going to a strange apartment."

But you had no trouble having sex with a strange man! I didn't say this aloud. I'd done the same with Marcus, Mr. I Have Kids After All. Nell would love to throw that in my face.

"So, are you going to see him again?" Grace asked.

"I might. I suppose it would be mostly for sex. I mean, what sort of adult woman sleeps with a man on the first date and then expects a relationship? Anyway, I'm not looking for a relationship. I won't call him but if he calls me . . ."

I was not at all happy with Nell's behavior. She sounded like, like a prostitute! "This is all Trina's fault," I said. "That woman is a bad influence on you."

"Her fault?" Nell repeated. "All she did was introduce me to Oscar. Anyway, nothing bad happened, Laura. I'm having fun, finally. It's a bit scary but no one is putting a gun to my head and forcing me to go out at night. This isn't middle school where peer pressure can make you do idiotic things just to be liked."

Grace shuddered. "Ugh, being a kid is not all it's cracked up to be."

"Okay, so who is this Oscar?" Jess asked.

"A friend of Trina, currently divorced, back in the game, and by the way, very attractive."

"Obviously!" Jess said. "He got the re-virgin into bed on the first try!"

Nell grinned. It was getting annoying, all this grinning.

"Actually," she said, "we never made it to the bed."

"Oh, my God! Give us some details, a highlight or two, anything. I'm living vicariously."

Before my sister could answer Jess's totally gross question, I said, maybe a bit too loudly, "Enough! I don't want to hear any more of this."

"Since when," Nell asked, "have you become a prude?"

"I'm not a prude," I snapped. "I just think what goes on between two people in the bedroom—"

"Or on the floor," Jess said.

I glared at her. "Wherever. I just think it's private. I don't think you should sit around talking about it, especially not when you're eating."

Grace suddenly looked to the empty pizza plate. "Hey, what happened to that last piece? It was mine. I only had one."

Well, you snooze, you lose, I thought. I turned to my sister. "Do you really not want to get married again?" I demanded.

"All I'm saying is that marriage isn't on my agenda at the moment."

I frowned. "You don't want to wait too long to get serious. It's much harder to get a man at fifty than it is at forty."

Nell gave me her angry look. Again. "What if you focus on your own life, okay?"

Jess and Grace were very quiet. Suddenly, I felt very tired and close to tears. I don't know why.

I reached for my sister's hand. "I'm sorry, Nell. I just don't want you to get hurt."

Nell squeezed my hand and slipped out of my grasp. "I've already been hurt. But thanks. I appreciate your concern."

I wondered if she did.

"I need to rant for a minute."

I looked at Grace. "I don't think I've ever heard you complain. Except about Simon, of course."

"Well," she said, "Simon's part of this rant, too."

Then she told us about how her interns had gotten all excited about meeting Simon Trenouth, Mr. Moody Art Guy.

"These girls were going on and on about Simon like he was a god or something," she said. "I felt like shaking them and telling them the ugly truth, which is that Simon is human just like the rest of us. On his good days. On his bad days he's more, I don't know, wolverine."

"He always reminded me of something reptilian," Nell said. "Maybe an iguana."

"Don't insult iguanas," Grace said. "They make excellent companions, which is a lot more than I can say for Simon."

"Anyway, Grace," Jess said, "a groupie wouldn't care what you had to say about Mr. Wolverine. A groupie thinks she's the one woman in the entire world who really understands his tortured soul, the one woman who's his true soul mate."

Grace laughed bitterly. "Just like I did. Boy, what a crock of shit. I'm sorry. I don't usually use foul language, but listening to them made me very angry. I hate the fact that otherwise intelligent, self-respecting women get so stupid about the emotionally abusive men, the artists, the musicians, the poets. It's ridiculous."

Really, sometimes I just didn't understand my so-called friends. I'd never fallen for any of those awful types. I might have made some mistakes, but at least I hadn't fallen for some guy with greasy hair, tattoos, and paint under his fingernails!

"It is ridiculous," Jess agreed. "But it probably will always be the case. No one really listens to sound advice when it comes to matters of the heart. Or hormones. All you can do is be there

for the women when they're left alone and drained of energy.
And money."

"I suppose. But that's enough, my rant is over."

"What about you, Jess?" Nell asked. "What's new and exciting
in your life?"

"Absolutely nothing. My life is pretty dull right now and I'm
glad. I work and I sleep and I watch an occasional DVD and
whenever my girlfriends' busy schedules permit, I see them for
dinner."

"Nothing lasts forever," Grace said. "A cliché but true. This
dormant period will end. Your life will be vital again."

"Sigh. I know. That's why I'm cherishing the peace while it
lasts."

"And then it's back in the game?" Grace said.

Jess nodded. "Once more into the breach, I suppose."

"When you put it that way," Nell said, "dating doesn't sound
very appealing, does it?"

"No, it doesn't. A battlefield is not a fun place to be."

"Speaking of ugliness," Grace said, "I witnessed another example of ageism just yesterday. I was in a café waiting at the
counter for my lunch order and standing right up by the
counter was a woman probably in her seventies. She'd come in
just after me and was nicely dressed, not exhibiting any crazy
behavior, just a normal person. Behind the counter were two
guys in their twenties, earrings, tattoos, no doubt convinced
they were very cool. And then in walks this girl maybe eighteen,
maybe not even, in the full standard outfit."

"Jeans so low slung they should be illegal," Jess said, "a
skintight tank top, belly ring exposed, messy hair piled on top
of her head."

"Messy blond hair."

"Of course."

"Anyway, she flip flops right up to the counter—you know
how young girls never seem to lift their feet?—and stands right
next to the older woman. That's it, it's only the three of us so
there was no possibility for confusion, and both guys charge
over to her, ask for her order, completely ignoring the older

woman who I know they knew had been standing there while they took their lazy time making my sandwich."

My sister made a face. "Disgusting."

"What did the woman do?" I asked.

Grace shook her head. "It was awful. I was stunned so at first I didn't say anything. The woman kind of raised her hand a bit, like she was back in school, and opened her mouth to say something, but I guess she lost her nerve. So, I stepped in."

"You didn't!" I squeezed her arm. "Good for you!"

"Well, I don't know how much good it did, but at least the woman was able to place her order. The girl just kind of looked bored and neither of the guys even apologized. You know what one said?"

"What?"

"He said, 'Oh, I didn't see you there.'"

"Of course he didn't," Nell snapped. "She was over thirty!"

"Ageism against women," Grace said, "is something vastly different than ageism against men. Somehow it's more humiliating. At least men once had the upper hand. At least they have their memories of social prominence. What do women have? Memories of a life-and-death struggle to earn respect in a world clearly skewed toward the penis."

I thought back to that horrible night with Barry, Happy Couples Match #1, and how his behavior at that bar had humiliated me. Ugh.

"I agree. For both men and women," Jess was saying, "aging is about loss of power—physical, intellectual, social. But for women aging seems much more unfair, much more lonely. Then again, maybe men feel the same way when their hair starts to thin and their belly starts to droop, that getting old is deeply unfair."

"I don't care about men," Nell said. "Let them suffer. I care about women."

"Our sexual appeal is a power we take for granted." Jess almost seemed to be talking to herself. She does that a lot. "Even women who aren't physically attractive by common standards have the power. It's innate and it doesn't go away inside us except that the world fails to acknowledge that power once we hit forty and fifty and sixty. We just don't command the attention we used to command."

"Some of that attention is unwanted or abusive," Grace pointed out. "Catcalls, whistles, crude comments. What woman needs that sort of thing?"

"No woman," Jess agreed. "But most women do want the appreciative glances and the romantically worded compliments."

I sighed. "Really! I mean, Duncan used to say things like, 'why do you care if guys don't look at you? I look at you, I love you, isn't that enough?' I'd tell him, no way!"

"Men," Nell said, "really don't want to hear that their exclusive woman appreciates the attention of other men. That information is far too scary for them to process."

"It's a macho thing," Jess said. "Woman as possession. Still, flirting with one man when you're married to another can go too far. It can become inappropriate."

Well, I thought, Jess should know!

"Simon used to flirt outrageously right in front of me," Grace said. "It's amazing what you can get used to or what you can ignore if you choose to. I'm embarrassed for myself retrospectively. I can imagine what other people were thinking about me. I'm sure they thought I was an idiot for putting up with Simon. I'm sure they thought I had no self-respect."

"Well," I said, "I wouldn't have put up with Simon. I would have killed him!"

"And gone to jail for murder," Nell pointed out. "I think Grace's solution was best, a nice legal divorce."

"Divorce," Jess said, "is never nice, but I know what you mean."

It's especially not nice when your soon-to-be ex-husband tells you he's fallen madly in love with another woman before you can have one successful date!

"The bottom line," Nell was saying, "is that we need to recognize our sexual power early and have fun with it. We need to use it to full advantage while we can. When we're young, we're ignorant. We assume we'll always be attractive and then we start to age and suddenly, we notice that we're being passed over, simply ignored, and we're shocked."

"No one's ever prepared for the future," Jess said, "no matter how carefully they plan."

"You know what I hate?"

"No," Nell said to me, "tell us."

"I hate how when an old man flirts with a young woman, everyone chuckles and says, oh, how cute, he's still 'got it.' But when an old woman says she's interested in a man, young or old, everyone shudders and says, 'Ugh, how gross.'"

Jess sighed. "I'm depressed again."

"Don't be," Grace said. "We're still a long way from blue hair and rolled stockings."

"True," Nell said. "But it never hurts to think ahead. Be prepared. Seize the day while you still have the energy to seize it, before your arthritis cripples you entirely."

"You've become pretty bitter," I said to my sister.

"No, no," Nell said, "not bitter, just pragmatic. Richard's leaving me opened my eyes to a world to which I was blissfully ignorant. Now it's either win or lose, no coming in second. I'm learning how to turn the dating game to my own advantage."

"That's Trina talking!"

"It is Trina. But now," Nell said, "it's also me."

I reached for my purse. "I need to go home," I said. "I feel kind of bloated."

Chapter 36

Jess

Just because your ex-husband slept with your best friend doesn't mean your relationship with her is over. Men are disposable; a good girlfriend is worth hanging on to. Besides, it was probably his fault in the first place.

—*He Slept with My Best Friend: What to Do When the Unthinkable Happens*

"Hello, Professor Marlowe."

I turned from the graduate student serving wine in plastic cups.

"Hello, Professor Morgenstein," I said. "I haven't seen you around."

Seth smiled. "And I haven't seen you around."

In fact, I hadn't seen Seth in almost five months. Our offices and the buildings in which we teach are on opposite sides of the campus.

We moved away from the drinks table. "I've been holed up in my office a lot lately," I said. "And I guess I haven't been into the campus social scene much. I'm only here tonight because my department head guilted me into making an appearance."

Seth laughed. "Mine, too. Had you ever met Dr. Maynard before tonight?"

"No."

"Me, either. So why are we at his retirement party?"

"Professional courtesy?"

Seth is very tall, almost six feet five inches. No one would call him handsome, but he has an undeniable appeal. It has something to do with his mouth, which the poets would call sensitive, and something to do with his eyes, which the poets would call soulful.

"Are you okay?" he asked, and suddenly I remembered his mouth on mine. It was a nice memory but it called up no real desire. "About the divorce?"

I smiled. "I will be."

"Good. You know, I still feel bad about—"

"Seth, please, it wasn't your fault, believe me."

Seth looked around to ensure our privacy before saying: "Are you sure you aren't even a little bit angry with me?"

"I'm sure. All you ever did was make me happy. While it lasted."

"Yes. While it lasted. And you made me happy, too."

I suppose I had.

"So, what about you?" I asked. "How's life been treating you?"

"Better than I deserve. I just got a grant for some research, and with Dr. Brown taking a sabbatical, I'll be teaching his genetics and genomics class this fall."

"That's great, Seth. Even though I have no idea what it is you'll be teaching."

"Thanks," he said. "It's a bit scary but I'm really grateful for the opportunity."

Scary.

Suddenly, thoughts of Dr. Neal Smith, he of the bondage-as-therapy school, popped into my head. A quick check around the room told me he wasn't at the party. Good. I remembered he said he'd heard I'd been around. Someone had been talking about me, but who?

"Seth," I said, "I'm curious. Did you tell anyone about us?"

"No," he said promptly and I believed him. "But people find out. I don't know how, exactly. That's more your department, no?"

"Maybe. Human behavior. Sometimes I think I know nothing

at all about it. I'm not even sure what I'll do ten minutes from now."

"Leave this boring party with me?"

"Excuse me?"

Seth smiled. "I miss talking with you, Jess. Do you remember the passionate discussions we had, about everything?"

How could I forget? When I met Seth I was so eager to talk and to listen, so needing to be heard, to engage in a relationship of words. Life with Matt was so—silent.

"I do," I said. "And I miss them, too. That was good stuff."

"Other stuff was good, too."

"Yes. But that's—"

"Over," he said. "I know. Seriously, Jess, let's get out of this place and go somewhere we can sit and talk for a while. If I hear Dean Roberts's cackle one more time, I might be forced to do something desperate."

I grinned. It really was a horrid cackle. "Like what?"

"Like stick this toothpick in my eye."

I put my plastic cup on the appetizer table. "Let's go."

Seth and I spent close to three hours over several cups of coffee and a shared monster cookie at a Starbucks. We discussed politics, both national and world. We admitted we'd both seen the latest Owen Wilson comedy and loved it. He ranted about the head of his department. I told him about a certain professor's penchant for S & M but didn't, of course, mention his name. Seth told me he was dating a woman from MIT, an associate professor, someone his own age and not married to another man. I congratulated him on his mature decision.

Seth was the same as he'd been back when I'd first met him—unassuming, attractive, intelligent, funny—but now I felt no sexual pull.

I was glad. We truly had exhausted the physical part of our relationship. There were no messy edges left to trim, nothing tricky to avoid.

It was a great night with someone who was becoming a real friend and it gave me some much-needed perspective.

When I got home at about eleven, I wasn't sleepy; blame it on the caffeine and sugar. So I decided to use my wakefulness to good purpose. In the bottom drawer of my desk I found a notebook, one with a brocade cover. Grace had given it to me for my last birthday but, never having kept a diary or journal, I hadn't known quite what to do with it.

Until that night. I picked up a pen and began to give form to some of the chaos that had been plaguing me since the divorce.

I'm not the first woman to have an affair and I certainly won't be the last.

Life is hard. Love, even harder. Relationships come in all varieties and sometimes they work and sometimes they don't. Clichés are often true. But am I relying too heavily on them?

I am intelligent. But do I lack the skills to be truly introspective? Okay, I can ask myself this question; I'm not entirely unconscious. But . . .

Should you work on a relationship even when you don't particularly want to? I suppose it depends on your reasons for not wanting to.

I'm not a lazy person or a fearful one. I refuse to believe my marriage fell apart because I was too afraid of the truth and intimacy it would have required to work things through with Matt. If something is worth fighting for, I believe I will fight for it. I've done so in the past. Haven't I?

I must think about that. Maybe I am afraid of emotional intimacy. And if I find that I am, do I want to change that? Or do I want to accept my shortcoming and make what life I can?

I hesitated, suddenly almost afraid. And then I wrote the words I'd been saying to myself for months. Difficult, painful putting them on paper, words I'd never seen in print, in my own handwriting, but necessary.

The simple truth, the bottom line, is that I didn't love Matt. When you don't love someone—when you never did or when you no longer do—why, why should you stay with that person?

Why? Can someone tell me an answer I can accept?

I know I was wrong to marry him in the first place. But would staying with him have corrected that wrong? No. I can't believe it would have.

Suddenly, I felt exhausted. I closed the notebook and got straight into bed.

It had solved nothing, the writing. I'd discovered no great insights. But it had helped in a way I couldn't define and I promised myself to pick up the pen again.

Chapter 37

Nell

She sympathizes with your need for a new pair of shoes for each occasion. He complains about the price. She understands the trials of PMS. He thinks you're faking. She doesn't care that you're ten pounds overweight. He gags when he looks at you. Is there really any question who makes the better partner?

—*Loving the Lesbian Within: Starting Over in Middle Age*

"I've been invaded."

Jess laughed. "The locusts have swarmed? The storm troopers have descended?"

"Yes, the kids are here." I glanced into the living room from the kitchen. "At this very moment Colin is sprawled on the couch playing some video game or whatever it is on some new machine his father bought him."

"And Clara?"

"Not in sight. Probably raiding my closet, though we don't wear the same size and our tastes couldn't be more different."

"I look forward to seeing them again. I think."

"Oh, they're okay," I said. "They've been having a great summer. They did some traveling with the families of friends. Clara took two summer courses just for fun, nothing that will work toward her major. Colin played on a summer hockey team."

"Still, they must be happy to be home, no?"

"I don't know," I admitted. "They can't really want to be around Richard and me after all that's happened. I really can't blame them. Frankly, I think it's nice of them to come home at all. I didn't expect it of them."

"It'll be fine," Jess said. "I've got to go. I'm going to catch a movie in Coolidge Corner."

"I've got to go, too. Trina and I are going out tonight to hear some music at Josephine's."

"Have fun."

"Thanks," I said. "I intend to."

I found Clara in the bathroom of the master suite I'd once shared with Richard. She had spread my makeup across the counter and was experimenting.

I'd redecorated that bathroom only two years earlier. I'd chosen what I thought was a more masculine color scheme, black and white, something that Richard might like more than the peaches and cream we'd had for so long. Ironic, isn't it?

"Those colors don't work with your complexion," I said. Clara has her father's darker, almost olive skin tone, while Colin favors me in being very fair.

Clara made a face in the mirror. "I know. That's why I like them. I'm creating a sort of sickening look. Just for fun."

"Oh," I said. It's at moments like these, when a twenty-year-old tells you that looking sickening is fun, that you realize just how old you are.

I selected a few tubes and jars from the mess and set to work on my own face.

Since Colin and Clara had been home, we hadn't talked at all about the new family dynamic. I found myself oddly unable to bring up the subject in a natural way. Standing with my daughter at the marble counter in my brightly lit bathroom, I decided to just dive right in.

"So," I said, "your friends don't care that Dad is gay?"

Clara looked at me in the mirror. "Are you kidding? They think it's great he came out."

Twenty years too late, but who's keeping track?

"And it really doesn't bother you?" I asked.

Clara groaned. "Mom, stop asking already! So Dad is gay, big deal. Good for him. I'm glad he's finally living his own life."

"After lying to me, to us, all those years," I retorted. I hadn't meant to get into an argument with Clara; I really didn't want her to see my bitterness or the depth of my pain. Or did I?

Whatever the case, Clara seemed unable or unwilling to understand her father's betrayal.

"Oh, Mom," she whined. "So Dad didn't tell you he was gay, so you had to find out for yourself. Can you blame him? You were always so uptight!"

I turned from the mirror and wagged the mascara wand at my daughter. "Don't tell me about uptight," I scolded. "Your father is the most uptight person I've ever met."

Clara shrugged the maddening shrug of the young. "Whatever. Anyway, I'm psyched you're dating again. You should just totally go for it. Totally embrace your sexuality. Take some chances. But use protection, okay?"

I cringed. How had our roles become reversed, my daughter counseling me on safe sex?

"Of course," I squeaked. "Now, let me finish up here alone."

Clara snatched a tube of lipstick and left. I put on a pair of leather pants, a fitted white shirt, and high strappy sandals.

I walked into the living room. Clara jumped up from the floor where she had been flipping through the current issue of *Vanity Fair.*

"Mom," she cried, "you look so hot!"

Colin was sitting on the couch, typing on his laptop. He looked up at me, and rapidly looked back to the screen.

I pulled at the hem of my fitted shirt to make sure it covered my stomach. "I won't be back too late," I said.

Clara sighed. "It's okay, Mom. You should stay out as late as you want."

"You have my cell phone number?"

"Yes, Mom. You posted it on the fridge, remember?"

Still Colin typed.

"I'll be at Café Montreal, then Josephine's. If you need me I can be home in fifteen minutes."

Clara made a pretense of stumbling in frustration.

"Mom, go already! We're fine, we're adults, we're on our

own all the time. You don't have to go all protective on us when we come home. Sheesh."

"Sorry," I said. "It's habit." I took a step closer to the couch. "What are you up to tonight, Colin?"

He shrugged, his eyes still on the screen, his fingers flying. "Nothing."

"You're not going out?"

"No."

"Colin," I asked, "are you okay? Do you feel sick?"

"I'm fine," he mumbled, eyes down. "Look, if it's okay, I'm going to ask Dad if I can stay with him and Bob."

Clara shot me a look. She knew as well as I did why Colin was acting so strangely.

Seeing his mother decked out for a night on the town bothered him; that was normal. It didn't mean he didn't love me anymore. It didn't mean he hated me.

It meant that Colin wasn't Clara.

I knew my son was angry with his father for destroying the status quo. But Richard and Bob had created a life that more closely resembled it than the life I was creating. Colin, always a bit of a homebody, never a rebel, needed at least a semblance of domestic tranquility.

I couldn't deny my son that very real need.

I swallowed hard. "Of course it's okay, Colin. I'm sure Dad would love to have you."

Clara ushered me out the door. In the hallway she gave me a hug.

"Don't worry, Mom," she whispered in my ear. "Everything will be okay."

Chapter 38

Laura

Etiquette be damned. There's no need to wait a proper period of time after filing for divorce before you have sex with your soon-to-be ex-husband's gorgeous and powerful boss. Hubby's fragile ego is no longer your concern.

—*Divorce in the 21st Century: It Ain't What It Used to Be*

"Look, I have to tell you something, but it's a secret, okay? You have to swear not to tell anyone until I say it's okay." Nell frowned. "I don't like the sound of this."

We were in Nell's kitchen. She was making a salad for our lunch. I was glad she'd put down the vegetable knife.

"Please, Nell," I said, "this is really important and I really need to talk to someone about it!"

Nell sighed and crossed her arms over her chest. "All right, all right. I swear. What's your big secret?"

I felt all nervous, like I used to feel just before gym class, just like I feel when I have to go to the doctor, kind of sick to my stomach. And then I just blurted it out. "I'm seeing Matt. Matt Fromer, Jess's ex-husband."

Nell dropped her hands to her sides. "You're what! Oh, Laura, come on, this is going too far!"

"Why?" I asked defensively. "Jess didn't want him. They're officially divorced. And Matt wants a family. He wants to get married again. He's perfect for me."

Nell kind of laughed. "Okay, wait a minute; I need to process this."

I waited. Nell stared into space, her eyes squinty. "Do you even like him?" she said finally, looking back to me. "You know, as an individual, as Matt? Or are you just interested in his stats?"

"Of course I like him," I said. "Okay, he talks a lot about football, but so what? While he's watching the games, I'll be taking care of the baby."

"I can't believe what I'm hearing!" Nell cried. "You're already assuming he's going to ask you to marry him?"

I really didn't see why she was so upset. Things between Matt and me were moving fast, but so what?

"I'm not assuming," I said. "But I do think we have a good chance of making it work."

Nell turned back to chopping vegetables and tearing lettuce. I hoped she had some bread or chips or something, too. The muffin I'd had for breakfast was long gone. I made a mental note to stop at the grocery store on the way home and buy another box of those donut holes I liked.

"Have you told Jess yet, about you and Matt?" Nell asked, her eyes on the cutting board.

"No," I said. "I want to wait until I'm sure."

"Until you're sure of what, exactly?" Nell looked up at me again, a strange smile on her face. "Until you're sure you love him?"

"No. Until I'm sure we're going to get married."

Nell has gotten so dramatic. She slammed the knife down on the cutting board.

"You've put me in a very awkward position, Laura. Jess is my friend. She's had a really tough time these last few months. I don't like keeping your relationship with her ex-husband a secret."

"You promised you wouldn't tell anyone!" I cried.

"And I'll keep that promise. But you have to promise me you'll talk to Jess soon. Within the week. Okay?"

"Okay," I agreed. My stomach rumbled. "But it won't be easy."

Nell laughed. "This is just occurring to you now? Of course it won't be easy. Jess isn't going to like this one bit."

"She'll come around," I said.

At least, I hoped she would.

Nell reached for a large bowl in the cabinet behind her. "I wouldn't count on having Jess over to dinner once a month. You know, once you and Matt are all settled into your life of domestic bliss."

Domestic bliss. Those are two very nice words.

"Everything will be fine," I said. "Do you have any chips?"

Chapter 39

Grace

If your divorce is particularly acrimonious, you might be tempted to burn your wedding video and album. Before you take a step that is truly irreversible—unlike your marriage—consider. Wouldn't it be more fun to replace your ex-husband's face with that of a baboon and send the improved photos to his bimbo girlfriend?

—Creative Solutions to Those Messy Post-Divorce Problems

It was almost eleven o'clock. I was in bed, reading, sipping a cup of tea. I was very comfortable.

Then, the doorbell rang.

I knew it was Simon.

I ignored it.

The doorbell rang again. And again.

There was no doubt in my mind at all.

I tossed aside my book and stomped to the front door.

"Who is it?" I demanded.

"It's me."

So, Simon still thought he had the "it's me" privilege.

I unlocked and opened the door. Simon stood there grinning that infamous lazy grin.

"I was just in the neighborhood and . . ."

Right. And you thought you'd make a booty call to your ex-wife.

"And?"

"Hey, can I come in? It's hot in this hallway."

Why had I opened the door if only to turn him away? I sighed and stepped back to let him pass. "Of course."

"You have anything to drink?" he asked on his way to the kitchen.

"Sure," I said, but he was already digging through the cabinet in which I kept what few bottles of liquor I had.

Simon reemerged with a bottle of scotch.

"Want one?"

I shook my head. "I'll have a bit of wine."

Simon opened the fridge and retrieved an open bottle of white wine.

"How's the prep for the show coming along?" I asked.

"Not bad," he said. "I've got a painting to finish but it's going okay."

Simon handed me a glass of wine.

Are you sleeping well? Do you need any money? How do you feel? Are your sinuses bothering you again? Can I get you another pillow?

"Cheers," he said. Simon downed his drink and poured himself another.

I took a sip of the wine, leaned against the counter, and observed my ex-husband. For all his bad habits and crazy schedule, Simon was aging well. His face was thin but virtually unlined. His hair was still dark brown and though his hairline had receded a bit in the past few years, the hair itself was still thick. No middle-aged belly, either, though that might be the result of his forgetting to eat regular meals. I was pretty certain Simon hadn't started an exercise program.

Simon grinned. "What are you looking at?" he asked.

"You. You look good, Simon. Life must be treating you well."

"Can't complain."

But you will, anyway.

Simon put down his half-finished glass and came to lean next to me against the counter. He looked into my eyes. "I miss you all the time, Gracie," he said. "You know that, don't you?"

I nodded. What was I supposed to say? Did he really miss me? Did it still matter to me if he did?

I inched to the right, away from his scent. Simon had always smelled good. He didn't wear cologne; it was something about his skin.

"Do you miss me?" he asked, his voice almost a whisper.

Do I? Maybe. Sometimes. I don't know.

And then before I could protest or even register what was happening, Simon was leaning down and kissing me, very softly.

And then I was kissing him back.

Simon took my shoulders and drew me against him. Pressed close to the body of the man I had once adored, I kissed him more hungrily. I felt Simon take the tilted wineglass from my hand and then we reached that dangerous moment when it seems foolish, absurd not to go on, that moment when turning back seems impossible and then, in the next moment, is impossible.

And in that moment something started to turn.

My body continued to respond to Simon's, but my mind was engaged in a struggle to justify what I was letting happen. By kissing Simon, my mind said, you're just fulfilling a physical need. There is nothing at all emotional or nostalgic or desperate about what is happening.

My mind recoiled from its own lame excuses.

What was wrong with me? Wasn't I supposed to be the mature one in our relationship?

That word. What relationship? I had no relationship with Simon, not any longer. Our relationship was in the past, the relationship in which I was the caregiver and Simon the greedy, needy little boy.

Or, not a little boy at all, but a crafty, manipulative man.

Maybe, just maybe, I hadn't been as in charge as I thought I'd been.

There was a time, a long time, when I thought I was indispensable.

And now Simon was doing just fine without me.

With every ounce of will, I pushed against Simon's chest and yanked my mouth away from his. "I can't," I cried raggedly. "I just can't do this. No, Simon, you have to go."

Simon's eyes were dull with passion. I felt like a high-school tease.

"What?" he mumbled, reaching for me again. He was breathing heavily. "Come on, Gracie, don't be that way."

I backed away and put the kitchen counter between us.

"You have a girlfriend," I said. "This is cheating."

Simon shook his head. He laughed. "Gracie. It's me. Simon. It's not cheating when it's you and me. We're classic, Gracie. We always come back to each other."

No. No, no, no. It couldn't be that way anymore. It couldn't.

I hugged myself and turned half away. "Simon. Go. I can't. I won't, not anymore." I said the words; I meant them, but I could no longer look Simon in the face. Not yet. I wasn't strong enough yet.

"I don't believe this," he said. "This is crap."

"Fine. It's crap. But that's the way it is."

It was time. I turned back to him and saw a man I once had loved. But not anymore.

"I get it," Simon cried suddenly, a smile spreading across his face. "You have a boyfriend and you feel all guilty. Jeez, Gracie, since when did you get all uptight?"

"No boyfriend. It's just me."

No Simon. Just me. Go.

"Gracie—"

"Go."

He was angry. He was confused. But he left.

Finally.

Chapter 40

Grace

The first anniversary of your divorce might bring a rash of un-expected feelings and behaviors, such as murderous rage, ex-treme nostalgia, or manic laughter. Go with the flow. Experience the pain. Pass through the hysteria. Only then will you learn not to care.

—*The First Step Is the Hardest: Recovery 101*

"Our waiter likes you, Grace."

I watched him walk away with our order. "He does?"

"Can't you tell when a guy flirts with you?" Laura asked.

"I can tell," I said. "Most times."

Except that at that moment I was thinking of Evan and there was no room in my thoughts for another man. Surprisingly, not even for Simon. Our last, messy encounter had further severed the bond that had kept me in a chokehold for so long.

"Grace is better off being oblivious," Jess said. "I think our waiter looks kind of smarmy."

Nell shrugged. "A little flirting never hurt anyone."

"I suppose," I said. "But he doesn't do anything for me."

"Speaking of men who do—or don't—do anything for us," Jess said, "I ran into Seth Morgenstein at a work function."

"How did it go?" Nell asked. "Were you comfortable? Was he pleasant?"

"We both were very comfortable and pleasant to each other. In fact, we skipped out of the party and sat in a Starbucks for al-most three hours, just talking."

"Did he make a pass?" I asked Jess. I could ask this of my friend but I wasn't about to tell her, I wasn't about to tell anyone, about my close call with Simon.

"No. And I'm glad. That would have ruined everything."

Oh, yes, I thought. Sex certainly can ruin everything.

"Anyway," Jess went on, "it got me thinking about how really miserable I was in my marriage when I first met Seth. It made me remember how I craved some real contact. I needed a level of intimacy that just wasn't there with Matt."

Yes. I knew all about real contact, and about not finding it. Maybe all of us did, Jess, Nell, and Laura, too.

"You can feel far lonelier when you're with someone," I said, "than when you're by yourself."

"Absolutely," Jess agreed. "Anyway, since the other night, since talking with Seth, I think I'm beginning to forgive myself for having the affair. It was wrong, I know, but I was acting out of despair, not coldheartedness. Suddenly I found myself married to someone I realized I didn't even love. I think it made me a little crazy, like how a trapped animal circles his cage madly, desperately clawing at the bars even though he knows nothing will be gained by it."

"A caged animal probably doesn't know his behavior is futile," Nell pointed out. "But I understand your meaning."

"Right. I should have gone to a therapist. I should have talked to Matt about how I was feeling. Those would have been reasonable ways to handle the situation."

"You and Matt still might have gotten divorced," I said.

"Of course. But there wouldn't have been the betrayal."

I also knew all about betrayal, and about tolerating it. I wondered what Evan knew about the subject. A person could hardly reach maturity and know nothing about betrayal.

"Jess," I said, "I'm so glad you're making progress."

Nell nodded. "We all are. It's about time. You were getting a little boring with all the agonizing."

"I know! I could hardly stand myself most days."

Laura had said nothing since Jess started to talk. I looked closely at her now. She was staring at her awful pink drink, too quiet, almost as if she was guarding a secret and afraid if she opened her mouth it would come spilling out.

"You know, Grace," Nell said, "there's something I've never asked you. I hope you don't think I'm being nosy, but have you ever wanted children?"

Laura choked on her drink and reached for her balled-up napkin.

"You really shouldn't drink those sugary concoctions," Nell said with what was probably false concern. Sometimes I wondered if Nell liked her sister at all.

"No," I said, "you're not being nosy. I've dragged you all through every other aspect of my private life, why not this? Frankly, children never seemed a real option when I was with Simon. Simon is enough of a baby for any woman, and he's six foot one, which makes him a very large baby."

Jess laughed. "A very large baby with a very large appetite for self-indulgence and other people's money."

"Right. I knew Simon would make a terrible father. Oh, he'd love a child to the best of his ability, which means the child would be like an afterthought. It wouldn't have been fair to any of us."

"Especially not to you," Nell said, "since it's likely you'd have wound up a single parent."

"With no financial help. Ugh. The court can order a deadbeat dad to pay child support, but if the money isn't there, it isn't there."

"So, after Simon, after the divorce, have you ever considered having a baby?" Nell asked.

Laura spilled her water.

I shook my head. "Oh, no, not now. It's way too late for me, maybe not biologically but emotionally. I'm not who I was at twenty-four or twenty-five when I really did want to get pregnant but at the same time realized it would be a big mistake. No, I'm fine teaching kids. That's enough virtual parenting for me!"

"It's great that you've come to terms with it all," Nell said. "Unfinished emotional business can be killing. And we all know about unfinished emotional business."

Laura dropped her fork.

"Yes, we do," I said. "What about you, Jess? I've known you all these years and I've never heard you talk about having a family."

"That's because there's really nothing to talk about," she said. "I never wanted children. I mean, maybe when I was little and playing with dolls, but once I started to grow up, I had no interest. I don't dislike children. I've just always known they're not for me."

"What about Matt, then?" Nell asked, her head cocked. "He mustn't have wanted kids, either."

Laura shot her sister a panicked look. Something was going on with Laura, all right.

"Oh, he was okay with not having a family. We talked about it early on, when we'd been dating only a few weeks. I think Matt would have made a fine father, though."

"Oh, he would have!" Laura blurted.

It was right then that I knew. Laura was dating Matt. Nell knew, too, but Jess didn't. And it wasn't my business to tell Jess what my instincts had just told me.

Jess eyed Laura curiously. "I didn't know you had such strong opinions about my ex-husband."

Laura turned very red. "I don't. I just—He seemed nice is all."

"He was nice," Jess agreed. "And he was boring. At least I found him to be boring. I'm sure lots of women would find him exciting."

"Oh, yes." Nell grinned. "Lots of women."

Laura dropped her fork again. I picked it up and handed it back to her.

"Matt does have that all-grown-up-boy-next-door appeal," Jess agreed. "I'm sure he's got his pick of beautiful women to date. Like the one I saw him with at Downtown Crossing. She was model pretty, tall and slim, great hair. She looked perfect with him."

Poor Laura. She looked absolutely miserable being taunted knowingly by her sister and unknowingly by Jess.

"Hey," I said, "sorry to change the topic, but I was wondering if anyone has seen that new Jim Jarmusch film that opened last week."

"Netflix has spoiled me for watching movies," Nell said. "I prefer to stay home and pop my own popcorn."

"You don't like popcorn," Laura said.

"It's just an expression."

"Well, I'd like to see it, if anyone wants to come along. You know, I haven't been to a movie in years. It's pathetic."

"I'll go," Jess said. "As long as we don't sit too close to the screen."

"Of course not. We'll sit right in the middle."

"Do people still make out in movie theaters?" Nell wondered.

"I don't know," Jess said. "I avoid looking too closely at what's going on in the back rows."

I thought back to my own teen years and the awkwardness and fear that had attended them.

"Kids are so open about sex these days," I said. "Our entire culture is dripping with sex. Do young people still have to sneak around?"

"Sneaking around is part of the fun," Jess pointed out. "It's arousing; it makes people feel they're involved with something illicit even if they're not."

Nell shot a look at her sister. "Don't you agree, Laura? That sneaking around is part of the fun?"

Laura glared back at Nell. "I wouldn't know."

Really, I thought. Nell was out of line torturing Laura like this.

"Some people still like privacy," I said. "Not everyone wants to be an exhibitionist. A back row, a darkened theater, it's a perfect place for some snuggling."

"Or more."

Nell looked to Jess. "Have you ever done more than kiss at a movie?"

Jess laughed. "You'll think I'm wanton, but then again you probably already think it. Yes, I once gave a guy a blow job. Not just some random guy, my boyfriend at the time."

I'd done an awful lot for Simon, but I'd never engaged in an act of public sex. He'd asked, repeatedly, but on that one point I'd stood firm.

"I'd never have the nerve to do something like that," I said. "What if I got arrested for lewd behavior or an even worse charge? How would I explain that to the principal of my school? I guarantee I'd never be allowed to teach again. My career would be over."

"Never say never. Hormones are very powerful." Again Nell shot a look at Laura. "They all too easily conquer reason."

"Not at our age," Laura replied quickly. "At our age we look before we leap. At least, I do."

Nell sighed dramatically. "Well, then, my dear, you are made of superior stuff. The rest of us are mere mortals, frail and capable of any sort of debauchery."

"Please, Nell, no more!" Jess put the back of her hand to her forehead, a silent-screen heroine. "I don't need reminding that I'm weak and susceptible."

Suddenly Laura stood, almost knocking over her chair in the process.

"I've got to go," she said.

"Feeling bloated again?"

I shot Nell a reproachful look. She caught it and shrugged.

Laura opened her mouth, then closed it again. Poor girl.

"I'll walk with you," I said. "Let's just pay the check."

"You don't have to walk me all the way to the T."

I glanced over at Laura. Her shoulders were hunched and her head was down.

"That's okay," I said. "I need the exercise."

"I'm really fine."

I laughed. "I know you are. I'm not saying you need an escort."

"Sorry." Laura looked up from the ground and to me. "It's just that Nell makes me so mad sometimes. I mean, why does she—"

Laura pressed her lips together and shook her head.

"Why does she what?" I pressed. "Why does she tease you in front of your friends?"

"Yes!" The word burst from Laura's lips. "But it's worse than teasing; it's like she really wants to embarrass me. Sometimes I think she hates me."

"She doesn't hate you," I said, but I wondered. Why did Nell feel she had the right to torture her sister the way she did? She might not hate Laura, but she certainly showed little respect for her. And if I was right, if Laura was indeed dating Jess's ex-husband and Nell was in on the secret, she was being cruel out of all proportion.

We walked on, the T station now in sight.

"Laura," I said, careful to keep my voice even and my tone not in the least bit accusatory. "Are you seeing Matt Fromer?"

Laura stumbled. I reached out for her arm. She shook away from my touch.

"What?" she cried. "Of course not! What gave you that idea? I mean, God, I mean, of course not!"

Her protestations confirmed my hunch.

"It's okay if you are," I said, though I wasn't quite sure it was okay or that I was okay with it.

"But I'm not."

We walked on in silence until we reached the stairs to the T station. Laura didn't quite meet my eye when she said, "Okay, I guess I'll see you soon."

I don't know why I couldn't let it go. Maybe because I thought that by telling me about her relationship with Matt, Laura might find some relief. The secret was burdensome: that was abundantly clear.

"Laura," I said, "look at me."

She did. Her eyes looked scared.

"At dinner tonight, well, I got the feeling that you are dating Matt. And that Nell knows and is giving you a hard time about it. Am I right?"

Laura opened her mouth and I felt sure it was to once again deny the fact of a relationship. But then she surprised me.

"Yes, it's true," she said, "I am seeing Matt and Nell thinks it's horrible and that Jess is going to be furious and that I should have told her right away and—"

I put my hand on her arm and this time Laura didn't shrug away. "Laura," I said, "slow down." Under my hand I could feel some of the tension leave her body.

"What do you think, Grace?" she asked. "Do you hate me?"

I shook my head at the pitiful nature of that question. "No, Laura, of course I don't hate you. But I do think you should tell Jess as soon as possible. Keeping the fact that you're seeing Matt a secret clearly isn't doing you any good." And, I thought, it's giving Nell the upper hand over you.

Laura looked to the ground again. "I know. I know I have to tell her. But I'm afraid. What if she hates me?"

Really, I almost lost patience with her then. I could almost—almost—understand why Nell felt compelled to harass her younger sister.

"She's not going to hate you," I said. "No one hates you, Laura. You really should try to stop thinking that way."

Laura nodded but I doubted she was taking my words to heart.

"Look," I went on, "Jess will probably be surprised and maybe she'll feel a bit uncomfortable around you for a while, but she's a reasonable person. She'll be fine. But the sooner you tell her, the better for you both. Okay?"

Laura looked up to me and, though the night was getting dark, I thought I saw a glimmer of a smile in her eyes. "Okay," she said. "I'll tell her right away. You really think she'll be okay?"

"I really do," I said. And to myself I added, "She had damn well better be or we're going to have a freak show on our hands."

Chapter 41

Jess

Punishment #57: Pay a brainy high-school kid to break into your ex's personal e-mail and forward it to all of his colleagues. He's sure to have a ministroke.

—*Revenge Is Sweet: 101 Fun Ways to Wreak Havoc on Your Ex's New Life*

"Remember Matt, your ex-husband?"

I looked up from the piece of bread I was dipping in a small bowl of olive oil. Really, Laura has the ability to bring ditzy to a whole new dimension.

Either that or she was nervous for some reason. I noticed she'd scrunched her napkin into a ball and was squeezing it tightly. She'd done the same thing the other night when the four of us had been at dinner. She'd also spilled her water, choked on her drink, and dropped her fork.

"Um, yes," I said, "I remember him."

Laura looked down at her plate. "Well, it's just that . . . it's just that I'm seeing Matt. We're dating."

I carefully put down my fork. So much for lunch.

"You're seeing my Matt?"

Laura looked up from her plate. "He *was* your Matt," she said a tad defensively. "He's mine now."

Yes. Of course.

"Why?" I said. "Why him? Why not some other average, decent single guy?"

"I like him."

Yeah, you like him. And you weren't doing too well in the dating game so why not poach your friend's ex-husband?

"How long has this been going on?" I asked.

Laura took a gulp of water before answering. "About a month," she said hurriedly.

"I can't believe you didn't tell me before now!" I took a deep breath. There was no point in getting thrown out of one of my favorite bistros for bad behavior. "Who else knows?" I asked.

"Nell."

I felt like I'd been hit in the stomach with a very large fist.

"But I swore her to secrecy," Laura said urgently, "and she's only known for a few days, I swear! It's just that I wanted to tell you myself. Please, Jess, don't blame Nell. She was really angry with me for not talking to you right away. She made me promise to tell you soon, and I just did."

I imagined Nell's reaction to the interesting news. I almost smiled at the thought. Almost. And then Laura said, "Grace knows, too."

I closed my eyes. I don't know why. I opened them after a moment to see Laura with her shoulders hunched and her face scrunched into that "please don't hate me" look.

"You told Grace," I said.

"She asked me. I mean, after dinner the other night, when we walked home, she asked me if I was seeing Matt. She guessed, Jess. I tried to lie but she wormed it out of me."

I doubted that worming was Grace's style, but I didn't argue with Laura's version of what had happened between them.

"Give me a minute with this," I said.

Laura picked at her hamburger. My own lunch was long abandoned.

"Were you attracted to Matt when I was married to him?" I asked finally.

"Oh, no! I had Duncan. I thought Matt was nice and all, but I really didn't give him much thought."

And then something occurred to me, just like that. "Until Duncan wouldn't take you back. Until you were desperate."

Laura paled. "How did you know about Duncan?"

"I didn't." I almost felt like grinning. "It was a good guess."

"Anyway," Laura said huffily, "I'm not desperate. That's not why I'm with Matt."

Yes. And I'm a three-hundred-pound pro-football tackle.

"Now I know why we're in a restaurant," I said. "You know I won't make a scene in public."

"Yes," Laura said. "I was scared you'd really explode."

"Oh, I'm exploding. Except it's all inside and if I don't leave this lunch with an ulcer, it will be with a migraine."

Laura winced. "I'm sorry, Jess. Really."

And right then I remembered once thinking that someone like Laura would be more of a fit with Matt than someone like me. Maybe I did know a little about human beings, after all.

"What are you sorry for?" I said. "You're right; Matt isn't my property anymore."

"Well, he's not really mine yet, either. I mean, we're not engaged or anything. We haven't even, you know, had sex."

This was way too much information.

"I don't know," I said, "if I want to hear the answer to the question I'm about to ask, but I'm going to ask it anyway. Does Matt talk about me?"

Laura shook her head. "No. We agreed we wouldn't talk about you."

"That's something."

"I'm not a complete monster, Jess. I wouldn't stay with him if he said bad things about you."

I didn't quite believe her. "You know he's obsessed with football."

"I remember your telling me. I'm sure I can handle it."

I realized I didn't really know what Laura was capable of handling.

"Yes," I said, "you probably can. You don't want much from Matt, do you? You don't want a soul mate."

Suddenly, Laura looked pained, sad, old. She looked me right in the eye. "I want him to marry me," she said with deliberation. "I want him to make me pregnant. And I want him to support me and my child."

I had expected to hear some such statement. Still, it felt like big news.

"So," I said, "Matt's changed his mind about having a family?"

"Yes."

"And in return for his sperm," I said, "what will you offer him?"

Laura's shoulders hunched just a bit under the blow. "The opportunity to be a father," she said. "My loyalty."

"What about your love?"

"People grow to love each other," Laura said. It sounded as if she'd rehearsed the line for just such situations. "Matt and I really like each other right now. We'll be fine."

No, I thought, they won't.

"I hope so. Matt doesn't need his heart broken a second time."

"I won't break his heart," Laura said, leaning over her half-eaten lunch toward me. "I'll try my best not to. Anyway," she said, sitting back, "I don't think I can go through another divorce. I feel I've aged ten years in the last few months."

"Yes," I said drily, "divorce can be murder on the appearance. Let's get the check."

I was very happy to get home that night and lock the door behind me. It had been hard to concentrate all afternoon after Laura's surprising and unsettling news.

I checked my machine—no calls—poured a glass of wine and sank into the comfy chair I'd bought on sale at Macy's when Matt took most of the living-room furniture for his new place.

Just when I'd begun the process of forgiving myself, this strange news from Laura. But what, really, did it mean for me?

There was no more need for guilt, was there? Matt had moved on, he would probably get married, and though I knew Laura wasn't in love with him, I thought he just might be in love with her. Matt needed to have a woman in his life; he needed to believe that he was in love.

And what did this one-sided relationship portend? It seemed likely that one day Matt would find himself suffering through another divorce.

Matt was one of the good guys, in spite of his flaws. He hadn't deserved me. I wasn't sure he deserved Laura.

But Matt's life was his own as was mine; our lives were no longer intertwined. He would fend for himself, as would I.

Suddenly, I felt very hungry. Laura had ruined my appetite for lunch but now, hours later, perspective had revived appetite. I reached for the phone, dialed the number of a local pizza place, and ordered a large pie with mushrooms.

One of the best things about living alone is that you don't have to share your junk food.

Chapter 42

Nell

Start poisoning your ex-husband's character as soon as he walks out the door. Make sure his kids know what a lying, cheating bum their mother had been duped into marrying. Only in this way will you be sure to have the kids on all major holidays.

—*Getting What You Want: The Post-Divorce Woman*

They were sitting at a table near the back of the room, Richard and Bob.

I took a deep breath and headed toward them.

I had been surprised when Richard suggested the three of us have lunch. It was the first time he'd ever suggested a meeting, at least to me. Maybe Richard and Bob had talked about it many times. What did I know about their relationship?

Nothing. And what I knew about Bob could fill a small Post-it. I knew that Colin thought Bob was "okay." I knew that Clara thought he was a "dreamboat."

And I knew that he had stolen my husband's heart.

Richard saw me coming and stood. He always was a gentleman. "Nell," he said, "it's good to see you."

"Hi," I said, and my voice sounded odd, a bit too high.

Richard and I took our seats. "Nell," he said, "this is Bob Landry. Bob, this is Nell Keats."

The man directly across from me extended his hand. I thought I saw it shake just a little.

"It's very good to meet you," he said, quite seriously.

I shook his hand. "Hello," I said.

Bob cleared his throat. He straightened his knife. He was nervous and that made me feel a bit more in control of my own nervousness. Which, of course, made me feel superior. Ridiculous, I know, but I can't always be noble.

We made small talk and ordered, though I wasn't at all sure I could eat.

"So," Richard said when the waiter had gone off. "I thought it would be nice for you and Bob to get to know each other a bit."

I smiled wanly. "Yes."

Bob said, "Sure," and nodded. Clearly, the lunch was all Richard's idea.

"Bob is an electrician, an independent contractor."

"Yes," I said. "I know."

Richard took a sip of water. "Oh. Yes," he said, "I suppose I told you that already."

"Richard tells me you're involved with the MFA and various charities around Boston." Poor earnest Bob, coming to Richard's rescue.

"Yes," I said. And then, "Have you ever been married? I mean, like Richard was."

Bob didn't flinch. My abrupt question seemed to have broken the ice.

"No," he said easily. "I came out in college. I did take a girl to our high school prom, but she was just a friend. And she knew that I was gay."

"So you didn't lie to her."

Bob shot a look at Richard. Richard blanched.

"I'm sorry." I shook my head, ashamed. "I shouldn't have said that."

Richard smiled a wan smile. "It's okay, Nellie. I know this is hard for all of us."

Our lunch was served and while I picked at my salad, Bob told me he was thirty-five and that he'd grown up just outside of Portsmouth, New Hampshire. He'd gone to Clark University in

Worcester. He had a brother and a sister, two nephews, and his parents had moved to Florida.

"That's really pretty much it," he said with a small, self-deprecating laugh. "I'm not a very exciting person."

Richard squeezed Bob's hand. "I think you're an exciting person."

Bob squeezed back. "Well," he said, gazing into Richard's eyes, "I guess that's all that matters."

I've never been keen on public displays of affection, whether verbal or physical. And to watch my ex-husband engage in a romantic moment with his lover . . . It was a terribly uncomfortable moment for me. If Bob had been a woman, I don't think it would have been any easier.

At that moment, as the third person at the table, a barely touched salad before me, I felt my loss more keenly than I'd ever had. There was no one in my life telling me that I was an exciting person, no one to greet me at the end of the day. There was no one to make coffee for in the morning except me.

We kept the conversation light for the rest of the meal. It was hard to find topics that felt entirely safe, and by the time the check was paid, I was exhausted.

The three of us emerged into the high midafternoon sun. I felt as if I could drop to the sidewalk and sleep. Bob extended his hand. This time, it was steady.

"It really was nice to meet you, Nell," he said. "Thank you again for joining us."

For joining *us.* The invited guest. Not part of the couple.

I took his hand. "It was nice to meet you, too, Bob," I said. I turned to Richard. In the bright sun I saw a weariness in his eyes. None of this, not the years of secrecy, not the divorce, not the coming out had been easy for him.

"And it was good to see you, Richard," I said.

Would he kiss my cheek or shake my hand or give me a hug?

"Thank you, Nell," he said, from a distance. "Thank you."

And then Richard and Bob left me there, alone.

Chapter 43

Laura

"I have got to get some new clothes!"

I threw a pair of jeans on the bed. Absolutely nothing in my closet made me look pregnant. And I really wanted to show up at the Mommy In Training class looking at least a few months pregnant.

Because I was pretty sure I wouldn't be allowed to stay if someone found out I wasn't pregnant!

I stood in front of the mirror and looked at myself from the side. Nell had oh, so helpfully pointed out that I'd gained some weight. I stuck out my stomach. I poked it with my forefinger. Well, I guess she was right; I had put on a few pounds, but not enough to make me look pregnant or anything.

In the end I wore an old pair of Duncan's sweats he'd left behind and the biggest T-shirt I could find. I was kind of hot by the time I got to the church basement where the class was being held, but I figured sweating was probably something a pregnant woman would do on a warm day in June.

I was also wearing my old wedding ring. It felt odd on my finger, too tight, as if my finger had already plumped up to match the size of the other fingers. By the way, lots of pregnant women get swollen fingers.

The room was large and painted an icky yellow. Crayon drawings were tacked to a corkboard along the left wall. Folding chairs were arranged in about six lines of six seats across. Not very comfortable for the pregnant woman! Only a few seats were open and I took one near the back.

A minute later an African-American woman in a sexy yoga outfit sat next to me. Her belly was as flat as a pancake.

"Hi," she said. "I'm Roberta."

"Hi. I'm Laura."

"First baby?" she asked, looking at my midriff.

I nodded and put my hand to my stomach as I'd seen a few of the other women do.

"So, when are you due?" Roberta asked.

"In—"

And then I panicked. I'd worked out the calendar just that morning, but now my mind was an absolute blank.

"Um, well, it's kind of unclear," I mumbled. "The doctor is . . ."

"Okay, mommies, listen up!"

Saved by the drill sergeant of an instructor!

I murmured "Sorry" and focused on the woman who stood before us. She introduced herself as Mrs. Beaker. She was squat, like a frog woman. Her hair was a sort of halo of very tiny, tight gray curls. She had a booming voice and a big smile. I thought she must be a grandma. I thought she probably made really yummy casseroles. I decided to get a grilled cheese sandwich for lunch.

Mrs. Beaker was a pretty good teacher. We learned about the importance of prenatal care. It didn't sound so bad, eating all those vegetables and fruit—you could make smoothies out of the fruit, at least—but I wasn't thrilled about the exercise thing. Maybe, I thought, I could try yoga for mommies-to-be; that didn't sound too sweaty and you got to sit a lot.

We learned about the importance of regular visits to the ob-gyn. Well, duh, I thought, of course. Okay, I hadn't gone to the gynecologist in a few years, but there was no big reason to go. I hadn't had any infections or anything. But I would go once I got pregnant!

Mrs. Beaker told us that there were a whole bunch of vitamins and minerals you had to get enough of, especially folic acid, whatever that is.

And then she outlined what sort of things we could expect to happen to our bodies and when. A lot of it sounded really awful, like diarrhea and nausea and swollen hands and feet. I shuddered from head to toe when she talked about sex during the last trimester. Nell says I'm squeamish and I guess I am. But what's wrong with being grossed out by the thought of a penis poking your unborn child? No way. Not for me. My new husband would just have to hold out.

Roberta had brought a pen and a notebook. She scribbled down every word Mrs. Beaker spoke; at least, from the way she was flipping pages it looked like it. I guess I should have thought to bring a notebook, too. But I just didn't know there'd be so much information!

Finally, finally, the class was over.

"Okay, ladies," Mrs. Beaker boomed, "next time I need you to bring—"

I scooted out of the room before Roberta could ask me more questions. And as soon as I got home, I made myself a grilled cheese sandwich and started working on the calendar again.

"See, what he doesn't understand is that I know what he's thinking. I know . . ."

I nodded and tuned out and Matt talked on. He talked for fifteen minutes—I discreetly timed him—about something going on in his office, something to do with some guy who wants Matt's job but who's really naive if he thinks he's going to get it and just last month he got off probation for—something or other.

I nodded a lot and made some sympathetic sounds and when Matt was finished, I said, "Wow. Your job sounds so important," and he kind of beamed.

"So," he said, "how was your day?"

I was on the verge of telling Matt about going to the Mommies In Training class that morning but decided he might think I was trying to pressure him. And we all know that men do not like to be pressured!

"It was very nice, thanks," I said brightly.

Men also don't like their mood spoiled over dinner.

"Good. You know, my buddy Greg got a line on tickets to the entire season and I'm thinking—"

Nod encouragingly and make sounds of sympathy or surprise. That was how to handle Matt. That was how to handle most men.

It wasn't, I suddenly remembered, how I'd handled Duncan. He hadn't needed handling. We just had a good time together.

I shifted in the seat as if to shake off the memory of my marriage. My happy marriage.

Jess and Matt hadn't had a happy marriage, I reminded myself. Which is why Matt is single and sitting across the table, carving steak and talking to me about football.

For the life of me I couldn't understand why Jess had married him. He was so not her type. I don't really know what Jess's type is, but I know that Matt certainly isn't it.

And then I wondered why Matt had married Jess. I wasn't going to ask him, but I was curious. I was prettier than Jess so it couldn't have been her looks. She is smart, smarter than me, but I don't think a man marries a woman because she's smart. Right?

"Should I get the check?"

I came back to life and smiled big at Matt. "Sure," I said. "Whatever you like."

Chapter 44

Grace

Of course he left you. You're vastly overweight, your hairstyle is completely outdated, you bring no money to the household, and your fashion sense died when you said, "I do." Get with the program. Lose the weight, cut your hair, get a job, and hire a personal shopper. Maybe you won't have to spend the rest of your miserable life alone after all.

— *"He Should Love Me the Way I Am" and Other Harmful Nonsense*

I was afraid he'd be there. I was afraid he wouldn't be.

"I should have called," I said to Evan. "You're probably busy. I'm sorry."

He smiled. "Not at all. It's good to see you."

"You, too."

I'd finally worked up the nerve to approach Evan. After our last phone conversation, the one in which I'd so rudely rejected him, I'd avoided even walking past the Auster Gallery, afraid I'd run into him, afraid of the look I might find in his eyes, anger maybe, or hurt.

But since that awful phone conversation, something inside me had changed; at least, it was beginning to change. I was tired of avoiding what might be my life.

Now, standing face to face with Evan, I found that what I'd felt that night in the restaurant, that intense draw, was still there. It hadn't been due to the surroundings or the wine. It was because of Evan. I felt very glad. Frightened but glad.

"So," Evan said, "are you interested in one of the works?"

"No. I mean, yes, of course. I love the small landscapes in the second room, but I'm afraid a teacher's salary doesn't allow me to collect much art."

"Starving artists, starving appreciators. The business of art is strange and unfair."

"Oh, don't get me started on the topic!"

"So, if you're not here to buy a piece . . ."

Steady, Grace. "Actually," I said, "I stopped by to say hello. I mean, I was hoping to run into you."

"Oh?" Evan asked. "Why's that?"

"No reason in particular. Just to, you know, say hello."

Did I imagine it or did Evan's eyes reveal some pleasure at hearing this?

"I'm glad you did," he said. "I've been wondering about your program."

"You have?"

"Yes," Evan said promptly. "Arts education is in such trouble in this country. I feel I've neglected to do my part in supporting it. If you feel your program is something worthwhile, I'd like to help in some way. I'll make a financial donation, but I'd like to do something more hands on. I'm good with a hammer and nails."

I didn't know what to say. Was Evan's offer to help out really just a way for him to spend time with me? And would that be so bad?

"Why are you hesitating?" Evan asked with a smile. "Do you think I'll make a mess of everything?"

"Oh, no, of course not! It's just . . . Just that you must be so busy with the gallery and the upcoming show and all."

"I am busy," he said. "But I want to make time for your program. I wouldn't offer something I can't deliver."

I thought of Simon. He always made offers he had no intention of delivering. It was his way of life, almost unconscious.

"Well, then, yes," I said, "I'd love your input. I'd like it. Thank you."

"Great. So, when should we get started?"

And then I took a further step toward liberation.

"How about we meet for dinner?" I said. "Maybe tomorrow. If you're free, that is."

Evan bowed slightly. "I am free and I would love to meet you for dinner. Why don't you choose the restaurant this time?"

I said I would. We made plans to meet at the gallery at seven the following evening. We parted with smiles. I felt the need to touch his arm but didn't. There would be time for that. I hoped.

I couldn't help grinning as I walked along Newbury Street. Let people think I'd lost my mind. Maybe I had, but if this was crazy, I liked it.

I stood at the next corner and waited for the light to turn green. The sun was warm, the air dry; potted flowers lined the patio of the café to my left. Suddenly, I was overcome with a desire to pick up a paintbrush, to prepare a surface, to produce something. It was a long-missing but still-familiar urge; its resurfacing took me completely by surprise. Suddenly, I couldn't wait to get home and work.

The light turned green and I dashed ahead.

Who was this brave new Grace Henley? Whoever she was, I hoped she wouldn't let me down.

Chapter 45

Jess

Get ready to reexperience all the miserable things you remember about dating in your teens and early twenties. Your stomach will clench when he rings the doorbell; your dinner will go virtually untasted because you'll be afraid of getting food stuck in your teeth; you'll laugh at all the wrong places. Rest assured you will be massively uncomfortable and therefore will make a fool of yourself.

—*Dating in Middle Age, or Life's Cruelest Joke*

"Well, let's put it this way," Nell said. "As I'm learning how to become my self, or how to redefine the old self, whatever it is I'm doing, I'm realizing that Richard has that exact same right. He has the right to be himself. I'm not saying it was easy sitting across from the man my ex-husband has sex with—"

"The man he loves," Grace corrected.

Nell grimaced. "That's even worse. Anyway, I'm not saying it was easy, but it was okay."

We had gathered for dinner at a very good bistro called Gabrielle's. Laura grumped about the prices until Nell pointed out that no one had forced her to come along.

"What was your impression of Bob?" I asked.

"Honestly, Jess, I thought he was very nice. He seems unassuming. He's got a pleasant face, though Richard is definitely more handsome."

"You two did make the perfect couple," Grace said, "at least as far as looks."

"Sure. We were a living, breathing Barbie and Ken. But might I remind you that Barbie and Ken don't have genitals."

"And," I added, "I heard they broke up after something like forty years together."

"So, Ken was gay after all?" Laura asked, eyes gleaming, as if relishing the thought.

"I don't know. I think their PR people thought they needed to be single for a while. You know, recapture the world's attention."

"Ah, yes." Nell grinned. "The media-created breakup. You know, it might be nice to have someone else make my personal decisions for me. Nell, it's time you dated a twenty-year-old. Nell, it's time to dump the twenty-year-old and get back with your ex-husband for six months. It'll make great press."

"Well," Laura said, "I don't know how you did it, meeting those two for lunch. If I were you, I wouldn't have anything to do with Richard."

"Thankfully, Laura," Nell said, "you're not me. You don't have to deal with Richard if you don't want to, but I would like to be his friend. I'd like to create a new dynamic, one that allows each of us to be comfortable."

"And you think Bob will be open to you and Richard being friends?" I asked.

"Absolutely. Bob might have accidentally wrecked my home, but he's not the home-wrecker type."

"Well," Grace said, "it's not like Bob has to worry about anything sexual going on between you two."

Laura put her water glass down with enough force to spill part of its contents. "I still think you're crazy. The man cheated on you! He lied to you. He humiliated you. And you want to be his friend?"

I supposed compassion and forgiveness were foreign concepts to the younger Keats sister.

"Yes, Laura," Nell said, "I do. And here's why. In a few years the kids will be graduating from college. Maybe someday they'll get married. Maybe someday they'll have children. I don't want to make occasions that are supposed to be celebratory miserable. For Colin and Clara's sake, if not for my own, I have to work on a relationship with Richard."

Laura rolled her eyes. I wondered how old her child would be when he started therapy. Probably about two.

A child.

"Have you wondered about Richard and Bob having kids of their own?" I asked Nell.

Nell laughed. "Oh, God, of course I have. Richard's only forty-four and he's in perfect health. If anyone has the energy for an infant, it's Richard. He was amazing when the kids were little. But I just can't bring up the subject with him."

"I don't blame you!" Laura huffed.

"Enough about me." Nell turned to Grace. "What's going on with you and the job?"

Grace's face suddenly became animated.

"It's been crazy lately," she said. "We've got so many kids, but Evan's been a real help. Of course, the money he donated is going to fund a buying spree at my favorite art supply store. The kids will be grateful, especially the ones who are really into making art. But it's his time I most appreciate. My interns are almost entirely without a work ethic. Most mornings they show up late and hungover. But Evan shows up when he says he's going to and stays until the job is done."

"Is there something you're not telling us about this Evan person?" I asked. "Like, are you two involved? Is this the same guy you mentioned when we met Trina at Nell's house?"

"Ah, yes," Nell said. "The 'real' man!"

"No! I mean, no, we're not involved, and yes, Evan is the 'real' man. And I think he might like me a little."

"And . . ." Laura prompted.

"And I think I might like him a little, too."

I know Grace. And at that moment I knew she liked Evan a lot more than a little.

"What's he like?" Laura asked.

"Well," Grace said, "he's very attractive. He's got a lovely smile and—"

"What's he like as a person," Nell said, "not what does he look like."

Laura protested. "I want to know what he looks like!"

"Look in a magazine," I said. "His picture is all over the local media."

"Let's just say that he's about as different from Simon as a man can be."

Nell raised her wineglass. "Hurrah!"

"Really," Grace went on, "he's responsible and independent and he's always doing things for other people, always thinking of other people."

"Especially you?" I asked.

"I don't know yet," Grace admitted. "I'm not sure I'm reading his behavior correctly. I'm not sure if I should take his words at face value or look for a more subtle message. In some ways with Evan I feel completely innocent, unschooled, almost as if I'd never learned anything about men and women and how they come together."

"Maybe that's a good thing," Nell suggested. "Maybe that means what's developing between you is special, unique."

"If something's developing between us. I'm still not sure of anything."

"Has he been married?" Laura asked. "Does he have children?"

Grace nodded. "Yes, he was married once for a long time to a woman he met in grad school. They got divorced when he was around forty. That much is common knowledge, but I haven't asked him about what happened. It's too soon for that. And he has no children. He told me that himself."

"So he's been single for how long?" Nell asked.

"About ten years," Grace said. "Of course, that makes me wonder if he has any intention of ever remarrying. Not that I'm ready to consider another marriage. Not yet, anyway."

"You'd probably know if he was a Casanova," I pointed out. "He's too much in the public eye to hide a wild reputation."

"True," Grace said. "Maybe he just hasn't met the next love of his life."

"And maybe that's you. I'm glad for you, Grace, really."

Grace laughed a rueful laugh. "Don't be glad just yet, Jess. I have no idea what will happen, if anything."

"All right," I said. "We won't jinx it. We'll change the topic."

"So, Laura," Nell asked, turning to her sister, "what's new with you and the quest for a sperm donor?"

Laura gave her sister a dirty look. Really, I thought, Nell should lighten up on Laura. She is what she is, and no amount of teasing is going to change her.

"I'm not sure I should talk about my relationship with Matt," Laura said. She leaned forward, as if about to impart a secret. "You know. Because of Jess."

Nell and Grace exchanged a look of exasperation.

I cleared my throat dramatically. "Laura," I said, "I thought we talked about this. You have every right to live your own life. If you want to talk about Matt, fine. Just don't expect me to listen to stories about what you two do in bed. I'm not that sophisticated or cosmopolitan."

"I told you, we haven't slept together yet."

"What are you waiting for?" I asked abruptly. I shouldn't have been mean; here I was thinking Nell was being mean, but something about Laura just calls up the nastiness in people.

Laura blushed.

"Oh," I said. "I get it."

"Get what?" Nell asked with a grin.

"Laura's revirginalized. No sex until marriage."

"Engagement," she corrected. "No sex until we're engaged."

"That night with what's-his-name," Grace said, "the one who lied about having kids, really spooked you, didn't it?"

"Yes," Laura admitted. "Besides, I think waiting makes the whole thing more romantic. More special."

"Does Matt know about this vow? That you'll only have sex in exchange for a diamond?"

"It's not like that at all! Nell, why do you always have to be so harsh?"

"Sorry."

I doubted she was.

"Anyway," Laura said, "Matt understands how I feel. He understands that doing things the right way is very important to me."

"He can be amenable," I said. "He did let me drag him to Paris on our honeymoon."

"Where are you dragging Matt on your honeymoon?" Nell asked Laura. "Babies 'R' Us?"

Laura sat up straighter. I couldn't help noticing the beginnings of a double chin. "For your information," she said, "if we get married, we're going to go to Cancun or some other tropical paradise."

No stuffy museums or dank old churches. No unpronounceable food and a foreign language to contend with.

Yes, I thought, if Laura doesn't break his heart, she'll be a much better match for my ex-husband than I ever was.

"Another round, ladies?" I asked.

Chapter 46

Jess

Before you feel all righteous and file for divorce, ask yourself the following questions. Who helped take care of your dying mother? Who brings you flowers on the anniversary of your first date? Who maintains the boiler and cuts the lawn? If the answer to these and similar questions is, "My husband," you might want to put down those divorce papers, get into the kitchen, and make him a nice meal.

—*Appreciating What You Have: How to Avoid the Biggest Mistake of Your Life*

That damned little ping.

I closed the file I was working on—an outline of a course I was thinking about suggesting—clicked on GET NEW MESSAGES and there was the important news that someone felt I just must have at that very moment.

An offer for a new Viagra substitute.

I deleted the message.

Checking e-mail has become a daily ritual I dread. No matter the safeguards the university has installed, the spam gets through—ridiculous requests for financial help from dethroned African royalty; prescription drug deals that just can't be legitimate; mortgage offers that scream fraud.

Colleagues send long, boring jokes or forward photos of their kids' every action—first time on the potty, first taste of ice cream, first birthday party.

I dread the day my mother finally gets an e-mail account. I'm sure she'll be forwarding articles about women who've ruined their lives by making foolish choices. Just for my edification, of course.

In fact, I am so tired of e-mails that waste my time, and have become so used to speedily deleting messages without opening them, that I almost missed the interesting announcement that came in later that day from Professor Rivers of the European history department. This is how it began.

To Friends and Colleagues:
In the interest of truth and honest disclosure, Mary and I would like to confirm the rumors that we have separated and are in the process of negotiating a divorce.

Rumors? I'd heard no rumors, not even a ping.

It must, I thought, be a prank, an unkind joke played on poor Professor Rivers by an angry student upset with a bad grade. But a quick call to the department secretary—I felt I should alert Professor Rivers immediately—corrected my erroneous assumption.

"No," Nancy said. She sounded as bewildered as I felt. "No, he really is getting a divorce."

"Oh. Okay. It's just that I've never, uh, seen something like this. The e-mail, I mean."

I imagined Nancy shaking her coiffed head. "Don't ask me what this world is coming to because I just don't know."

That made two of us.

I hung up and read through the rest of the message.

Mary and I are parting amicably and with the greatest respect and admiration for each other. We have every intention of remaining close friends and supporting each other in future choices, relating both to career and personal happiness.

I shook my head. No doubt about it, the announcement read like the press releases celebrities issue when they've cheated on their wife or fiancée or when they're getting divorced or when they've been caught doing something really naughty, like breaking parole or punching a photographer. I wondered if Professor Rivers had written this announcement himself or had paid a professional PR person to write it. It certainly sounded nothing like the awkward academic language he was notorious for using.

I read on.

Mary and I ask for your understanding and support as we go through this most difficult of times. Thank you all.

I sat back, bewildered. Who did Professor Rivers think he was, Jude Law publicly apologizing to Sienna Miller for having sex with his kids' nanny? Brad Pitt and Jennifer Aniston asking their fans and the media for privacy in their time of pain? Renée Zellweger denying that her request for an annulment has anything to do with the character of her country-music-star husband?

If privacy was such a concern, I wondered, why issue the press release in the first place? Well, I know next to nothing about the nasty workings of Hollywood, but I suppose that old adage holds true: any publicity is good publicity.

But why was Professor Rivers, a lowly and by all accounts second-rate professor of European history, in need of publicity, especially of this kind? And why would he suppose that anyone would care about the personal trials of someone they barely knew, someone of no real interest to them at all?

I scrolled through the e-mail announcement again.

What was the etiquette in a case like this? Was I expected to respond to Professor Rivers's e-mail? And if so, what was I expected to say? Was I really expected to care? Was I expected to pretend to care?

Since when, I wondered, had the personal lives of the average Joe and Jane become fit subject matter for every other average Joe and Jane?

Oh. Right. Since the explosion of reality TV, of course.

And then I laughed out loud. Was Professor Rivers hoping for a TV contract? I could see it now: Real Life Divorces of the Middle Class and Unknown. Prime-time stuff for sure.

I wondered. Had divorce become the new must-have accessory?

Something that had once been hushed up and associated with shame had become so common, so ordinary that it seemed almost coveted. Couple Number One has a high-end condo, a Mercedes SUV, and a very public divorce. Couple Number Two has the condo and the SUV but not the divorce and are rumored to be jealous.

Ah, how the world has changed.

I forwarded the e-mail to Seth in case he hadn't yet received it. Of everyone I knew, he would most enjoy the absurdity of Professor Rivers's bid for fame.

Chapter 47

Nell

Never in a million years did you expect to be invited to your ex-husband's wedding. But the invitation is in hand and you're wondering what you should do. Stop wondering. Throw the invitation in the trash. His gesture is far more of a "Ha, ha!" than a "Isn't it nice we can be friends?"

—*Post Divorce: Tricky Situations and How to Handle Them with Aplomb*

"I said no!"

"Jesus Christ, Nell, you practically broke my nose!"

Brian stumbled into the dining table. I grabbed my blouse and held it against my chest. I tried not to think about what might have happened if Brian were a bit taller, a bit stronger.

"Good!" I cried.

I'd known Brian Kennedy for years. Richard and I had had dinner with Brian and his former wife several times. I'd seen him at parties and fundraisers. And not once had I suspected the ugly truth about him.

Fear and disbelief were rapidly being replaced by fury. I struggled not to throw something at him, a lamp or the phone or a kitchen knife.

"I should report you to the police," I spat.

Brian laughed and reached for his tie; he had tossed it on a side table. "They wouldn't believe you. I'm a respected citizen. People in this town know me, important people. They'd think you were out for my money."

It was probably true. Brian Kennedy was rich and powerful enough to be considered the target of a lonely, grasping woman. I felt sick to my stomach.

"You're right," I said. "They might not believe me. So I'm not going to report you. I'm going to do much more damage to you. I'm telling everyone I know, everyone we know, about your disgusting behavior. I'm going to blacken your reputation beyond recognition."

This time Brian gave me a look of amusement. "It won't matter. Enough women won't believe you. I know women. Some will think you're just angry because I wouldn't call you again. They'll go out with me."

I watched as Brian calmly buttoned his cuffs. I tried to comprehend this man.

"You really don't care that you're using violence to get sex, do you?"

Brian looked up at me. He took his suit jacket from the back of a chair.

"No," he said, "I don't. And enough women don't care, either. I've been around, Nell. You'd be surprised at what a man can get away with."

No, I thought. I wouldn't be surprised. I stopped being surprised when my husband told me that he's gay. He'd gotten away with twenty years of deception. And what had he gotten from me in return? Twenty years of devotion and two children.

"Get the hell out," I said. "Before I change my mind and call the police."

Brian turned away from me. He started for the front door. "You don't want your name dragged through the mud, Nell. I know your type."

This time I laughed. "You have no clue who I am, none. Get out."

Without looking back, Brian left.

I took a long hot shower, after which I poured a large shot of scotch, turned the living room lights low, and settled in my favorite chair. Richard had bought it for me early in our marriage. It was early nineteenth century, in good condition. I don't know how he afforded it at the time, but that was Richard. Always trying to make me happy.

Happy and protected.

I took a first sip of scotch and breathed deep.

From the age of nineteen when I started to date Richard, I'd been protected from the world of menacing men. Of course, all women are subject to crude remarks and gestures and possibly worse from men on the street. But not all women are subject to attempted date rape.

I was completely unprepared for the encounter with Brian Kennedy, stunned that someone would attempt to force me into sex, me, Nell Keats, intelligent, well educated, financially stable, mother of two.

It was an embarrassing admission to make to myself. I had made a terribly harmful assumption, one I never suspected I'd made, that victims of rape were somehow complicit in the crime. That victims were foolish or careless, that they teased men, led them on until . . .

I put my hand over my eyes in shame.

And then I realized that if it had happened to me, it must have happened to other women in my circle, other decent women. But why hadn't anyone spoken about Brian? Why hadn't I heard warnings? And was Brian the only one in our social circle abusing women, or were there others, many others?

I took another slow sip of the scotch and let it burn its way down my throat. The sensation felt good.

I wondered. Maybe Brian's other victims were scared of the nasty publicity exposing such a powerful man might bring. Maybe Brian had threatened or bribed other women into silence. Or maybe there had been talk about him, just not when I was in the room. Mrs. Richard Allard, happily married; there'd be no reason for her to know about a predator like Brian Kennedy.

I thought of Trina then and determined to ask her what she knew; I felt sure she knew more than most. And then I was going to ask why she hadn't warned me, single, available Nell Keats, to reject all offers from Brian Kennedy at the outset.

I got up, went into the kitchen, and poured another scotch. What did it matter if I got a little drunk? There was no place I had to be in the morning. No one was expecting me; no one needed me. I walked back to my favorite chair.

And I wondered. What sort of nerve did it take to completely ignore the pleas, the needs, the desires of another person? What was the thought process of such a predator?

And right then I recognized another stupid assumption I'd been holding for way too long, that rapists of any sort were drug addicts or murderers, young, uneducated men from bad neighborhoods. I'd never imagined them as middle-aged, well-educated, socially respectable men.

Suddenly, I felt like the most naive forty-two-year-old in the city of Boston.

Why was Brian the way he was?

Enough women would willingly have sex with a man who seemed smart and funny and successful. What sick need made Brian choose violence over love, even over passion?

There had to be an answer.

I wondered then if I had encountered evil for the first time. Brian was amoral; that was clear. Was amorality the human, earthly equivalent of evil? I'd never given much thought to the concept. There'd been no personal, compelling need to think about evil, not in my daily life, not outside of a college philosophy class.

Oh, Nell, I told myself, you have been a very, very lucky woman. No one, I thought, deserves such luck.

"I wanted to tell you in person, Nell."

Richard had asked me to meet him for lunch. I asked if Bob would be joining us. Richard said that no, he wouldn't. I accepted his invitation.

"Tell me what?" I asked when the waiter left with our lunch order. Oh, please, I thought, don't let him be sick. I scanned his face for signs of illness. But Richard looked almost robust, better than he'd looked for some time.

"Bob and I are getting married."

"Oh," I said. No beating around the bush for Richard.

I don't know why I was so surprised. Richard and Bob were in love. Wasn't marriage simply the next logical step in their relationship?

Richard cleared his throat. I noted a new pair of gold cuff-links. I wondered if they were a present from Bob.

"I know I can't expect you to be happy for us, for me . . ."

"No," I snapped, remembering Brian Kennedy, remembering the night I had found the love note from Bob, remembering the day I had first met Richard. "You can't."

"But I hope that in time you can be happy. For me and for Bob."

If I hadn't believed before that Richard was gay and in love with a man and that I was no longer his wife, I believed it in that moment. Finally, finally, the truth hit home in a way it hadn't yet hit home.

And it felt awful. The truth is awful.

I looked at Richard with a brittle smile. "I still find it hard to believe I lost out to a guy with a permanent five o'clock shadow."

Richard sighed. "Nellie, please don't be that way. It wasn't a contest; you didn't lose anything."

"Oh, yes, Richard," I said, "I most certainly did. I lost my identity. I lost my confidence. I lost you."

The waiter placed our lunch on the table and asked if we needed anything else. I shook my head and stared blindly at the salmon steak in front of me. When the waiter was gone, Richard leaned across the table.

"You didn't lose me," he said softly, "not entirely. You can have my friendship if you want it. You'll always have my love."

But not in the way I need it.

I looked up at the man who had taken my virginity all those years before. "Is this why you wanted the three of us to have lunch a few weeks ago?" I asked. "So I could get to know Bob? So the big news would somehow be easier to take?"

Richard sat back. "Yes."

"I suppose I should thank you for the effort. It didn't work, though."

"I'm sorry. Bob didn't think it would."

So, I'd been set up. The only one not in the know, the ignorant one. I'd been ambushed.

"Have you told the kids?" I asked.

Richard picked up his fork and put it down again.

"Of course not. I wanted you to be the first to know. I'll call them tonight."

"Okay. When? When's the big day?"

"The Saturday after Labor Day. You'll be invited, Nellie. And the children, of course."

What, I wondered absurdly, does one wear to the wedding of one's former spouse?

"I don't know if I can come," I said.

"Try."

"Maybe. Just don't expect anything of me."

"I don't," Richard whispered.

But what did I expect of Richard? And what did I expect of myself?

"I can't eat," I said. "I'm sorry."

"I'll get the check. I'll ask the waiter to pack up the food."

I could hardly murmur my thanks.

I spent another night alone in the dark with a glass of scotch. And I remembered.

Just after Richard had moved out, I'd asked him point-blank if he had ever been sexually attracted to me. He told me that yes, he had. He said that in the beginning it was fairly easy for him to kiss me and to touch me.

Fairly easy.

Sure. I was young and pretty and slim. How could I have repulsed anyone? I'm sure sex with me had been tolerable.

Tolerable.

It came to me just after that conversation that not once in my life had I been touched by a man with real desire. I hadn't dated much in high school, and the few fumbling efforts I'd endured didn't count. Those randy adolescents would have grabbed for any port in a storm, even a blow-up doll. Especially a blow-up doll as she's a one-time expense; you don't have to buy her sodas and burgers every time you want a little action.

It was an accident of fate that at forty-two I found myself single and doubting my ability to inspire passion in a man. Or was it? For a long time after Richard's confession, I couldn't help wondering if I lacked some essential quality that men needed in order to feel passionately about a woman.

And then came Oscar. But I wasn't in love with Oscar and he wasn't in love with me. At least, I didn't think we were in love with each other. What, I wondered, was love with passion like? That night, after my lunch with Richard, after he announced he was getting married, and as I sat alone in the dark, I seriously doubted I would ever know.

I got up from my chair, tossed the rest of the scotch down the kitchen sink, and called Jess. It was late and I woke her up but she said it was fine, that I'd been there for her often enough. I told her about the incident with Brian Kennedy. And then I told her about Richard and Bob.

"Are you going to be okay?" she asked gently. "I could come over and stay with you tonight."

"No," I said. "I'll be fine. Really. Thanks again for listening. I needed to hear a female voice. I've got all these male voices clamoring in my head."

"Male voices can be harsh. Good night, Nell."

I hung up the phone. And then I cried like I hadn't cried since the night of my parents' funeral.

Chapter 48

Laura

Your ten-year-old daughter thinks her father's girlfriend is prettier than you. Your best friend runs into your ex and the girlfriend at a party and tells you the girlfriend is a lot smarter than she looks. Your ex informs you his girlfriend owns a small chain of specialty cheese shops. Face it: the better woman won.

—*When You Just Can't Win: Accepting That You're Second Best*

"Matt and I have been talking about getting married just as soon as my divorce is final."

I'd stopped by Nell's apartment on the way home from work. She doesn't like when I just come by without calling, but I forget every time.

"But no ring yet?" she asked.

I looked at my naked finger. "No. But he'll propose. I just know he will."

Nell poured us each a glass of wine and we took them into the living room. Nell sat on a straight-backed chair. I sat in a corner of the couch. Its arms were high so you could really lean against them. I really needed to lean against something.

"Think about this carefully, Laura, please," my sister said. "You talk about your relationship with Matt like you're talking about hiring a new secretary at the office."

That bad? Well, Nell had become kind of dramatic since her divorce.

"I'm not stupid, Nell, in spite of what you think. I—"

"I don't think you're stupid."

Yes, you do. "Let me finish," I said. My sister has such a big mouth. "I know the reality. When I was fifteen, I was ripe and juicy and all the boys wanted a taste of me."

Nell cringed. "Fruit metaphors?"

My sister can be so annoying. "Anyway," I went on, "at twenty-five, I was cute and curvy and the boys were still pretty much crowding around. Now, I'm almost thirty-five. I mean, I'm still kind of sexy, but the cute part is long gone. And the crowds of boys? Ha. They're long gone, too. Now I'm lucky if I get a quick glance from some dumpy middle-aged guy in the T station."

Nell waved her hand dismissively. "Oh, come on, Laura. You're still adorable. You're—fine."

I took a sip of wine and wondered how many calories were in a whole glass. There couldn't be that many, right? Grapes were natural.

"Thanks, Nell," I said, "but I'm not buying it. At forty I'll have the body of a turnip. I'm built just like Mom; I can't help it. It's now or never for me. I have to get married again before it's too late and I've got that wide rear load of a middle-aged matron and the only thing a guy thinks of when he sees me is a pair of sensible white cotton underpants."

"You should have thought of that before dumping Duncan."

My sister always has to have the last word. Even when we were kids, she was so bossy.

"Thanks," I said. "You know, for reminding me of the huge mistake I made. Thanks for reminding me how badly I screwed up. Thanks a lot."

Nell shrugged. "Your butt will be uglier after a pregnancy, you know. Your whole body will change for the worse."

"Probably," I said, thinking of all the cottage-cheese thighs you see at the beach and how I'd always sworn I'd never have those thighs, but of how now I did. "But I'll have my baby. What's an ugly butt compared to a bundle of joy?"

"And a husband to pay the bundle's bills. Or child support once you get tired of the husband."

"I won't get tired of Matt," I said. I almost believed myself.

Nell's tone suddenly turned angry. "How can you know? No one can know anything for sure, other than that they're going to die."

"You're not in a very good mood," I said.

"Should I be?" Nell demanded. "My ex-husband, the love of my life, is getting remarried in a few months. Excuse me if I'm not jumping up and down with glee."

I looked closely at Nell, really closely, for the first time in a long time. She looked so sad.

"I'm sorry," I said, my voice breaking. "I'm really so sorry."

Nell shrugged and wiped a tear from the corner of her eye. "Don't be. No one ever said life was going to be easy."

No, I thought, finishing my glass of wine. They certainly didn't.

I couldn't sleep that night. There was too much on my mind, what with Nell being so unhappy and my body getting fat and all.

At eleven o'clock I watched the late local news. It was more of the same, some leak in a tunnel, some fight over a cop who shot into a rowdy crowd outside some bar after a ball game, a fire in one of the suburbs with a lot of old wooden houses. And then there was this segment about this little boy living in foster care. Every week the news ran this segment, about a different child, of course.

Usually, I just tuned out or went to the kitchen for a soda. But that night I had my soda already in my hand, so I found myself paying attention.

This little boy was two and very cute. He couldn't really speak for himself, of course, but the announcer talked about his personality and stuff he liked to do. She said he had a sister, five, in another foster home and that it would be great if someone would adopt them both. They showed a picture of the little girl. She wore glasses and looked very solemn, way too serious for a five-year-old.

When the segment ended, I didn't turn off the TV. I just sat there, thinking.

Maybe, just maybe, I had been too quick to dismiss the idea

of adoption. There were all those adorable babies and toddlers just begging to be taken home by some nice couple, or by some nice single person, someone with a lot of money for childcare or a live-in nanny.

Besides, some of the stuff I'd learned in that mommies-to-be class and from reading magazines was pretty scary and disgusting. Pregnancy wasn't all rosy glow and eating lots of ice cream. It was hard. And don't even get me started about childbirth!

Maybe, just maybe, it was all too hard for me?

No. I changed the channel. No more thoughts about adoption. I was going to get pregnant and have my own child and if all sorts of women could do it, women out in the fields of, you know, wherever, then why couldn't I?

Still.

If for some reason I couldn't get pregnant . . .

No. I changed the channel again. Nell had had no problem, so why should I? Okay, she had been in her early twenties when she had her children, but at thirty-four I wasn't exactly ancient! I wasn't exactly dried up.

Right?

I turned off the TV. In a kitchen drawer I found my phone book and flipped to the Ls. I'd gone to Nell's gynecologist once, a few years back. She was nice. Dr. Lakes. I left the open book by the phone. I'd call in the morning for an appointment. She would tell me that things were okay.

As long as she didn't try to fix me up with an eighty-year-old!

Chapter 49

Grace

The first thing to remember is that your kids will hate his kids and vice versa. There's nothing you can do about this but to let the kids figure it out. Over time the shoving matches will become less bloody and the sobbing will quiet down. Remember: this is your life, not theirs.

—*Introducing Your Kids to His: Let the Fireworks Begin*

"Let me help you with that."

Evan reached for the large cardboard box I was lugging across the room to a worktable.

"Oh," I said, "thanks. It's heavy, be careful."

I felt Evan's hands slip over mine and linger as he took the box from my arms. For a long moment we shared the burden and looked into each other's eyes. We spoke no words; none were necessary.

A slamming door brought us back to the moment. Probably one of the kids arriving early for class.

Evan smiled and took the box from me. I smiled back, a bit dizzy with desire.

Oh, yes. There was something happening between Evan and me. Now I knew for sure.

The message light was blinking.

I knew, somehow I knew before even playing the message, that it was from Simon. Things had been too quiet recently; my life had been going too nicely. It was time for Simon to enter with a flourish and wreck it all.

It was time for the old routine to revive.

I put down my bag and got a cold glass of water. I drank the whole thing before walking to the machine. I pressed the play-back button and Simon's harried voice was; in my apartment.

"Gracie, pick up! Pick up if you're there; this is important."

Wasn't it always?

"Oh, man, all right. Listen, Gracie. I'm locked out of my place. The idiot landlord changed the locks and I can't get my work; it's all in there, Gracie. I'm two lousy months behind on rent and he changes the freakin' locks."

I almost laughed. Simon's entire being was absurd.

"I need those paintings, Gracie. I'm supposed to start mounting them at the gallery on Thursday."

There was genuine panic in my ex-husband's voice. I almost enjoyed it. Almost.

"Gracie, you have to help me, you have to. I am royally screwed this time; everything's all fucked up."

I thought: Whose fault is that? Not yours, certainly. The land-lord's, the president's, the postman's, even my fault, but never yours.

"Call me at Rob's. My cell isn't working. Call me, Gracie."

That was the end. No please or thanks. Not that I was ex-pecting gratitude.

And then the full meaning of Simon's latest predicament hit me.

If I didn't help him, if I didn't come up with the money for rent, Simon's paintings would remain locked in the apartment. His show would be cancelled. Simon would never get another offer from Evan. Evan's reputation would suffer; he would lose money.

I went into the kitchen and poured another glass of water. In a cabinet I found an almost-empty bottle of aspirin. The expi-ration date was some time the year before, but I took two any-way. I felt the headache sneaking in like a cat burglar, swift and dark.

I didn't want Evan to suffer.

But if I did help Simon, if I did bail him out, would this time really be the end? I'd sworn, I'd promised myself not to ride to his rescue ever again, and here I was considering doing just that.

But it would be for Evan.

Save Simon, save Evan, save myself.

I stretched out on the couch; I tried to relax.

It was hopeless.

Chapter 50

Nell

It's a fine and noble thing to trust your husband to organize and manage your finances. Good luck to you. But it's a far smarter thing to hide as much money as you can against the day when he decides he's fallen in love with his secretary. Consider an offshore account, a strongbox buried under the rose bushes, even cash stashed in a place he'll never look, like the closet full of cleaning products.

— *A Penny Here and a Penny There: Planning for Your Single Future*

"I need some advice."

I laughed. Poor Grace. "Well," I said, "you've come to the right place. We three have made such huge successes with our lives, I'm sure we can be of some help."

"Oh, please," she said. "You guys are doing wonderfully. Unlike me, you seem to be able to keep your exes out of your lives."

We'd met for brunch at a popular spot in the South End. I don't particularly like the idea of brunch; it seems somehow renegade and disruptive to the day. But Saturday morning was the only time the four of us were free to meet, so I made the sacrifice.

"So, what's your problem?" I asked.

Grace told us about Simon's predicament and about the predicament in which it had landed her.

"Simon is the proverbial bad boy," she said finally. "I fell for him absolutely. And I kept taking him back and helping him financially because I believed in his work. I still believe in it. That's why I want the show to be a success."

"You didn't take him back because of love?" Jess asked. "Or because of sex?"

"Love, of course, for a while. But even after I fell out of love with him, I still believed in his talent."

"And?" I asked. "The sex?"

Grace laughed. "Honestly? The sex wasn't so great. Simon is very self-centered. It was usually about his pleasure. But for a long time I didn't mind that. Simon was somehow 'worth it.' Just being with him felt worth—I don't know, felt worth being ignored, mostly."

"I can't stand to be ignored," Jess said. "I don't mind being alone because there's no one around to ignore me. But if I'm with a man, I want him to know I'm there. And I want to know he knows I'm there."

"I agree. Now. But in the old days? Like my mother always told me, 'Grace, you're a pushover.'"

"Gee, thanks, Mom." I laughed. "Now, how about teaching me how not to be a pushover?"

"We never got that far in the conversation. My father would holler for something and off she'd scurry."

"Let's get back to your current problem," I suggested.

Grace considered before speaking. "I think the real question I have for myself is this. Can I ever have a real relationship with a real man if Simon's still in my life? Is it fair to Evan—or to whomever—to rush off to Simon's rescue every time he has a problem?"

"If you're really involved with Evan," I said, "you won't have the time to be at Simon's beck and call. I think the real question is, do you really and truly want to build something with Evan, knowing it will mean cutting Simon loose?"

"Yes," Grace said promptly. "I wasn't sure of my answer for a while, but now I am sure. I want an adult, healthy relationship. Hopefully I can make one with Evan. If not, I want to find another man, not a boy like Alfonse, not a leech like Simon."

"Talk to Evan," I said. "Tell him what it's been like between you and Simon. Avoid too many gory details, but make sure he understands you don't want to be Simon's mommy any longer. You want to be Evan's partner."

Jess nodded. "Right. Work this out together. You'll learn a lot about Evan and about yourself and about how you might function as a couple."

"I'm scared," Grace admitted.

"Of course you are," I said. "Most things really worth doing are hard and scary. It stinks but it's the truth. Like my having to deal with Richard's wedding."

"Is he still asking you to be there?" Laura asked. "Why doesn't he just take no for an answer?"

"Yes," I said, "he's still asking. It seems to mean a lot to him, but I'm just not sure I can handle watching him marry someone else."

"I thought you liked Bob," Jess said. "I thought you said he was nice."

Very nice and, according to Richard, also exciting.

"Oh, he is nice and I suppose I do like him. It's not about Bob. It's all about me."

"Have you seen Oscar again?" Jess asked.

I shook my head. "No. I haven't really been in the mood to socialize. Except with you all, of course, because with you I can be grumpy or dull and it doesn't matter."

"So, he's called?" Grace asked.

"Yes," I said. "He asked me to dinner last Saturday, but I lied and told him I already had plans. I suppose I should go out with him again. I did have a wonderful time that night."

"It might take your mind off the wedding," Grace suggested.

"By 'it,'" I asked, "do you mean sex?"

"Well, I meant the whole date, starting with dinner, but I suppose you could boil my meaning down to sex."

I grinned. "We shouldn't talk about sex with Laura being a virgin and all. It might upset her delicate sensibility."

"Ha, ha," Laura replied. "It's just that I'm not obsessed with sex the way you three are. I can do without it."

"She's master of her domain, all right," I said.

"How are things going with Matt?" Jess asked. "And I'm asking as a friend, sincerely."

"Fine."

"Just fine?" Grace asked.

"What? No matter what I say, Nell will make fun of it or twist it somehow to make me look bad or silly, so I'm just not going to say anything."

I shrugged. "Okay."

It took about thirty seconds before Laura burst out with: "This is so unfair! I wanted to ask Jess about Matt's family and now I have to wait until we're alone and—"

I raised my hand. "Laura, calm down. You have my word of honor, on our parents' graves, that I won't say a word. Really."

Laura eyed me with suspicion. I suppose she had a right to.

"On Mom and Dad's graves, Nell, remember."

I nodded. I didn't even say, "Okay."

Laura turned to Jess. "I guess I just want to know, you know, what to expect from Mr. and Mrs. Fromer. When I meet them, that is. Assuming I'll meet them someday. Like, are they nice?"

Admirably, Jess answered my sister's question without mockery. "Yes, Laura, they're nice. They are very average people, completely unpretentious. I can't say I ever found their conversation stimulating, but that's me."

Laura, I thought, will probably think they're rocket scientists.

My sister smiled and seemed relieved. "Okay, but do you think they'll like me? You know, assuming I meet them someday."

Jess looked to Grace for help.

"Well," Grace said, in her careful tone, "given their son has been through a divorce, I think you should be prepared for them to be a bit—cautious—in welcoming another woman into the family."

"But I'm nice!"

Grace considered. I stuck a nail in my palm to kill the grin dying to break out. Jess took a long sip of wine, no doubt to hide her own grin.

"You're very nice," Grace said then, ever the diplomat. "But that's not the point. Their son was hurt. They're going to want to reserve judgment on his new girlfriend until they get to know her some. It's very normal."

What isn't normal, I thought, is my sister wanting to marry someone she doesn't love, just to have a baby.

Laura frowned. "I want Matt's parents to like me. I want them to accept me."

"They will," Jess said. "Just be patient, Laura."

Patient? My sister? The woman who tossed her marriage in the garbage can without even taking the issue to therapy? Not happening.

"It's Matt's brother Mike you want to stay away from," I said.

Laura whipped her head around to me. "I thought you weren't going to say anything!"

"Don't be mad. I'm showing concern here. Jess said he's bad news."

"He's a bum," Jess confirmed. "He'll try to weasel money out of you the first time you meet, just to see what he can get away with. Don't give it to him. You'll never see it back."

Laura nodded. "Okay. I'll remember to stay far away."

I finished my glass of wine. Now, I thought, if only I could convince my sister to stay far away from Matt.

Chapter 51

Jess

Just because you were married once before doesn't mean you can't look fresh and beautiful on your second wedding day. Spend the money on a gown. No full skirts, short sleeves only if you work out regularly, and remember, white can be harsh but ivory is universally flattering.

—*Fashion Advice for the Second-Time Bride*

I slid the notebook toward me and opened to the next fresh page. Only five or six fresh pages remained. The writing had become a habit; the notebook went with me everywhere, even to the office. I began to write.

In the early days of a romance, how do you distinguish love from lust? Maybe you can't. Maybe they are inextricably bound together in a symbiotic relationship, each helping the other to survive.

There is nothing so energizing as desire, and nothing so exhausting. I need to feel desire. For me, desire isn't a luxury. Maybe if I'd never experienced it so intensely, I wouldn't be this way. You don't miss what you've never had. Right?

Have I ever really been in love?

Yes, I have been in love. And eventually love is distinguished from lust in that when you're in love, you want and need to look

*deeply into a man's eyes. You need his eyes to hold your own, you
need absolute connection—*

Absolute. The word made me stop for a moment and think.
What did I mean by absolute? Completeness, entirety, something undivided.

*I don't remember ever, not once, looking deeply into Matt's eyes
or wanting him to look deeply into mine. I do remember smiling
brightly and blandly, then looking away, and then, after a time,
avoiding even the sight of him walking through the room. That's
not love, it's—what? Disgust? Indifference? A combination of the
two, an impatience to be done with the person, to be alone again.
An irrational feeling? But are any feelings rational?*

*Yes, of course. Fear in the face of real, tangible danger. That's
understandable; it makes sense; it's about self-preservation, the
will to live.*

*But isn't the death of the spirit a real danger, if not a tangible
one?*

*Was I afraid while I was married to Matt, afraid that I had
signed a sort of death warrant by agreeing to live with him as his
wife? Afraid that if I kept my promise to love, honor, and cherish
him, I would destroy myself in the process?*

*Or is this convenient hindsight? Am I creating a reason in retro-
spect for the crime I committed, just trying to let myself off the hook,
just*

"Jess?"
I looked up, startled, and closed the notebook with a slap.
"Oh," I said to Seth. "Sorry. I didn't hear you come by."
"You okay?" Seth leaned against the door frame and crossed
his arms.
"Yeah. I am. Just—preoccupied." I slid the notebook away
and smiled.

"I just wanted to know if you've had lunch yet. I thought I'd run down to that new Chinese place for some takeout."

"Just give me one minute," I said. "I'll meet you by Tom's desk."

Seth went off to wait for me in the department's reception area. I slipped the notebook into my bag and, after a minute, followed.

"I've been keeping a sort of journal," I said. "I've been exploring what happened with Matt and me, trying to figure out the truth."

Nell didn't respond right away. Conversations over the phone are faulty. Hesitation makes the listener wonder if she's been heard. There are no facial expressions and body gestures to help her understand those words that are being spoken.

"Nell?"

"I heard you," she said. "I was just thinking. I think you have to be careful about journaling, or whatever it's called in professional circles."

I took a sip of the wine I'd poured earlier with my dinner and asked, "Why?"

"I'm sure that in some cases and maybe for a short time, writing about something big that's happened in your life can be productive. Maybe it can help you understand things, give you some insight into your motives, whatever."

I nodded to the kitchen sink. "Right," I said. "That's what I'm hoping, anyway."

Nell went on, "But I think that in other cases, or after a certain amount of time, journaling can result not in helping you move on but in keeping you tethered to the past. You know, sometimes rehashing a subject becomes a symptom of laziness or an unwillingness to let go. Not that I'm saying that's what's happening in your case," Nell added hastily. "Only you can answer that."

I felt a tiny rush of annoyance, self-defensiveness, but let it pass. It did, quickly.

"It sounds as if you've given this topic a lot of thought," I said. "Have you ever kept a journal? Have you ever used writing as a sort of therapy?"

"Once," Nell replied. "When the doctors thought I might have cancer. It helped. But that was a very different sort of situation from the one you're facing now."

"So, not when Richard left?"

"No. I didn't keep a journal, but I did fall into a sort of obsessive way of thinking about my troubles. It happens. It's not unusual, but it can really hurt you in the end."

I put down the empty glass of wine and wondered. Had I really learned anything from all the scribbling I'd done in the past weeks? I couldn't say for sure that I had.

"So," I said, "you see journaling as self-medicating? Something better left to the professionals?"

"It seems to me that talking to a professional counselor is a far more productive way to recover. If she suggests you keep a journal, fine. I imagine she'd offer guidelines to help make the exercise worth your while. Of course," Nell added with a small laugh, "if therapy isn't appealing, you could always talk to your friends."

"Which, of course, I've been doing for far too long," I replied.

"That's okay, we've all been talking obsessively about our lives. It's what friends do. People need perspective on their problems. People need advice, especially in times of crisis."

"Unless the advice is ridiculous," I said. "If you listened to Laura, you'd hold a grudge against Richard for the rest of your life."

"I learned long ago not to take advice from my sister. You have to carefully consider your sources."

I walked into the living room and sank into a chair. I suddenly felt very tired.

"So," I said, "what do you think was the key to your being able to move on? And don't say Trina or leather pants. It has to be something more powerful than gossip and cowhide."

Nell laughed. "It was. It is. The answer, Jess, is forgiveness. I had to forgive Richard in order to live. You, my friend, have to forgive yourself. It's that simple."

"It's that hard."

"Yes. But I know you, Jess. You're strong. You can do it. You've already begun the process."

"I slip back a lot."

"So do I," Nell admitted. "Right now I'm having a hard time remembering that I don't hate my ex-husband. But no path is perfectly straight. Lord, listen to me: I sound like some two-bit guru or a poorly written fortune stuffed into a cookie."

"Only a little bit. Look, Nell, thanks again for listening. And for the advice."

"So, you consider me a reliable source?"

"I do," I said. "Good night."

I went to bed soon after that. I didn't open the notebook. I thought a bit about forgiveness and what that really meant, and then I slept quite soundly.

Chapter 52

Nell

You know what they say—the third time's the charm. Don't be afraid to look fabulous on your wedding day. Take the time to have a facial and to have any unsightly growths removed. Practice posing for the camera in a way that minimizes the obviousness of your sagging chin. Consider a mother-of-the-bride gown as they are generally excellent in hiding the time-ravaged body.

—*Fashion Advice for the Third-Time Bride*

It was about ten o'clock in the evening. I was already in my nightgown and robe when the doorbell rang. I jumped when it did; no one I knew just stopped by unannounced, especially at night.

I pulled my robe tighter around me—an instinctual protective gesture, though what a fold of terrycloth would protect me from, I didn't know—and tiptoed to the door. I couldn't remember when I'd last had occasion to peer through the peephole. I felt a bit afraid to look.

"Who is it?" I demanded in a voice so aggressive I hardly recognized it as my own.

"Nell," a male voice, far less aggressive, answered, "it's me, Richard."

"Shit," I said. "Shit, shit, shit."

"Nell?"

I thought I heard a note of pleading in my ex-husband's voice. Good, I thought, let him plead. Let him stand in the hallway and plead for all the neighbors to hear.

"What do you want?" I shouted.

Richard hesitated a moment before answering. "Nell," he said, almost too softly for me to hear, "please open the door."

Now I hesitated a moment before answering. It wasn't lost on me that I was behaving badly, like a woman scorned; worse, like a bitchy teenaged cheerleader mad at her dumb jock of a boyfriend because he bought her the wrong color roses.

It wasn't lost on me, but I didn't much care. Still, I did have a reputation to maintain as a good neighbor, and having a public fight with my ex-husband wasn't going to help me maintain that reputation.

I unlocked the door and opened it partway.

Richard stood there in a rumpled trench coat. The collar of his shirt was half in and half out of the coat. He wore a beat-up pair of loafers. He looked sad, or maybe like he hadn't slept well, but I had no sympathy to give.

"What?" I asked.

"I had to see you, Nellie." Richard made a move to step forward but then didn't. "You haven't returned my calls. I know my announcement about the wedding must have come as a surprise and—"

"You don't know anything." I began to close the door. Now Richard stepped forward and put his hand against it.

"Please, Nellie," he said. "Please, can we talk about this?"

Suddenly, I felt tired, absolutely exhausted. If I couldn't spare myself, at least I could spare the neighbors this ugly little scene. I turned away from Richard, heard him follow, and then heard the door close quietly behind me.

I walked into the kitchen. It was my domain, always had been, since Richard and I were first married and I was learning to make chicken without killing us with salmonella. I turned back to face him and leaned against the concrete counter I had installed only months before I learned that Richard had a secret life.

Innocent times.

"Can I take off my coat?" Richard asked.

I shrugged.

Richard sighed and folded his coat over one of the stools at the counter.

"I'm sorry it's so late," he said. "I mean, I'm sorry that I came over so late."

"And unannounced."

Richard nodded, pulled out the stool on which he'd laid his coat, and sat.

"I suppose I should offer you something to drink," I said. The sudden thought of coffee or tea, even water, made my stomach flip. I remembered those first horrible weeks after I had found the note from Bob, Richard's lover. I remembered how I could hardly eat, how my clothes began to hang off me, how I only could sleep with the aid of a pill.

The memories made me feel angry all over again.

"Okay," I snapped, "so what do you have to say? I'm tired. I want to go to bed."

"Nell—"

"Wait," I interrupted, "let me guess. You feel bad and you want me to make you feel all better. Okay, you know what, Richard? I'm as happy as a clam for you and Bob. Okay? Feel better now?"

Richard shook his head. "No. I won't feel better until you do."

"Oh, pressure!" I laughed, shocked at the nastiness in my tone.

"I didn't mean it like that," Richard protested. "You know I didn't."

I walked around to the far side of the counter, putting a physical barrier between us. I stared hard at Richard; he looked away, toward the calendar hanging on the refrigerator door. I flashed on how when the kids were little, the fridge would be covered with their drawings and scribbles.

"You still feel guilty for lying to me," I said, "for cheating on me. And now you want to move on and marry your lover with a clean conscience and you want me to give that to you, but I can't, Richard. And even if I could, I'm not sure that I would."

Richard rubbed his forehead and looked back to me. "I do

still feel guilty," he said. "I probably always will. I know you can't absolve me of the guilt, but you can forgive me, Nellie. If you choose to. I thought you'd already started."

I remembered what I'd said to Jess just the other night, about forgiveness and how to move on in life you had to forgive if not entirely forget. But who was I to preach to anyone?

"You're asking too much from me," I said, and I heard my voice waver.

Richard didn't reply for a moment, and when he did finally speak, I heard something new in his voice, something stronger than I'd heard for over a year. "Maybe I am," he said. "Maybe I am asking too much of you, but Nell, maybe I've been asking too much of myself, too."

Richard stood abruptly and leaned over the counter toward me. His eyes were dark. I took a step back.

"I'm tired of apologizing and I'm tired of groveling, Nell. I can't do it anymore. I'm flawed, yes, and I made some big mistakes and I hurt you, but you know what, Nell? I have to live my own life, with or without your approval." Richard shook his head, then laughed. "You know," he said, "I shouldn't have come here tonight. I shouldn't have bothered you and I shouldn't have bothered myself, either. You're right. I'm asking too much all around."

Richard straightened and took a step away from the counter. An uncomfortable silence settled on us. Absurdly, I wondered if I was strong enough to knock him down. I wondered if I were brave enough to slap his handsome face.

And then the words just came, without forethought.

"God, I hate you."

Richard flinched as if I had indeed hit him physically.

And I felt sick. I ran to the sink and gagged but nothing came up. With shaking hands I wet a paper towel and held it to my face. There was a heavy silence behind me, Richard's damaged presence.

Finally, I turned back to my ex-husband, the father of my children, my first and only love. But I had nothing to say.

Slowly, Richard reached for his coat. I had, indeed, defeated him. Isn't that what I had wanted to do all along?

Richard slipped into the coat and then our eyes caught. And I realized that I'd never, ever seen him look as sad as he did right then, not even when I'd told him ten years earlier that I might have ovarian cancer.

Suddenly, he was no longer the enemy.

The tears came in a flood. I dashed around the counter. "Oh, Richard," I cried, "I'm so, so sorry."

Richard took a step forward and then we were in each other's arms. I hugged him so hard my arms hurt.

After a while—it felt like a long time—we pulled apart enough to look at each other. Naturally, as we'd done for over twenty years, we shared a tender kiss, the kiss of friends.

I was finally ready to let him go off into his new life, his real life.

"I still love you, Richard," I whispered. "How can I not?"

"And I still love you, Nellie," he said, his voice pleased.

"I'm glad."

"Will you come to the wedding?"

"I will."

"Thank you."

"But," I said, "I am not going to try to catch the bouquet."

Richard laughed and it was lovely to hear. "Fair enough."

Chapter 53

Laura

The cost of legally changing your name back to the one you were given at birth should be absorbed by your ex. After all, if it weren't for his philandering ways, you wouldn't be waiting in line at the DMV and posing for an unflattering passport photo.

—*It's His Responsibility: Getting Every Last Cent Out of the Bum*

"Laura, will you marry me?"

It can't be, I thought. It can't be, he wouldn't.

But it was. I know jewelry. It was definitely the same diamond he had given Jess when they'd gotten engaged.

Matt and I were sitting on my couch, side by side, knees touching. In his left hand he held an engagement ring, a brilliant-cut diamond flanked by six smaller diamonds, three on each side. The setting was yellow gold. The band was decorated with filigree.

I continued to stare at it.

Matt shifted a bit closer to me. "I know what you're thinking, Laura," he said. "But this diamond has been in my family for generations. I—I know you've seen it before, but the ring is entirely new. I sold the—other—setting and had this one made just for you."

I understood. I did, Matt's family and all, but still, it felt weird.

"It's fine," I said brightly. "I'm just surprised, that's all." I kissed Matt's cheek. "Yes," I said. "I'll marry you."

Matt hugged me. And then he started to kiss me. I felt my lips responding, but my mind was still on the ring. Maybe, I thought, Jess won't notice the diamond I'm wearing now used to belong to her. Maybe no one will notice and I won't have to tell anyone I'm wearing a recycled stone.

Matt's kissing got more intense and before long we were in my big bed. We had sex.

It was fine.

"Matt asked me to marry him."

I called my sister the next morning while Matt was out getting bagels. I felt weird. Empty. Like there was nothing left to look forward to.

"I'm assuming you said yes." Nell sounded sleepy. I wondered if she'd been out the night before with that Trina person.

"Yes."

"Well, congratulations are in order."

"Thanks."

Neither of us said anything for a moment.

"I thought you'd be happier," Nell said finally. "You're getting what you wanted."

What I wanted. Be careful of what you wish for. Was it too late to back out now?

"I am happy," I said. "Really. It's just . . ."

The teapot on the stove. Duncan had given it to me. It had a whistle that he couldn't stand but that I loved. He had endured its shrill sound for me.

"Just what?" Nell asked. "Say it."

I turned away from the stove. I walked into the living room.

"Look," I said, "I'll admit that it's not the perfect situation."

Nell laughed halfheartedly. "It's far from ideal. Marrying a man you don't love just to have his baby. Just to have your baby."

Matt's brown oxford shoes sat by the front door. His briefcase sat alongside it. It was also brown.

"Things could be worse," I said.

"Yes, they could. Matt could find out that you don't love him."

I laughed, though nothing at all was funny. "I'm not so sure he'd care. I'm not so sure Matt loves me. We're like—we're like two people doing each other a favor."

Nell sighed. "Please, Laura," she said, "please reconsider this."

I walked back into the kitchen. I took the butter out of the fridge. Matt would be back in a few minutes.

"You think," I said, "that I'm settling by marrying Matt."

Nell hesitated before answering. "Not settling. I think you're trying to negotiate. I think you're trying to distinguish what you really need from what you really want."

"Are they ever the same things?" I asked, though I didn't expect Nell to have the answer. "What you need and what you want?"

"Sure," she said. "I guess. I don't know. Maybe for some people. It's too early in the day for me to be philosophical."

I tossed the dregs of Matt's first cup of coffee in the sink.

"Will you support me in this?" I asked.

"Haven't I always supported you?"

"Well," I said, "not really. Mostly you've been nasty. Mostly you've made me feel like an idiot."

"I'm sorry, Laura. Really. From this point on you have my full support. I won't criticize or judge or say 'I told you so' if things don't work out."

Nell sounded genuine enough.

"Mom would be happy for me. Dad, too. Don't you think so, Nell?"

"Sure," she said. "I'm sure they would be happy for you."

I heard a key in the lock of the front door.

"Matt's here," I said. "I have to go."

Chapter 54

Grace

Every once in a great while you'll be introduced to a couple who have been married for fifty or sixty years. So what? Like staying together is such an accomplishment? Let them try going through the hell of a divorce and then you'll offer congratulations.
—*Married People: Friends or Foes?*

"Simon's locked out of his apartment."

I stood in Evan's office, just inside the door. Evan sat at his desk, legs crossed, a cup of coffee in his hand. "I see," he said.

"He hasn't paid his rent in two months."

Evan put down the cup, uncrossed his legs, and leaned forward over the desk.

"Let me guess. The paintings are inside."

I walked farther into the office and sat in one of the guest chairs. "How did you know?" I asked.

"I've heard stories. Everyone has."

Okay, I thought. Here we go. I looked steadily at Evan. "Then you know about me," I said.

Evan smiled. His expression was kind. "All I know," he said, "is that you went above and beyond the call of duty to help an artist create his work."

"Yes, well, that's a nice way of putting it."

And then I painted a broad-stroke picture for Evan of the

past seventeen years. The spending sprees, the cheating, the damaged furniture, the good and the less good work, the missed opportunities, the divorce, and its aftermath. Evan listened quietly and with sympathy.

"That's my sorry story," I said finally. I thought: How can you want someone like me?

"I'm very glad you told me," Evan said. He got up and came around to the front of the desk where I sat.

"Simon was very lucky to have your love."

I stood. "Was he?"

Evan reached for my hands. "Yes."

And then we kissed. It happened naturally and inevitably and it was wonderful.

And oh, I felt the burn.

"Simon, it's Grace. And Evan. Let us in."

Simon was holed up in his friend Rob's apartment. Techno music was blaring into the hallway.

Evan banged harder on the door. "Simon! Open up!"

The music shut off. "It's Grace, Simon," I called again.

Chains slid. Locks turned. Slowly, the door opened and Simon peered out from behind it.

I held out my hand.

"Here's the new key to your apartment. Your landlord gave it to us."

Simon came out from behind the door. A smile spread across his face. His hair, I noticed, needed cutting. He needed a shave. He snatched the key from my hand.

"Gracie, I knew you'd come through!"

He put out his arms. I took a step back into the hallway.

"No, Simon," I said, "I didn't come through."

Evan took my hand, squeezed it, then let it go. I was sure Simon didn't notice.

"What?" Simon said, scratching his stomach.

"I paid your back rent, Simon," Evan said. "And I'm taking it out of whatever sales the show brings. And if the sales don't cover it, I'm holding the paintings until they do sell."

I almost laughed. The look on Simon's face was priceless. I
don't think anyone had ever held him responsible for anything.

"Wait," he said, a trace of panic in his voice. "That's not in
my contract. That's totally bogus!"

I kept my mouth shut and let Evan do the talking.

"You're a good artist, Simon. I'm happy to be showing your
work. It's too close to the opening for me to cancel this show, so
I'm bailing you out. But I'm not a fool, and I won't bail you out
again. Understood?"

Simon looked downright sheepish. He nodded and mumbled something I thought was "yes." Was it really that easy to
control him?

Evan smiled. "Good. I'll see you tomorrow, Simon, as planned.
You remember our meeting?"

Simon nodded again. "Three o'clock."

"Excellent."

"Good-bye, Simon," I said.

And we walked away.

Chapter 55

Laura

It's a fact: unmarried women over the age of thirty-five make for the least desirable dinner guests. Their unattached status makes married women nervous and married men curious to learn if they can 'get some' without strings. The hostess is put upon to dig up a single male to even the numbers at her table. Finally, the never-married single woman can't participate in general conversation about topics that really matter, like your kids' tuition bill, their school plays, and their amazing feats on the soccer field.

—*The Single Woman as Social Pariah*

"**D**id I ever tell you that Richard tried to come back after he'd moved in with Bob? It was about two weeks after he'd moved out of our apartment."

I shook my head. "That's sad." And pathetic, I thought.

We were having dinner at one of my favorite restaurants. It's called Big Bowl and it's a chain, but the food is really good and the portions are huge. I had to drag Nell to Big Bowl kicking and screaming, and I get a feeling Jess and Grace aren't as into the giant nachos as I am, but I'm not going to some high-end restaurant, paying a fortune, and eating something I can't even pronounce.

"It is sad," Nell said. "He actually thought he could, I don't know, repress it all again, go back to being 'hetero'—or, at least, to being perceived as heterosexual."

"Poor Richard." Grace sighed. "It must have been a horrible time for him, and for Bob."

Poor Richard! Ha, I thought. He's not getting my sympathy.

And why should I care about Bob? "You told him no right away, right?" I asked my sister.

"Well," she said, "I have to admit the idea was tempting. For a split second I thought, sure, why not? We'll just go on the same way we've been going on for all these years. I'll have my best friend back as my roommate. And then I came to my senses."

"You did him a favor," Jess said, "by cutting him loose."

"Did I?" my sister said. "Did I help him by not letting him re-treat into his phony past? Maybe. It certainly wasn't my inten-tion. I hated him in those first days, really despised him. I lost my best friend and my husband in one fell swoop."

"It must have been awful," I said with passion. "It must still be awful."

Nell shook her head. "Actually, not so much anymore. I guess it's true that time does heal everything. At least, it dead-ens the pain somehow."

Yes. Time did do—something. I still dreamed about the crash that killed my parents, but only once or twice a week now. That was a big improvement.

I tuned back into the conversation. Nell said: "Can you imag-ine if Richard asks me to stand up for him!"

I was shocked. "You wouldn't say yes, would you?"

Nell laughed. "What a bizarre thing my life has become. I don't know if I could officially—release—him again. Signing the divorce papers was bad enough. I know he's no longer mine. I don't want to have to, I don't know, play out the act of severing again."

"He'll always be yours in some way," Jess said. "Your first love, the father of your children. You and Richard and Colin and Clara will always be a family."

"How disgustingly sentimental you've gotten."

"Sorry." Jess shrugged. "I'm just trying to help."

"And I do appreciate it, really. Thank you."

"I wonder if they'll register?" I said. I for one was looking forward to my own second registry. There were so many things I wanted, like a set of fancy dishes, maybe with gold trim, and some Waterford crystal, and maybe even a new vacuum.

"Maybe," Nell said. "Richard left without a lot of the things he'd bought over the years. His stereo, his projection TV. I didn't want them—I still don't—but he insisted I keep all the accoutrements of a successful house. I don't know what Bob brought to their place. I don't know what they've bought together."

"So, do you think we'll all be invited to the wedding?" Grace asked.

"Oh, yes. I told Richard it would be easier for me to be there if my friends were there, too. I'm bringing Trina as my date, by the way."

"Well," I said, "I'm not going!"

Nell gave me one of her annoying looks. "Fine. You can explain to your niece and nephew that you hate their father. I'm sure they'll love to hear it."

"I'm trying to be loyal to my sister!" I protested.

"Then don't cause further strife for my family."

Jess raised her eyebrows at me. Everybody has an opinion!

"All right, all right," I said, "I'll go for the children's sakes. But I won't enjoy myself."

"Fine. Just show up and behave. And make sure Matt behaves, too."

Right. Matt. My fiancé. Of course he'd be my date to Richard's wedding. Of course Jess would be there, too.

I slipped my hand under the table. No point in causing trouble.

Did Jess recognize the stone? The setting was so different from the one Matt had given her. Mine was yellow gold; Jess's had been platinum. Mine was kind of busy and old fashioned. Jess's had been very simple and contemporary.

"So," Jess said, "I assume from the rock you're trying to hide from me that you and Matt are, at long last, intimate."

I nodded, embarrassed, and put my hand back on the table. Why had I ever opened my big mouth about my personal life?

My sister shot a scolding look at Jess. Sometimes, not often, she comes to my rescue. "So, when's the big day?" she asked.

"Some time early next year," I said. "I'm still shopping around for venues."

"You'll be a winter bride," Grace said.

Yes, I thought, a winter bride. And maybe I'd buy a dress trimmed in white fur! Maybe I'd wear a white velvet cape with a hood and carry all white flowers.

"Are you going to do a big event?" Grace asked. "Bridesmaids and a sit-down dinner and a three-piece band?"

"Isn't that a bit much for a second wedding?" Nell asked.

"Not these days," Grace told Nell. "It's common for third- and fourth-time brides to stage elaborate weddings. There seems to be no embarrassment about remarrying with all the fanfare. The first wedding is conveniently forgotten."

"Who pays for all these big weddings?" Jess said. "Do people really have that much money, or is every new couple in debt for years to come?"

I nodded. "I've been checking out photographers, and you wouldn't believe how expensive they are!"

"But photos of the big day are worth it." Nell shook her head. "What am I saying? They're only worth something if the marriage lasts. After Richard left, I put my wedding album at the back of the closet. Do you know our official portrait had been in a frame on my dresser for over twenty years? When I put it away with the album, the whole bedroom looked alien."

"Simon and I didn't have official pictures taken," Grace said. "Some of our friends took snapshots. I have only a few; Simon spilled red wine on most of them one night when he was drunk. Honestly, I never look at the photos. I'm not even sure where they are at this point."

"I know exactly where my album is. I look at it every week or so and I try to figure out what went wrong, as if somehow the pictures will provide a clue as to—" Jess turned to me. "I'm sorry, Laura. This must be uncomfortable for you, listening to me talking about my marriage to Matt."

"Yes," I said. I realized again there would be a lifetime of un-comfortable moments between me and Jess.

"This is what I want to know," Nell said suddenly. "Does a divorce invalidate all that went before? Does what happens now change what happened in the past? Is my history irrevocably altered by what happened last week or last month?"

"Your perception is definitely altered," Jess said. "But the reality itself? I think it's one of those unanswerable questions. You know, on the order of 'if a tree falls in the forest and there's no one there to hear it, does it make a sound?'"

Nell nodded. "Okay. But I have to at least try to answer it. What if I learn that what I thought was true wasn't really true. Do you see what I mean? Maybe I was happy with Richard because I thought he was happy with me, but if I find out he wasn't actually happy—was I actually happy?"

No one said anything. Really, what did Nell expect us to say? Talking about the past always causes trouble. Stupid Nell! Now I couldn't stop thinking about Duncan!

All those years together. I wondered: What are you supposed to do with the memories? Where are you supposed to put them?

Grace cleared her throat. "I'd like to talk about the present for a minute."

"Yes, please!" I said.

Grace told us that she'd talked to Evan about her relationship with Simon. And that Evan had bailed Simon out for one time only. And that she and Evan had finally kissed.

"It was a wonderful first kiss, really," she said, "the kind you remember, the kind you still feel days later."

"Wow." Jess sighed. "I'm jealous. I wonder if I'll ever have one of those magical first kisses ever again."

Grace grabbed Jess's hand. "Oh, Jess, of course you will!"

She might not, I thought. My first kiss with Matt was okay but nothing special. And that was my last first kiss. Suddenly, I felt very sad. Would I feel any happier after the wedding? I pushed the worry away. Besides, what's so great about happiness?

"And Evan was great with Simon," Grace was saying. "He stood up to him, and I don't know why, but Simon seemed to listen. Who knows? Maybe next month he'll screw up again, but he won't be my problem or Evan's."

"Congratulations," Nell said. She raised her glass. "To Grace, who really, finally cut the cord."

"To Grace!" Jess echoed.

Slowly, I raised my glass. At least one of us was in love.

Chapter 56

Jess

Particularly if you have children, there might come a time when you are in the position of having to introduce your ex-husband to your current partner. Say your ex shows up early for his afternoon with the kids and your partner answers the door. Keep your cool. Be polite and resist the temptation to tell your ex you're having better sex than you ever had with him.

—*Keeping the Peace: We Live in a Civilization*

"Heads up!"

I ducked in my beach chair. What was flying at me now? A wild Frisbee, a kite out of control, a bocce ball accidentally lobbed too high?

"Sorry about that."

I looked up to see a teenaged boy bending down to retrieve a large plastic ring.

"That's okay," I said as he trotted back to his buddy. For half a second I wondered if I should point out that he was playing a beach game in the zone restricted for sunbathers, but it was far too nice a day to be grumpy.

A perfect summer day at the beach.

I looked out over the water and thought again about the last time I'd been on Ogunquit Beach, the day the water was so blue and calm, the day the pink beach ball drifted along lazily. The day I somehow knew I would be divorced from Matt.

Strange, how life works.

My meditative thoughts were interrupted by a caravan slog-

ging past me under the awkward weight of chairs and bags and
coolers and umbrellas. The caravan consisted of a balding father,
an overweight mother, a moody, reluctant adolescent daughter,
and a blissfully oblivious younger brother.

I smiled. Unlike seasoned beachgoers who pack their
gear neatly into nifty little carts and wagons, this family
looked like they had stumbled into foreign territory. I
hoped they didn't mind sand in their ham and cheese sand-
wiches. Suddenly, the father let out a curse; seems he'd
stepped on a broken shell. The daughter rolled her eyes.
The mother ignored her hobbling husband's accusatory
whines. The young boy dashed past them all and into the
wide tide pool.

And I hoped the McFamily settled far away from me. A nasty
argument was sure to erupt before long. These four people did
not want to be with each other.

Just then, being alone seemed like heaven.

Still, on the drive up to Ogunquit I had experienced a brief
stab of loneliness, followed by a wee bout of self-pity. I found
myself imagining the assumptions people might make at the
sight of an adult woman all by her lonesome.

"How sad. That poor woman must have no friends."

"Just look at her all alone. Poor thing, she must be so
lonely."

"Mommy, why is that lady all by herself?"

"Don't stare, Timmy. She might be crazy."

Sometimes I can be so morbidly self-centered. Well, I suppose we all have our moments.

The McFamily finally settled near another disheveled group
that included a grandmother and possibly an aunt or two.
Aside from an older man whose toasty skin color betrayed him
as a professional sun worshipper, I was the only person in view
without a companion.

But did a companion ensure companionship? No, it certainly did not.

Consider the couple with the matching beach towels. The
woman was reading a big, fat paperback novel. The man was

sleeping, his legs sprawled and his mouth open. He let out a ferocious snore and I felt a moment of sympathy for the woman, though she didn't so much as flinch.

Consider the couple with the bright yellow umbrella. She was listening to something—music, a talk show—on an iPod, earphones blocking the sounds of her children's whoops and cries. The man was twisting the dials of a transistor radio that must have been forty years old, that or a good reproduction of an old machine.

Consider the couple that had brought their gear in a little red wagon, or the three girls in bikinis, or the two older women in floral print one-piece bathing suits. Each of these people was talking on a cell phone.

Not one person in sight was having a conversation with the person next to them.

"Heads up!"

I ducked again. It was the same teenaged boy, retrieving the same plastic ring.

"Sorry," he said again.

"That's okay," I said. "Have a nice day."

Yes, I thought, it's okay to be alone.

"Another round of oysters?"

I laughed and held up my hand. "God, no! A dozen is my limit."

The bartender smiled. "I love those Malpecs, man. Can't get enough of them."

I'd stopped into a restaurant in Perkins Cove for a light dinner before the drive back to Boston. The view from the upstairs bar was spectacular. I felt utterly relaxed, if a bit sandy.

I ordered another glass of wine and was considering the mixed berry dessert when a man in chinos and a dress shirt opened at the neck sat on the stool next to mine.

"Hi," he said.

"Hi," I said back.

We smiled. I liked his face. He ordered a dozen oysters and a glass of the same Pinot Grigio I was drinking.

The bartender nodded at me. "You two know each other?"

The man looked puzzled.

"We ordered the exact same thing," I explained.

The man smiled again. "Ah, great minds and all. I'm Nick, by the way."

I introduced myself. Nick told me he was a real estate agent with a large local group. I told him I taught sociology at Northeastern. From there, the conversation rambled along nicely.

"I really should be heading out," I said finally. "It's about an hour and a half to Boston."

Nick reached for his wallet. "Me, too. I've got an early showing tomorrow." Then he turned completely in his seat so that we were face-to-face.

"I suppose we should consider each other geographically undesirable," he said, "you living in Boston and me living in South Berwick."

I laughed. "I've never even heard of South Berwick."

"It's not far from here. It's south, close to the New Hampshire line."

"Oh."

"That means nothing to you, does it?"

"Well, I do drive through New Hampshire to get to Maine. So I know where the state line is. But beyond that . . ."

"A New Hampshire virgin. Have you ever been to Portsmouth?"

"I confess that I have not."

"Ah," Nick said, "here's a perfect opening for my big question! Would you be interested in getting together some time? I could show you Portsmouth, or some of southern Maine. Unless you're really opposed to dating someone from where life is the way it should be."

I laughed. "I'm not opposed to Mainers on principle. How do you feel about Bostonians?"

"I'm neutral. You seem nice but I don't care for the mayor."

"What about the Red Sox?" I asked.

Nick put his hand over his heart. "They're my gods."

"Sure," I said, keeping to myself the fact that I don't care one way or another about sports. "Let's get together some time."

Nick walked me to my car and waved as I drove off.

Yes, I thought, it's also okay to be with someone.

Chapter 57

Nell

In matters of love it is best to follow your instinct. In the matter of marriage, however, it is best to follow your reason. Sure, he may make your heart flutter and your blood race, but is he on a solid career track? Can he support you in the style to which you would like to become accustomed? If the answer is no, sleep with him and move on.

—The Business of Marriage: Choosing Your Partner Wisely

"The men here, darling, are a sorry bunch. You see that one over there, by the ice sculpture?"

Trina and I had stopped by a party being held in one of the MFA's large galleries. I wasn't really in the mood for a formal event, but Trina had enticed me with the notion of dinner afterward at a new restaurant at which it was almost impossible to get reservations. Of course, Trina, with all her connections, pulled off a table for two at nine.

"The one standing with the woman with a puff of white hair?" I asked. "I don't think I've ever seen hair that—round."

"That's his wife," Trina said with a little snort. "A pathetic little thing, really. Anyway, I slept with him last year. Was it in the spring or the summer? I can't remember exactly, but I do remember being bored almost to death."

"Why?" I asked, stunned. "Why did you sleep with him? He looks old enough to be your much older father. What did you see in him?"

Trina shook her head at me as if to say, "Will this woman never learn?"

"Well?" I asked.

"He's fabulously wealthy, Nell. And looks have been known to be deceiving." Trina sighed and looked in the direction of the cheating husband again. "Unfortunately, not in Stanley's case. Well, I might have expected it. At some point most married men lose the no doubt little sexual skill they had in the first place. Years and years of sex with the same woman dulls their instincts."

Did it? I realized I wouldn't know. I'd never had years and years of sex with anybody, not even myself. Sex was still a largely foreign territory.

"Still," Trina went on, "a certain few married men don't lose their capacity to please. You might consider having an affair with Dan Collins, for example. I've heard good things about his prowess in the boudoir."

After months of knowing Trina, she still had the ability to shock me.

"I can't have an affair with a married man!" I whispered, though there was no one close enough to eavesdrop. "Especially not after what I've been through with Richard. It's so horrible to be the one cheated on. I just couldn't do to some other woman what Richard did to me."

Trina sighed. "Yes, Nell, that's very nice of you, but you're assuming the wife cares about her husband and what he does when she's not around. There are plenty of wives in this town, in every town, who are more than happy to turn a blind eye to their husbands' infidelities. As long as he comes home eventually and continues to pay the bills, he's allowed to have his fun on the side."

I glanced around the room. The women were well and expensively dressed. Their voices were low and modulated. No doubt they had beautiful homes and vacationed on Nantucket. But how many of these wealthy, pampered women lived lives of quiet desperation?

"I can't imagine being that sort of woman," I said. "It sounds like such a painful and lonely life."

A waiter glided up with a tray of champagne and we exchanged our empty glasses for full ones. When she had glided off, Trina touched her glass to mine.

"You can't imagine being that sort of woman," she said, "because you lived with a man you loved. Don't assume all wives love their husbands. For any number of reasons they might welcome their husbands' attention otherwise directed."

"I suppose," I said. "It just seems so horribly sad, so wasteful. Why would a woman rather settle for a loveless marriage than look for happiness?"

Trina laughed lightly. "Dear Nell. Again you're assuming the wives of whom we speak are unhappy with their lot. One hopes—and suspects—that they are having their fun on the side, too. Take Catherine Harrington, for example. See her standing by the huge floral treatment in that appalling green dress?"

I nodded. The dress really was appalling. How had I not noticed it before?

"She's been married for almost twenty-five years and for the last five has been madly in love—and involved—with her doctor. Her husband goes his way and Catherine goes hers. She has her cake, darling Nell, and she's eating it too, passion with one man and financial stability with another. One really could be envious."

One could be envious or one could feel slightly ill.

"The sanctity of marriage. What a joke."

Trina drained her glass of champagne. "Marriage is what you make it," she said. "It's not inherently good or bad. Really, I wish morality would be eliminated from the notion of marriage."

"Then why get married in the first place," I argued, "if there's no moral imperative to remain faithful?"

"Financial reasons, darling Nell. Companionship. Social acceptance. As marriage was in the beginning, it is now and ever shall be. Human nature without end, Amen."

"Doesn't anyone play by the rules anymore?" I asked foolishly.

"No one ever really did, darling Nell. Ah, here comes our waiter. I am parched."

I didn't believe that, of course, that nobody had ever played by the rules. It was just Trina overstating her case again. Consider my parents. Neither had ever cheated on the other. I didn't know that for a fact—I'd never asked them such a bold question—but I knew they were faithful to each other the way I knew . . .

I took the offered glass of champagne.

The way I knew what? The way I knew that Richard was faithful to me? Until, of course, the night I learned that I knew nothing at all.

I turned to Trina. "You were married to Miles when you had sex with that old man, Stanley. Do you always have affairs while you're married?"

"Of course," she said, as if again surprised I'd ask such a silly question. "How else am I supposed to entertain myself? How else am I supposed to find my next husband?"

Of course. Always looking to improve on the current situation. The grass is always greener.

A thought suddenly occurred to me.

"What happens if a husband cheats on you?" I asked. "What happens if he falls in love with someone and wants a divorce? What happens if he discovers you're having an affair and throws you out?"

I thought I saw a flicker of something dark, fear maybe or suspicion, cross Trina's face. I might have imagined it.

"None of those scenarios has played out yet," she replied briskly, "but I daresay any of them are within the realm of possibility. But as long as I have a good lawyer—and I do—I'm sure I will be just fine."

"You might be just fine, but how will you feel?" I pressed.

Now I thought I detected a flicker of annoyance dash across Trina's unlined face. "Nell, darling, I appreciate your concern, if that's what this is, but I assure you I will feel fine, too."

"You never know how you're going to feel until you feel it," I told her. "Trust me, Trina. Everyone underestimates or overestimates her emotional capacities. I certainly had no clue as to my own strengths and weaknesses until Richard and I divorced."

Trina studied me for a long moment. I didn't look away. I wondered what she was seeing. Finally, she said: "There's a lot more to you, Nell, than there is to me. You're sensitive. I simply am not."

I studied the woman I had begun to consider a friend in return. "Yes," I said after a long moment, "I don't believe that you are."

Chapter 58

Laura

If you find your interest in your spouse waning over time, don't despair and waste money on a therapist. Everyone gets bored with the same old same old. Recall that old adage: Familiarity breeds contempt. Watch the great actors of our time and take notes on how to fake it.

—*101 Tricks to Help You Survive the Inevitable Decline of Love*

"None of those weird names. I can't stand that."

"Oh," I said, "I agree."

Matt and I were at his new condo in Charlestown. He liked us to be there rather than at my apartment. He thought it was too small, and he didn't like sleeping in a bed where another man had slept with me. It made him feel bad, he said; it made him remember that his wife had had sex with another man.

I didn't ask Matt how many other women had slept in his bed, after Jess and before me. In any case it was different; those women hadn't been his wives, so I really didn't care.

Anyway, we were talking about baby names.

"What about family names?" I asked. "You know, like people name their child after their grandmother's maiden name or something. Like, I don't know, Finnerty."

Matt made a face. "Finnerty? As a first name? It sounds ridiculous."

I kind of liked it; it was my mother's mother's maiden name. But with Matt I was all about keeping things calm and happy.

"Well, okay," I said, "maybe that's not a good example. But, well, how about Keats? In honor of my parents."

Matt sighed. "Laura," he said, "I don't want to be difficult here, but Keats is a last name. Keats Fromer? It sounds—it sounds stupid. Even stupider than Finnerty Fromer."

"Oh."

"Do you want a soda or something?" he asked. I shook my head. Matt walked to the kitchen. I noticed the very top of his head was just beginning to go bald.

Matt came back from the kitchen with a Diet Coke and slumped back on the couch.

"What about your parents' first names?" he asked. "What were they again?"

I felt the sting of tears. I'd told Matt like a million times. How could he have forgotten?

"Mary and Lucas," I said, and it was really hard not to scold him.

Matt nodded and took a sip of his soda. "Oh," he said finally. "You know, here's another option. Your diamond originally belonged to my great-grandmother Alice. That's a nice name, don't you think?"

My daughter was going to be named Alice.

"What if we have a boy?" I asked dully.

Matt scooted to the edge of the couch, excited. "Here's the beauty of it," he said. "My great-grandmother's last name was Alexander! We could name a boy Alexander and call him Alex. It's perfect. Even better, if we have a boy and a girl we have Alice Alexander all over again!"

I forced a smile. "Okay. That sounds good."

Matt beamed; at that moment he looked about twelve. It annoyed me for some reason.

"Wow, Laura," he said, "I am so glad we're on the same page with this!"

"Me, too."

"And I was thinking," he went on. "I was thinking that I really want our son to play football. Now, before you say anything, just hear me out."

I wasn't going to protest. There was no point.

"Okay," I said.

Matt drained his soda before going on. "I know the moms don't like the idea of their boys playing football, but trust me, it's no more dangerous than soccer, and every mom these days wants their kids to play soccer. I want our son to be an all-American kid, a football and apple pie sort of kid, you know?"

I nodded and Matt talked on. And I wondered if he really knew that I, Laura Keats, was in the room with him, listening to his plans for his children. I suddenly had the feeling that any woman could be sitting in this chair, any woman of childbearing age, tall or short, dark or light, it wouldn't matter because in the end, all Matt really wanted now was a family.

Any woman would do.

Matt, I realized, was using me as totally as I was using him.

When Matt had gone to bed, I went online—he has a home office that's really mostly a shrine to football—and started to research local suburban school systems. This was the sort of information you couldn't find in a phone book; since leaving Duncan, I'd become a bit better at the computer.

Winchester. Brookline. Marblehead. Cape Point.

Yes, Cape Point looked very nice, a great place to raise children. A good school system, beautiful houses, a country club, some pretty white churches. (Even though I don't go to church, it would be nice to have a pretty one nearby.) The only problem was that it was pretty far from downtown Boston. I estimated that it would take about two hours to get into the city on a weekday morning, and two hours to get back home.

I wondered: Was that too far for Matt to commute to work every day?

I looked again at the house. By the time we were ready to buy something, this particular house would be sold. But I bet there would be another just like it in the area.

Four bedrooms; two full baths and one half bath; a finished basement—maybe I could get a Ping-Pong table!; a big back-yard where I could have Matt set up swings and a jungle gym

and maybe even an above-ground pool—and of course, a bar-
becue; a living room; a dining room—I was glad I'd registered
for so much new stuff, including a set of fancy china!; a totally
renovated kitchen, which meant I'd have to learn to cook more
than pasta, but being a stay-at-home mom, I'd have lots of time
to learn, right?

Best of all, the house had a fireplace, a real stone fireplace
with a mantel where I could put pictures of my mother and father and my children!

And I decided right then, thinking about that fireplace, that
I didn't really care if Matt had to commute a total of four hours
to work five days a week. He was getting the baby names he
wanted. Fine. Then I was going to get the house and the loca-
tion I wanted.

I thought it was a fair enough trade-off.

Chapter 59

Grace

Your parents can't accept the fact that your marriage is over. As often as you assure them that a divorce is the right thing, they just can't believe a woman would willingly end her marriage. Deal with it. And know that by the time your own daughter gets her first divorce, it will be the norm.

—*The History of Divorce: From Aberration to the Norm*

"So, you really don't know where he is?"

I sighed and looked at the clock. This fruitless conversation had been going on for almost five full minutes, interrupting me just as I was about to attempt a small exercise using the cobalt violet paint I'd bought the day I met Alfonse.

Jake, one of Simon's longtime buddies and a fellow artist, couldn't seem to understand that I was no longer Simon's keeper.

"No, Jake," I said into the phone. "I told you already, I don't know where he is. I'm assuming he's at his apartment. Have you tried him there?"

"Yeah, I practically broke down his door knocking. And he's not answering his cell."

Probably because he lost it, I thought. It's probably lying on the sidewalk somewhere.

"Oh," I said.

"Aren't you worried?" Jake demanded.

"No," I said. "I'm not." Not anymore.

"But you know how he gets."

Yes, I know. Better than anyone, I know.

"Jake, Simon's just not my problem anymore. Why don't you call his girlfriend, Jane somebody-or-other?"

Jake snorted. "Jane's history. Last time I talked to Simon, he was with some chick named Bella. He told me she's into voodoo."

Of course she was. "Then why don't you call her?" I said, hoping Jake would hear the impatience in my voice. "Maybe she can, I don't know, do some magic and find him."

Unless he's right there in her apartment, eating her food, and splashing red paint on her walls.

"I don't know where she lives," Jake said. "I'm not even sure she has a last name."

I sighed heavily. "Look, Jake, I don't know what you want me to do. I haven't heard from him in weeks. I really can't help you."

It was a moment before Jake responded. When he did, his tone was reproachful.

"You know, Grace," he said, "Kara and I thought you and Simon would be together forever. I mean, I know you guys have been divorced for years now, but still. I've got to say it's hard to deal with your just cutting him off like this."

"Life is full of surprises, Jake," I said testily. "I really have to go. Say hi to Kara for me."

I hung up before Jake could further scold me for taking back my life.

I looked again at the clock. I was meeting Evan for dinner at seven. There was a little over an hour to get ready. I went into my bedroom to choose an outfit.

Simon would surface. Or he wouldn't. Evan was in possession of the paintings: they were locked away in the gallery's storage vault. Simon's presence at the opening wasn't necessary.

I inspected a new blouse I'd bought just the day before. It was a bit of a splurge, but I felt no guilt about the purchase.

I felt no guilt about anything.

* * *

"You look lovely in that blouse."

I felt myself blush. This is what Evan did to me: a simple compliment and I felt as if it were the first I'd ever received.

"Thank you," I said.

Simon never noticed what I wore. He never noticed anything specific about me. I'd come out of the shower, hair plastered to my head and dripping water all over the bathmat, and Simon would look right at me and ask: "Did you take a shower yet?"

"Grace?"

I blushed again. "Oh, I'm sorry," I said. "Was I staring at you?"

"It felt more like gazing. But I don't mind at all."

The conversation went like that all through dinner. We both knew that night was the night, though it hadn't been openly discussed. But that's the way things were with Evan and me; increasingly we were living our lives in synch.

"You've hardly touched your food," Evan said.

"Oh," I said. "Right." I realized I was holding my fork and knife over the plate. I cut into the piece of chicken.

Oh, yes. Romance over thirty-five induced lunacy. I felt thoroughly addled, eager to be alone with Evan and yet almost scared, too.

I took a bite of the chicken and chewed. Since when, I wondered, had sex become so important, so full of meaning?

Since Evan had come into my life.

We finished our dinners and opted to pass on coffee and dessert, which was fine because my stomach was a riot of butterflies, and even the relatively bland chicken dish I'd eaten wasn't sitting too easily.

Hand in hand we walked back to my apartment. With my free hand I held on to Evan's arm. I wanted to touch all of him.

We reached my building and I suddenly remembered the first night Alfonse had walked me home. Oh, I thought, Evan is so much more right.

No more boys, Grace. It's time for a man.

"I want to kiss you," I whispered up to Evan.

He lowered his lips to mine and we kissed, slow and long. Finally, still holding me close, Evan said, "Grace, may I come inside?"

"No," I said definitely. My apartment was thick with memories of Simon. I wanted to start fresh with Evan. "I'd rather go to your place. If that's all right."

Evan smiled and kissed me again. "It's perfect," he said. "Let's grab a cab."

I'd never been to Evan's apartment before. I wasn't at all surprised by what I found there—lots of art, of course, all beautifully hung; clean Danish modern furniture with the occasional Asian accessory; a well-appointed kitchen with sleek metal fixtures.

And the apartment was spotless! No wads of dirty tissues on the floor, no crumpled clothes thrown over chairs, no overflowing garbage cans. In at least this respect, Evan was entirely different from my ex-husband.

"It's a beautiful home," I said when Evan had finished giving me the tour.

Evan smiled. "I like that you said *home*. I want it to feel lived in and enjoyed."

"But clean!"

"Ah, yes, thanks to the cleaning service, very, very clean."

And then there came that awkward moment. We all know the one, the moment when you and the one you love find yourselves—waiting. Waiting for the first touch, wanting it more than anything, waiting and feeling almost shy and—

"Grace," Evan whispered. And then he took my hands and I raised my face to his and for a long moment we looked at each other with a kind of wonder and then, Evan kissed me, gently at first and then with a passion I'd never known, not even in the early days with Simon, not ever.

Evan made love to me that night. I say that—made love to me—because that's what he did and that's what it was, not just sex, but something intense and intimate and loving and so, so thrilling.

Hours later, deep in the night, I lay awake, Evan's body against mine, content in his sleep. I was simply too happy to close my eyes.

Chapter 60

Grace

Finally, you can watch your favorite TV shows without ridicule. Finally, you don't have to pick up his dirty underwear. Finally, you are freed from the boring Saturday night routine of a movie you don't really want to see, followed by dinner at a restaurant you don't care for, followed by sex you pretend to enjoy. Live it up, girl, and don't rush into another marriage.

—*It's All About Me: A Woman's Life After Divorce*

"So, what's Richard wearing at the wedding?" I asked. "Is it a formal occasion?"

Nell nodded. "Oh, yes, it's formal, not officially black tie, but Richard and Bob are wearing tuxedos with brocade vests. Richard's will be a sort of mauve and Bob's will be a muted green."

"I guess the flowers are also mauve and green?" Jess asked.

"I suppose. Richard's always had a good eye for color. I'm sure everything will be lovely. Come to think of it, Richard chose the color scheme for our wedding, too."

The four of us had gathered for dinner at Chez Bernadine. Laura made a face when I ordered rabbit. What, I wondered, would she be like when she was pregnant and experiencing "morning sickness"? Maybe she'd simply stay at home.

"Sometimes," Jess was saying, "I wonder if Richard would have stayed in the closet if you hadn't found evidence of his affair."

"I don't know," Nell said. "I think he might have. All those years and I never found one other clue. Richard was comfortable in some ways, I think."

"I think he wanted you to find the evidence," I surmised. "I think he wanted to get caught so he'd be forced to stop lying and live his real life, finally."

Nell smiled ruefully. "No matter what pain it caused me."

Yes, well, love is painful. So is the truth.

"Richard's basically a good guy," Jess said. "Confused, yes. A coward in some ways, yes, but you almost can't blame him. What an enormous thing, to come out at his age."

Laura snorted. She might have agreed to go to Richard's wedding, but her attitude toward him hadn't changed.

"Yes, yes," Nell said, "a coward. It's odd to think of him as a coward, though. Since the day I met Richard he was so responsible, so adult. I believed he could accomplish anything. He really was my knight in shining armor."

"But did he ever really love you?" Laura asked. Her mouth was set in a grim line.

"Yes," Nell said promptly. "He did. If I allow myself to remember the good things about our relationship, I find a million and one ways in which Richard demonstrated his love for me."

"He was cheating on you for most of your marriage. Doesn't that make you furious?"

"I thought," Jess said, "that we'd gone through all this before, Laura."

"My sister is stubborn." Nell turned to Laura. "Of course it made me angry that I was duped. But after a while, I just got tired of being angry. How many times could I yell at him or hang up on him? Being angry didn't get me anywhere; it didn't change anything. I know you can't comprehend this, Laura, but I really do forgive Richard. I really do feel compassion for what he suffered."

"Good for you, Nell!" I cheered.

"That's very mature and unselfish," Jess said, "in spite of what your little sister thinks."

Laura made a face.

"Maybe," Nell admitted. "But there's something in it for me, too. All the anger was making me old. I could see it in my skin. My GI tract was a mess. I started to lose my hair. And for what? For something I'll never be able to change. Anyway, I just want to be happy again. And I can't he happy unless I move on. And moving on means learning how to forgive."

Laura made a huffy sound. "Well," she said, "you're a better woman than me. I don't think I could ever forgive someone for cheating on me, not even if he did it only once."

"Well," Jess said with a bitter little laugh, "now I feel horrible all over again."

I frowned at Laura. "Life's complex," I said. "Don't you think you're being a bit naive?"

Laura frowned back. "This from the woman who forgave her husband every time he banged some idiot model type who fawned over him at a show? I think you were being a bit naive all those years with Simon."

Nell cleared her throat. "I apologize for my sister. My mother did her best, but I suspect the doctor dropped Laura on her head when she was born."

"No, it's okay," I said. "Really. I can talk about it now."

"Because she's grown," Jess said pointedly.

I turned to Laura. "I wasn't being naive. Right from the start I knew all about the affairs and it hurt. I never once thought, well, he's my husband and I made a vow for better or worse, so I have no other option but to take his abuse. I didn't excuse his behavior, either. It's just that I wanted the marriage to work. I thought I was doing the smart thing by letting Simon have his flings. They were meaningless. He always came back to me. And I thought—I hoped—that after a time he'd get tired of fooling around and realize what he had in me, a wife who understood his artistic nature, a wife who wasn't interested in stifling his soul. Well, I was wrong. Wrong but never naive."

Laura was silent for a moment. Then she said: "Excuse me. I'm going to the ladies' room."

When she was gone, Nell laughed. "My sister didn't understand a word of what you just said."

"I know. But I felt the need to say it anyway."

"You know," Jess said, "and in spite of my past I'm not advocating trickery, sometimes I wonder why Laura didn't just go ahead and get pregnant. Maybe Duncan would have accepted a baby once the baby was a fact."

"It wouldn't have worked. I know my brother-in-law. Duncan would have been furious with Laura. He'd have known he was tricked and he'd have left her. He'd have done the right thing and supported the child, of course, but Laura would have been pregnant with no husband."

"I thought that's what she wanted," I said. "Sorry. That was mean."

"Anyway," Jess said, "that kind of subterfuge is despicable in anyone over the age of sixteen. And even then it's the desperate act of a desperate child."

"Sssh." Nell nodded to her left. In another moment Laura took her seat.

"What did I miss?" she asked.

Nell sighed. "Oh, nothing. We were just discussing the half-life of subatomic particles."

Laura's mouth dropped.

"Laura," I said, "she's kidding!"

"I knew that." Laura fluffed out her napkin before returning it to her lap. "Nell is always making bad jokes."

"Speaking of bad jokes," Nell said, "Trina tells me she's experiencing perimenopause. She's very upset. She called me three times yesterday to report on her symptoms. Suddenly, she has them all."

"What's perimenopause?" Laura asked.

"It's a sort of premenopause," I explained, "a hormonal imbalance."

"Does everyone get it?"

"You don't get it, Laura." Nell shook her head. "It's not a disease. You experience it or go through it."

"So, what makes Trina think she's premenopausal?"

"Let's see. Yesterday it was hair loss—she's convinced she's going bald—and dry skin and anxiety."

"But those could be symptoms of stress. Isn't she going through a divorce?"

"Trina doesn't experience stress," Nell informed us.

"What about the anxiety?"

"Good point. But she's probably just feeling anxious because she thinks she's losing her hair."

"Has she seen her gynecologist?" I asked.

"I convinced her to make an appointment. It seems she's been poring over Internet sites about women's health and self-diagnosing."

"That could make you nuts," Jess said. "Most people misdiagnose themselves. It's the power of suggestion. Read about dry skin and suddenly, you start to scratch."

"I, for one, would be happy not to have periods," Laura announced. "They're such a pain. Cramping, bloating, irritability, staining, ugh. Who needs them?"

I thought Nell was going to scream; her self-control is admirable. "Women who want to have children. Women like you."

"Duh, of course. I just wish there were an easier way."

"Not having periods will be great," Jess said, "but it will also mean vaginal dryness and estrogen loss and a thickening middle. I, for one, am not looking forward to sex becoming a difficulty."

Nell took a sip of her wine. "As long as I bleed, I feel young," she said then, "like I'm still useful as a woman. Is that terribly old-fashioned to admit?"

"Of course not," I said. "It's not a crime to be proud of your ability to conceive and bear children."

"It's not as if I define myself entirely by my being a mother."

"Even if you did," Jess said, "it's your life, Nell. Define yourself however you like."

"And how do you define yourself, Jess?" I asked.

Jess laughed. "Depends entirely on the time of day!"

"What about right this minute?"

"I'd say that right this minute I am first and foremost a friend. Which is a very nice sort of person to be."

Nell eyed Jess. "You sound unusually upbeat. What's going on?"

So Jess told us about the guy she was seeing in southern Maine.

"I'm far from being in love," she said, "but I am enjoying the time we spend together."

"So?" Laura asked. "Does he have husband potential?"

"For some women, yes. But not for me."

"Why not?" Nell asked. "What's wrong with him?"

"Nothing's wrong with him," Jess said. "He's smart and funny and I find him attractive. But it's just not ever going to be anything serious. I can't even say why, exactly, but I think we both know that. I suppose it's sort of a grown-up version of a summer fling, or an affair without the betrayal, something very fun and a bit decadent."

"You don't mind driving all the way to Maine?" Nell asked. "I'm still angry at myself for driving to Waltham to meet a man."

Jess shrugged. "It's only about an hour and a half north. Anyway, I feel like I'm on a minivacation when I'm in Maine, especially if I stay overnight."

"Of course," I said, "the lure of the overnight trip. Do you ever get to the beach or do you two stay holed up in his bedroom all day?"

Jess laughed. "We see the beach on occasion. Honestly, because he's in real estate I spend a fair amount of time on the beach alone. He's always getting calls from panicked buyers and sellers who need him to get them some document or another. It's a tough life, real estate. Definitely not for me, but Nick seems to like the high-energy aspect."

"Well," I said, "speaking of high energy . . ."

"Grace is being dramatic," Nell said. "It must be about sex."

"It is," I said. "Evan and I finally spent the night together."

"Congratulations," Jess said. "I'm guessing from the grin on your face that things went well."

"They did. It did, the whole evening. There was some of that first-time awkwardness, but we laughed about it and it became part of the fun."

"But he's, like, old, isn't he?"

Nell rolled her eyes. "My sister is so subtle."

"He's only fifty, Laura," I said. "He's hardly decrepit."

"And you know what they say, the older the vintage, the sweeter the wine. Of course," Nell added, "I couldn't bring myself to taste the seventy-nine-year-old vintage Dr. Lakes set me up with, so what do I know?"

"As men age," Jess said, "the good ones, anyway, the ones worth having sex with, they get better at it. They've got experience and they don't rush through like they have a plane to catch. Or so I'm told. Nick is only forty-five and as far as I can tell, he's still in his prime. Come to think of it, Nick is the oldest man I've ever slept with. Huh. All those sixty-year-olds to date and so little time!"

"Older men can't rush through sex," Nell pointed out. "Everything takes longer to happen. Still, I suppose there's some merit to the experience argument. I don't think I could tolerate some groping youth."

"Old men are probably totally grateful to be having sex at all," Laura declared. "Maybe they're good—if they really are, and I have my doubts!—because they want to show their appreciation for a woman's having said yes."

"Old and grateful?" I shrugged. "Maybe. Whatever the case, Evan is not old and he's incredibly fit and I'm incredibly happy."

"And Simon hasn't reared his ugly head?" Jess asked.

"Not since we showed up at his friend's apartment to bail him out of trouble."

"Maybe the sight of you and Evan together shocked him into some sort of coherence."

"It's possible," I admitted. "But I'm not expecting any miracles where Simon is concerned."

"Some people don't change."

"Some people won't."

"Some people can't," I said. "I suspect Simon is part of that group."

"More's the pity," Nell said. "Unless, of course, what he's got going on continues to work for him."

"It might not always work, not when he's lost his physical appeal," Jess noted, "but who knows? There's always a groupie desperate enough to attach herself to the formerly famous."

"A leechlike relationship," Nell said.

Jess shrugged. "Hey, it's someone to do the housework and bring in the groceries when you're an old and feeble has-been."

"I think Simon's kind of yucky."

I turned to Laura. "Yucky?"

She wrinkled her nose. "I don't like that two-day-old beard thing. It seems so, I don't know, so—"

"Yucky." Nell smirked. "Yes, we know."

"Well," Jess said, "be thankful then that you're with Matt. He's an expert shaver. He could teach that grooming master from the Fab Five a thing or two."

"Is it pathetic that we're talking about facial hair?" I wondered. "At our age? Shouldn't we be talking about world events, local politics, something of substance?"

"I am mired in substance all day," Jess replied. "When I'm with my friends, I want to float on fluff. As it were. Besides, not all of our conversations are so banal. You know, there's divorce and all the dreadful realities that go with it."

Nell grinned. "Besides, if we talked about the current situation in the Middle East, my sister wouldn't be able to participate."

"I would, too!" Laura protested. "I read the paper. Not every day but a few times a week."

I sensed the evening coming to its natural end.

"Shall I get the check?" I said.

Jess immediately replied. "Yes, thanks, you shall."

Chapter 61

Jess

It's important to maintain a semblance of professionalism in the courtroom or the mediation room. Resist the urge to spit in your husband's eye or to give him the finger. Acting out will only hurt your case. Save the bags of burning feces on his doorstep until after the divorce is final.

—*Anger Management and the Divorcing Woman*

"**I**'m falling for you, Jess."

We were at Nick's apartment in South Berwick. We'd just finished dinner and had moved into the living room and onto the couch. Nick wasn't a terribly creative cook, but he managed to make perfectly tasty simple dishes. That night he'd prepared homemade tomato sauce with mushrooms and poured it over fresh pasta. I'd brought in bread and wine.

A simple dinner, followed by a not-so-simple conversation.

Falling for me. What did that mean? Did it mean Nick was falling in love with me? Or just . . .

"Oh," I said.

Nick traced his fingertip along the back of my hand.

"Does that upset you?"

Only a little, because here I was assuming we both viewed our dating as more of a summer fling than as a prelude to a serious relationship.

"Of course not," I said. "No, it's great. Of course. It's just that . . ."

Just that what? I lowered my eyes as if the answer were to be found in my lap.

"Just that what?"

I looked up again at him. "I can't promise anything, Nick." It was all I could think to say.

"Why not?" he asked. He took back his hand and rested it on his thigh.

Nick's thighs were one of his best physical features.

"Because I can't," I repeated. "And if you need a more specific reason, let's just say I can't promise anything because I'm too soon out of a messy divorce."

Nick's eyes trapped mine. His eyes were an interesting shade of green.

"But that's not the real reason?" he asked.

"It's a real reason," I said. "It's just not the only one. Please, Nick, don't press me on this."

Nick reached for my hand again. I let him take it.

"I'm sorry," he said. "I don't mean to sound as if I'm rushing things. I just don't want to lose you so soon after finding you."

"I'm not going anywhere," I said. But how could I be sure? Was it ever right to promise anything to anyone?

"I've never been married," Nick said suddenly. "I'm the only one of my friends from college who didn't get married. The only reason I can come up with is that I was just too busy. I've always been too busy with work and with travel and with my own interests. It sounds insane, doesn't it?"

"I wouldn't call it insane," I told him truthfully. "Too many people get married for the wrong reasons. Maybe it was better that you didn't make a commitment you might not have been able to keep."

Listen to me. Talking like I knew what I was talking about.

Nick sighed. "Maybe. But I'm not a kid anymore, Jess. I know what's good for me when I see it—or when I see her. I feel I just don't have any more time to waste. Life's too short."

I laughed, hoping to lighten the mood. "Nick, you're only forty-five. That's like the new thirty-five. Or so say the magazines."

But Nick wasn't ready to lighten the mood. "Yeah, well," he said, "I don't feel thirty-five. I don't remember having chronic back pain when I was thirty-five. I don't remember falling asleep every night by eleven o'clock when I was thirty-five."

I wondered. Did Nick want a wife or a nurse?

"Eleven o'clock is pretty late," I said.

"Do you know," he said, ignoring my lame remark, "that two of my friends have already had heart attacks? One guy is only forty-eight. Okay, he isn't in the best shape of his life, but he doesn't smoke and doesn't drink much and still, wham, major heart attack."

Illness happens, I thought. And the possibility of it happening increases with time. Thanks, Nick, I thought, for further darkening the mood.

"Is he okay?" I asked.

Nick shrugged. "He survived, if that's what you mean, but Jess, his life will never be the same. It was a major wake-up call. He's been reevaluating everything: his career, his marriage. I guess I don't want to wait until a crisis forces me to focus on the rest of my life. I want to start making choices and changes now."

I wondered if Nick was also thinking about starting a family. He certainly wasn't too old to be a father. But if he was considering children as part of his future, then he definitely had set his sights on the wrong woman.

"I understand," I said. I did understand. I just didn't share Nick's urgency to seize his life and shake it into place.

But maybe I was wrong not to be thinking of my future.

Nick was a good man, a decent man, a man now with a mission. Was I insane to resist the love of such a man?

I thought then about Matt, also a good and decent man, and about how I'd said yes to his proposal of marriage, and about how it had turned out to be a very, very bad decision.

There are times when it's far more important to act from one's heart, rather than from one's head.

"Do you really understand, Jess?" Nick pressed.

I wanted to leap off the couch and run for my life.

I nodded. "I admire your determination to live a fulfilled

life," I said carefully. "But as I told you before, I just can't make any commitments right now. I'm sorry, Nick."

Why is it so terrible when a man looks hurt? It wounds me to see a man wounded.

"Do you care about me at all, Jess?" Nick asked, his voice somehow changed.

I shifted a bit closer to him on the couch.

"I like you, Nick," I said. "I like you a lot. That's all I can say right now."

Nick tried to smile. "I guess it will have to be enough. For now."

"A relationship grows and changes," I said, for lack of anything more consoling to say. "You can't force it to be something it's not. Let's just wait and see what happens down the line. Okay?"

Nick shifted away. "Do you want to watch a movie?" he asked.

"Sure," I said. "Your choice."

I stayed with Nick that night instead of driving back to Boston as I'd planned. It felt somehow wrong to leave him after our conversation earlier that evening. It seemed somehow cruel.

But by staying with him, was I leading him on? Would Nick consider my earlier protestations about a serious relationship minor female skittishness? Maybe he'd think I wanted him to press harder, to work to win me over, to buy me expensive jewelry and dinners.

Somehow, it seems, I'd gotten myself into a relationship.

I left for Boston around ten the next morning, hoping to avoid the heaviest traffic. Nick had been gone since nine; he had a showing in Wells at nine-thirty. Before he headed out, he had kissed me on the lips and hugged me hard.

"When will I see you again?" he asked.

"I'll look at my schedule and call you."

"Promise?"

I pulled away just enough to look him in the eye.

"Promise," I said.

Some things, I thought, you can promise. The small things, like a phone call; you can promise and deliver a phone call.

But anything larger?

I was glad to get to my desk that day.

Chapter 62

Nell

It's a tired old cliché, but it's worth keeping in mind. The way to a man's heart is through his stomach. Bone up on your culinary skills and your husband will be less tempted to stray. And remember: if he gets fat enough, no other woman will look at him. He'll be all yours until he drops dead of a stroke brought on by type 2 diabetes.

—*Keeping the Man You Have: Secrets of the Trade*

"I want to vet the guy you next decide to marry. I want to do a background check and ask him his intentions."

Poor Richard. So old-fashioned. So protective of the women in his life.

"Well, this might come as a shock to you, Mr. Marrying Kind," I said, "but I'm not getting married again."

"You don't know that, Nellie. You're a wonderful woman. You're smart and beautiful and—"

"Stop it, Richard," I said. "I know I'm a wonderful woman; I don't need you to tell me that. It's just that I don't want to settle down again, for a long time, maybe ever. I'm having fun. I'm having sex, Richard." I lowered my voice and whispered, "Sex. It's not just for gay men anymore, you know."

Richard, my fastidious ex-husband, and I were having dinner at Tristan's. Now, he cringed. "You are being careful, I hope."

"Of course! Clara asked me the same thing. What do you two think of me?"

"I think the world of you, Nellie," Richard said earnestly. "And so do our children."

"Thanks," I said. "Just don't be such a worrywart, okay?"

"I'll try but I can't promise anything."

I wondered: Who can promise anything and mean it?

Richard's face took on a funny look. I'd seen it before.

"What?" I said. "You look like there's something you want to say."

"I shouldn't."

I laughed. "After all we've been through together, you're getting shy now? Come on, Richard."

Our waiter appeared with cocktails: a vodka tonic for Richard and a scotch on the rocks for me.

"Okay," Richard said when he'd gone off. "I know I probably have no right to say this . . . But I have to admit it makes me uncomfortable to know you're having sex with other men."

"You're right," I said, a bit surprised. "You have no right. But I'm curious. What exactly about the situation offends you? Besides the possibility of my catching an STD, of course. And wait a minute. You tried to set me up with one of Bob's friends. You seemed pretty comfortable with doing that."

"I don't know why I did that," Richard admitted. "Maybe because I knew the guy and trusted him. Still, I was glad when you said no." Richard hesitated. "I know you'll think I'm crazy, Nellie," he said finally, "but the reason I don't like the idea of you having sex with other men is that you're the mother of my children. Our children. And you're the first woman, the only woman, I've ever loved. I'm sorry, Nellie. You know I want a wonderful life for you, I really do, and I do hope that life includes love."

"Just not sex?"

Richard shrugged. "What can I say? I'm an old-fashioned guy."

"I know. I remember when Clara brought home her first boyfriend. You went into a deep depression."

"I know men, Nellie. I know what we're like. We're a trouble-making bunch."

I laughed. It felt good to be laughing with Richard. "Don't I know it!"

"Speaking of trouble," Richard asked, "how's Laura? Has she forgiven me, just a little? Or does she still think I'm the Devil?"

"Oh, you're still the Devil. Laura is—"

"What she is," Richard said definitely. "And she is loyal to her sister."

"I know," I said. "And yet I give her a hard time about pretty much everything. She's so—unconscious—and she's getting worse as time goes by. I guess I should ease up on her, but when I see her making ridiculous decisions, I just can't control myself."

"Maybe Matt will be good for her in the end," Richard said. "I remember him as a pretty stable guy, no?"

"Duncan was a stable guy, too," I reminded him. "But his stability didn't seem to rub off on Laura."

"Your parents' deaths hit her hard. We have to keep that in mind."

"It unhinged her," I said, "but she won't admit it, least of all to herself."

Richard nodded. "I guess you never really know how the death of a loved one will affect you. Remember when my parents died? I hardly felt a thing."

I remembered. I'd felt so bad for Richard.

"But that wasn't a surprise, was it?" I asked. "You were never close to them. Frankly, they hardly noticed you. They hardly noticed anyone but themselves."

"That's true," Richard admitted. "Still, I always thought that when they died, I'd experience some sort of, I don't know, catharsis. I thought I'd realize I'd always loved them. I thought I'd miss them, even a little. I never expected to feel—nothing."

I leaned across the table and took Richard's hand.

"Some people aren't cut out to be parents. I don't know how you wound up becoming such a good and normal person growing up with such self-centered people."

"I could be gooder," Richard joked. "But thanks."

"You're welcome." I released his hand and sat back in my chair.

"Do you think your sister is one of those people who shouldn't have kids?" Richard asked.

I thought about that for a moment. "I don't really know," I

admitted. "I do know that you were—that you are—a great father. You're a natural, Richard."

Richard gave me a funny look. "You're just full of compliments tonight. Okay, Nellie, what do you want? I already told you I'm picking up the check."

"Nothing! Really, I'm just so happy I don't hate you anymore. I feel like I want to tell you over and over how I recognize the fact that you're not a demon. All those months just after I found out about Bob, I treated you with such anger, such disdain."

"I had it coming, Nellie," Richard said. "I think your reaction was justified. I'm surprised you didn't shoot me in the back."

"I was tempted, believe me! Well, not really. I didn't want you to die because then you wouldn't be around for me to yell at."

Richard raised his glass. I raised mine.

"Here's to being alive," he said.

"To being alive."

Life, I thought, could be pretty okay.

Chapter 63

Laura

Think of your divorce as an opportunity to upgrade. For example, say your ex-husband was poorly endowed. After years of wondering if it was already in, this is your chance to find a man hung like a horse and really have fun!

—*Looking on the Bright Side of Divorce*

I had just buttoned the last button on my blouse when someone knocked on the door to the exam room.

"Come in," I called.

Dr. Lakes came into the room holding a yellow file folder. She wasn't smiling.

"Am I okay?" I blurted.

"Well," she said in that careful way doctors have, like anything they say can and will be held against them, "we won't know about the Pap results, of course, for another few days."

I nodded. I felt sweat break out under my arms. I remembered that I'd forgotten to buy a new brand of deodorant at the drugstore the day before. The old one wasn't working like it used to.

"I am, however, a bit concerned. There's evidence of scar tissue. You stated on my forms that you've never had surgery. Correct?"

I nodded, again. Now my lower back was sweating. I wondered if you could use deodorant on places besides your underarms.

"Have you been treated for infections?" Dr. Lakes asked next. "Any STDs?"

"No," I blurted. "No. I mean, I've had some yeast infections, but who hasn't?"

"Uh-huh. Any pain or discomfort of any sort, maybe something you ignored, something that should have been treated?"

I shook my head. And then I remembered that yes, on and off over the past ten years or so I'd had some weird pains. Once I thought I felt a lump right through my skin. And a few times it had been so hard to pee I thought I would die. But I'd always hated going to the doctor, ever since I was a little girl.

"Well, maybe," I said.

"Any family history of endometriosis?"

"What?"

Dr. Lakes scribbled something in my file.

Oh, boy. Now the back of my neck felt wet. How was I going to go back to the office all dripping and smelly?

"Is it dangerous?" I asked. "Scar tissue?"

Dr. Lakes gave me a funny look, kind of like the look Nell gives me when I ask a simple question. Can't anyone just answer without making a face?

"No, not dangerous," she said. "It could cause some problems down the line."

"But I can still get pregnant, right?"

Dr. Lakes hesitated a moment before answering my question. I really felt I was going to freak out.

"Are you currently trying to get pregnant?" she finally asked.

"Not yet," I said. "But I will be, very soon." I held up my left hand. "I'm engaged."

Dr. Lakes leaned against the counter with the sink built into it.

"Yes," she said. "I noticed. Laura, when was your last gynecological exam?"

I scrunched up my nose and thought. Scrunching helps me to remember.

"Um, about three years ago," I said. "No, four. I think."

Dr. Lakes shifted a bit. "You know you should be having a Pap test every year."

Yes, yes, I knew. But if you did everything you're supposed to do when you're supposed to do it, you wouldn't have any time left for other important stuff, like shopping or going to the beach. Besides, like I said, I hate going to the doctor's. Doctors scare me.

"I'm sorry," I said, for no good reason. I wasn't really sorry.

Dr. Lakes wrote something else in my file. "You don't have to apologize, Laura," she said then. "But you might want to start being more responsible about your health, particularly since you're hoping to have a family."

I nodded. Now I felt sorry, really awful, like when my third-grade teacher kept me after class and told me that if I didn't stop whispering to my friends while she was trying to talk, I would be suspended.

"Think of the child you hope to have the next time you're tempted to put off a doctor appointment," Dr. Lakes was saying. "If you learn you have an advanced medical condition that might not have been so serious if you'd caught it in its early stage, you're going to feel horrible. And your child is going to suffer."

"Okay," I said. I felt like I might start to cry. "What should I do? You know, about the scar tissue."

Dr. Lakes smiled that soothing smile my own mother used to give me when I'd get all nervous the night before gym class. "There's nothing you can do right now," she said. "We'll see what happens when you start trying to get pregnant. There are surgical options, but we won't talk about them now. Are you eating right?"

I thought of the hot dog I'd had for lunch, and the French fries. And the candy bar. And the soda.

"I think so," I said. My voice trembled just a bit.

"Hmm." Dr. Lakes gave me the suspicious look Nell gives me when she thinks I'm not telling her the whole truth. "Well," she said, "I'm going to prescribe some dietary supplements. Start taking them right away. We want you in good shape for the future."

I nodded.

Then Dr. Lakes told me to go to the reception desk for my prescriptions. When she was at the door of the examination room, her hand already on the knob, she turned.

"And Laura?"

"Yes?" I said nervously.

"One more thing. I'd like you to lose about ten pounds. For health purposes, of course."

And then she was gone.

Matt was working late that night. I decided to stay at my place and go through my clothes. For some reason a lot of them weren't fitting right. It was annoying me.

After trying on three pairs of pants I could hardly button, I just gave up. Okay, Dr. Lakes had told me to lose ten pounds, but there was no way I'd actually gained ten pounds! I mean, really.

And then I remembered that skinny thing at the phony dating agency, Ms. Berber, had told me the same thing!

I looked in the mirror. I thought I looked okay from the front. I turned to the side. That didn't look too bad, either. I mean, I guess I had put on some weight but really, I was under a lot of stress!

And then an idea came to me. I wondered if the weight gain was hormonal. Maybe my body was, I don't know, sort of getting ready to be pregnant. I wondered if that was even possible but then thought: hey, anything's possible, right? Just about anything.

I left the three pairs of pants on the floor of my bedroom and went into the kitchen. Just that afternoon I'd bought a pint of chocolate chocolate-chip ice cream. Dairy is good for you; everyone knows that. Women need calcium and even the fat can't really be bad; it's not like the fat in a cupcake or anything unnatural.

I took the pint from the freezer and dug in. Yum. I went into the living room and flipped on the television. There was a rerun of an old *Three's Company* episode. I love that show, but while I watched, my mind wandered.

I wondered what sort of medical insurance Matt had. Mine was not great. I was planning to go on Matt's the minute we got married. I guessed that would be okay with him. We hadn't talked about every little detail yet, like how I was going to stop working right after the honeymoon so I could really concentrate on getting pregnant. You know, have sex and then when Matt wasn't around, rest up and eat right and stay really calm so that my body would be ready.

My body. It was not going to betray me if I had anything to say about it.

I scooped up another spoonful of ice cream. There were at least ten chocolate chips in it! An individual chip can't have that many calories, I thought. A chip is so small. Dr. Lakes would probably frown, but Dr. Lakes, I thought, is supposed to frown. Doctors are such party poopers; it's their job, I know, but how about dealing with reality!

A commercial for some toilet-bowl cleaner came on and I remembered I needed to clean the bathroom. Matt liked a sparkling clean bathroom.

Matt.

Matt might ask me about the visit to the doctor. If he remembered I'd gone. He didn't seem to remember a lot of things I told him I was doing. Of course, I never bothered to tell him what I was thinking or what I was feeling. Even I know that would be a waste of time!

The show came back on. It was one with Suzanne Somers as Chrissy. She was my favorite.

Matt liked blondes. I don't know why he'd been attracted to Jess.

I ate another spoonful of ice cream. It was nice and melty. Matt hated melty things; he didn't like mess.

I supposed I should just tell him about the scar tissue.

But how could I? I mean, really. How could I possibly tell Matt that I might have trouble getting pregnant? What if he decided to call off the engagement?

No. Better to keep my little secret a secret.

I'm not dumb. I was never under any illusions about Matt

and me. I knew we weren't getting married because we were deeply in love. We were getting married because it was convenient. Advantageous, too. That's what Nell had said. It was to our advantage to get legally married. We each had something the other wanted. It was as simple as that.

Matt wanted my ability to give him a child. If somehow I lost the ability, what would stop him from leaving me?

I ate the last spoonful of ice cream and tossed the empty container in the trash.

And there was another thing. I just couldn't be single any longer. I just couldn't. I just couldn't go on another awful date with another awful man and be humiliated yet again. There's only so much humiliation a girl can take before she loses all self-respect.

No, Matt and I just had to get married, the sooner the better.

You know, it's a lot harder to get divorced than it is to dump someone you're not legally tied to.

In my bedroom I kicked the stupid pants under the bed.

Chapter 64

Grace

You've spent ten years looking at the same face across the dinner table. Ten years without Chinese food because your husband says it gives him gas. Ten years putting up with his nagging mother. Enough! Life's too short for that sort of agony. File for divorce and move on!

—*What Are You Waiting For? Make Divorce Your New Best Friend*

"I like Evan," Nell said. "He's got the right stuff."

"And," Jess said, "he's very handsome. He's got that sophisticated thing going on, but he's not at all stiff."

It was the night of Simon's opening. An hour into the event and so far there'd been no crisis, at least that I was aware of. Simon, though his usual social, manic self, hadn't yet jumped on top of the drinks table to perform an impromptu jig, a Simon Trenouth trademark act.

"No," I agreed. "Evan isn't at all stiff. He's actually kind of fun. I never would have suspected fun from someone with his prestige, someone in his station. Shows what I know about people."

Laura joined us then, a glass of sparkling water in her hand and a frown on her face. "I don't get Simon's stuff," she said abruptly. "It looks like something a kindergartener could do."

Nell opened her mouth, no doubt to insult her sister, but thought better of it. Like Nell, I'd long ago given up any hope of educating Laura in art history or appreciation.

"Well," I said, suppressing a smile, "Simon's work is not to everyone's taste."

"Matt would hate it," she said. "I'm glad I didn't ask him to come."

"Where is he tonight?" Jess asked. Of course, she knew the answer; we all did.

Laura shrugged. "Oh, there's some stupid football thing on TV, or maybe one of his friends has a video of some game; I don't know. They get together and watch these old games over and over. It drives me crazy. I mean, how boring!"

"Well, I won't say I told you so, but I told you so."

Laura stuck out her tongue at Jess. "I'm going to the ladies' room and then I'm going to head off. I'm in the mood for a hamburger."

"I see Laura's given up alcohol," Nell said when her sister was out of earshot. "She must be purifying the vessel."

I nodded. "She's gained a lot of weight lately, but otherwise she looks okay. I just hope she's happy."

"Me, too." Jess frowned. "She's known Matt for such a short time. It's awfully soon for her to make a commitment to marriage."

"Well," Nell said, "the wedding isn't for months yet. Hopefully she'll come to what few senses she has before then and call it off."

There was a moment of awkward silence. Then Jess said, "You know something we don't know, about Laura and Matt."

"I might. But I've promised to support Laura in this craziness and I will. Now, if you ladies will excuse me, I'm going to strike up a conversation with that tall fellow by the door."

"She's amazing," Jess said when Nell was gone. "She's gotten past the Richard crisis so quickly."

"Nell's a lot tougher than she looks. I don't worry about her like I worry about Laura."

Jess raised an eyebrow. "Do you worry about me?"

"I did," I admitted. "For a while, but not so much anymore. I think you're over the worst part of the post-divorce trauma. Am I right?"

"I think so. Yes, probably."

Laughter that sounded more like a series of shrieks broke out behind us. We both turned to see Simon with his arms around two college-aged girls in almost identical outfits—a flouncy, low-cut, sleeveless blouse; low-slung white jeans; and spiky sandals. Each girl held a glass of white wine and was gazing adoringly at the artist.

"Jess," I said, "meet Brittany and Brianna."

"Your interns?"

"Yup. I don't know how they got into a supposedly private party. Well, I wish them luck, whatever happens after hours."

We both turned away from the spectacle.

"You know," Jess said, "now I almost want to warn them about getting involved with Simon. But I suppose the best way to learn a lesson is to go ahead and make the mistake."

I laughed. "Ah, yes, the joys of experience."

The shrieks erupted again, but this time neither of us bothered to look.

"Does Simon know about you and Evan?" Jess asked. "I mean, that you're a couple."

"I don't know," I said. "I kind of doubt it. Simon is so self-absorbed he doesn't notice the majority of what's going on around him."

"Someone might have told him, though. One of his friends."

"I suppose," I admitted. "But they're not the most perceptive bunch, either. Which, I suppose, is an odd thing to say about a group of artists. Besides, it's not as if I've made a formal announcement that Evan and I are dating."

A waiter offered us a scallop wrapped in bacon, which we declined. When he'd gone off, beckoned loudly by Simon, who knew how to stuff himself with free food, Jess said, "But it's obvious when you two are together, even when you're not touching. It's the way you look at each other."

I smiled. "I love looking at Evan. I never thought I'd be in this place again and I'm so grateful to . . . I don't know, the universe, fate, whatever, for giving me a second chance on real love and passion."

"I'm so happy for you, Grace, I really am. You so deserve this."

"Deserve?" I said. "I don't know about that!"

Jess nodded over my shoulder. I looked to see Evan. He winked, smiled, and went back to a conversation with a man he'd introduced to me earlier as a gallery owner visiting from New York.

"Simon's never seen you with another man, has he?" Jess asked.

I thought about that for a moment. "I guess not," I said. "I doubt he knew about Alfonse. And there wasn't anyone else in my life of any significance. Gosh, how pathetic!"

I snuck another look at my ex-husband, who was at that moment downing a glass of red wine as if it were a soda.

"Is Simon the jealous type?" Jess asked.

I laughed. "I wouldn't know! I don't think it ever occurred to Simon while we were married that I might fall in love with someone else or that another man might find me attractive. Simon believes he's the most important person in the world. I don't think it's ever crossed his mind he might need to be on guard against other men. I don't think it's ever crossed his mind he might have to work on a relationship."

"But when you divorced him," Jess said, "he must have felt rejected. No one is that impervious to pain. No one is that self-assured."

Not even Simon?

"Well," I said, "it's not like the divorce meant the end of our relationship. Simon might have felt rejected at first—though honestly, I saw no signs of it—but before long, I was at his beck and call again. Nothing much changed for a long time. Not until these past few months."

"Oh, these past few months have seen a lot of change for all of us!"

"Mostly good, I hope."

Jess shrugged. "The good has been slow in arriving, but it will come. I have to believe that or go nuts."

"No going nuts allowed. Hey, speaking of changes for the

good, I've started to paint again. On my own, I mean, not for use at school."

"That's fantastic, Grace! You're an inspiration, you and Nell. Life gave you lemons and you made lemonade."

"Not to rely on a cliché . . ."

Nell rejoined us. "What cliché?" she asked.

"Nothing," Jess said. "So, how was your chat with the tall man in the navy blazer?"

"Very nice. He seems to be a good conversationalist. And he asked me out for a drink after the opening."

"What did you say?" I asked. Nell really was an inspiration. She'd gone from naive wife to independent woman about town in a few short months.

"I said yes. He's a friend of Evan's. At least he says he is. I'll give him a mini third degree and if I smell a rat, I'll hop a cab home."

"I'll ask Evan about him right now," I said, "if you like."

Nell shook her head. "Don't bother. I'm sure he's fine. I'm just being more cautious these days."

"After that awful episode with, what was his name, Brian something or other?" Jess asked.

I thought I saw an uneasy look in Nell's eyes, but it passed. Maybe I imagined it.

"Oh, yes," she said. "You know, Trina still swears she had no idea he was such a horror show."

"And you believe her?" I asked.

"I do. Since I told her that Mr. Kennedy deserves to be behind bars, she's made it her personal mission—well, aside from divorcing Miles, of course—to get his victims to go to the police."

Jess smiled. "Good for her. I bet she can be very convincing. But what about you, Nell? Are you going to help the cause?"

Nell hesitated. "I'll do what I can," she said finally. "Even if all it means is that I help pay for a lawyer if something goes to court. I'm sorry if that sounds weak. Maybe I'll find more courage in time."

Before either of us could answer—and honestly, I wasn't sure what to say—Nell excused herself to go to the ladies' room.

I spotted Evan at the door, greeting a group of three quite elderly people, two men and a woman. His graciousness and social ease continued to impress me.

"I think I can take back my jewelry now," I said suddenly.

Jess looked a bit surprised. "Are you sure? It's no problem at all for me to hold on to it."

"I'm sure," I said. "I'm really finally over Simon and our sick little dynamic. I'm working on a healthy relationship with Evan." And then I laughed. "Besides, look at my ex-husband now."

Jess turned to where Simon was standing by the largest of his canvases. He was surrounded by fawning women, young and old, including the elderly woman who'd just arrived. Brittany and Brianna stood on the periphery of the group, pouting. Brittany's face was an alarming shade of red. I suspected that before long, Brianna would be holding her friend's hair while she vomited in the nearest alley.

"I think," I said, "that Simon will meet his next mommy tonight."

Jess turned back to me. "So, you're never opening your door for him again."

"Nope."

"Good for you. I'll bring the jewelry over tomorrow evening if that's okay."

"It is. We'll celebrate my liberation with a glass of champagne. Evan gave me a bottle for a special occasion with a friend. Isn't that a thoughtful gift?"

"He's a keeper; there's no doubt."

I looked closely at my friend. During her messy divorce and for a long time after, she'd looked a bit worn out, as if she'd hardly been eating or sleeping. Now, I thought I saw more animation in her features. There was something brighter about her all around.

"And you, Jess?" I asked. "Anyone on the horizon aside from Mr. Real Estate?"

"No," she said, "no one else on the horizon. Nick would like to get serious, but I'm just not ready to commit myself again. In fact, I'm really not sure how long he'll stay with a woman who's not interested in getting married any time soon. So, the future stretches out before me like an open road. It lies before me like an empty book or a—well, you get my meaning."

"I do. Sometimes it's nice not to have a plan or a goal. It's nice just to live each day and see what happens. Of course, I don't really know what I'm talking about because all my life I've been busy as a beaver, plotting and planning for myself and for Simon."

Jess gave me a considering look. "Evan's not entirely Simon's opposite, is he? I mean, he's not a control freak, I hope."

I looked around the crowded room for Evan. I spotted him listening to the animated chatting of a tiny man everyone knew as "that tiny man who shows up at every art-related event and never buys a thing!"

I looked back to Jess. "I don't know for sure," I admitted. "I don't think he's a control freak, but I suppose I'll learn in time. Like you, I'm in no mad rush to make a commitment I'm not ready to make."

Jess raised her almost-empty champagne glass. "Here's to enjoying the moment."

I raised mine to hers. "Here's to independence, in all its many forms."

Our toast was cut short by a loud thud and the shattering of glass.

I laughed. Simon had finally crashed his way up onto the drinks table.

"For the first time in my life," I said to Jess, "I'm going to enjoy the show. Because this time, I don't have to clean up after it."

Chapter 65

Jess

Love is patient and kind; love is not jealous or boastful; it is not arrogant or rude. Love does not insist on its own way; it is not irritable or resentful; it does not rejoice at wrong, but rejoices in the right. Love bears all things, believes all things, hopes all things, endures all things.

—*First Letter of Paul to the Corinthians, verses 4-7, the Holy Bible, Revised Standard Version*

O that you would kiss me with the kisses of your mouth!

—*Song of Solomon verse 2, the Holy Bible, Revised Standard Version*

"**B**y the power vested in me by the Commonwealth of Massachusetts, I now pronounce you married. You may kiss each other."

And they did, Richard Keith Allard and Robert Thomas Landry. When they parted and turned to face those of us gathered in the church, a wild applause broke out.

I so hate crying, but I couldn't stop the tears from flooding my cheeks.

"I brought makeup," Nell said into my ear.

I nodded and continued to dab at my face with a wad of tissues. Nell was crying, too, but not nearly as much as I was. Trina, to Nell's other side, was dry-eyed. Grace, to my left, quietly sobbed into a handkerchief Evan had given her midway through the service. Behind us, Laura sat with Matt. I don't know how either of them reacted to the ceremony. I couldn't even guess.

Slowly, the guests filed out of the church.

"It was a lovely service, wasn't it?" Nell said as we walked down the aisle.

I nodded again, still not sure I could speak without inducing another torrent of tears.

It really had been a lovely service. Clara read a poem special to her father and Bob. One of Bob's nephews read from both the Old and the New Testament. The minister, a middle-aged woman, made mention of Richard's deceased parents being with him in spirit. (Nell harrumphed quietly at that.) Bob's parents beamed through it all. But what touched me most, I suppose, was the surprise fact of Colin being his father's best man.

Nell, Grace, and I made a beeline to the ladies' room before joining the receiving line out in front of the church. Trina stayed with Evan, hanging on to his arm and chattering about some woman's awful taste in wedding attire.

"Here," Nell said, unloading her purse. "I've got everything we need for repairs."

Grace sniffed. "Good, because for some stupid reason I forgot to wear waterproof mascara. I know how I get at weddings; I don't know what I was thinking."

I looked in the tiny mirror over the tiny sink and burst out laughing. My face looked like a clown's after being sprayed by the business end of a high-powered hose.

"It's pretty bad," Nell agreed. "Weddings are murder on the appearance. It's a good thing people look only at the bride."

It took a moment for the absurdity of that observation to hit the three of us, and then we were all laughing.

"They make an attractive couple," I said.

It was the cocktail hour, and Richard and Bob were circulating among their guests. A classical guitarist played softly while waiters carried trays of delicious hors d'oeuvres.

"They do," Nell agreed, "don't they?"

Trina joined us with a fresh glass of champagne. "Darling Nell. This is a wonderful affair. The champagne is marvelous."

"Richard has good taste in wines."

"And good taste in women." Trina raised her glass.

"Thanks," Nell said. "I won't deny it."

Trina let out a little squeal. "Oh, darlings, they're passing around more of those wee nibbles I adore!" And off she tripped.

"How are you holding up?" I asked Nell when Trina was gone.

"Not bad," she said. "I'm okay. I'm glad the ceremony is over, though. I was dreading it. Now I feel mostly—spacey. As if this isn't quite real. I suppose it's some sort of self-preservation instinct. I suspect the reality of it all will hit me again late tonight. I'll be all alone in my cozy bathrobe, sipping a cup of herbal tea, and it will hit me like the proverbial ton of bricks that my former husband is now legally married to a man."

"I think you'll be fine," I said hopefully. "I think you really are past the shock element."

"Maybe. Let's hope so. Now that I've cleared this hurdle, I'd really like to concentrate on my own future. Speaking of future, will you look at my daughter!"

I followed Nell's eyes to find Clara obviously flirting with one of Bob's nephews.

"Oh, Lord," Nell said. "She had better not get involved with another Landry, or I'm afraid I will have to kill her."

Life, it's been noted, is strange.

"At least Colin is behaving," I noted. In typical Colin fashion, he was off by himself in a corner, staring into the middle distance meditatively.

Nell smiled. "He's probably mentally designing a new computer program or something else incomprehensible to his dear old mother."

Just then we were joined by Grace.

"Where's your better half?" Nell asked.

Grace pretended to shudder. "Isn't that a horrible phrase? In the men's room, if you must know. And what about you, Jess?" she asked. "I thought you might bring Seth or Nick as your date."

"I considered it. Either would have come if I'd asked. Nick

would have loved being at a wedding with me. He'd hope it gave me ideas. But, I don't know, it just felt right to be here on my own."

"I think I understand," Grace said.

A waiter offered us another glass of champagne. It would have been rude to refuse. When he'd gone off, Nell turned to me.

"And how are you doing seeing my dear sister with your ex-husband?" she asked.

"It's strange," I admitted. "It's strange seeing her take his arm, but it's something I'll just have to get used to."

"Oh, look, there's Evan. Excuse me."

Grace hurried off to reattach herself to her new love. Nell left to say hello to one of Richard's colleagues. And I took the opportunity to observe the engaged couple from afar. Laura and Matt stood off to themselves. They weren't talking. Laura was working her way through a plate piled high with food. Matt was nursing a bottle of beer, likely the only one he'd had in months. An attractive woman in her twenties crossed the room and Matt followed her with his eyes. Laura didn't notice.

I turned and walked out to the enclosed balcony overlooking downtown Boston. I like cityscapes, night or day. And I thought about change.

My friendship with Laura had never been terribly deep; I thought of her mostly as Nell's sister. And once Laura and Matt were married, I knew that what friendship we'd had would wane. It was okay. It was more important for Laura to build her new life than it was for us to spend time together over dinner once every few weeks.

As if summoned by my thoughts, there was Matt, suddenly on the balcony with me.

"Oh," I said. "Hi."

Matt nodded. He looked not at me but at the city spread before us. I waited but it seemed nothing more of a response was coming.

"Nice wedding," I said finally.

"I got your e-mail." Matt blurted the words, as if they'd been crowding against his front teeth, fighting to get out.

I swear, for a second I didn't know what he was talking about. And then I remembered.

"Oh," I said.

And I waited. But Matt said nothing more. He took a sip of his beer and kept his eyes straight ahead.

"Okay, then," I said after a while. "I'm going to go talk to— someone I know."

Matt nodded and I bolted back into the room, just in time to greet the happy couple. We all kissed. They looked so relaxed.

"Congratulations, you two," I said. "It was a lovely ceremony."

Bob nodded. "I thought so, too. The part I was conscious of. I've never been so nervous in my entire life."

"Really? I couldn't tell." I laughed. "Then, again, it's amazing I saw anything through the flood of tears streaming from my eyes."

Richard reached for my hand. "Thank you, Jess," he said.

"For what?"

"For everything. For being here, but mostly for being Nell's friend."

I squeezed Richard's hand. "You're welcome, Richard. It's been my pleasure."

The newlyweds continued their rounds and then dinner was served.

Celebrating hope.

What a wonderful way to spend an afternoon.

EPILOGUE

Chapter 66

Jess

To every thing there is a season, and a time to every purpose under the heaven.

—*Ecclesiastes 3:1*

"Last one in the water's a rotten egg!"

I laughed and darted past Bob into the waves. "Ha, ha, you lose!"

Bob splashed in after me. The midafternoon sun was warm but the Maine coastal water was not.

"Brrr! Remind me why we're doing this again?"

Bob grimaced. "Because we're idiots? Because we're thirty- and fortysomethings desperately trying to hold on to what's left of our youthful exuberance?"

"Ah, right. Idiots. Let's get out, now."

Bob and I sloshed our way back to shore and our beach towels. A half hour later we were back at the Ogunquit house Richard and Bob had bought just that spring, warm, dry, and enjoying crab rolls, fruit salad, and cold beer for lunch.

Across from me sat Nell and Oscar, recently engaged. Bob sat to my right and Richard to my left. There was much laughter and good feeling. And if anyone had told me only three short years ago that I'd be sharing a pleasant meal with Nell, her fiancé, her ex-husband and his partner, I would have dismissed the idea as ridiculous.

But life is all about surprise, isn't it, both good and bad. She who bends, survives and all that.

Here's another tidbit I like, it's printed on T-shirts all around town: "Women who behave rarely make history." I don't know who said that, a feminist leader or some savvy marketing guy, but I'm trying to adopt that as my motto and stop worrying about fitting into a created notion of who and what I should be.

Like, a respectable married woman.

Anyway, now that I'm over forty and still single, I'm considered a lost cause, aren't I? My chances of finding a man to marry are abysmally low; I'm more likely to be hit by a train or struck on the head by a passing Frisbee or something.

Oh, well.

Nick and I didn't stay together for long. He was serious about settling down and I began to wonder if it really mattered to him who he married. I wondered if he was in love with me or with the idea of me, a single, available woman.

So, we split, amicably, soon after Richard and Bob got married, and I haven't heard from him since. I wouldn't be at all surprised to learn that he's married, maybe even on his way to becoming a father. I wish him well.

Seth and I are still friendly, but since he started living with his age-appropriate girlfriend, I see him only occasionally. Our worlds are so different in some ways. He's really just starting out, and me? I'm entrenched. Plus, he's young and in love, and when you're young and in love, you don't need friends, or you think you don't.

And then the road gets bumpy and the first thing you do is look for those friends you misplaced and wonder why you misplaced them at all.

Lost friends.

I haven't seen Laura since Alex was born, but I hear about her from Nell. It's not my place to judge or even to comment on someone else's life. I'll let Nell do that. Suffice it to say, I feel sorry for them both, Laura and Matt, and though I'm the last person to suggest a divorce, in this case I can't help wondering if it isn't the right thing to do.

Divorce. You think you're not going to survive it and then, you do. And you survive largely thanks to the support of your friends. Really, without Nell and Grace—and even, on occasion, Laura—I don't know how I'd have come to this point of contentment.

Friends and my career. A research project I'd worked on for some time has become a book. It will be published by a small university press, which means the distribution will be low and the sales even lower. But you don't write this kind of book for the money; you write it for the professional recognition as well as—hopefully—for your own fulfillment.

I sent an advance copy to my parents, on some level always the dutiful daughter. I wasn't expecting either of them to be impressed, so I was pleasantly surprised when my father called me one evening to congratulate me warmly. My mother then got on the phone, reluctantly—I could hear her protests in the background—and after a mumbled acknowledgment of having received the book, she said, "You don't expect me to read it, do you?" I told her that no, of course I didn't expect her to read it. She replied, "Good. Do you want it back, then?"

I took a deep, steadying breath. It helped a little. And I said, "No, Mom, keep it. Use it as a coaster or something." And I got off the phone as quickly as I could.

Some things never change.

Some things do, like the turning of the year and with it, the arrival of a new birthday.

When I turned forty, Nell wanted to give me a party but, not being much of a party person, I said no, thanks. Instead, I suggested Nell, Grace, and I spend a weekend in Paris. We did and it was a seminal time for us, not one fight over who paid for what or what museum to go to before lunch, just three good friends enjoying each other's company in the City of Lights.

Of course, I thought once or twice of my honeymoon with Matt, but the memories were no longer painful or poignant. Some were downright amusing, like the look on Matt's face when I ordered escargot one night at dinner. He didn't know that escargot meant snails; I don't know what he thought they were, but when I told him, his face turned green, absolutely green.

"Plans for the afternoon?" Nell asked the group gathered on the flagstone patio behind Richard and Bob's lovely new home.

"No more swimming," Bob said with a laugh. "But I'd like to walk the beach for exercise."

Nell looked to Oscar. "Is it a terrible thing," she asked, "to forgo the beauties of nature for a quick trip down to the outlets in Kittery? Say, 'No, dear, it's a wonderful choice.'"

"No, dear," Oscar repeated, "it's a wonderful choice. Personally, I see a nap in my immediate future."

"I'll join Bob for a walk." Richard looked to me. "Jess? How about you?"

I smiled. "If no one minds, I'm going to sit right here with a good book, and when I'm not reading, I'm going to watch the wind in the trees and admire the lovely garden."

"That's what this place is for," Bob said. "A place where friends and family can gather and feel entirely comfortable doing what they please. Unless, of course, doing what they please involves paintball tournaments."

Lunch broke up soon after that. I cleared the table and loaded the dishwasher. When Nell had driven off, Oscar had retreated to their room, and Richard and Bob had walked down to the beach, I settled on a lounge chair, book in hand. Truth be told, I felt too lazy to read, but not too lazy to appreciate all I had in my life: generous, loving friends; a fulfilling career; and when the mood struck, romance.

It's enough for now.

Chapter 67

Nell

But what minutes! Count them by sensation, and not by calendars, and each moment is a day, and the race a life.
 —*Benjamin Disraeli, Earl of Beaconsfield*
 Sybil. *Book 1. Chap. 2*

"No, you can't have more money and I will not put your father on. Clara, you're over twenty-one, legally an adult, and it was your choice to move to Seattle without a job, not mine."

I rolled my eyes at Richard. He put out his hand for the phone, but I shook my head.

"Yes, that's terrible, Clara, it's a terrible shame that you can't afford to spend the weekend at the spa with your friends, but I'm sure you'll survive."

Richard was starting to look pained.

"I'm going now, Clara. Yes, I'm a horrible person. Goodbye."

I ended the call.

"Would it be so terrible if I sent her the money?" Richard asked. "She deserves a little fun, and I know she's working hard at those temp jobs."

Poor Richard. Wrapped nice and tightly around his daughter's little finger.

"Richard," I said, "we've been through this a million times. If you keep giving in to her, she'll never learn how to be responsible for her own well-being."

Behind Richard, Bob nodded at me. Poor Bob. Forced as a stepparent to keep his mouth shut and his opinions to himself.

"Would anyone care for a cocktail?" Bob said.

I smiled warmly at the man. "Yes, thanks, that would be wonderful."

"Did I hear the offer of a cocktail?"

Oscar appeared in the door to the kitchen. He was tan and fit and wearing the white linen shirt I'd given him for his birthday.

"You're like Nick Charles," I said, laughing. "You hear the sound of a cocktail shaker a mile away."

Richard joined Bob at the concrete counter. "What'll it be, everyone?"

So, Oscar had asked me to marry him and, with little hesitation, I said yes. He gave me a cushion-cut diamond in an antique platinum setting, and I absolutely love it. More, I absolutely love Oscar. I don't know how it happened, but it did. Who says a man won't respect a woman who sleeps with him on the first date?

It won't be a marriage like the one I had with Richard. It will be different and in some ways, it will be far better because now I'm aware, now I know things I didn't know at nineteen, now my expectations are more reasonable and yet, more precise. I know what I need and what I want and I know what I can give and what I can't.

I would never call my marriage to Richard a trial run; that would trivialize the most important years of my life to date. But it did turn out to be a good training ground for this second phase of my life.

Colin and Clara like Oscar well enough, though they've met him only a few times. Last Christmastime we four had dinner together at my apartment. It was only minimally awkward for me; Colin was his usual reticent but polite self; Clara bombarded Oscar with questions but not in a belligerent way. Oscar made it out alive and ready for another round, which came the following spring when he scored prime tickets to a Red Sox vs. Yankees game at Fenway. Neither of my kids is particularly into sports, but every Boston-area person has a soft spot for the Red Sox. Oscar, I learned, is one of those loud, enthusiastic fans. It was very amusing to watch him shout and leap from his seat whenever a batter hit a ball or someone completed a good play. That day Colin and Clara saw a side of Oscar they'd not seen before, and I think it further endeared him to them.

As for Oscar's children? Honestly, his is not a particularly close family, which I suppose will make it easier for me in the long run. I met them all twice, once at a small dinner party at Oscar's apartment, once at a symphony concert. His two sons, Malcolm and Oscar, Jr., work in the technology field; what, exactly, they do is a mystery to me, though Oscar gamely tried to explain it all to me. His daughter, Sara, has followed in her father's footsteps and is an attorney. I know Oscar hopes that someday she'll join him in his firm but, not wanting to pressure Sara, he keeps that hope to himself.

Anyway, all three adult children were perfectly pleasant to me and to each other and later, they received the news of our engagement with nary a ripple of emotion. Sara sent a card with a brief personal note to the effect of, "I wish you happiness in the future." Malcolm and Oscar, Jr., actually called their father to congratulate him. Oscar heard nothing from his ex-wife, but that was to be expected.

"Has Colin called?" Richard asked.

Speaking of communication! I laughed. "Who? Do I know someone named Colin?"

Bob shook his head. "Even when he does call, he hardly says more than hello and good-bye."

"Colin has always been a man of few words." Richard came around the counter and handed a martini to me and one to Oscar.

It's true; Colin was always better with numbers and equations and graphs than he was with words, written or spoken. Currently, he's in graduate school for a degree involving computers. As with Oscar's sons, I have no idea what it is Colin studies; I suppose he got his mathematical talent from someone in Richard's family because he certainly didn't get it from anyone in the Keats clan.

"Is there any left for me?"

Jess came into the spacious kitchen in a pair of chinos and a fitted tiny T-shirt. Lately she's been dressing less conservatively than she had been for years, and I think it suits her.

"Of course," Richard said. "Name your poison."

"I'll have whatever it is the rest of you are having."

Richard reached for the bottle of vodka. "A dry martini it is."

Jess leaned a hip against the counter and smiled. "Trina should have been with Bob and me on the beach this morning," she said. "The number of men wearing those thonglike swimsuits was astonishing."

"They're called banana hammocks, dear," I pointed out helpfully.

Jess cringed. "Ugh, that's a horrible term! Still, I must say, many of these men were quite fit. And some of them weren't kids, either. And then again—"

"Then again," Bob cut in, "some of the men in those skimpy suits were just disgusting. You've got to know your body type. The mirror doesn't lie."

"Yes," I said, "but people do, especially to themselves."

And then again, I thought, some people are brutally honest with themselves, people like Trina.

I haven't seen as much of her since Oscar and I have deepened our commitment, but we still try to get together once a month. She remains amusing even when life throws her a curveball, as it did just after her divorce from Miles was final.

Trina had fully expected to marry the New York tax attorney. Imagine her surprise then when he ended their affair—one could hardly call it a relationship—and announced he was marrying a twenty-five-year-old Ukranian model. But ever the survivor, ever the optimist, Trina forged on and within four months or so had found herself husband number five, a real-estate bigwig named Kent Caroll. Oscar and I attended their wedding. It was hard to sit there and listen to Trina pledging her eternal love when I knew full well she meant no such thing, that she wasn't even going to try to make the marriage work, that before the honeymoon was over, she would be plotting her escape and her next happy landing.

Still. Trina is a friend, if an unusual one, and I applauded along with everyone else when the minister announced Trina and Kent husband and wife.

And who knows? Maybe this one will stick. Maybe Trina will get tired of the game she's been playing for most of her adult life and settle into a version of domestic contentment.

Ah, yes, talk of domestic contentment leads me to give you the update on my sister.

Laura is a mess. I don't think she ever really recovered from the death of her infant daughter, Alice, and just as the deaths of our parents unhinged her, this tragedy has led her to some very strange behavior. Sure, she saw a therapist and was put on an anti-depressant, and though that combination probably saved her life at the time, it didn't provide any lasting solutions; it didn't give her the skills she'd need to cope with the years ahead, with troubling things.

Like Matt having an affair.

Okay, I have no proof, but I just know it's true. The signs are all there; I've seen them clearly, but my sister has no idea at all. I've been tempted to talk to her about my suspicions, tempted to shake her into reality, but thus far I've held my tongue. I suppose I'm a bit afraid of what might happen should Laura have to deal with another emotional trauma.

And, there's Alex to consider. Though Laura pretty much smothers the poor little boy with affection, and he'll probably need serious therapy later in his life, hopefully before he becomes an axe-wielding, woman-hating serial killer, he is well cared for. Laura might be letting herself go to rack and ruin, but Alex is thriving. Should something happen to Laura, should she break down again, what will happen to Alex? Well, of course I'd take him if Matt wanted me to; he doesn't seem to care all that much about his son. Don't get me started on that topic, men who still think children are the sole province of women.

I'm very concerned about my sister's health. She's not even forty, but at the rate she's going, she's not going to make it to fifty. Well, maybe I'm exaggerating. I've been known to exaggerate, seeking dramatic effect. Still, Laura has gained an enormous amount of weight and is very sedentary. It's heartbreaking to see, especially when I look at pictures of her when she was a little girl and then a happily married woman, when Duncan was in her life, before my parents' car accident.

I ran into Duncan a while back. He's remarried and his wife was pregnant; if all went well, she's had the baby by now. And Duncan was in the process of officially adopting Anne's little girl from a previous marriage. He seemed very happy, content. He asked me to give his best to Laura. I said that I would, but I didn't. I didn't think my sister needed to hear about her ex-husband's joyful new life.

"I almost forgot!" Richard's usually placid face was suddenly animated. "I heard fantastic news yesterday, just before leaving Boston to come north."

"Well," I said, "don't keep us in suspense. What is it?"

But Richard was enjoying his role as keeper of a coveted bit of information. "Remember our friend Brian Kennedy?"

Oscar put his hand on my shoulder. Jess scowled. Bob blurted, "You heard something about that pig and didn't tell me?"

"Richard," I said, "if you don't tell us right this minute I'll—"

"He's been arrested on charges of attempted rape."

A collective shout went up in Richard's glossy new kitchen.

"Trina must have succeeded after all in rallying the victims," Jess said. "I think we should toast her."

Richard grinned. "Actually, it was a new victim who turned him in, one of the young social set. It seems you don't mess with the twenty-year-olds of today. Anyway, once word is out, I wouldn't at all be surprised if the women Brian succeeded in intimidating come forward."

"Man," Bob said, "I'd hate to be his defense attorney."

Oscar squeezed my shoulder. I reached up and put my hand

over his. "The problem is," he said, "that Kennedy's got more than enough money to buy the best representation."

"I won't believe he'll be acquitted," I said. "I can't allow myself to believe that. And, yes, I know how I can help. I'll come forward. I'll testify. God."

Jess nodded. "That's very brave, Nell. I admire you."

"We all do."

I smiled up at Oscar, the man soon to be my husband. And then I looked to Jess, my dear friend, and to Richard, the father of my children and my first love. Finally, I looked to Bob, a sweet man and a friend to my family.

"If I'm in the least bit brave," I said, "it's all because of you."

Chapter 68

Laura

Children begin by loving their parents. After a time they judge them. Rarely, if ever, do they forgive them.
  —Oscar Wilde, *A Woman of No Importance*

"I don't know why you don't listen when I'm talking to you. Matt! Look at me!"

Matt unglued his eyes from the screen and the football game showing on it. "What?" he said with a scowl. "I'm busy, Laura. You just can't start talking to me and expect me to hear you."

"You're always busy," I complained. "It's like I have to raise my hand and wait patiently until you notice me, until it's convenient for you, before I'm allowed to say anything."

Matt's eyes drifted back to the screen.

"Forget it!" I shouted. I stomped out of the living room and headed for the kitchen. There was half a chocolate cake left over from last night, and though it was supposed to be Matt's half because I'd already eaten mine, it suddenly seemed very important that I eat all of it, every last crumb, and leave nothing for Matt. He couldn't listen to me? Fine. Then I'd eat his cake!

I sat down at the small round kitchen table and stabbed the cake with a fork. Lots of icing, just the way I liked it. Just the way Matt liked it, too, but he wasn't going to get any!

Sometimes he drives me so crazy I swear I think I could kill him and not care. Except, of course, there's my baby to consider, and no child wants to grow up with his mother in jail.

My baby. I wonder if he's going to like chocolate icing when he grows up.

So, I got pregnant after all, about a year after Matt and I got married. There were a lot of problems and I had to have two surgeries before the doctors realized the only way I had a chance of getting pregnant would be if I was injected, you know, in vitro. Well, that didn't work the first two times, but it worked the third time, you know, the time they say is the charm.

I got pregnant with twins. Matt wasn't too happy about that, but I was thrilled. He told me we couldn't afford two children at once, but I said pooh. Four people can live just as cheaply as three. Matt pointed out that since I'd quit my job and insisted on going through all the infertility treatments and in buying a house in Jamaica Plain—okay, not Cape Point, where I really wanted to move, but nice enough for now—that our financial situation was strained.

Twins. A boy and a girl. I was so excited. I would finally be able to use that adorable pink sweater and leggings set I'd bought at that fancy shop.

Well, Matt got his wish for just one child in the end. Alice lived only a few days. She was seriously small even though she was born at full term; of course, the doctors had warned me she might not be okay, after doing sonograms and all where they could see her. But size wasn't what made her so weak. The real problem was with her heart, some congenital heart defect.

I went into a really bad depression when Alice died, and nothing Matt or the nurses or the doctors could say helped me, not even the bouncing baby boy who did survive, Alexander, whom we call Alex. I didn't even want to touch him at first, but the nurses kind of forced me to, though neither of us took to the breast-feeding thing, which was just fine with me as lots of people had told me it hurts.

Anyway, Matt got me to see a therapist and while I was clawing my way out of the pit, he hired a live-in nanny to help me. I don't know what he thought I was going to do to Alex, forget to feed him or something? Let him drown in the baby bathtub? Anyway, in the end the nanny was okay and after about seven months we were able to let her go as I was feeling much better and was even allowed to stop taking the pills. Well, the therapist wanted me to stay on them for a while longer, but I thought I was fine and since she couldn't force me to take the pills, that was that.

Matt shouted from the living room. Someone must have scored a touchdown or something. In the first months of our relationship and up until the babies were born, Matt used to talk all the time about football. I pretended to listen and to care, nodding and saying things like "wow" and "oh, yeah?"

But since Alex, Matt doesn't bother to talk to me about football. Well, about much of anything, really. Which is fine because with Alex, I'm very, very busy. Not that Matt notices . . .

I know Matt loves Alex, but he never seems to want to help me with him. He likes to say good night to Alex because then he's all scrubbed and in his clean jammies, but forget about cleaning up vomit or changing diapers. He has almost no patience reading books to his son or trying to understand him when he talks, which I admit is hard, but if you really listen, you can make out some of what Alex is saying. Matt doesn't come right out and say it, but it's pretty clear to me he considers babies women's work.

Which is fine, really, because I love hanging out with Alex all day and Matt does have to work long hours at the office. Sometimes he doesn't even get home until almost midnight. It's a little strange that I haven't seen any big change in his paycheck these past two years, and you would think that for all the extra hours he's been putting in, they would have given him a raise or a promotion or something.

But I don't complain about his not being home. Honestly, I prefer to be alone with Alex, just us two, and even though the pediatrician says I should probably put Alex in some sort of day care thing so he can learn how to socialize and stuff, I'm going to keep him home for as long as possible. I'd keep him home forever and ever if I could, but at some point the law says he has to go to school.

Anyway, what I do complain about is when Matt is here and I have to take a number to talk to him! He'll look right at me and I think he's listening and then he'll say, "What?" And I'll say, "Weren't you listening?" And he'll laugh and say, "No," or maybe, "I was thinking about something. You need to get my attention before you just start yammering at me."

Yammering? I don't even know what that means!

Sometimes I'm tempted to just give up and stop trying to get his attention. Because let's face it, even when he does listen— or says he's listening—he forgets what I've said like three minutes later. So, why bother?

But I haven't given up yet, though now it sounds like I'm nagging all the time when I'm just trying to be heard!

I put the last bite of cake in my mouth. I remembered that Nell and Oscar and Jess had gone up to Ogunquit to spend the weekend with Richard and Bob. They hadn't asked me to come, but I understood. The whole Jess and Matt thing probably made them uncomfortable and some people don't like having a baby around and . . .

"What are you doing?"

I looked up and there was Matt, standing in the doorway to the kitchen, a scowl on his handsome, boy-next-door face.

I put the fork down on the empty plate.

"Was that my cake?" he demanded.

I couldn't talk with my mouth full, so I just nodded.

"That was my dessert," he said. "You had your half last night. You know I was saving that."

I swallowed. I didn't feel bad, not at all. But I said, "Sorry."

Matt continued to glare at me.

"What?" I said.

"You're fat, Laura. You eat too much. You should go on a diet. It's not healthy."

And then he walked out of the room.

You know what? I wasn't even mad. Really. I felt—nothing. I

remember just sitting there at the kitchen table with the empty plate and smeared fork and feeling nothing.

I sat there for a long time.

I heard the front door open and slam shut.

I heard a delivery truck pull up and my neighbor, Mrs. White, laughing.

I heard the beating of my own heart.

And then Alex cried out from his room.

Chapter 69

Grace

But at my back I always hear/Time's winged chariot hurrying near;/And yonder all before us lie/Deserts of vast eternity.
   —*Andrew Marvel, 1621–1678, from "To His Coy Mistress"*

"Thanks, Evan."
   I reached up to take the glass of Prosecco from Evan's hand. I let my fingers linger on his for a moment.
   "To us," he said, raising his glass.
   "To us. And to vacation. I'm so happy we were able to get out of the city this weekend."
   Evan and I had been invited to Ogunquit with Nell, Oscar, and Jess, to spend a long weekend at Richard and Bob's new three-season home. As tempting as the offer was, we decided to sneak off on our own for a few days to Nantucket. Evan has a friend who owns a small but charming house there. He and his wife were traveling to see family and offered us the use of their home.
   Now, enjoying the twilight from the house's front porch, I was very glad we'd made the choice we had.
   As if reading my mind, Evan asked, "No regrets about not joining the others?"
   "No regrets. Besides, there'll be other gatherings."

"I wonder why Richard and Bob didn't invite Laura and Matt," Evan said. "You did tell me they weren't invited, right?"

I nodded. The mention of Laura always makes me sad.

I last saw Laura about a month earlier. I was walking along Newbury Street on my way to the gallery when a woman up ahead caught my eye. She was standing just to the left of the entrance to a high-end clothing store, holding a bundle in her arms and staring into the middle distance.

My first impression was one of sadness. I felt that I should look away but I couldn't. I slowed my pace just a bit as I approached, wondering for a moment if the woman was homeless—her hair was long and unkempt, she was overweight in the way life on the streets can make some people, and maybe, I thought, that bundle in her arms contained her only possessions.

Just as I was within a few yards of the woman, a young teenager on a skateboard came out of nowhere from behind me and passed within a foot or two of the woman. This served to startle her; she jerked and stepped back against the glass window of the store.

And in that moment I recognized her as Laura.

I felt sick to my stomach with grief.

I came to a dead halt on the sidewalk and watched as she whispered down to the bundle. And I realized that her son, Alex, too old to be carried like an infant, was wrapped in that blue blanket.

Her only, her most important possession, indeed.

I knew I had to go up to Laura, preferably before she became aware of my staring at her. And just as I was unlocking my knees to take a step, Laura turned and almost ran down the street.

I could have called out to her, but I didn't. I just watched her go.

When I got to the gallery, I went immediately into Evan's office and called Nell. I told her what I'd seen. With a sigh, Nell promised to check in with her sister. Laura had experienced several setbacks since the crippling depression she'd experienced after Alex's birth and Alice's death. So far, she'd recovered from each one, but what I'd seen that day on Newbury Street scared me.

Since then I've sent Laura a few e-mails and a card for her birthday, but I haven't heard anything back. I just hope that Nell, as far as I know Laura's only living family member, is taking her sister's predicament seriously. In my opinion, Nell too often dismisses Laura as a fool or a dimwit, almost a cartoon of a person, and fails to see that Laura is not a figure of fun but a real woman with valid thoughts and feelings.

"I think," I said finally to Evan, "I think that Laura is happiest when she's with Alex."

Evan frowned. "But couldn't she have brought him with her?"

I reached for Evan's hand. "Evan, I guess Richard and Bob had their reasons."

My answer seemed to satisfy Evan, at least for the moment. He picked up a magazine and resumed reading the article he'd started earlier.

Several months ago the magazine had carried an article about Simon.

As I predicted back at the opening of his first show at the Auster Gallery, Simon is doing just fine. About a year ago he married a woman named Cassandra Cole. Cassandra is sixty-five if she's a day, fabulously wealthy, and deeply eccentric. Let's face it, she bought Simon and he allowed himself to be bought and obviously, he's enjoying his new life. Recently, Evan and I ran into Simon and his new bride at an opening. Simon was clean shaven. He'd put on a few pounds and looked healthier than I'd ever seen him look. And he was dressed in designer clothes from leather blazer to Italian loafers.

Simon's work has garnered a lot of attention since he joined forces with Cassandra. Her connections are paying off nicely and I'm glad. Simon is a good artist, maybe even a great artist, and deserves to be seen and known.

I looked at Evan. His profile in the fading light brought a smile to my face. He hasn't revealed himself to be Simon's complete opposite, a control freak, someone who tries to live my life for me. Instead he's proved to be a real partner, supportive but not intrusive, especially when it comes to my painting.

All on my own, without any help from Evan, I managed to get a small show in a South End gallery. It's a group show but four of my paintings are going to be hung and if I'm lucky, at least one will be sold. But the money's not the point—though money is a good thing—the painting is the point. Some of my students are all excited to have their parents bring them into "the city" to see their teacher's work. I'm very happy about that.

I'm happy about a lot of things these days.

Evan and I have been living together for a year. Last month he proposed with a simple platinum band in which is set an utterly clear diamond; he had it custom made for me.

Of course, I said yes and we're planning to tie the knot next spring. I know I'm probably too old to make a big fuss about a wedding, but given the fact that my first wedding was such a washout, I'm going to make this one really special. I won't wear a white dress, but I will have lots of flowers and a big, beautiful cake, and there'll be music and I'll walk down the aisle. Jess is my maid of honor and Evan's nephew is his best man. A professional photographer will take pictures and I'll put the best ones in a leather-bound album. Simon and Cassandra will be invited to the wedding. Why not? He's no threat to me now—and I'm no threat to me, either.

I'll invite Nell and Oscar, of course, as well as Richard and Bob. And I'll also invite Laura and Matt. I hope they can be there; at least, I hope that Laura is in good enough shape to be there.

I miss her.

"Interested in dinner?" Evan asked, bringing me back to the moment.

A summer night on Nantucket with the man I loved.

"I'm starved," I said. "Will you start the grill?"